Th

When he had finished reading, Mulcahy looked around him at the men in the Count's office. There were no smiles. Liebo, who rocked nervously in a chair, said, 'Now read this,' his slim finger indicating the promissory note, which contained the figure of $840 *million* as the indebtedness. Then Mulcahy read the first page of the mortgage, in which the figure of $840 *thousand* appeared.

It took him two trips through the documents even to notice the discrepancy in the fine print. Then he looked back at the Grenade letter, and his eyes opened wide.

'Some typo,' he said.

Educated at public school in Norfolk and thereafter at Harvard, Sabin Willett is a trial lawyer who practises in Boston. He lives outside the city with his wife and four children.

SABIN WILLETT

The Mortgage

Mandarin

A Mandarin Paperback
THE MORTGAGE

First published in Great Britain 1996
by Mandarin Paperbacks
an imprint of Reed International Books Ltd
Michelin House, 81 Fulham Road, London SW3 6RB
and Auckland, Melbourne, Singapore and Toronto

A CIP catalogue record for this title
is available from the British Library
ISBN 0 7493 2182 2

Printed and bound in Great Britain
by Cox & Wyman Ltd, Reading, Berkshire

Qui dono lepidum novum libellum
arido modo pumice expolitum?
Léonie, carissimi, tibi.

Acknowledgements

Bill Haney chided me by example; Alex Beam by an early, caustic remark and a deft touch. I acknowledge a debt to each. Errol Willett read early, and was kind; Michael Flood also read early, and wasn't, particularly. Thanks are due them in equal measure: a tyro needs both reactions. Wayne Bennett and Marty Murphy gave technical advice which saved me from many howlers. They are gratefully absolved from responsibility from those that survive. Leonie indulged me, as always she has. Special thanks to the matchless Stephanie Cabot, without whose audacity this book would still be a photocopy, and to Hugh Mullens, who taught me that, time being precious, and books many, a book should stand the test of a hundred years before one invests the time to read it. I hope he makes an exception.

Prologue

It takes just nine minutes. At 3.32 a.m., the terminal is activated, and the cursor begins to thread its way through the libraries and menus. The screen shows the text. At its head is the word 'Mortgage'. The cursor moves down through the paragraphs of legal prose until it comes to rest on a single line of type:

> To secure repayment of the sum of eight hundred
> forty million dollars ($840,000,000) (the
> 'Indebtedness')

The cursor finds the word, 'million'. With a click, it is gone, and in its place, the word 'thousand' appears. Mouse and cursor move again, entering the parentheses. With a click, a comma becomes a period, and seven zeros become six. Now the line reads:

> To secure repayment of the sum of eight hundred
> forty thousand dollars ($840,000.00) (the
> 'Indebtedness')

Three forty-one. The mortgage, one among two hundred ninety-six documents in the closing agenda, returns to its electronic home, there to rest for a few hours until, just after sunrise, the signature copies would be printed. By day's end, it would join the other documents destined for the six leather-bound volumes, each four inches thick.

There stand the facts. They are known with certainty. Beyond them lies only the broader region of inference.

In the darkened law office, the only illumination would have been the shimmer of the computer screen, a ghostly light. Around about would have been silence, except for the rattle of gloved fingers on plastic keys, and the tock, tock, tock in the darkness, steady and stately, as the pendulum moved in its leaded case. And after that, just the faint sound of footsteps fading away down the corridor.

In a few hours, the lawyers would gather in a conference room, to do a last review of two hundred ninety-six documents. The tens of thousands of words which had come to rest in those documents were meant to define every contingency in a $900 million leveraged buyout. One of the documents would be the mortgage. It would contain this error. But the lawyers were exhausted. They had worked almost without sleep for eight days. No one would be looking for this. And there were other points of contention left. Small points, but points which had to be resolved before the sand ran through the glass on 31 March. Even the most contentious, the most nervous, the most careful attorney in the room would secretly be thinking about being done. About the closing dinner. About sleep.

It was, after all, a single line of type. The odds were reasonable that it might elude them. Perhaps, when they left the conference room, with its stacks of documents freshly signed, none would suspect that a time bomb lay there, ticking in the bank's portfolio. And in Freer Motley's practice.

And so, long after the event, as Ed Mulcahy struggles to comprehend this, as he recreates the mental picture of the blank CRT screen fading to darkness, he tries to catch a face in its disappearing reflection, tries to see the eyes. But he cannot.

In every case, you begin with facts, and proceed to inferences. If you are a trial lawyer, you wrestle long with those inferences, trying to pin them, trying to make facts of them. That is what Ed Mulcahy did. But some inferences are stubborn. Some remain grey even after the jury comes back.

Part I

1

On the last day of March, dawn broke east of Boston, the sun peeking up over Spectacle Island, with a pale light tickling the steel-grey clouds over the rim of the Atlantic. A fishing boat headed up the harbour, so far away and dim in the half-light as to appear motionless; as though it were fixed in place on the still waters. The morning sun just caught the pennants rimming the World Trade Centre. Beyond it, the container ship cranes stood motionless.

As the first fingers of light poked into the office towers in the financial district, John Shepard sat alone in the Freer Room, the conference room which, as befitted its name, was the largest at Freer, Motley & Stone. His back was to the windows, and before him extended the vast conference table. On it were heaps of documents and cartons of congealing Chinese food.

Shepard sat with eyes closed, leaning back in his chair, although he was not asleep. His fingers worked slowly at his beard, stroking it. Before him on the table was a document with the words 'Closing Agenda' typed at its head.

At just a hair over six foot two, John Shepard's broad shoulders tapered to the same narrow waist he'd had at twenty. Even in a suit, and even with the first traces of salt flecking his curly sideburns, the man looked like an athlete. His face, like his torso, was long and lean: no fat on it, no sign of contentment in it. His mouth was usually cast in an ironic smile, a mouth that at an instant could go wide with laughter in its brown-bearded thatch: but an ironic laughter, a harsh laughter.

It was his eyes that most compelled you. It wasn't that they were deep, or that they were fiery, or that they were merry, or that they could pierce right through your head and seem to take note of whatever was behind it, and it wasn't just the way the man had of leaning down into your face while his eyes were doing it, as much as it was all of those things. John Shepard's eyes made you wonder whether your shoe laces were tied. His eyes could fix a man in mid-sentence and put him in mind of mouthwash. It was a body for work, a mouth for laughter, and a pair of eyes for making people nervous.

At about 6.30, others began to arrive in the Freer Room. Clusters of lawyers began to form at different parts of the table. Most looked drawn and tired, their eyes red, the chins of the men unshaven. Among them were Timothy Ogle, a first-year associate, and Mike Mitts, a paralegal. They were the two most junior Freer Motley people on the team: the proofreaders, the gofers, the all-night rewrite men. Shepard nodded and smiled as they walked in and parked at the far end of the table.

Timothy Ogle's powerful eyeglasses scanned the room. His was a narrow face, with thin tight lips, and those lips formed a thin tight smile. God, the money, think of it! There wasn't enough money in the whole world for Timothy Ogle, but a lot of it was going to flash in and out of this room today. He was so excited he couldn't swallow coffee. His adam's apple rocketed up and down.

Ogle might have been the skinniest adult male in Boston. His belt end wrapped crazily, obscenely around his waist. The oversized lenses in the tortoise-shell frames perched on his nose, dominating his face. The powerful convexity of the lenses shaped the long narrow face like an egg timer, with too much fore-head at one end and two thin lips at the other. In the last eight days, he had been on the receiving end of what seemed to him like a thousand orders. 'Ogle, you got that draft? Run a covenant change! Get me the schedule. No, the other schedule, goddamn it!' And so on. Now it was almost over.

Ogle looked at Mitts with relief, reminding himself that there was someone in this deal junior to him.

A moment later, he nudged Mike Mitts. 'Ms Seven Fifty,' he whispered, nodding towards the woman who had just walked in, flanked by two of her associates. Ogle sighed under his breath. Seven fifty, and a knock out. Elizabeth Russell, recently a partner at Fletcher, Daye & Symmes, represented the buyer. She was the only person in the room who looked fresh. A striking woman, tall and slim, with thick dark hair pulled back in a ribbon behind, and skin

11

lightly tanned, she usually did. On this particular morning, she arrived perfectly coiffed, wearing a suit of fine blue wool. About her throat was an Hermès scarf. Her eyes were of a riveting pale blue, wide and penetrating.

'Good morning, John, a pleasure to see you ... *and* your dinner,' she said, indicating the cartons of congealed Chinese food scattered around the table. She turned to the others in the room and smiled their way, too, to show the teasing was in good fun.

Shepard nodded back to her, with an exaggerated, ironical bow of the head. A smile creased his eyes as he sparred back. 'Now comes Elizabeth "Women's Libby" Russell to give me a raft of shit in my own goddamn conference room at my own goddamn closing. Always delighted to hear from buyer's learned counsel,' he said.

Mitts looked at Ogle curiously. 'Seven fifty?' he mouthed.

'Her fee,' Ogle whispered. 'Seven hundred and fifty thou for this deal.'

Mitt's eyebrows shot up. 'For eight days?' But Ogle, nervous now, shushed him.

'Do you have last night's revisions?' she asked.

'Last night's revisions,' Shepard sighed. Then he looked up, his eyes twinkling. 'You'll get 'em, Libby. Be here soon,' he said.

At about seven a young woman arrived from the copy centre with a cartful of drafts. She began to arrange twenty stacks of them around the table. She set one of the piles before Shepard, but he did not respond, or look at it. He leaned back in the chair, and his hand stroked his beard, moving up and down on his cheek.

12

Soon Russell and the other lawyers were poring over the fresh drafts.

It grew lighter. The day would be clear. The ribbon of the Central Artery winding round the district had already choked with the morning commuter traffic. Below the office, Congress Street was snarled. At Freer Motley, others began to drift in. Today would see – or would not see – the largest closing in the history of Depositors' Fidelity Bank, N.A., or 'DeFi', as it was known ('Dee-Fi', as it was pronounced), Freer Motley's largest client. And it would happen – or wouldn't happen – here in the Freer Room.

A consortium headed by Sidney Weiner, the New York financier, was seeking to buy Idlewild Industries, a widespread holding company based in Boston. Idlewild's roots lay in the Bassett family's mill holdings along the Merrimack River, but very little of its business now involved either shoes or textiles, the nineteenth-century mainstays. Now its holdings included electronics, bio-tech, and real estate nationwide. The jewel in the crown was Idlewild Tower – a gleaming obscenity on Fifth Avenue in Manhattan: fifty-four floors of new commercial real estate.

By the end of the day, if all went well, a partnership headed by Weiner would own Idlewild, and DeFi would have loaned $840 million towards the transaction.

The bankers from DeFi, led by Mark Barbieri, its aggressive young Division Head from Asset-Based Finance, arrived next, a pair of deputies flanking the red-headed banker. Ogle winked at Mitts from their outpost at the bottom of the table. 'If we close this, fifty K in a bonus for Barbie!' he whispered. His eyes widened behind their lenses.

On they came: the borrower's accountants, the Idlewild CFO, several directors, various aides and assistants. Among them was Phil Owens, from Bunker House, the venture firm putting up the subordinated debt, and his team of assistants and lawyers. Owens, an owlish little man, had not slept, and looked to be suffering from a digestive malady.

Mitts looked questioningly at Ogle.

'Two fifty,' he whispered.

More of the Idlewild partners arrived. Bond counsel, two of the Tennesseans from the Knoxville Redevelopment Authority, and a team from Chemical, one of the bank group participants. As the men and women arrived in ones and twos, the Freer Room, great as it was, began to fill with bodies, overnight bags, briefcases, chatter. And, of course, a full brace of investment bankers, the so-called 'IBs', soon entered to salivate over the fees they hoped to earn by day's end.

When the first set of golfing suspenders crossed the threshold, a great smile lit across Ogle's face. He turned to his co-conspirator Mitts. 'Meet Mr Twenty Mil,' he whispered.

Twenty mil! Think of it! Platt's firm would clear twenty mil! Today! Ogle did think of it, a triumphant smile crossing his face as he luxuriated in the idea of all of that money. He was still smiling when he looked up into John Shepard's gaze. He saw Shepard's eyes lock on his own, saw the index finger, saw it crook, saw it beckon him to come. Ogle's

Adam's apple bobbed. Shepard scared the shit out of him.

He bolted from the seat. When he had reached Shepard's side, his boss turned slightly, and said softly, 'Oggles?'

Ogle hated that name. He had been in the top 10 per cent of his class at Columbia Law! 'Yes?' he whispered.

'You two boys plan to do any work today, or just issue press releases on the fees?'

Ogle felt his face flush. 'Sorry,' he said.

Shepard turned away. 'Better focus on the credit agreement. And the subdebt agreement. That's where all the changes were yesterday.' Returning to his seat, Ogle buried himself in the documents. Mitts leaned over. 'What did he . . .?'

'Fuck off!' he whispered, his eyes darting up the table.

More of the business people gathered. Around the room, Ogle, Mitts, and the buyer's lawyers continued to frown over the revised drafts. Looking up, Libby Russell noticed that Shepard's stack of documents went untouched.

'Are you going to proof those?' she asked.

'Reckon I've seen enough of 'em.'

Her smile, if it was a smile, was inscrutable. She returned to her stack.

By 7.45 the noise of conversation had increased. A Freer Motley paralegal arrived with a couple of closing racks.

As the crowd gathered, John Shepard remained seated at the centre of the table, his back to the window, with nothing before him but a cup of black

15

coffee, his closing agenda, and the untouched stack of revisions. He nodded at each new arrival, and sat stroking his beard. By 8.15, the crowd had swollen to about thirty of the forty-five or so people who would ultimately attend this closing. Shepard now seemed suddenly to wake. He looked down at his watch, then up at the room about him.

'All right, folks,' he said. The chatter stopped. He spoke loudly now, but with the same rich drawl, still laconic, but authoritative. The room fell silent.

'We are seven hours from wire transfer deadline, and a lot to do. Lot to do. We got a lot of bodies here, more coming, and this isn't going to happen without co-ordination. So get your coffee, and here are your rules.

'*First*, we go by agenda item. Wait for your issue.

'*Second*, no bullshitting on phones in this room. You need to call somebody, go to the receptionist. Don't use my phones to call New York for your goddamn messages. I got three phones in here and I need them all.

'*Third*, this room is for work, people. Those who want to gab about restaurants, golf, who got laid last night, or the Red Sox, head for the lobby. Any IB heard discussing his condo at Hilton Head will lose his commission.

'All right, let's get after it. Oliver, do the agenda, startin' with what's done. Long list, people. Speak up if you think it ain't done. Your silence will close the discussion. Mary?'

Mary Oliver, a mid-level corporate associate at Freer Motley, began reading through the closing agenda – the list of two hundred ninety-six items

16

which had to be signed and delivered to close the transaction. She read out only those items which appeared to have been settled.

When the various investigators later tried to reconstruct this part of the closing, they asked whether anyone could remember discussion of the Idlewild mortgage. In fact, it was one of more than two hundred items which, over the next hour, Oliver read out. But if anyone grunted or nodded over coffee or said anything at the time, no one remembered it later. As Oliver identified the documents, Mitts lined up the execution copies in the closing rack.

The room began to buzz again. Small talk sprang up, punctuated by Mary Oliver's recitation, 'Agreement of Limited Partnership of Idlewild Partners, L.P.,' she said, 'Agreement of Limited Partnership of Idlewild Associates, L.P., Certificate of Limited Partnership of Delaware Limited Partnership, Articles of Incorporation of Idlewild Associates, Inc., a Delaware Corporation, Certificate of Secretary of State of Delaware . . .'

Shepard looked up and noticed a silver-haired man, flanked by associates, standing in the conference room doorway. He watched Russell rise to greet him. They began conversing pleasantly. The buyer was here, he thought. This must be a closing.

On went Oliver. 'Real Estate documents. One Texas Place Mortgage. 7078 Volunteer Drive, Lexington, Kentucky Mortgage, Collateral Assignments of Kentucky leases, "a" through "l". Estoppel Certificates. Certified copy of Texas Place Deed. Certified copy of Kentucky Deed. Idlewild Mortgage . . .'

'John Shepard. Welcome to my closing, Mr

17

Weiner,' he said when he reached Russell and her client. 'Hope you brought your Cross pen? We better get started on the signing.'

'*Your* closing?' said Sidney Weiner. 'I thought *I* was buying these companies.'

'With my client's money,' said Shepard, smiling. 'Until we wire, it's my closing. Do as I tell you and you'll own the companies by dinner – and, after dinner, the biggest tab since the last British Coronation.

'Oggles!' Shepard barked. 'Get this man some coffee. And a Danish. Get him two Danishes. He came all the way from New York to buy some companies.' Ogle stood poleaxed for a moment. Get a Danish? he thought. Mitts is a *paralegal*, I graduated in the top 10 per cent of Columbia Law, and *I* have to get the Danish . . .?

'Oggles?' Shepard prompted.

He was off, muttering dark – but silent – imprecations. *Oggles* indeed! Top 10 per cent at Columbia Law! Barely missed law review! He scuttled down the hall to find the kitchen.

John Shepard turned and resumed his centre field perch at the table as Oliver read on. 'Bassett Board resolutions. Resolutions of Affiliated Subsidiaries . . .'

One by one, the documents passed left to the closing rack and autograph alley. Oliver read on until 9.30.

Conversation was now buzzing all over the room.

'. . . Impossible to get a reservation there. I was in the Back Bay last . . .'

'It's skinny at base plus two. Second quarter this

18

would not be a doable deal. I would not want to be in committee again on these coverages.'

'. . . Mark, I have a problem with this . . .'

'. . . You got language . . .?'

'. . . Where is the Cooper's estoppel, has that been faxed?'

'. . . Jim, you got the schedules to the Security Agreement yet?'

'. . . Shit, are we out of coffee, already? Somebody get housekeeping!'

'. . . Where's Dick Lewis?'

'. . . Judy said he was getting here this morning . . .'

'People!' It was Shepard again. The buzz settled. 'We got some signing to do. Messrs Weiner, Fallon, Heckster, and Ms Cohen, get at it. Oggles, help 'em out. All right, Mary, how many open documents?'

'Twenty-nine.'

'Jesus. Okay, read out the journal of comparative scatology. People, listen for your issues. We're going to tick 'em off. No argument yet. We'll come back after roll call.'

At the bottom of the table Mike Mitts whispered to Ogle: 'Scatology? What is that? Like, jazz?'

'No,' Ogle whispered back. 'Like, shit. Big shit, big problem. Little shit, little problem.' He shrugged. 'It's a Shepard thing.'

Up the table, Oliver was beginning. 'Okay, number one,' she said, 'the Cooper's estoppel, we don't have it yet.'

'Worm shit,' said Shepard. Looking down the table at the real estate partner – technically, his senior at Freer Motley – he said, 'Tom where the hell is it?'

'They said they'd overnight it . . .'

19

'I thought this was roll call only,' someone said from the other end of the room.

'Roll call subject to the Shepard exception,' he said, then turned back to Tom Ruggerio. 'Well, have them fax it too. Call the sonofabitch.'

'I called him last night.'

'Call him again. Speak peace unto that heathen. Get a fax of that thing. All right!'

'Two,' continued Mary Oliver, 'the Paducah real estate opinion. Counsel won't give an opinion on an old railroad easement.'

Barbieri looked at Shepard. 'Mouseshit,' he said. 'Mark, you don't care. Next.'

'Three,' said Mary. 'Credit Agreement. We got covenant issues still?'

'What issues?'

'Comparative inventory covenants.'

'Ant shit. Jesus H. Roosevelt Christ, is that still around? Mark, Gary, get on that and fix it, will you, please?' Shepard barked at the junior banker – his own client. 'We've only put the goddamn thing through seven hundred drafts. Next issue.'

A young banker went to the end of the table with the company's CFO as Mary Oliver continued. 'Four . . . Five . . . Six . . .' The issues were read out, with Shepard ascribing to each issue the excrement of a greater or lesser order of animals, as the issue struck him in importance.

'. . . Eleven, Opinion of Borrower's Counsel.'

'What?'

'Yes, we still have an issue with . . .'

'Libby,' said Shepard, cutting her off before she could speak. 'Really. For eight forty mil, you folks

20

ought to opine to anything. I'm sure Sid will see it that way, too. Chicken shit.'

'Aw, John, make me a mammal at least, please?' she pouted, winking at him.

Mary Oliver pressed on. Men and women were now passing quickly in and out of the conference room, which was fast taking on the air of an eastern souk, with papers in a jumble, and the rumble of arguments in every corner.

'I need a phone, I need a phone,' someone was saying.

'Can we get a secretary in here?'

'Seventeen,' Mary Oliver was saying. 'The subdebt documents . . .'

'Where the hell is Lewis?' Shepard interrupted. 'Libby, you plan to close this deal?'

'He's coming,' she said.

'So's Christmas,' said Shepard. 'We're not funding without that knucklehead's autograph. Yeah, all right,' he continued, returning to Mary Oliver's list, 'we know about the subdebt issues. Mastadon shit.'

'Let's cut to it now, John,' said Phil Owens, the irate venture capitalist who had been waiting since eight for his moment. Bushy eyebrows emphasised his scowl. It was now nearly 9.45. 'Right now you people have no acquisition because you people have no subdebt. We *will* kill this deal on these documents, guys,' said Owens. His voice had a nasal, New York whine. 'Dick,' he said, turning to the banker, 'we are not funding.'

'Potential whale shit. Wait your turn, Phil, god-damn it,' said Shepard. 'Oh, and Phil?'

'Yes.'

'That was a good speech. Not great, but good. Next!'

When they had finished the roll call and finished sorting out the little issues, it was almost lunchtime. Three hours to go.

It was this part that people remembered most clearly later, when the investigations began. The subdebt negotiation. The question was arcane, and all of the specialists in the room thought Shepard's position was unusually aggressive. No one expected Bunker House to give on it. Why was Shepard being such a hard ass?

Depositors' Fidelity Bank was going to lend $840 million, at an interest rate which would be 2 per cent over the prime rate of interest. Bunker House would contribute another $40 million, as a loan which would be beneath the bank loan in priority. To compensate for its greater risk, Bunker House's interest rate would be much higher – about 15 per cent. But its agreement with DeFi would provide that DeFi would get paid back first.

So far, so good. But the devil is in the details. What would happen, for example, if the holding company went into bankruptcy? Under bankruptcy rules, subdebt can team up with the shareholders to wreak havoc with the bank. Shepard wanted to block that – he wanted a provision which would allow DeFi to exercise Bunker House's voting rights in a bankruptcy.

That's where the negotiation had broken down two days before. Owens vowed that they simply would not lend the money under those terms. At $40 million it was going to be the largest subordinated loan they had ever made. They would not take that risk in a bankruptcy.

'Phil,' John was saying, 'you may have forty in this thing, but I got eight hundred and forty in a goddamn LBO, and if it tanks and I want a liquidation, I want a goddamn liquidation. Why'n hell you think you've got a 15 per cent coupon!'

'What the hell are you worried about?' Owens demanded. 'You've got a first mortgage in Idlewild Tower, for Christ's sake!' He turned to the banker. 'Mark,' he said, 'we are not doing it. We are *not* doing it.'

'Well, I am a little concerned if DeFi is raising at this late date . . .' Sid Weiner started to say.

'We ain't committed except to documents acceptable to us, so don't even think about it,' Shepard cut him off.

'*Reasonably* acceptable,' said Libby Russell. 'John, what kind of grandstanding is this? We have a deal to close, and we have to close it now. Enough with the fun and games.' And for the first time, Russell looked nervous herself.

'Yes, Libby. But even reasonable people got to be careful about eight forty mil, now don't they?' said Shepard. She scowled at him and was about to interrupt when he turned to cut her off. 'Mark, you can't close without this provision. You'd be a lunkhead to close without it. You can't do it.'

Now Barbieri's eyes were bouncing back and forth between Shepard, Russell and Owens.

'You show me, John, another deal of this size where the mezzanine gave that up!' said the little birdlike man. His voice was high, and his eyebrows pumped up and down. Now he wagged a finger. 'You go downstairs, get the binder and bring it up here!'

Before he could answer, Shepard looked up. Others looked up too, for in the doorway stood Samuel Boylston Whitaker. He was the senior corporation law partner at Freer Motley, its former managing partner, and the nominal head of the DeFi team. His brush cut and cool blue-eyed gaze had, for a generation, inspired anxiety at Freer Motley. He stood in the doorway in a charcoal suit. Tall, erect, he surveyed the room over the top of a pair of bifocals. A venerable bow tie of white and blue silk was tied in just that way that sent the tie ends in an elegant droop. He nodded at Shepard.

'Lemme talk to my guys about this,' Mark Barbieri was saying to Owens. He had seen Whitaker too. 'Sam, can you join us?'

'Sam, *please* do,' Russell said. 'John's testosterone is about to croak a billion-dollar LBO.' She smiled, but looked careworn. It was time to close.

It was at that moment, all later agreed, that the call came in, the Good Lord providing a diversion. Or light entertainment. Or both. As Shepard was leaving the room, someone said, 'It's Lewis.'

He stopped and turned. 'Shit incoming,' Shepard said to himself softly, 'potentially major mammal.' And then, more loudly, 'He better be at Logan.'

The man on the phone shook his head. 'Pittsburgh,' he said.

'Jesus, give me that phone,' said Shepard. 'Lewis? Goddamn it, what in the nation are you . . .?'

There was a pause. The room watched as Shepard rolled his eyes, listening to the telephone. 'Missed his fucking plane . . . all we like sheep have *missed* our *fuckin'* planes, I can't believe . . .' he said to the room. He returned to the phone.

'I got a nine hundred million dollar closing and you can't find the airport? . . . What? . . . John Shepard at Freer. Look, you mighta had your ass here last night, sunshine. It's only your nine hundred million dollar acquisition . . . DeFi is not funding without your signature . . . yeah . . . yeah. Well, listen, I got about forty-seven people willing to rip your eyeballs out right now . . . Yeah . . . Hold on a damn minute . . . Don't move from that phone!

'People,' he said, this time to the room, 'listen up, will you!'

The room fell quiet.

'People, we have a knucklehead in Pittsburgh. He needs a law firm. Who's got one?'

'Janson Kohl,' someone said.

'Yeah, they'll do,' said Shepard. 'Get 'em. Get somebody there. This poster child's gonna be there in twenty and is gonna need a fax.' He returned to the phone and barked instructions to the hapless director. 'All right, all right,' he was saying, 'get into a cab and get over to Janson Kohl . . . Hell, I don't know, *find* it . . . What? . . . Janson, Kohl, somebody and somebody . . . Yeah . . . Call this number back when you get to their receptionist. Think you can catch a cab all right or do we need to send somebody to do that for you? What?'

'That's really helpful, John,' Libby Russell interjected.

'Yeah . . . yeah.' Shepard was still on the phone. 'Well, I'll be happy to oblige, after we close. Get to

25

that damn law firm. The Mouth of the Lord hath spoken it, motherfucker!

'Jesus!' he said, as he slammed down the receiver. 'Sid, it's a helluva partner you got there. Is he the guy who's gonna remember to pay back my debt?' He shook his head. 'Oggles!'

Oggles again! In front of the whole room! 'Yes?'

'Is a faxed signature binding under Pennsylvania law?'

Ogle shrugged.

'Well, find the hell out, son, and if it ain't, check Ohio and make some cab driver's day.'

At that point Shepard left the Freer Room to join his client, Barbieri, and Samuel Whitaker in an interior conference room. They were gone for some time.

When he returned from the library, Timothy Ogle hovered outside the glass wall of the interior conference room. He saw Whitaker sitting impassively. Shepard was pacing, gesticulating, shaking his head. Barbieri sat looking at his hands.

Ogle knocked, hesitantly.

'What is it?' Shepard said.

'About that faxed signature, I checked, and . . .'

'Oggles, just make the problem go away. And make yourself go away.' Shepard eyed him critically. 'For Jesus's sake, Oggles, eat some Danish. You're too goddamn skinny!'

'Sorry.' As Ogle backed out of the room, he saw Shepard looking at his watch.

'Look, it's your goddamn billion dollars, Mark,' he heard Shepard say, and then the door latched shut.

It was one o'clock. The Freer Room was now a nervous place. There was barely time to flog the secretaries through the mechanics of incorporating the remaining changes in the documents. There was no time for more of this foolishness between the bank and the venture capital firm. The buyers and sellers, the bankers and lawyers, the accountants and advisers, even the secretaries, stopped milling and took seats when Shepard resumed his post at the centre of the table. The room fell silent. He pressed his fingertips together, looking at them distractedly for a moment, and then returning Owens's gaze. There were now more than forty people wondering whether this closing was going to happen.

Shepard's eyes narrowed and he stared at Phil Owens, his mouth in a tight, ironical smile. 'Phil,' he said, 'you are one cheap motherfucker. And I don't mind tellin' you your eyebrows are buggin' the shit out of me.' He paused. 'We give the point,' he said. And that was that.

Except for a frantic, breathless rush to amend the subdebt documents and obtain the final signatures and fax out wire transfer authorisations, to collect Lewis's signatures from the Pittsburgh law office, and to put the key mortgages and UCCs on record at forty-three offices nationwide. The room became a blizzard of paper, of secretaries hurrying in and out, faxes being snatched from machines and rushed into the crowd, of throngs of lawyers huddled over documents, nodding, scribbling in the changes.

At 2.53 p.m., it had come down to the money. Once again the room was hushed, elbow to elbow with lawyers, bankers, deal men, accountants, investment bankers. Half-eaten sandwiches littered the table, in and amongst the piles of drafts. Ties were askew, jackets flung over chair backs and the HVAC vents. The air was close. All around the room were reddened eyes and sweat-ringed armpits. Sid Weiner paced by the window. Even Libby Russell looked dishevelled. With her jacket off, she stood by Mark Barbieri, one hand on her hip and the other brushing hair from her forehead. She bit her lip as she strained to hear Barbieri, who stood with a telephone to his ear.

'Yeah . . . yeah . . . uh, huh,' he was saying. 'Yeah, we can wait.'

He waited. They waited. And then a small arch appeared in the banker's eyebrow, and a smile spread slowly over his face. He looked up from the phone. 'Sid,' he said, 'Bankers has just acknowledged receipt of eight hundred eighty million dollars.'

Someone let out a whoop, backs were slapped, laughter spilled into the halls, and eight days of tension, sleeplessness, and doubt ended. Idlewild had closed.

The news had raced round the office. Shepard had done it again, pulled off the biggest closing in the firm's history, and in just eight days. Ed Mulcahy had to see for himself. At just after five, he took an elevator upstairs to find the conference room.

The Freer Room had all but emptied: Mitts and a somewhat crestfallen Ogle were cataloguing the documents. All that money, Ogle was thinking. But it had all gone. And he was left with this mountain of paper. Him, a graduate of Columbia Law – a near miss for law review!

Libby Russell was packing up her briefcase. Shepard leaned back in his centre seat, his size twelves on the table, and sang out as he recognised a familiar face at the door, 'Ed Mulcahy! What the hell brings you out of the Doberman cage, boy!'

'The word is all over the office, John. Something about you and a billion-dollar LBO. You pull it off?' Ed said.

'He pulled it off,' said Libby Russell, turning to greet him. 'Hello, Ed Mulcahy, it's been a long time.' She smiled broadly at him. He hadn't seen her for years, and, once again, he was disarmed. She was a beautiful woman, showing a little eyestrain now, perhaps, but when she turned her head slightly to the side and flashed her model's smile, it was difficult to concentrate.

Any pretence at eloquence fled. 'Hi,' was all he could manage.

'Damn, Mulcahy,' said Shepard, 'for a pot-bellied Celt, you know all the pretty girls. Lots of sides to you.'

'Ed and I were prosecutors together,' Libby said. 'Right, Ed?'

'I see,' said John, before he could answer, 'before old Women's Lib here got a real job. Well, the lady is too kind. *She's* the one pulled it off. I just represented a bank, is all. Her guy owns Idlewild tonight.'

'The credit is all *yours*, John,' she said, as if determined to have the last shot in this tennis rally of mutual admiration. 'Anyway, I'll see you later.'

But he shook his head. 'Naw,' he said, 'won't be there.'

'No? John Shepard pass on a closing dinner?'

'Got some business to attend to, Libby.'

'Oh, yeah, right. Look, John, I'll speak to the headwaiter. You won't have to use a fork or anything. We'll just bring you a big slab of meat and let you tear into it with your fingers. Okay?'

Shepard had his hands clasped behind his neck and was leaning back looking at the ceiling. 'Mul-ca-hee, is the bitch funnin' with me? Are you taking note of this? Mul-ca-hee is my litigator, Lib. I'll have him all over your ass one of these days. So to speak.'

She teased him back, winking at Ed and goading Shepard. 'Foaming jugs of beer, John, you great big man, you, served by chesty young chatelaines, even a few of consenting age, maybe, just as you . . .'

'I hope you will reconsider,' said a sharp voice from behind Ed's shoulder. They were all caught short, not needing to turn or look to know that it was Samuel Whitaker's voice. Instantly the banter ceased, and the room went cold. A moment ago there had been a pillowfight, and now a dorm parent had surprised the slumber party. Shepard turned from the older man's gaze.

The exchange which followed lasted less than a minute. For long afterwards Ed Mulcahy would remember the coldness that came so swiftly over the room the instant Shepard heard Whitaker's voice.

'Whatever has happened between us, John,' Whitaker said, 'you should enjoy yourself this evening. And I want you to know that I am deeply grateful to you. This transaction could not have been closed without you.'

Libby Russell, regaining her own composure, looked up at Whitaker, who directed a courtly half-bow to her. 'Elizabeth,' he said. 'Congratulations.'

'Thank you, Sam. And to you.

'John,' she said, turning back to him, 'Sam's right. You've earned it. You did an extraordinary job putting this deal together. It was your deal. You should come tonight.'

But none of this warmed the chill in the room, and Shepard merely waited for it to be over, looking away through the windows towards the airport silently until they were finished. With the diplomacy come to its clumsy conclusion, Whitaker stood by the door and Shepard remained motionless, across from Libby Russell, the three of them under the gaze of old Simon Freer, looking out above his starched collar in the portrait over the credenza. At the far end of the room, Mitts and Ogle had stopped shuffling papers.

Shepard broke the silence. 'I got other plans,' he said.

His hand slipped into his breast pocket and withdrew a blue envelope. Mechanically, he placed it on the table and gave it a push. The envelope glided across the silky table top and came to rest before the senior partner. Their eyes met then, and remained locked as Shepard rose, stepping around the table towards the door, locked even as he reached the threshold. Now they were eye to eye, and even Whitaker seemed to retreat a hair, a fraction, as

Mulcahy wondered, for a moment, whether the confrontation might become physical.

'What I *earned*,' Shepard said, when he was within six inches of Whitaker's face, 'wasn't any goddamn steak dinner. I earned loyalty. And I earned a partnership. But I didn't get either, did I?'

There was no answer. He turned for the door. But before taking his leave of them both, the senior partner of Freer Motley and the rising star of its cross-town rival, Fletcher Daye, his eyes had narrowed and Mulcahy could see by that ironical grin that he was going to get off a parting shot.

'I was just the associate. This mess,' he said, his arm indicating the stacks of closing documents at the far end of the table, 'was y'all's deal.'

Then he was gone. He was gone, and the rest of them were left to wonder just exactly what they were doing in that room together. The blue envelope rested on the table for a moment more before Samuel Whitaker retrieved it. Later, of course, after the investigation began, long after Whitaker had opened the envelope and read the letter, and sent it on to Human Resources to close out their personnel file, Ed Mulcahy would find it, and read John Shepard's one-sentence announcement of his resignation.

2

It was the sort of club where the silver, and the china, and even the linen, has a certain heft to it. Waiters do not come, and they do not go. They materialise and then vanish. Conversation is muted, and there is a decorous clinking of the silver on the china, and a decorous lady at the door, and there are on the walls decorous prints of old New York, and the chairs are polished to a deep and decorous sheen, and there is, to the north, an exceptionally decorous view of Central Park.

The lady stepped forward to greet Sid Weiner when he arrived, and he acknowledged her with a smile. Weiner dressed impeccably in a Glen Plaid suit. The starched handkerchief, the silk foulard, the spread collar, the cufflinks, the white hair, the deep tan – far too deep to have had any relationship to April in New York – they all belonged in the Parkview, and were content there. He stood with his hands clasped behind his back, admiring the prospect from the top of the tower. He liked everything about the Parkview

Club: he liked the menu; he liked the cut flowers; and he particularly liked the view from his usual table, up Fifth Avenue to the park – a view which recently had become his view. For the Parkview was on the 54th floor of what was now *his* tower: Idlewild Tower.

Weiner turned to meet his guest, who stepped through the door just as the clock was sounding one. 'Good to see you again,' he said. 'I didn't expect to see you – and here, of all places.'

They were seated at his usual corner table, and he gave his guest the seat with the unobstructed view towards the park. Weiner recommended the vichyssoise, and the waiter brought a bowl for each of them.

'I was surprised by your call,' he said. 'Pleasantly.' He discoursed for a bit about the view, the tower, the weather.

His guest smiled.

After the waiter brought the fish, his guest said, 'You enjoy your new building.'

'I do enjoy this building.'

The guest separated flakes of fish one from another before asking, with an air of distraction, whether Sid Weiner might enjoy it more if he held it debt free.

Weiner smiled. 'I must tell you about my trip to St Lucia,' he said.

Throughout his adult life, Sid Weiner had found himself in unusual negotiations, and he had long ago learned that sometimes it is best to seem not even to notice a surprising offer. At any rate he rarely confessed surprise, or even interest, in anything surprising or interesting. So they chatted idly about his trip to the islands as if he hadn't heard the remark. A waiter materialised and vanished with the plates. Another materialised in his place with the dessert cart.

'Coffee?'

His guest declined. Weiner asked for an espresso and waved off the desserts.

Now Weiner's guest circled back to the subject. 'Debt free, this building would generate, what, about ten million a year in free cash flow?'

'You must have studied the pro formas very well,' Weiner said. The coffee was there. It was time to talk. 'But what has ten million a year in free cash flow to do with the real world?'

'The world is what you make of it, Sid. And the world could be a better place.'

He smiled. 'My dear friend,' he said. 'May I call you that? I congratulate you. You now have my undivided attention.'

But his guest was looking off towards the park, still, to all appearances, distracted.

'Supposing that a dear friend,' his guest went on, 'were able to reduce your debt here: to save you four or five, or even ten million a year in free cash flow from this building. A prudent businessman might determine that it was worth his while to retain that friend. To have that friend on his side.'

The guest looked straight at Sid now, and the businessman felt himself disarmed by the steadiness of the gaze. 'A prudent businessman might want to put such a friend on retainer. I would think, for savings of better than five million a year in cash flow, the businessman would be happy to invest a retainer of two million a year. For, say, five years. That's the term of the mortgage, isn't it?'

Weiner was frowning. He was a man accustomed to circumlocution, but not at this level. 'Two million dollars is a lot of money.'

'Yes, it is. And right now you have the privilege of paying it to a bank. It's also a lot less money than five million dollars.' And his guest smiled again, that unsettling smile.

'I'm glad you enjoyed the lunch,' Sid Weiner said. 'Well, let's suppose I was interested in a little debt relief. That's American after all, isn't it? What would I have to do?'

'To begin with, I would recommend hiring a good lawyer.'

3

In the shaving mirror the very morning of the Shanklin meeting, Edward Xavier Mulcahy had taken inventory. Height: still only five foot eight. Hair: one head of dark and curly, now thinner, with hairline inching back. Teeth: still on the shelf, like a good book, but like a good book, yellowing. ('You mean I need to floss more?' he had asked an inquisitive dentist at his last check-up. 'What exactly do you mean by "more"?' the dentist had cross-examined.) Eyes: blue. Midriff: oh, Lord. Ed Mulcahy had played a little ball in his youth, but had never amounted to much as an athlete. At thirty-six, he could still remember the feeling of twenty. He just couldn't *feel* it any more.

He looked down at the counter. The morning *Transcript*, opened to the sports section, was splotched with drops of water. Mulcahy liked to read while he was shaving – always had. From through the wall, he heard a low moan. The moan acquired a baseline intelligibility.

'Eddie!' said the voice.

'Yeah?'

'Seen my story yet?'

'Yeah.'

'Whaddaya think?'

In a matter-of-fact sort of voice, Mulcahy replied, 'I think it's . . . ah, not your best.' He screwed up his face into a contorted pout as he brought the razor underneath his chin.

'Thank you. Thank you for your support,' said the voice.

Ed looked down at the newspaper, scanning the Celtics story, by Victor H. Reggitz. 'No, I mean it, Gitz,' he said helpfully. 'It's not your best. Objectively.'

'Thank you, kind sir,' said the voice through the wall. 'Why don't I ever learn?'

'Man's gotta tell the truth,' Mulcahy grunted, and went back to pulling the razor through the foam.

The voice grunted back. 'That's my business, not yours.' Gitz was now awake.

'Not so,' Mulcahy said, 'not so. I'm a great believer in the truth. Makes life easier.'

'Please die,' said Gitz. 'Soon. Today would be acceptable.'

'How come I have to read twelve paragraphs to know it's a basketball game?' Mulcahy asked back.

''Cause you're illiterate and you have no life. Did you make coffee?' Now there was stirring in Gitz's room.

'Yeah,' Mulcahy said.

Gitz stumbled into the bathroom. He was a skinny man, with curly red hair and droopy eyes. 'How come,' he said, 'it's important to you to tell me my story is lousy? Can't you just go off and bill some hours or something? Isn't that what you do?'

Mulcahy stared into the shaving mirror, rubbing his hand across his freshly shaven chin.

'Is that my shaving cream?'

'It is your shaving cream,' said Mulcahy.

'You are shaving with my shaving cream when you criticise my story?'

'You've got me there,' said Mulcahy. 'You have absolutely got me.'

'Ed, lemme ask you something,' said Gitz, scratching his belly.

Mulcahy looked over at his room-mate.

'I've been your room-mate for, what is it, six years? I've seen you through, what, three women? I told you to drop the ones you kept. I told you to keep the ones you dropped . . .'

Mulcahy grunted. 'The ones dropped me, you mean.'

'Right. Anyway, six years, right? So I know you pretty well, right? I have this question. Just exactly what the hell is it that you *do* do?'

When he boarded an elevator just after 10.30 a.m., Ed Mulcahy knew only that he had been summoned to a meeting with Cain and Shanklin in Shanklin's corner office on 24. Shanklin was the managing partner, and Cain the chairman of the litigation department, and so Mulcahy knew something unusual was astir. He did not guess, could not have guessed, at the course on which he would so soon be set. But days and decisions which seem dramatic in hindsight often are accretive, gradual in the doing. They are like a river. If you float for even a little while, it carries you downstream, and each passing yard brings less and less hope of getting back.

In Shanklin's office he found the Gang of Three awaiting him: 'Texas Tim' Cain, head of litigation; 'Liebo', or Daniel Liebowitz, a cultivated, urbane tax lawyer who seemed to know all of the most prosperous of the city's Jewish community, and to have brought half of them aboard as clients; and then there was the Count, Albert Shanklin, whose nickname sprang from his uncanny resemblance to Bela Lugosi. The Count had few friends, but he had the ear of DeFi's Chairman, and he had parlayed that connection and a great talent in financing law to become head of Freer Motley's management committee.

All these Harvard people always made Mulcahy a little uncomfortable. The white shoe firms of downtown were still in the hands of the Harvards, and when you come from Northeastern, as Mulcahy did, you sensed you had a little more to prove.

Shanklin's office was always dark. He used only a desk lamp, and its low-wattage bulb was a symbol of the Count's fixation on firm overhead. On that morning, he looked as grim-faced as his namesake, frowning from behind the polished stone slab which held his telephone and which went by the appellation of 'desk', though it looked more like an altar. His companions, sitting before this monstrosity, appeared no less dyspeptic. Shanklin put before Mulcahy the letter which was later referred to as the 'Grenade', and had him read it before they began.

On its face, it was not much: simply a note,

addressed to Depositors' Fidelity, dated 1 May, delivered by hand. It read:

> Enclosed please find our cheque no. 1106 in the amount of $848,500.00, representing $8,500.00 in interest payable as of 30 April 1992, and payment in full of the outstanding principal on the indebtedness secured by that certain Mortgage by and between Depositors' Fidelity Bank, N.A., as Agent, and Idlewild Tower Partners II, L.P., dated as of 31 March 1992 (the 'Mortgage').
>
> Also enclosed please find a form of discharge for the Mortgage. Please execute the discharge and return the same to the undersigned.
>
> Very truly yours,
>
>
> Idlewild Holdings Group II, Inc., General Partner, Idlewild Tower Partners II, L.P.
> By:
> Sidney R. Weiner
> President

When he had finished reading, Mulcahy looked around him at the men in the Count's office. There were no smiles. Liebo, who rocked nervously in a chair, said, 'Now read this,' his slim finger indicating the promissory note, which contained the figure of $840 *million* as the indebtedness. Then Mulcahy read the first page of the mortgage document, in which the figure of $840 *thousand* appeared.

It took him two trips through the documents even to notice the discrepancy in the fine print. Then he looked back at the Grenade letter, and his eyes opened wide.

'Some typo,' he said.

No one was smiling. Mulcahy said that he supposed Freer Motley had drafted the documents, and when Shanklin said, 'Of course,' he looked up.

'Whose deal was this?' Mulcahy asked.

'Whitaker's,' hissed the Count.

Mulcahy waited. 'What are we planning to do?' he asked. 'What does DeFi want?'

'DeFi wants our balls on the bull's eye at the local shootin' range,' Tim said.

'I don't know,' said the Count. 'We're looking at it.'

Mulcahy's eye returned to the document. 'This can't work,' he said. 'It's just a *typo*. A scrivener's error, something like that. There'll be an equitable defence.' He added questions. 'Doesn't this number show up in fourteen other places in the documents? Wouldn't that show it is an error? I mean, they wired eight hundred forty mil, right? Doesn't it have to be an eight hundred forty million dollar mortgage?'

The words had barely left his mouth when he reflected on how absurd they must have sounded. This group hadn't summoned him for his legal analysis of a case which could cripple the law firm's relationship with its largest client. He was its junior litigation partner.

'Naw,' said Texas Tim, 'you ain't a deal guy, Ed. Sumbitches *defahn* everything, you know? So the number gets defahned as the "Indebtedness", and then all the other cross references are to the "Indebtedness". So that don't work.

'And the problem with yo' other argument is the money being loaned don't have to match up with the mortgage in a deal like this. See, Idlewild Tower was the key collateral, but there was, I dunno, Al, thirty, forty other pieces a collateral, right?'

Shanklin nodded. Texas Tim went on.

'Other real estate, stock of half a dozen companies, assets here, there, ever'where. It don't matter that all that other stuff don't amount to a billion dollars. Value is negotiable. So Sid Weiner will say that that was the deal, y'all – that Idlewild was only supposed to secure a little bitty eight forty thousand of the debt, and all the other stuff secured the rest. See? Now that's bullshit, of course. But it probably is plausible enough to git 'em into their legal argument.

'There you got the Parol Evidence rule, right? Where the parties express their agreement in an unambiguous writing, evidence to contradict the writing is inadmissible. Ain't nuthin' more goddamn unambiguous than a number, wouldn't you say?'

No one answered him. It was quiet for a moment, before Texas Tim went on. 'Funny, you know, litigatin' for the bank, I dunno how many times I've relied on the rule. Some ole boy who cain't pay his debt is always wantin' to say there was a side deal of some kind. Hell, I probably got briefs fahled in ever' court in the state which'd be waved in my face if we litigated this. If DeFi guesses wrong, it's an eight hundred thirty-nine million dollar guess. DeFi don't like that kind of ante. Neither does the OCC. 'Sides, Ed, to defend the bank case, you got to prove our own malpractice, and we've only got a hundred mil in coverage.'

Mulcahy nodded.

'Ed,' said Cain, 'we've got you here for a slightly different reason. We need to investigate this matter. Find out what happened. We're looking at a huge malpractice exposure either way.'

'Well, have you spoken to Mr Whitaker? I assume somebody didn't proof his document, right?' Mulcahy asked.

There was an uncomfortable silence at the mention of his name. 'Maybe,' said the Count, after a moment. 'Maybe not. But find out. If it was, find out who made the mistake, and how, and who read it, or who didn't read it and should have. How did this get through a Freer Motley closing?

'And,' he said, 'if it wasn't a mistake, find that out too.'

What was the real agenda here? Mulcahy wondered, looking around the darkened office. Was it just as they said? Or was it a vendetta against Whitaker? Mulcahy glanced from one to another, but their faces were set. No one moved except Liebowitz, who continued to rock back and forth in his chair.

'Wasn't this John Shepard's deal?' Ed asked, remembering suddenly that strange meeting in the conference room on the last day of March.

'Yes,' said Shanklin.

Mulcahy removed his glasses, and rubbed his eyes. This was not proving to be a good assignment. 'John Shepard is a friend of mine,' he said. 'A good friend.'

'He may have left his good friend's partnership with eight figures of liability,' said the Count, cutting him off acidly. 'Maybe nine figures. Just look at this. See where it goes. And get on it as fast as you can.'

Cain added, 'Ain't nobody convicted John of anything. He probably had nothing to do with this.' He paused, as if to let the silence acknowledge that Shepard's stunning rejection for partnership had to be on everyone's mind. It had happened on 15 March, only days before the frantic eight-day marathon Idlewild negotiation and closing.

'Does it make sense for me to do this? John Shepard and I were, well, close. We once, well . . .' Mulcahy's voice trailed off.

But the Count wasn't listening. 'You are on this,' he said, and then raised his eyebrows to punctuate the conclusion of the meeting.

Mulcahy wanted to say something further, but it was clear that the matter was closed. In later days he would task himself for not confronting it then. But they had left him no opening. They had caught him unaware, unprepared for a stand.

He rose, uncomfortably, and left them, wandering dizzily from the corner office into the corridor and down to the elevators. So they wanted the Coloradan, the maverick, the one who, good as he was, brilliant as even his enemies had to concede, would never quite fit in because he was foul-spoken and ruder and cockier than all of them. Yes, he was smarter, too, and even smoother with a client, when the moment called for it, and cleverer in negotiations. But he wasn't one of them.

Shepard had come to the firm out of Harvard Law School in the early 1980s. When Mulcahy got there five years later, Shephard was already ensconced as a rule to himself, a brilliant iconoclast, and a canny deal lawyer. Quickly Mulcahy had been drawn to his flamboyance. It was so alien to everything about Mulcahy's manner, so deserving of a comeuppance it never found. The Friday afternoons – he remembered those best. He would pick up his phone to hear the country-western yodel of Shepard hollering: 'Get your ass down here, boy!' And Shepard would have gathered two or three others, popped the frosties out of his credenza, and the stories would begin.

Those were the best times: Shepard, his feet up on his desk, beer bottles all over it, the door wide open – he didn't care who knew about it – rattling off his caustic review of the firm's powers and potentates, Mulcahy drinking in the stories with the beer. He could break every rule, every convention, and nobody touched him. And one night, three years ago, Shepard had said to Ed Mulcahy, 'Vacation time, mother-fucker. Grab those skinny boards – we're going to Colorado!'

An odd thing had happened early in Shepard's career, a thing no one would have predicted. Samuel Whitaker, the strait-laced Yankee senior partner, product of three generations of Yale and two of the Harvard Law School, had become his mentor. And Shepard looked up to Whitaker, too, a thing perhaps equally unlikely. Perhaps each man saw in the other something which he could not be, but secretly admired. In the quixotic manner of law firms, the link proved a bad one for Shepard. Whitaker's star had waned at just the time he came up for partner, and the war drums beat for a sacrifice. Shepard's manner had offended so many lesser men that enough dissenters were rallied to oppose him at the partner-ship vote, in part out of distaste at his style, in part for fear of his abilities, in part as the opportune moment to stage a coup against Whitaker's control of the firm. Shepard was the offering, and he was passed over at the vote on 15 March.

That was the night they elected Ed Mulcahy.

And so that second day of May, Ed Mulcahy began his assignment with a gnawing ambivalence. He sat for most of the afternoon in a conference room overlooking Post Office Square, as paralegals gathered the files from every corner of the office, and the stacks of paper grew on the table around him: the loan bibles, the drafts files, the research files, the due diligence. They wanted the Coloradan, and they had deputised Ed to bring him in. Welcome to the partnership.

He sat distractedly for several hours, but by day's end took consolation in this: the facts are the facts. All he had to do was investigate them, and report on them. Investigation Ed Mulcahy was good at, and perhaps there was no betrayal in reporting the facts. So he began.

Mulcahy looked about himself at the files on the table. The stack of drafts of the mortgage began with the first, dated 24 March 1992, at 8.59 p.m., and proceeded through to the tenth, or execution, draft which was dated 31 March 1992, the day of the closing, at 06.49 a.m.

He saw that the early drafts contained moderate mark-ups, reflecting the lawyers' skirmishes over details. In later drafts, the comments dwindled to sporadic. But none of this involved the key point. In the first nine drafts, the paragraph identifying the amount of debt secured was simply blank. Only the tenth draft, which was circulated only three hours or so before the parties began signing, and the final, executed version, which was identical, contained the error.

He did some quick calculations. The wire transfer deadline would have been 31 March at 3 p.m., and the wires had to clear by 31 March to permit the loan to be booked in the first quarter. Where to begin? He'd start with the people. Hunting through a file picked at random, he found a cover memo and ran his finger down the list, and a moment later had dialled a number on the telephone.

'Mary,' he said, 'Ed Mulcahy.'

'Oh, hi, Ed,' said Mary Oliver.

'Mary, did you hear about Idlewild?'

'The Grenade? Yeah. Sheesh.'

'I've been asked to look into it. I wonder if you have a few minutes?'

She paused. 'Sure.'

When she joined him in the conference room a few moments later, he had the circulation list in front of him. 'This was the deal Libby Russell led, right?'

She rolled her eyes – the special revolution of the female pupil reserved for the subject of other females, that feminine optical gesture which says, 'Ask me about her. I'm begging you.'

'You two not friendly?' he asked.

'Libby-I'm-late-for-a-reception-Russell? Libby Will-the-gentlemen-kindly-restore-their-tongues-to-their-mouths Russell? *That* Libby Russell? Oh, yes, Snow White and I are old knitting buddies,' said Mary.

She folded her arms across her chest and set her pudgy face into a frown, her glasses slipping down her broad nose, and her curls lying rather too flat on her head.

Mulcahy was shaking his head. 'Snow White?' he asked.

'Sure. The dark-haired beauty with the seven male dwarves carrying her bags for her. And all the princes of finance just want that one kiss.'

Mary Oliver had busted her rather considerable backside for every advantage, and for most every day of the last six years at Freer Motley. A little heavy, a little frumpy, a little left out when the bankers grabbed up pals to share a drink with after a negotiation, a little lonely, she bore grudges. And first among them was a grudge against any woman who got somewhere by short cuts. Mary had worked the long hours, answered the phone calls, proofread the documents. She had paid dues.

'You know, Ed,' she said, 'she was something to pull off that deal, I'll say that.'

'What?'

'She doesn't know bupkus about corporate law. To do a billion-dollar LBO when you don't know corporate law – to arrange enough people to cover for you – you've got to be pretty . . .'

'Smart?' he asked.

'No, just . . . pretty,' she said.

'We *are* venting this afternoon.'

'Well, I am. But hear me out. I'm good on Snow White once you get me started. Ed, I'm all for women making it, but women making it because they're connected and a bunch of third-rate loan officers have wet dreams about them, that doesn't help the

49

cause. We caught her once, though. She didn't know what a Deprizio waiver was.'

'A what?'

'A Deprizio waiver.'

'Mary, I hate to break it to you, but the world is full of people who don't know what a Deprizio waiver is. One of them is in this room.'

'Well, you're a litigator. You're allowed. Leading an LBO, you know Deprizio. Basically, it's this whacked-out case that says, in a bankruptcy, a lending bank may have preference risk if you have insider guarantors in a deal. Which this one did.'

She could see the blank look on his face, so she went on. 'In a nutshell, it's this, Ed. You're the bank, you've got the collateral, everything is fine. But, same bank, same collateral, if you have guarantees from the owners, then payments you get prior to a bankruptcy, you might have to give back. There's this weird case Deprizio, and it leads to that result. The point is, you draft around it. Which this deal did. So, one morning we're sitting in the Freer Room, Shepard, me, a bunch of bankers, and Snow White. And she says no to my Deprizio clause. "Give up subrogation claims," she says to me, "you understand that we certainly can't agree to that." Well, lah-dee-dah! Shepard pulls on his beard and he looks over at me and I look over at one of Snow's flunkies and he looks back at Shepard, and we all proceed to look around at our clients, and I'm hoping John will nod at me so I can cut her knees off. I'll be honest. It would have made my day to cut her knees off. But Shepard – he doesn't. He leans over, and he says, real

50

quietly, "Libby, do you really think a national bank is gonna take Deprizio risk in a billion-dollar LBO?"

'Well, she looks at him, and what can she do but the old reliable? Smile sweetly, Snow White! She knew she didn't know what the hell Deprizio was! And she knew we knew. She realised everybody in the room knew what it was. The clients knew what it was! The receptionist in the lobby probably knew what it was! Everybody except her. And she didn't even know how to spell it! So she gives the room about a megawatt of eye power and says, "We'll table the issue for now, and come back to it." We'll come back to it just as soon as one of my love slaves explains what it is!

'Sheesh!' said Mary Oliver, re-folding her arms.

'Okay,' said Mulcahy. 'Enough on Libby Russell. I need to . . .'

'. . . she's probably frigid, too,' Mary interrupted.

Mulcahy smiled. *That* would be a pity, he thought. 'I need to ask you some questions about the mortgage.'

Now Mary Oliver's face fell. 'Ed,' she said, 'I wasn't the real estate person, okay?'

'Mary, there was a typo, a big typo. The mother of all misprints. My job is to figure out how it happened. That's all.'

They talked until late in the afternoon. She told him that a first-quarter closing had been vital to DeFi's commitment. The last drafts weren't circulated until nearly 7 a.m.. They still had to be reviewed by Fletcher Daye, Ellenberg, Shipley, the bond lawyers, and the principals. Finals weren't generated until close to noon. It was tight, too tight: so tight that there was barely time to get the last changes typed.

'A deal like this,' she said, 'almost never closes in a day. Usually you preclose it for a whole day. The lawyers run through it, organise it, make sure there are no outstanding issues, you fine tune the last details, you fool with the closing adjustments, and so on. The lender's lawyer runs through the closing agenda, okay? Have we got this, have we got that, have we got the other thing? And you know, there's usually a few nits you have to do still. A line or two in the opinions. That kind of thing.'

Mulcahy nodded his head.

She went on: 'The clients sit in one room and bullshit. The lawyers sit in another and negotiate. You bring the clients in after a while. Somebody gives the last point or two so everybody can go. Then the next day, the actual closing, is all mechanics. It's all wiring instructions and co-ordination with the guys you've got out in the registries to put the UCCs on, and so forth. I mean, you've got two hundred and ninety-six things to sign, in counterparts, you know? That's the usual big deal.

'But Idlewild . . . Idlewild, Jesus, this deal didn't preclose. And more than that, we were still negotiating deal points, I mean negotiating down to the wire, you know what I mean? It was absolutely crazy. We were still negotiating the subdebt documents at lunch!'

'Why?' he asked. 'Why was it so crazy?'

'Ed,' she said, 'it was a nine hundred million dollar deal. We closed it in eight days.'

'I guess that's right,' he said.

'So you're the executioner,' she said, after a moment.

'No,' he said. 'No. I just need to understand it.'

But she didn't believe him, and he wasn't sure he believed himself. 'Look,' she said, 'was I in the room on 31 March? Yes. Could I have read the mortgage? Yes. But a lot of people were in that room, a lot of people. And I'm not the real estate associate. It wasn't my job, Ed!'

'Mary,' he said after a pause, 'I really am just trying to understand it. I'm not a deal lawyer.'

They were silent for a while, until she had calmed down. At length he asked, 'The mortgage starts out, I mean in the early drafts, with the amount blank.'

'Yeah,' she said, 'that's not unusual. You have to understand, the amount is not in dispute, you know? All the drafting, all the negotiating, all the red-lining and the late nights, is over details, the stuff people are fighting about. But it's an eight hundred forty million dollar loan, right? You are going to get an eight hundred forty million dollar mortgage. It was never an issue.'

He nodded. 'The blank never gets filled in until the last day.'

'Well, that's a little late. But it was an eight-day deal. Nothing was quite by the book on this one.'

They went through that part next. When Sid Weiner struck his bargain with the Idlewild board in January, he structured the acquisition as an $860 million dollar loan from the senior lender, with $20 million of subdebt. But committee would approve only $840 million, and only if it closed in the quarter.

So, as of February, the deal looked dead. At the eleventh hour, Weiner brought in Bunker House, which agreed to take a larger piece of mezzanine debt, and, as of 23 March, the deal came back on track.

Mary Oliver explained to Mulcahy how Sam Whitaker had summoned the team of eight lawyers late in the afternoon of 22 March, how a series of conference rooms had been commandeered.

'It was pretty amazing,' she said. 'We were sent home to get suitcases of clothes and Whitaker booked rooms at the Faulkner.' She was referring to the elegant hotel across Post Office Square. 'We were told that we would be at the office straight through, and we could go over there when we had to sleep. And the Fletcher Daye guys, they had office passes and basically lived on 26 in the conference rooms upstairs.'

'They had office passes?'

'Yeah,' she said, 'a bunch of them.'

He hadn't known that. Mulcahy asked her next how the responsibilities had been divided. Ruggerio was the real estate guy. Mary had been the main corporate lawyer, focusing on the credit agreement. A guy named Eilford handled the subdebt negotiations. And Shepard?

'He was in the whole deal,' she said.

Mulcahy shared a fourth-floor apartment out on the Green line towards Boston College. That night he sat in the kitchen and opened a copy of the mortgage before him. He reminded himself that it was a simple case history of the erroneous creation of a line of text, one line among hundreds of thousands. But as he reread the document, the type began to swim. His mind would not stay focused. It began to shake loose and roam. It was still cold by night, as he sat late with a mug of coffee and the kitchen window open. Gitz was out somewhere. Steam wreathed around Mulcahy's face. On the CD player in the living room a tenor sang softly. The melody burst joyously into his consciousness, then faded. Mulcahy's thoughts drifted and bobbed to the stories, the stories of John Shepard. Between Shepard and Whitaker, there were no two personalities of sheer greater size in the law firm – perhaps in his life experience. They occupied the centre ground of his imagination.

Mulcahy's thoughts came back to the present. He had finished his coffee and it had grown cold in the kitchen. It was past one in the morning. As he looked about himself, he realised that there was something else, too, a thought which was struggling to surface into his consciousness. Somewhere in his subconscious it glimmered faintly, and it had something to do with this case. He sat at the table, trying to draw it out. But it would not come.

And then another thought came, a thought with which he was all too familiar. He walked down the corridor to the bedroom, opened the closet, and shoved the winter suits to one side, to look at them again. The Karhu telemark skis stood leaning against the back of the closet wall, where they had been for three years. The P-Tex on the left ski was still scarred from the branches which had been lashed to it for the last desperate miles. You could see where paint had chipped off the three-pin bindings, and the edges were orange with rust.

He shut the closet door before surrendering to the memory of it, and sat down on his bed. Hell, he thought, it was just a misprint.

4

For three days, a medium-sized conference room overlooking Post Office Square was Ed Mulcahy's terrarium. He arrived there before dawn, and stayed long into the night. The rest of his law practice was shipwrecked, and the little pink mound of telephone messages grew. He emerged for the men's room and for coffee, and for little else. The project began to overwhelm him, as his search for the simple explanation of a misprint wound inexorably into the anatomy of a billion-dollar deal. He spoke only to those summoned there to give him information, and via incessant requests for more files, more deliveries from storage, more news clips, more interviews. By the end of the week the conference room's windows were choked with banker's boxes, and it had become a sort of lawyer's museum of the lives of Whitaker and Shepard.

It was frustrating because, at first, none of it seemed to lead anywhere. There were nine drafts of the mortgage. In all but the last draft, which was created the morning of the closing, the number was blank. In the last draft, the erroneous number appeared. Apparently, no one had picked it up. The heaps of drafts, notes, letters – none of them touched on this.

Of course. You don't negotiate typos.

He sighed. Time for a walk. He looked at his watch – it showed about 4 p.m., and he had pretty well been through the files now. Perhaps he could just write a quick report, conclude that the thing was a misprint which everyone missed, and move on. But he was puzzled. He had that sense he remembered from associate days when, having been sent to research a question, he was resigned to report that there was no case on point. That always bothered him – that sense that there *was* a case, out there somewhere, and he just hadn't found it.

At frustrating moments during his stint at the US Attorney's office, he had often gone for a walk – sometimes a long one, through the narrow streets of the North End, or along the waterfront.

It was a bright spring afternoon in Boston, but brisk. The grass was beginning to turn green, and a few hardy souls sat at the café tables in Post Office Square park, wrapped in their raincoats, huddling outdoors for a peek of sun. April is the month which breaks your heart in Boston, but May is still capable of duplicity.

Mulcahy turned into Milk Street and walked on. He thought he would head under the Central Artery and watch the seals in the outdoor tank at the Aquarium. At the corner of Broad and Milk, he came round the corner distractedly and almost tumbled over a man in an electric wheelchair, buzzing along the sidewalk close to the building.

'Sorry,' said Mulcahy.

'Asshole!' the man said, and buzzed on, rolling quickly down the sidewalk.

He stopped at the corner, with one foot on the kerbstone and the other in Broad Street as a smile stole across his face. The person whom he needed to see was obvious, but he hadn't thought of it before.

At a workstation in the furthest corner of the word processing department, which housed the firm's mainframes and hard drives, sat a pale-skinned man in a wheelchair. His blond hair had thinned, and was drawn ineffectually over his crown. He stared out at the world through spectacles with perfectly round lenses. His disability was so pronounced, and his face so unprepossessing, that one didn't notice, at first, how very broad the man's shoulders were, and how thick biceps showed even through a dress shirt. Years of getting about by wheelchair had thickened his shoulders and chest, and even his forearms were stoutly muscled.

George Creel had left his legs behind in Vietnam, along with whatever limited sociability he may once have had. Never an attractive man, always uncomfortable in human relations, his loss drove him to a solitude unrelieved except by computers. He lived alone in an apartment in East Boston where computers were the main furnishings.

A man of fixed routines, Creel left his third-floor apartment, rode the elevator to the street, and then guided his chair six blocks to Maverick Square, where he would board the number 30 bus for South Station.

From South Station, he chaired in to the office, arriving each morning at about nine, and usually staying until late in the evening. Tuesdays and Thursdays he swam at the YMCA. On Saturday night, he bought groceries. But mainly he lived unencumbered by personal contact.

The youths in Maverick Square had a name for the figure in the wheelchair debarking from the number 30. They called him 'Stumpy'.

'Yo, Stumpy!' they would shout, and then dissolve into snickers and giggles. 'Yo, Stump, get some air, man!' Then laughter.

One summer evening several years before, Creel had stopped in his chair, listening to the catcalls and the laughter as he was making his way home from Maverick. Maybe it was the heat that day. Or maybe it was the bug he hadn't been able to find in two thousand lines of code. Whatever the cause, that was the day he spun the chair rearwards, and advanced on the group of teenagers hanging under the streetlight at the end of the block.

As he came close it was his eyes that brought them up short, the coldness of the eyes behind the round lenses, the one that fixed you and the one that wandered. Their talking quieted as he approached. When he was six feet from the semicircle, he stopped. There were six of them. He appraised them in silence.

'Got a problem, Stump?' said the largest boy, standing in the middle. His eyes had narrowed. All the jocularity had gone from their faces. Violence was near.

Creel indicated towards the speaker. 'Follow me, please,' he said.

He spun the chair and wheeled behind the T Station towards LaFobbia Park. The tyres on his chair crunched over the litter and past the graffiti to a picnic table where Creel nimbly swung himself out of the chair and on to the bench.

They followed.

'Sit down,' said Creel to the leader, indicating the seat across the table.

'Dafuck you at, man, you wanna picnic?'

The boys snickered.

Creel loosened his tie. Then he unbuttoned the right sleeve of his shirt.

'Can you beat a cripple?' he asked the youth. His voice was flat as he presented his right arm, cocked for arm wrestling, the elbow on the deeply grooved surface of the table.

'Shee,' said the boy, and made shift to get up and go. But his companions had sensed possible hilarity in this.

'C'mon, Jamal,' said one, 'c'mon, he be callin' you out. He be callin' you out! You scared?'

There were snickers. Jamal was not finding this amusing now.

'Awright, muhfucker,' he said, and his eyes narrowed. He brought his arm to the ready.

It was over an instant after the white hand clasped the black. Creel's arm drove Jamal's to the table with no more hesitation than that of a high-speed stamping machine driving a template upon its medium. Jamal, no weakling, was astonished at the man's strength. So, too, were his gang. Although arm wrestling is not a black boy's game, they'd all thought Jamal could beat him.

'Jamal,' said Creel, as the boy rubbed his biceps, 'you know how I got to be a Stumpy?

'I'll tell you,' he went on, as the youth looked at him morosely. 'I was walking along one day in the rice paddy, looking for a few Viet Cong to kill before breakfast, when pop, off goes a mine. Kills the man in front me, blows off my legs.'

The boys were silent. 'But you see, before they can get a Huey to old George so that he doesn't bleed to death, we come under fire from the enemy. Bullets everywhere. VC fellow comes near me. Sees the stumps, thinks I must be pretty harmless. So I brought my M-16 sharply up to his solar plexus, and when he tumbles over me, well, do you know what I had to do then?'

They were staring at him now.

'Had to kill him, with my hands. I've always had strong hands.'

He shifted back into his wheelchair. 'Good night, boys,' he said, and pushed off for home.

The boys in Maverick Square paid Stumpy more respect after that. 'Yo, Stumpy,' Jamal would call out to him on summer evenings, 'kill some muhfuckers today, man?' And he would smile. A smile that said, I'm kidding. I'm *kidding*! 'Yo, Stumpy,' he once said. 'Smile, man, it won't kill you!'

But it didn't change things really. George Creel knew that people on the street looked at his stumps, not his eyes.

On the Internet, no one looked at Creel. Nor when, as he put it, he went for a ramble in the firm's private files. On Creel's terminal there were no staircases.

Indeed, on Creel's computer, the handicaps were

62

all in the other direction. Perhaps that was its secret appeal to him. Passwords, private files, concealed reference numbers, all were barriers effective against other people. But not against Creel. Depending as the fancy took him, he browsed in the management committee's memoranda, the firm's finances, the partnership struggles, or the occasional office E-mail flirtation.

As time went on, and the world began to awaken to computerised information and communications systems, George Creel even became jealous of activity on what he regarded to an increasing degree as *his* system. He wanted to know who sent E-mail to whom, which client's bills remained longest unpaid, how much money the partners made and when they made it, who telephoned whom, and for how long. Each piece of information whetted his appetite for more. He became obsessed with tailing the network's users down electronic corridors they thought were private.

The system was a better friend to Creel than most human beings. It was thoroughly reliable. And logical. It never betrayed. It never dissembled. It never pretended to care about him.

When the hullabaloo began over Idlewild, Creel knew. Throughout May, he had tracked the E-mail communications between members of the management committee. He pulled up the closing documents, digested all of the computerised material in the personnel files of the lawyers on the deal, searched records of inter-office phone call dates and times. I'm like Diggory Delvet, he thought, amending the nursery rhyme:

> A little old man in black velvet
> He digs and he delves.
> You *can't* see for yourselves
> The mounds left by Diggory Delvet

Because there were no mounds left by Creel, no electromagnetic trace of where he had tunnelled.

It was shortly after 4 p.m. on 6 May when Mulcahy came to Creel's computer terminal. He was clicking through menus with his mouse. Mulcahy hadn't seen him in some time.

'I was wondering when you would be here,' he said, scarcely acknowledging his visitor. He sat staring at his screen, typing in a set of commands, fingers working furiously.

'Why was that?'

'You're the in-house gumshoe on Idlewild, aren't you?'

'How'd you know that?'

'Must have heard it somewhere.' He turned and wrinkled his lips into a half-smile. 'I like to keep informed about firm matters,' he said. Then, just as quickly, his eyes returned to his computer screen.

When he had explained what he wanted, Mulcahy paused, waiting, while Creel finished his program. Then Creel looked at Mulcahy. One eye wandered, while the other seemed to bore right in on Mulcahy's retina. He found the coldness of that stare disconcerting.

'Have they sent you to investigate John Vincent Shepard, Esquire? Or is it Samuel Boylston Whitaker, Esquire? Or both of them? What do you think?'

Mulcahy was uncertain how to respond. Shepard, Whitaker? I thought it was a *misprint*, he was thinking. So he said nothing.

'Oh, well,' said Creel, 'no matter. But if you're going to catch *Shepard*, you've got to learn to ask the correct questions.'

'What would those be, George?'

'Oh, I don't know. You have to ask. Ask and look. Ask and look. And ask again. The trick is to know what to ask, you know. You have to know what to ask.' Creel rocked back and forth in his chair, smiling to himself.

'And then, of course, you have to know you've seen him when you've seen him.'

'I've seen him. It's ah, it's kind of hard to confuse him with anyone else.'

'Really?' Creel looked past Mulcahy again with that wandering eye. 'Let's have a little test.' His fingers lashed at the keys. He clicked his mouse through a series of icons and a short memorandum appeared on his terminal. Creel keyed the print function, and a moment later a copy was in Mulcahy's hand.

'How many clues do you see?' Creel asked.

'Clues?'

'Study the document, Mr Mulcahy. Tell me how many clues. You can call me later. I have things I have to do.' And he turned back to his screen, one hand brushing a lock of hair back to where it had slipped from its perch atop his perfectly round head.

5

In his conference room once more, Mulcahy stared at the page Creel had given him. It was a copy of a cover memorandum used in the Idlewild transaction, dated 31 March, addressed to a list of bankers, borrowers and lawyers. At the head of the list was Samuel Whitaker's name. Fifteen names or more followed. The memorandum listed fourteen documents which, it said, were in final form and expected to be signed that afternoon.

The memorandum seemed wholly unremarkable. It was a routine piece of paper. Mulcahy stared at it. Nothing came to him. So he turned to the files, unearthed several earlier cover memos, and sat comparing them. After a few minutes, he picked up the telephone and called Mary Oliver again.

He was engrossed in a stack of cover correspondence when her arrival startled him.

'Jesus,' he said. 'Mary, take a look at this.' And then, 'Seen this before?'

'Probably.'

'Anything strange about it?'

She read the memorandum. 'No,' she said. 'No, not really.'

'Not *really*?'

'No, no it's nothing.'

But the other cover memos had suggested something and so he said, 'Let me ask you, why is Whitaker on the list? I've looked at some of the other cover memos, and it doesn't look like he was copied on everything.'

'No. He wasn't going to go through every draft. I mean, it was his deal theoretically. But was he there at midnight, was he negotiating drafts, was he even reading drafts? No. Was he copied on everything? No, I'm sure he wasn't.'

'So why copy him on this one?'

'I'm not sure,' she said. 'Would I have copied him? Maybe not. Did other people in the deal send him drafts? No. But he was still the senior lawyer on the deal and a senior partner at the firm and the guy who was DeFi's lawyer for thirty years. And so, you're John Shepard, and this is the biggest deal in the history of the firm, and it's about to close, it's allee-allee-in-come-free time, and you want Whitaker to know you're the guy who got it done. So you copy him, I guess. Maybe.'

She pursed her lips in a frown and stared at him. 'Why is this important?'

'I don't know,' he said. 'It probably isn't. Mainly I have a headache and I'm just asking questions.' He sat silently.

'I'd better go now,' she said.

As she was leaving, he said, 'Mary, don't talk about this, okay?'

'Sure,' she said. But on the point of leaving she stopped and returned to the table to look again at the memo. 'Yes,' she said, 'there's another thing.'

'What?' he asked.

'No red-lining.'

'What do you mean?'

'Well,' she said, 'usually, you'd have the drafts red-lined, you know, marked with those funny carrots and underlinings which show the reader what has changed since the last draft. So you can compare the changes quickly, without having to read the whole thing. Anyway, the usual cover memo says, "Enclosed are the drafts of blah blah, marked to show changes from the drafts of blah blah." Only this one doesn't. Check the drafts from that morning.'

They examined several of the drafts from the morning of 31 March. 'Yeah,' she said, 'they weren't red-lined. Funny, I never noticed at the time. Too tired, I guess.

'Red-lining,' she went on, 'would have put a nice underline . . .'

'. . . under the number in the mortgage.' He finished the sentence. 'And not red-lining it left it buried in text.'

They both thought about it for a moment. 'So how unusual is this?' he asked.

'A little,' she said. 'Of course, John would say, "Yep, should have red-lined the bastard, but there was so *damn* little time." You know the way he talks?

' "We had to close that goddamn day," ' she went on, affecting his drawl. Not badly, either.

'Plausible?' he asked.

She nodded her head. 'Sure. But persuasive? I don't know.'

When she had gone, he sat on for a moment. That thought he had been struggling to regain was closer now. It must have found a synapse or two. Not enough of them yet. He sat with eyes closed, trying. It didn't come.

He returned to his own office to log on to the computer. Slowly he tapped out an E-mail.

G.C.C. – Re the 'clues': Thanks. I'll be in touch.
E.X.M.

Turning to a pile of correspondence which had been ignored over the past three days, he wondered how much longer he could baby-sit his practice while this investigation went on. How would he get time to do interviews? To dictate the reports? He was awakened from this gloomy train of thought when his computer beeped at him scarcely a moment later. He looked up at the screen.

Laboriously, he called his E-mail back up.

E.X.M. – How many, please?
G.C.C.

So he mailed back:

G.C.C. – Two.
E.X.M.

This is silly, he thought. Why don't I just call the guy? On the other hand, Creel was likely more talkative on his computer. Mulcahy had mail again.

> E.X.M. – I count three.
> G.C.C.

He tapped back a message.

> G.C.C. – Help! Here's what I've got: Whitaker as an addressee, and no red-lining.
> E.X.M.

He had mail.

> E.X.M. – Very good. What library was the document in, please?
> G.C.C.

What library was the document in? He puzzled again. What computer file was the document opened under? Was that what Creel meant? Like all computer-generated documents, it carried an identification number in the lower left-hand corner. It was document number Corp 57664.1. So what? Weren't they all Corp documents? He tapped a message back.

> G.C.C. – Corp. So?
> E.X.M.

The reply was back almost instantly.

> E.X.M. – Must I spell everything out? What library *wasn't* it opened under? And why?
> G.C.C.

Where wasn't it opened? It wasn't a litigation document or a probate document or a . . . He stopped. Or Junk. It wasn't Junk. He looked back through the piles on the table to his chronological file. Nine cover memos to the circulation list. All opened in the 'Junk' file, the file which the computer automatically purged once a week. All except this memo.

Mulcahy looked up at the stack of banker's boxes on the table, and for a moment it was as though Shepard was there with him, there in the room, now hidden behind the stack of boxes, now reclining with his feet on the table, laughing at him openly. His mind wandered from the computer legends he had been focused on, and as he sat silently daydreaming, he recalled a late night, some years before, when Shepard had come around a corner to find Mulcahy in the firm's library.

'Hey,' Mulcahy said.

'Hear that, man?' Shepard asked, a wide grin on his bearded face.

But Mulcahy could hear nothing, and shook his head.

'The hum, hear it?'

Mulcahy listened, tuning in, after a moment, to the background whir of the HVAC system, the sort of sound which can be heard only when one is directed to it.

When Mulcahy nodded affirmatively, Shepard said, 'That's the sound of a fuckin' money machine, humming away. Ain't it something?

'That is this place,' he went on. 'You could win the biggest case in the decade, or get mugged walking across the Common. I could close a billion-dollar deal, or be hit by a truck. Doesn't matter a goddamn. Not a goddamn. The hum would still be there.'

Mulcahy smiled, shaking his head.

'I do a deal, and what happens? Computers: bits of information on light-emitting diodes, that's it. We close, and some computer tells some other computer that something has happened, and everybody has dinner. Helluva thing, ain't it? Chips of lucite and stacks of documents in binders. You litigate a case three years and what happens? Paper. None of it is *real*, man. None of it matters a tinker's damn to the almighty hum,' he said in that earnest, half-jesting philosophical manner of his.

Mulcahy shook his head again. 'Have a good night,' he said.

Shepard had smiled back. 'Remember, none of this other is real. The only real thing is the hum. The hum is the Way, the Truth and Life, man! No man cometh unto Freer Motley but by the fuckin' hum!' And he had gone.

Mulcahy's attention returned to the present. He stood up and watched the passers-by on the sidewalk far below. Across the park was the dirty grey of the federal courthouse. He stared at the little windows set in stone, remembering the bonhomie of his office there, the delirium of the convictions, the joyful conspiring late at night among bags of hamburgers and stacks of the FBI's 302s. The decisions seemed easier, then. The FBI had evidence someone had trafficked in narcotics or robbed a bank. You represented the United States. So you went after him. Now, nothing was so simple.

With his back to the door, Mulcahy didn't hear

anyone come in. But all at once he felt a presence behind him.

'Mr Whitaker,' he stammered.

Whitaker inclined his head. His bifocals were perched on his nose, his narrow bow tie tightly knotted, the pale yellow silk tie ends drooping elegantly. His deep blue suit looked as crisply pressed as a dress uniform. His hair was still naval officer short, and he looked about the room with mild distaste, like an officer certain to be disappointed by inspection. 'You have been asked to investigate the Idlewild transaction,' he said, without apparent emotion.

'Yes . . . sir,' said Mulcahy.

The older partner looked at him. 'I would be pleased to be kept informed of your progress,' he said. 'Would you come and see me in a couple of days? Say, Tuesday next?'

'Yes, sir,' stammered Mulcahy again.

'Very good,' said the older man, and then he was gone.

Mulcahy still stood sheepishly, with a vague instinct to salute. Instead, he returned to his documents. When, after some moments, he was again able to concentrate, he called Mary Oliver. 'Mary,' he said when she picked up the phone, 'I need to ask you about something. Remember we were talking about that cover memo from Shepard enclosing the last drafts, the ones with the mistake?'

'Yeah.'

'That cover memo,' he said, 'was opened in Corp, not Junk. Do you usually put a cover memo in Junk? You know, the purge file?'

'Sure,' she said.

'Why wouldn't you?'

'Why wouldn't you?' she repeated. 'I don't know. I guess if you didn't want the computer to delete it.'

'And why wouldn't you want the computer to delete a cover memo?'

But he thought he might have guessed the answer to the question. 'Mary,' he continued, 'does this mean anything?'

'Maybe,' she said. 'How about the other cover memos? Sometimes you just call up the last one and change the date. Have you looked at them?'

'They're all in Junk. I checked. They all have the same number.'

'Well, that makes sense. There was a new set of drafts every day, sometimes more than one go-around. So somebody opened the first cover memo in Junk, and they would just call it up again and change the date. It never was purged because the seven-day window restarts every time you activate the document.'

'So why,' he asked again, 'would the last one be in Corp?'

'I dunno. Who knows? But,' she said, choosing her words slowly, 'if you wanted to be certain there was an electronic record somewhere linking the recipients of the memo to the draft with the error, even if someone threw out all the hard copy, you might do it this way.'

'Which would be consistent with a change which was not a misprint.'

'I guess I won't comment on that. But one thing is

pretty sure. It wasn't an accident that this memo was in Corp.'

'Why do you say that?'

'Well,' she said, 'you could do a cover memo two ways. One is, you might call up the last one and change the date. Only, you said all the old ones were all in Junk. If you did that, the new memo would be in Junk, too. And the other is, you could open a new memo.'

'Suppose you opened a new one.'

'The computer would default you to Junk.'

'You're saying someone at a computer screen had consciously to put this thing in a permanent document library?'

'I think so,' she said.

He hung up. She was right. A little thing like that, who knows? Still, sometimes it is the little things that won't leave you alone. And George Creel's sardonic questioning was sending him back over the little things.

Just before five, he had another conversation with George Creel. Creel confirmed that *of course* he could, from a review of the hard drive records, identify the terminals used to call up and edit loan documents. In that, 'of course', Creel might as well have said, 'Why did it take you so long to ask?'

Once again the thought was stirring, a long distance away in his subconscious, something, a faint glimmer, struggling for a synaptic pathway to Mulcahy's consciousness. He sensed it was there, like a child crying somewhere in the distance in a rambling Victorian house. He just couldn't identify the room. He looked about himself again, at the stacks of boxes, the paper chase he had been assigned.

Mulcahy reopened the personnel file, began paging through it. Amazing what they kept. There was Shepard's Harvard Law School transcript, stapled to his resumé. He looked through it. Old John was a lot of things, but not law review material. He chuckled when he saw the one 'A+': Negotiation Workshop. Somebody got that right.

The phone rang.

'Estella,' he said, 'hold the calls, will you, I've . . .'

'It's him,' she said.

'Who?' Mulcahy asked.

'Him. John Shepard.'

He drew a breath. 'Damn,' he said, softly. 'Okay, put him through.'

The voice hollered over the speakerphone and rang out into the corridor. 'Motherfucker!'

It was him all right. 'Hey, John,' Mulcahy said half-heartedly, picking up the phone.

'Listen, man,' he said. That voice again – after all of this! 'I'm sorry I haven't called you. Things broke kind of fast on me and I just didn't get round to it. But I wanted to say goodbye before I left town, and tell you to look me up if you ever get your sorry ass out west again . . .'

'John, I . . . listen, thanks. I guess I can understand that.' Mulcahy looked up and saw Ogle hovering at the threshold. He had summoned him for an interview. He waved him away. The goggle-eyed face disappeared from the doorway.

'Listen, John, I'd like to talk to you, really, I would, but you don't want to talk to me.'

'Why not?'

''Cause I drew the assignment to investigate the Grenade.'

'The Grenade?'

'You haven't heard about it?'

'Shit, I haven't talked to anybody.'

And so Mulcahy told him the story.

When he had finished, there was a long silence on the other end of the phone. Looking up, Mulcahy noticed that Ogle hadn't shut the door behind him. At length he heard Shepard's voice again. 'Ed, can't you see what this is all about? They want my ass. Why'd you take this one, man?'

'I tried to get out of it –'

'Well, you didn't try too goddamn hard! Aren't you a partner of that place? Jesus Lord,' Shepard sighed. 'I guess you're right. I guess I don't want to talk to you either. Or any of 'em. Goddamn it. Best of luck to you, man.'

The phone went dead.

Shame washed over Mulcahy. He stared at his hands, then at the files stacked all around him. Surprised, he glanced up to see Ogle, still hovering in the doorway.

Mulcahy snapped at him: 'What are you doing here?'

'You . . . I thought, didn't you . . .'

'Go away. I'll call you when I need you.'

Mulcahy sat in silence, his mind distracted again. He scribbled out a note to Shanklin, then crumpled it and tossed it in the wastebasket. He wrote another one. Then he sat, staring at the simple words on the foolscap. The note survived a few minutes more, but met the same end.

He sighed, and reached again for the file of annual reviews. It just wasn't in him to quit a job.

6

Tuesday morning found Ed Mulcahy perched uncomfortably on the edge of one of the cream-coloured Queen Anne chairs in Samuel Whitaker's corner office overlooking Boston Harbour. Whitaker had turned to the side and was leaning backwards in his desk chair, his fingertips pressed together, his gaze fixed out across the water toward the airport. While Mulcahy reported what he had found Whitaker said little, except an occasional, 'Go on.'

But Mulcahy felt like a schoolboy in the parlour making small talk with his date's father. His voice sounded like an adolescent's – halting and faraway. It was hard to concentrate, for one thing, what with the ticking of the grandfather clock in the corner, and the walls of photographs, plaques, tributes, degrees. While he was bumbling through an account of computer files, the black-and-white photograph of Whitaker with Attorney General Kennedy brought him up short. His gaze wandered to the photograph of Whitaker's destroyer in the Pacific or the photograph of his racing yacht; the degree from Jesus College, Oxford . . .

But there was another reason: Creel's analysis was in.

Mulcahy began by explaining that he had isolated the draft upon which the mistake first appeared and the time of its circulation on the morning of closing. He said that he had spoken with the computer people and they had determined that the document had been opened only three times in the twelve hours prior to its printing on 31 March. Two had been on John Shepard's terminal.

'Do you mean his secretary's machine?' Whitaker asked.

'No, sir, his were on his own machine. The one on his desk.' He referred to notes. 'The document was opened on Vicky Ippolito's machine – that's Ruggerio's secretary – at 4.10 p.m. on 30 March. It was printed out at 4.54. That was the eighth draft, the one which was circulated about 6 p.m., and it contained a blank for the indebtedness. After that, the document was opened on Shepard's machine twice prior to its being printed out the next morning. Once for about half an hour at 9 p.m. Again around midnight for a couple of minutes.

'You said there was a third time?'

'Yes, sir. At approximately 3.30 a.m., on 31 March, the document was edited for the last time. It took a couple of minutes.'

'On what terminal?'

'Yours, sir.'

Whitaker swivelled round to face the young partner. 'This one?' he asked, beckoning towards the computer terminal on his credenza.

'Yes, sir.'

'I see.' Whitaker turned back to face the harbour. He sat in silence for a moment, his face a blank. Then he turned back to his desk and looked at Mulcahy again. 'What do you make of this information?'

'I'm not sure,' he said. 'But I have one scenario, based on some additional information. You see, Shepard opened eight documents between about 7 and 10 p.m., each for twenty minutes to a half hour. Then he goes back and opens five of them, each for only a few minutes, between 11.30 and 1 a.m.

'So, I come up with this hypothesis. About dinner-time, he gets a set of the last revisions of the key documents. He reads them for an hour or so. Then he goes into each one, making the last changes he wants to make. This takes a while for each one. One of them is the mortgage. He's tired and he makes a mistake. He goes on to the other documents. It's around 11 when he finishes, and he's tired. He takes a break. He makes two phone calls. Oh, I forgot to mention, he places two phone calls to Colorado between 11 and 11.40 p.m. An hour or so goes by. Now he decides to give the documents a last read. He finds a few nits in four of the documents, including the mortgage. He goes back in each one, fixes it, and stops. He prepares a cover memo.'

Mulcahy stopped there. Whitaker raised his eyebrow as if to say, 'Continue.' Mulcahy said, 'At that point, I'm not sure.'

Whitaker nodded. 'Mr Mulcahy, do you suppose that I inserted this error?'

He stammered out a response. 'I wouldn't presume to suppose, sir. It's my job to investigate.'

'Well, I don't even use that thing,' said Whitaker, beckoning at his computer terminal with disdain. 'Why my learned friends on the management committee thought it a legitimate expenditure of the firm's capital to outfit us all with secretarial stations, I do not know.'

Mulcahy made a note as Whitaker continued. 'Eight documents are worked on by Shepard after the dinner hour, and this group includes the mortgage, is that right?'

'Yes, sir,' said Mulcahy.

'And then four more are also worked on, this time for a short period, and this group also includes the mortgage?'

'Yes.'

'And at 3 a.m., how many documents are opened on my terminal?'

'Just one. The mortgage.'

'I see,' said Whitaker. 'Have you a copy of the Ruggerio draft of the mortgage, the 30 March draft?'

He hadn't. But one was soon brought to them. Whitaker studied it. 'Yes,' he said, after a time, 'there were very few changes at this stage. What,' – he turned again to Mulcahy – 'do you suppose the three sets of changes were that John went in to make?'

Mulcahy confessed he could not see that there was much to do on the document. It was a matter of guesswork.

'Yes, indeed it is. But I can imagine a different hypothesis to explain these events, can't you? Let me put it this way,' Whitaker said, after he had allowed the remark to sink in for a moment. 'Would these events support a theory that the change was deliberate? That, perhaps, the change was made at 3.30 a.m., after the rest of the documents had been completed?'

It was an obvious possibility, and one that Mulcahy wanted to avoid. He sat in silence.

'And if that were the case, if the insertion was deliberate, do you suppose John might have been bright enough to use another terminal to do that?'

There could be no argument on that point. 'I guess,' Mulcahy said, 'I find it difficult to believe that of John.'

'I see,' said Whitaker, returning his gaze to the airport across the harbour. 'Do you find it difficult to believe of me?'

Mulcahy stammered, looking down at his hands. 'Yes, I do,' he said.

Whitaker continued. 'Do you suppose your regard for John Shepard is influencing your judgment?' The question was asked in a matter-of-fact tone, as though Whitaker were inquiring as to the departure time of the next train to Wellesley. Mulcahy made no response. Whitaker went on: 'You must have known that he was exceedingly disappointed over the partnership decision.' He shook his head and expelled a breath slowly.

The senior partner folded his hands on his desk, and dismissed Mulcahy. 'Keep me advised,' he said, as Mulcahy left.

7

It was a grey-suited, grey-headed herd which gathered in the ornate Fitzgerald Room at the Faulkner, and its mood was as darkly grey as the colour of its suits. The lawyers milled about the chairs, murmuring in anxious knots, fidgeting as they waited for Shanklin to begin the meeting.

Mulcahy arrived at they were taking their seats, and chose one near the back. In the middle of the room, he could see Sam Whitaker, flanked by empty chairs.

'I'll be brief,' said the Count, when he had called them to order. 'You have all heard about Idlewild. For those of you who may have been on a different planet, let me summarise. The Idlewild Tower mortgage contains an error, an eight hundred thirty-nine million one hundred sixty thousand dollar error. This office,' he said, pausing, as every eye stole towards the impassive man sitting alone in the centre of the room, 'drafted the mortgage. And Idlewild now claims it is entitled to discharge the mortgage. Suits have been threatened by both sides, and DeFi has advised us of a malpractice claim.'

'Malpractice?' sputtered one of the older partners.

'As I said, Myron, we drafted the mortgage.'

'I didn't draft anything!'

'We are a general partnership, Myron. You are your brother's keeper.'

Someone asked, 'Surely Idlewild doesn't deny the debt?'

'No,' said the Count. 'They do not deny the debt. Let me explain. The total bank debt is eight hundred forty million. There are a number of items of collateral, the most important – and valuable – of which is Idlewild Tower. That tower is supposed to secure all of the debt. But the mortgage on it is only for eight hundred forty *thousand* dollars. Idlewild paid that amount on the first of the month, and they claim now to hold the building free and clear. Without the building as collateral, DeFi faces a great risk that the debt will not be repaid from the other collateral. And that risk, if I understand Tim's analysis, may be quantified as our malpractice exposure.'

Tim nodded. There were frowns around the room.

Another interruption from the back. 'Have we received a formal demand?'

'We heard from DeFi's lawyers Monday,' the Count replied.

A small sad voice from the front said, 'I thought *we* were DeFi's lawyers.'

'We were, Fritz. One of the questions before us tonight is whether we will be again.'

The mood in the Fitzgerald Room grew bleaker, as the Count recited the details of the negotiations. The charcoal herd hunched further over in its seats, retired more deeply into its grey suitcoats. There was muttering around the room.

The Count went on. 'Tim and I,' he said, 'have been in meetings all week with the 35th floor and with Fletcher Daye. There is a proposal for global settlement. It is not pretty. But for reasons I will explain, the management committee strongly recommends it.

'Idlewild,' he went on, 'will stipulate to a six hundred million mortgage on the tower. DeFi will drop its claim against us. Our carrier will execute a one hundred million dollar collection guaranty, contingent upon exhaustion of the bank's other remedies. And everyone will execute a confidentiality agreement. No lawsuits. No publicity.'

'And us, what about us?' someone asked.

'We will guarantee collection of the last $140 million, again contingent upon exhaustion of DeFi's other remedies, with a call option on the . . .'

But the Count did not get through explaining the complex mechanism which had been devised to give Freer Motley power to intercede in a workout. For the room was in an uproar. A $140 million guaranty by the firm?? He'd lost his mind! Shouts came from every corner. Only the man in the centre sat impassively.

'Please, please!' The Count had his hands up. 'Please listen very carefully.' The shouts subsided to murmuring again, and he went on. 'It is a guarantee of the collection of the last $140 million only, and only after exhaustion of collateral and insurance. We have thought very carefully about this. If we do not accept this proposal, DeFi will begin serving its malpractice suit Monday. Under Massachusetts procedure,' he went on, turning to Texas Tim, who nodded, 'each of you will be personally named as a general partner. Further, we will, as of Monday, lose DeFi as a client. That is twenty-two, almost twenty-three per cent of gross revenues, on last year's numbers.'

Now the room fell silent. Numbers they understood, numbers and being named in law suits. 'There's more. Bank counsel advises that they will immediately seek prejudgment attachments on all of your assets: your homes, your automobiles, your bank accounts. While Tim feels somewhat bullish on our chances of resisting prejudgment attachments in court, there can be no guarantee. Further, this is a global settlement. If we do not settle, Idlewild does not settle.'

No one was interrupting him now. 'And in that event, we might face a judgment for the shortfall in collateral values, which I am told may exceed two hundred million.

'I'm afraid we have no choice,' he concluded.

'What if we don't vote for it?' Another voice from the back.

'We have considered that. It is my duty to advise you that if the proposal has not been accepted by 80 per cent of the partners voting, as required by the partnership agreement, all partners on the management committee will execute and file a chapter 11 petition on Monday.'

Again the room was in uproar. 'Blackmail!' someone shouted. 'Bastards, bastards!' said another. Francis Spencer, a real estate partner, was on his feet.

'You bastards on the committee – all you care about is protecting your personal net worth. That's all! I've got a daughter in college, and a son who will be going next year!'

'Francis . . .'

'No, I won't be quiet, Albert. You have sold us all. You have sold us all! You people on the committee all work for DeFi, and you have sold us all to save your practices. Well, I can get along without DeFi, and I can damn well get along without a one hundred forty million dollar guarantee!'

'Now hold on a minute, Francis.' It was Leibo. He sat in a seat at the front of the room, rocking to and fro. 'Albert hasn't sold anyone. What he's done is negotiate the best arrangement the circumstances will permit. What would happen to your practice, Francis, if this all becomes public? If we all are sued on Monday? If DeFi abandons us, what do you suppose other clients will do? Imagine the field day the *Transcript* will have with it!'

There were nods throughout the room. Most of Leibo's partners shared his contempt for the newspapers.

'Francis,' said the Count, icily, 'I understand your frustration, but I resent your remark. The members of this committee have been dealt a crisis the likes of which this firm has never seen. And we have done the best that can be done. If you accept this proposal, nothing will be attached, at least not yet. If you reject it, that college tuition will, I suspect, be in greater peril.'

Now a realisation began to sweep through the herd: a hundred forty million dollars – *their* dollars – and it had all been decided. It was as done as a judgment, as final as an execution. Instinctively, the herd began to search out its leaders, and the charcoal-suited bodies shifted and twisted in the seats as men and women hunted the room for those seven or eight partners in the ascendant. The herd tallied their faces, their expressions, and saw that it had been decided. It had been decided and scripted, and this meeting was as formulaic as a meeting of the Cuban Parliament. It was a ritual blessing. The shouts, the anger, the hysteria came from the older partners, the hangers-on, the ones who had grasped power in the institution once long ago, but held it no more. It was going to happen. And then fear began to ripple through the herd, the fear of standing up to the leadership, the fear of standing alone.

In the centre of the room, Samuel Whitaker had risen. The group fell silent.

'This transaction,' he said softly, 'was my transaction. This happened on my watch. I am puzzled by this. I shall be as interested as anyone in the results of Ed Mulcahy's investigation. But whatever the outcome, I am full of sorrow. I apologise to you all.

'I am out of management now, but I would say one thing more to you. There is much anger in this room, much hastiness, much fear. And I think that you have forgotten, those of you who ever knew, what it means to be partners. It means that you meet adversity together. A partnership is an institution of great strength, when the partners stand together. But it is weak and pitiful when they war with each other.

'Those of you who served this country in its armed forces, as I did,' he said, 'have seen real adversity, and have learned that it cannot be met with cleverness only. It must be met with courage.'

The soft voice had quieted them. He went on. 'In 1954, before my day, before all of our days, Daniel Stone took on as a client a frightened little teaching assistant from MIT named Harold Kripsky, a man with no money and no prospects, facing the full fury of the Senate UnAmerican Activities Subcommittee. Those of us who were alive in that time remember the contagion of fear which swept this country. Everyone knows, today, of Stone's epic confrontation with Senator Epps. It has become the stuff of legend. And everyone in this room knows that Kripsky went on to become, among other things, Chairman of Synsemics.

'But you do not know the feelings that were abroad when Stone took on that client. Every partner of the firm was audited by the IRS. Did you know that? The litigators couldn't win an uncontested continuance in the Suffolk motion session. Boardrooms, banks, our clients, began to close their doors to us. That was all before Stone's marvellous victory, of course. But the point is that the institution stood by him. It stood by him through adversity, and we were all better for it. Had Daniel Stone and had Daniel Stone's partners made their calculations rashly, based on the prevailing breeze of the moment, they never would have taken on Kripsky, nor remained steadfast in his defence.

'Now there is a new difficulty. In my judgment, Albert's proposal to you is hasty. It lacks moral force.

It lacks courage. Any good judge will see through this play by Idlewild and its counsel. So, while I concede that the committee's proposal is clever, I think it is immature. We should meet this challenge head on. We should meet it together.'

'It's all very well for you to talk about courage, Sam!' someone shouted from the rear. 'You've cut your severance deal! You've paid for your house! Your kids are through college!'

There was a murmur of assent. Samuel Whitaker sighed and looked around. He too could gauge the decision from the faces of the firm's leaders. 'So pointless, so pointless,' he said softly. And then, more loudly, but not much more so: 'Perhaps the problem is that there are too many of us. My judgment has not, I fear, been meaningful to you all for some time now. Perhaps my usefulness to this group is at an end.' He looked about him, and then, gathering his coat and striding from the room, he said, 'I wish you all well.'

There was, for a moment after the door swung to, a stunned silence. And then the flow of voices rose again. Shanklin cut it off. 'Given his involvement in this fiasco,' he said, 'it is hardly surprising that Sam won't face the reality of our exposure. But Sam wasn't on 35 today with the Chairman. The OCC is crawling all over this. They have threatened cease and desist proceedings. If this deal doesn't happen, they will go to discipline. DeFi's stock will take a bath, and this firm will have seen its last financing from that client.

'Now Sam is correct. A judge probably would find a way to do the right thing. But does anyone here want to bet eight hundred thirty-nine million dollars on a Superior court judge?'

There were no takers.

'No one imagines,' the Count went on, 'that we can afford a $140 million dollar judgment, if it ever comes to that. But in our view, it might come to that *today* if we don't agree to this proposal. And the firm would take a body blow to its revenues. On that you may rely. We do better to avoid the day of reckoning. Remember, to reach us, they have to exhaust the collateral and exhaust the insurance. There would be no such limit on a malpractice judgment, I'm told. And if Idlewild pays its debts to the bank, it may all go quietly away.'

He had brought them quiet again. The sting of shame they'd felt at Whitaker's remarks was swiftly replaced with the more pungent and customary instincts of fear and conformity.

'The Chairman assures us,' Shanklin said, 'that if we co-operate, we can put this Idlewild matter behind us, and continue our practices as before. The ballots will be delivered to you in the morning. The box will close at 5 p.m.'

The meeting adjourned. It had been managed skilfully, and the objective had been achieved. The charcoal herd rose dutifully and shuffled out of the room.

The ritual was completed the following day when the ballots were counted. But it had already been decided. The settlement had been approved.

There was one more meeting with Samuel Whitaker. According to Mulcahy's time sheet it was on 12 May.

He was nearing the end of his reconstruction of events. He had left for almost last the task of interviewing Whitaker himself, and entered the senior partner's office still steeling himself. Before he could ask questions, he found himself again grilled about the computer terminals. Mulcahy had spent the better part of an hour taking the older man back through the results of Creel's findings.

At a pause, Mulcahy said, 'Mr Whitaker, as a part of this investigation, I need to ask you some questions too.'

Whitaker turned towards him, fixing him with a steady glance. His face betrayed a momentary flash, but it was quickly controlled.

'Questions?'

'Yes, sir.'

He turned back to the window. 'Perhaps this is a part of Albert's extravagent severance package?'

'Sir, I'd prefer it if you would just let me ask you some questions.'

'Very well, young man,' Whitaker replied, 'ask your questions.'

Thus began the strangest interview of Mulcahy's career.

'Let me . . .' he began with discomfort, 'Let's begin with the borrower.'

'The borrower?'

'Well, yes, the borrower. There is an economic incentive for this, I think you would agree.'

'But how would the borrower engineer the mistake? We controlled the drafting.'

'As I understand it, one of the unusual aspects of this transaction was that the borrower's lawyers were in the office literally twenty-four hours a day. They had office passes.'

'You are suggesting that one of their attorneys planted this?'

'Please, Mr Whitaker,' Mulcahy interrupted. 'Leave judgments of persuasiveness for later. The question is, simply, what facts do you know which makes this either likely or unlikely?'

Whitaker frowned, and nodded. 'All right. The Fletcher Daye attorneys, the attorneys for the borrower, while tenacious and sometimes personally difficult, struck me as honourable people. The kind of thing you suggest, sneaking about the law office to plant this kind of thing, would of course if detected make a lawyer liable to disbarment, not to mention prosecution. And there would be no direct reward to the lawyer. I must say I find that quite unlikely.'

Mulcahy sighed. Whitaker was arguing. Well, where the witnesses were lawyers, what could he expect?

Perhaps sensing Mulcahy's reaction, Whitaker continued. 'But as to facts, wouldn't this person have to have access to the machine's password, in order to operate my computer? Shepard, it seems to me, could easily discover what my password was, particularly since I have never bothered to learn to operate the machine and program my own password. The person would have to come to this floor. If this was attempted during the day, it would certainly be detected. Even at night, there were many people involved on the transaction in the office.' He shook his head. 'Certainly, I don't recall ever hearing of this kind of suspicious behaviour on their part.'

These were, in fact, important points against the thesis, and Mulcahy had already pondered them. He asked another question. 'Can you comment on the hypothesis of deliberate acts by John Shepard?'

Sam Whitaker turned and held his eye. 'John felt betrayed about the partnership decision. He held me personally responsible. And when the transaction closed, on 31 March, that partnership decision was a still-fresh wound: less than two weeks old. I should think Shepard's anger was uncooled.

'As I say, he held me personally responsible. The morning after the decision was announced, he was in this office. He was angry, loud – well, you know John. It was an extraordinary half hour. That was on 16 March, I think.'

'What did he say to you?'

'He called me, "spineless" several times, and other things rather less elegant. He challenged me to justify the decision. I said I would not comment on the decision. He said he expected loyalty from me: that he had given me his loyalty and that he felt I had betrayed him. I told him I would simply not comment on the decision. I can tell you, since you have been admitted to the partnership, that it was very difficult for me. I supported him and felt that the decision was an error, but I was unable to command enough support. It is my belief that Shepard may have been sacrificed to a larger political struggle between myself and certain other partners. But of course that is only speculation, and I did not share it with John.

'He became abusive. He left in a fury, slamming the door, abusing my secretary Mrs DeSantis. It was quite extraordinary.'

Mulcahy nodded, but remained silent.

After a time, Whitaker said gently, 'Idlewild was, of course, my transaction.'

Mulcahy nodded again. Whitaker continued, 'There are many troubling circumstantial facts. First, it appears, from what you've told me, that the error was made on this computer terminal. That seems telling evidence on its own. I don't know many people whom I would credit with the brass for that, frankly. Second, if one had wanted to expose the error to the least opportunity for detection, it would have been inserted exactly when it was. Shepard was, of course, familiar with the extreme time pressures. Third, the negotiation on the morning of closing with the attorneys for the subordinated debt holders might be interpreted as a deliberate distraction. It was, in my experience, inconsistent with Shepard's negotiation style. Fourth, I have never known Shepard to make an error of this magnitude. His flamboyance was well known in the firm, but as flamboyant as he was, he was a superb lawyer for precision in drafting. Such an error was highly unlike him.

'But more important than any of that is the obvious motive. It was, of course, my transaction, and the embarrassment to me would be enormous. Shepard gave his notice the evening of the closing, if I recall correctly – on what would have been the very day the error was made and the transaction closed. In my view, he was acting impetuously – that had so often been his brilliant manner, of course, but it would appear to have got the better of him here.

'That is, at any rate, how I see it,' he concluded. In the room the only sound was of the steady, inexorable tock, tock, tock of the grandfather clock, which lulled Mulcahy into assent with Whitaker's utterly persuasive, utterly sensible argument. He had come to gather facts but, but – not for nothing had Samuel Whitaker been the Ayatollah of Freer Motley for close on twenty years.

'If I can ask you, sir,' said Mulcahy, 'why did you put him on a transaction as large as this so soon after your argument with him?'

'An appropriate question, of course,' Whitaker began. Later Mulcahy reflected that the answer seemed to come with too much fluidity. 'John had had the relationships with the bank officers in question for months, as this transaction wound through term sheets and came undone several times in committee and during the due diligence process.' This was all true, and well documented. 'It was Mark Barbieri's appointment as head of the new bank division which unlocked the gates, provided that it could be closed within the quarter. It all came on with tremendous rapidity. If the truth be told, the transaction probably could not have been accomplished without John. Both because of his history in the transaction and his skill.'

'Did you talk about the partnership issue?'

'We had one conversation,' the senior partner said. 'At the outset. I told him that I regarded him as a professional, that the client had an extraordinary need, and that in my view no one else could deliver the service. He said, "I'll finish it."'

'Just, "I'll finish it"?'

'That's all. That's all he said.'

They talked for a few minutes more about the

investigation. 'There is,' Mulcahy said as he was finishing, 'one more thing that the computer fellow is running down . . .'

'What is that?' Whitaker asked.

'Well, I'm not sure. He's kind of an odd man. His name is George Creel, I think I told you?'

'Yes, yes, I remember.'

'He likes to speak in riddles. He's an odd duck. So I confess I don't really know what he's up to. But he has been hinting that there might be some other way to get at whoever might have had access to the computer terminals. He said to me, "Let's see if we can find the guest book." '

'The "guest book"?'

'That's what he said.'

'The guest book,' Whitaker repeated to himself. 'Do you think he means the book kept in the lobby by the security people?'

Mulcahy shook his head negatively. 'I'm sure he doesn't. Actually, I've already checked that, and there's nothing of much interest. Since most people either come in during business hours or have a pass, there's not much in that book. Besides . . .'

Whitaker turned back from the window to look at him. His pale blue eyes were watery now, but steady. 'Yes?' he asked.

'Well, Creel is a hacker, a computer whiz. The guy has no interest in anything that is handwritten. I'm sure he's talking about some computer gimmick. He told me that he thought he'd have this "guest book" shortly.'

'I see,' said Whitaker.

They talked for a few moments more. Before

Mulcahy left, he said 'Sir, I need to ask you one more question.' He stammered it out as quickly as he could. Had Samuel Whitaker been at the office at about 3.30 a.m. that morning, 31 March 1992?

'It gives me no pleasure to ask the question,' he added apologetically.

'Of course,' said the older man, 'you must ask the question to do your job. Mr Mulcahy,' said Whitaker, staring sternly at him, 'please make a note of the following. I did not sneak into the office on the morning of 31 March 1992. All right?'

Mulcahy stammered out another apology, and left. Whitaker sat in silence for a few moments, and then picked up the telephone. 'Mrs DeSantis,' he said, 'could you find me a number for . . .'

That was the last time Ed Mulcahy ever spoke with Samuel Whitaker. It was only long after that it occurred to him that the senior partner had not directly answered his question.

8

On Saturday nights, Creel shopped at the Maverick Square Purity Supreme. The crowd was thinnest then. A cab would pick him up at his apartment, drive to the market, and then a second cab would pick him up at 9 p.m. for the return trip.

Before leaving his apartment that Saturday, Creel looked out his front window again. The car was still there. The man in the Taurus, the one Jamal told him about when he got off the bus Friday, had been parked across from his apartment last night. Jamal said he had been asking around about him. Now, today, he'd been parked across the street, a block up, all day.

He was still there when the taxi arrived to take Creel to the market at about 8.15.

He noticed the car again in the parking lot at about 9.15, while he waited for the cab to arrive to bring him home. Creel saw, through the cab's rear window, the Taurus pull after him from the lot. It followed them to his apartment building again.

'Keep driving,' he said, as the cab pulled up to the building.

The cab pulled back into the driving lane. A moment later, Creel saw the Ford pull out after it.

'Damn,' he said. 'All right, Maverick Square again.'

'Anything the matter?'

'Never mind. Just take me to Maverick Square.' The headlights loomed large in the rear view mirror now. The cabby saw it too.

'What the hell is going on, if you don't mind my asking?'

'Just get to Maverick Square as fast as you can.'

The cab driver obliged.

When they screeched to a stop in front of the T Station, Creel was relieved to see the boys there. And a Boston patrolman. 'Officer,' he shouted at the cop, who was standing by the entrance. 'Officer!'

The cop ambled over to the cab. As he approached, Creel saw the Ford pass by and turn the corner.

After a moment of conversation with the police officer, Creel was back in his chair on the sidewalk.

'Yo, Stump!' hollered one of the boys.

'Hey, what about the groceries?' asked the cabby.

'You'll have to deliver them,' Creel said. He rolled back over the sidewalk to hand the cabby a twenty. Creel turned his chair, and rolled away to the T Station. He pushed his chair out of the light, and looked around. He could not see the Ford. Perhaps the ostentatious chat with the patrolman had scared off whoever it was. The cop had gone back to his patrol car. Now what?

'Yo, Stump wha's happenin'?' hailed one of the boys.

Creel looked back at him. It was Jamal.

'Jamal, I need a favour.'

'I dunno, Stump, busy night.'

Jamal leaned against the brick front of the T Station. He had on a Walkman, and his trunk pulsed forward and back. Three or four of his friends hung loosely about him. They smiled.

'I've got to go to a friend's,' said Creel, 'but I'm a little tired. You think you might give my chair a push over to Chelsea Street? I'll pay you ten dollars.'

Laughter from the boys. 'Shee, Stumpy, what you think I am, a orderly?' Jamal asked. He rolled his eyes, and went back to his music.

'Well, look here, let me tell you the truth. That guy you told me about? He's still around, been parked in front of my place all day and following me tonight. I have a bad feeling about this. I need a little help. I figure if I have you with me, they'll leave me alone. You are a pretty intimidating young man.'

Tio, one of the boys, liked the sound of that. In an impersonation of white speak, he said, 'I say, Jamal, you are a pretty intimidating young man!'

Howls of laughter. The boys held their sides.

'Hey, Stumpy, you need some help, man, why don't you just axe me for it? Don't be offerin' me no chump ten dollar!' Jamal strolled slowly towards the chair.

'Appreciate it,' said Creel.

'Don' worry 'bout it, man,' said Jamal. The youth took up the handles and guided the chair across the intersection to South Street, heading toward the water.

Eight blocks from Maverick Square lived an old

friend of Creel's. He was rummy and broken down, but he might have a couch to sleep on until Creel could figure out what was going on.

They never made it. Two blocks from the water, Creel heard them – footsteps racing round the corner in the last block. He grabbed the wheels, spun and faced back up the street. A block away, a dark-haired man was running at him, something in his hand.

'Shit,' shouted Jamal. 'Dat him? What's goin' down, Stump?'

'Not now!' Creel spun the chair again. 'Run, Jamal, left off to Prince, fast as you can.'

'What you gon' do?' he asked, anxiously.

'Never mind, Jamal, get down Prince!'

The chair raced down the street, and Creel heard the footsteps as Jamal peeled off left at the last intersection. Creel flew through the intersection without pausing. Still the footsteps came on. Ahead was the last block of the street. It dead ended in the three-foot concrete abutment which separated the street from the harbour wall.

Creel's heart raced. He sped down the last block of South Street.

When the chair struck the abutment, it was travelling at better than fifteen miles per hour. The force of the collision sent Creel's body flat against the concrete. His arms grasped the top and levered him over.

He heard a gunshot as he jack-knifed over the top, and another as he plunged into the greasy darkness of Boston Harbour, fifteen feet below.

9

The paper was folded against the sink, splotched with water, and Ed Mulcahy was reading it and shaving. It was early Monday morning, 16 May 1992. The day he had been dreading had arrived: this morning he would have to start writing his report to the Count. That meant he would have to make the call which he had put off for as long as he could, the call to John Shepard. How in hell do you begin a call like that? Hey, John, good to talk to you again! Just wanted to chat with you about this fraud memo I'm writing!

He stared at his face in the mirror, and began to pull the razor through the shaving foam again. It looked like a smooth snow field on a brilliant Colorado morning. He looked down at the newspaper. The Sox had dropped another to Baltimore. Elko had been shelled. Their ace. Mulcahy sighed.

'Gitz!' he shouted.

'Emph?'

'Elko. What happened?'

He heard a stirring from the next room. 'All done. Kaputsville. Toast. His arm is meringue. Day old pasta. Didn't make it out of the third. He's finished. Did you see my story?'

'Yeah, pretty rough on the guy.'

'I'm in vulture mode, pal. The big buck is stumbling, and I'm circling. I can juice this story for months.'

'What if he throws a no hitter?'

'I'll be in the front row of the cheering section.'

Mulcahy chuckled, squinting at the shaving mirror. 'Gitz, are you a moral man?'

'Not even close, pal. But Ed?'

'Yeah?'

'He won't.'

At that moment, across the city, across the harbour in East Boston, a youth, about sixteen, dressed in baggy jeans and high top sneakers, a baseball cap turned backwards on his head, the tag still hanging from it, beckoned to his companion as they ambled down South Street towards the water.

'Check it out,' he said, indicating the wheelchair, which was lying on its side by the harbour wall. The other boy looked at the chair. Their slim dark hands ran across it. Below the wall, the water lapped against the abutment. The other boy turned the chair right side up and sat in it. 'Be Stumpy's all right,' he said. The two boys leaned over the abutment, looking down at the water.

'Man be shootin' at Stumpy?'

'Mmm, hmm,' Jamal said.

'At *Stumpy*?'

'I ain't lying to ya, man.'

'Damn. Stumpy. Man be fulla surprises.'

They stared down at the water. 'Think he dead?'

'Mmm, hmm.'

'Dey fine him?'

'No uh uh. Dey ain't found nuttin.'

The other boy pushed himself back from the abutment, and as he did, his perspective pulled up. A mile and a half away, across the open water, the downtown towers glittered in the morning sun, backing the aquarium.

'You think Stumpy could swim dat?'

'Naw,' said Jamal.

'He a strong muhfucker. Whipped yo' ass.'

Jamal shook his head in agreement. 'Yeah, he did. But Stumpy a cripple, man.' Sadly, he turned and pushed the wheelchair up the street.

Two hours later, in Freer Motley's office downtown, Ed Mulcahy went looking for Creel. But he had not come in, and had left no message. No one knew where he was.

John Shepard didn't answer, either. Mulcahy exhaled with relief when he heard the answering machine click on.

10

Late that evening John Shepard's rust-scarred 1984 Subaru wagon was headed westbound on the Massachusetts Turnpike, its tired, rusted undercarriage ready to say farewell to the Commonwealth's salty roads for the last time. Shepard fiddled with the radio dial and found a country and western station loud enough to compete with the muffler, the first of a series of stations that would carry him through New York, Pennsylvania, Ohio and Indiana, out through Illinois and Missouri into Kansas and the desolation of Eastern Colorado, through two nights of motels and long days of coffee and driving, until the tips of the Rockies would peek on to the horizon somewhere near Denver.

The station wasn't loud enough to drown his thoughts. His mind was racing. Nine years, he thought, nine wasted years. The song shuffled on in endlessly predictable G and C chords, about how she done walked out on him for the last time. He filled in the last words of each line before they came tinnily over the speaker. Still his mind raced.

'Fret not,' he said to himself, 'thyself because of fuckin' evildoers, For they shall soon be cut down like the grass, and wither as the green herb.'

But he continued to fret, his back hunched over the wheel.

In an hour or so he passed the exit for Hartford and New York, checking his watch. The station had faded out, and he switched it off. The two words, 'New York' on the green exit sign sent Shepard's mind back to one of the earliest deals he had done, his first big out-of-town closing for Samuel Whitaker, the one where they sat in Trader Vic's and drank Scotch long after the bankers had drifted off, and Shepard listened, fascinated, to stories of Whitaker's service in the South Pacific.

'Fuck 'im,' Shepard said audibly, and banished the thought.

But at that moment, the expression was superfluous. About three hours earlier, Samuel Boylston Whitaker had fallen to the floor of the study in his Sheringham farmhouse, dead from a single gunshot wound, fired at close range.

The dead man was dressed in a flannel shirt, a cardigan, and the moleskin trousers he typically changed into to roam his back fields on a spring evening. Not far from his body, his bifocals were found on the carpet. A plate of cheese and crackers had evidently sat on the coffee table before him, and been scattered by his fall. A glass of beer, half-consumed, was on a sideboard at the end of the room. The fatal shot had entered the right occipital portion of Samuel Whitaker's skull, exploded through the left parietal area, blowing out a skull fragment of over fifty square centimetres, and a vast quantity of brain matter. The force of the impact had thrown the man's head and shoulders forward, and the momentum had toppled his body on to the floor.

The next morning, the police would find, in Whitaker's right hand, the sidearm which had been issued to him as a young naval officer. Its firing chamber was empty, and the ballistics report would later conclude that it had fired the projectile which killed its owner. By his side, the ejected casing was found on the carpet. On the desk in the study was Whitaker's old Smith-Corona typewriter. In the carriage the detectives found a note.

By 10 a.m., the state police cars were stacked up like playing cards, and a team of detectives pored over the house. Meanwhile, the Subaru was crossing into Indiana.

11

The death of Samuel Whitaker stunned not only the little town of Sheringham, but the whole business community in greater Boston. It commanded days of headlines in the *Transcript*, was covered in the New York and Washington papers. Tributes poured from the financial and legal communities. Reporters pressed police for information beyond the initial, sketchy details of the apparent suicide, but there was little.

Whitaker was buried on Thursday, 19 May, at St John's Episcopal Church in Sheringham, where lilies cascaded from the dark stained glass window sills and five hundred mourners spilled out of the sanctuary and into the clear spring morning. It was a gathering of old Boston, Old Harvard, Old Beacon Hill, such as was rarely seen in those days. The Dean of the Faculty of Arts and Sciences at Harvard read from *Isaiah*. The Boston Bar Association president read from the New Testament. Anna Whitaker rocked silently in the front pew, supported on each side by her daughters, past hearing the benediction or the eulogy, stricken with shame and grief. She had been widowed only two weeks before her thirty-seventh wedding anniversary. Her daughter Beth stared at the casket, resting only several feet from the place she had stood the day Reverend Sillsbach had confirmed her, and a few feet more from the spot she stood when he presided at her wedding.

Mulcahy had been uncertain about whether to go. Shocked by the news in his Wednesday *Transcript*, he had wandered into the office where many of the partners and staff had gathered in a community of universal dislocation. The halls were filled with tears. No one had any idea of what to do when the telephone began ringing. Mulcahy's 'war room' lay as he had left it that Tuesday afternoon, stacks of files and yellow pads, chronologies, memoranda, all unfinished, all puny and insignificant. And the sickening thing, the thing that roiled the pit of Ed Mulcahy's stomach, was the sense that somehow he had been used to force this. Like a good soldier, he had carried out the Count's bidding, and pressed the old man with the questions. And he had put Creel on to the computer sleuthing, and found that the mortgage had been tampered with on Whitaker's terminal.

Mulcahy left his work untouched, deciding that he would attend the funeral Thursday. He felt a part of these events now. And so he drove west to Sheringham.

When the service was over the bells rang through the quiet spring air. The crowd shuffled slowly from the sanctuary, some pausing to grasp the widow's hand, or to embrace her, or merely to stand helplessly before her. In the press Mulcahy noticed virtually all of the Freer Motley partners, and a number of associates and staff. He saw Kate Maher, an associate with whom he often worked. He hadn't known that she knew Whitaker, and they smiled at each other sadly and helplessly across the crowd. He hadn't spoken to Kate since the investigation had begun.

Outside the church Frannie Dillard, the A-Team reporter, was recording a story for the TV news as Mulcahy walked past. He left the church, and followed the procession past the community tennis courts to the hillside cemetery. Above the cemetery, Rouse's apple orchard was in bloom. The cemetery was lovely, except for the new gash in the earth, and the hearse which pulled alongside. Mulcahy lingered near the back of the crowd.

When it was over, Mulcahy found Dover Street. Some few minutes later, he pulled his car to the shoulder and stared out across the road.

Set back from the road by about fifty yards was a sprawling farmhouse, with two extensions, one to the side, another off the back. The white paint of the clapboards and the black paint of the shutters gleamed in the midday sun. In front, between the house and the stone wall along the road, was an apple orchard. A small flock of sheep was grazing there. To the sides and rear, and behind the great white barn, the house was surrounded by fields. A herd of cows was visible at the end of the farthest field, gathered around a sileage feeder. They lowed gently, off in the distance, and apart from that, and bird song, only the occasional interruption of a passing car was heard.

Mulcahy crossed the road to the gravel drive. One of the sheep, startled, looked up, munching grass, its face a blank as the lower jaw moved from side to side, and then stopped. It turned and trotted towards the back of the pasture. The herd followed. Two or three sheep bleated, and then they trotted, tumbling one against the next, for the far wall. There they milled together, looking back at him.

He stood by the pink plastic strip, with its 'Crime Scene' legend. It streamed between the corner of the stone wall and a maple across the drive. He caught the sweet scent of manure on the breeze up from the barn. For a few moments, he looked out at the scene. Except for the police car parked in the drive, it was so peaceful that it still scarcely seemed as if this could be real. It was as though someone had strung a police barricade across a painting. There was no other car, nor sign of anyone. The shades were drawn. The mourners must have gone somewhere else after the funeral. Mulcahy's hands fingered the plastic strip for a moment. He looked up and saw that the sheep had returned to grazing, at the rear of the pasture.

He looked once more at the silent house, and then at the tape in his hands. Crime scene? he wondered. Didn't think suicide was a crime.

The return to Boston took almost an hour. Mulcahy tried to distract himself, pressing the radio buttons and leaping from one idiotic talk show to the next. These people who make the calls, do they work? he wondered. Do they have lives? Do they know that Samuel Whitaker is gone?

Freer Motley had closed again. Some kind of instinct compelled Mulcahy, nevertheless, back to his

113

conference room. Perhaps he thought he might find an answer there. Or at any rate that he should look for one.

The team of prosecutors sat around the elegant table in the great corner office, listening quietly as the detectives finished their presentation. Two of them took notes, while one, a large man wearing an impeccable blue worsted suit – he was the only man in the room wearing a jacket – thick, prematurely greying hair sweeping back from his forehead, sat impassively at the end of the table, his hands folded before him. Rising from the other end of the table, District Attorney Mike Connell walked to the window, and looked out at Pemberton Square, where he stood with his back to the group. 'Fellas,' he said to them, when they had finished, 'we are going to need a maximum effort on this one.'

He turned and faced them, the table full of state police and assistant DAs, with a twinkle in his bright blue eyes, and although he was smiling, it was a politician's smile, which looked like it might be assumed or discarded like a hat. Part of Mike Connell's success was due to his knack of seeming to be one of the fellas. And part of it, the part on display now, was the way he could smile at you so as to guarantee he might cheerfully discard you, too, with that same smile.

'Fellas,' he said again, 'I don't think I need to emphasise how important this case is going to be. I want to take it to the grand jury next week. That means we need maximum effort. We all know what year it is.'

The men and women around the table studied their hands. Though every one was a civil servant, and technically indifferent, they all knew what year it was. 'Let's have no fuck ups this time, okay?' Connell said. 'No Din Baos. Okay?' He was smiling at them still, but no one mistook that smile for affability.

'Paul, stay here for a moment,' he said to the lawyer in the elegant suit as the gathering broke up.

Part II

12

News of the indictment three weeks later was carried over the fold in the *Transcript* and on the front page of the *World*, with almost as much coverage as the report of the apparent suicide had been given. Ed Mulcahy flicked on the TV to find Frannie Dillard leading the A-Team Evening News with the story. 'High-flying corporate lawyer John Shepard,' said Dillard, with Pemberton Square as his backdrop, 'has been charged with murder in the death of his senior partner, Samuel Whitaker, according to an indictment returned today by a Suffolk County grand jury.'

It was a shock to see and hear it, but the shock of inevitability, not surprise. Rumours began leaking all over the legal community almost as soon as the funeral was over, rumours, questions, suggestions that the 'suicide' of Samuel Whitaker had been staged. And then the subpoenas came. It seemed as if half the office was summoned before the grand jury. The tenor of the questioning was widely discussed, notwithstanding the admonitions regarding grand jury secrecy. For Shepard's few friends at Freer Motley, it was as though the long watch had ended and the hurricane had finally battered the shore. By the end, no one doubted Paul O'Hanlon's intention.

'So Eddie,' said Gitz one night, as Mulcahy sat before the television. 'What gives with this? You know Timmy Serota? Good guy. He could use a break, you know?' He stood in the kitchen doorway, wearing grey sweats, a beer in his hand.

'Gitz, let me get this right,' said Mulcahy. 'You want me to leak information about this to one of your pals at the paper?'

'Can't a guy ask? Off the record. You know. He's a good guy.'

Mulcahy shook his head.

'So did he do it?' Gitz asked.

Mulcahy looked up from the television. 'How do I know?' he said. He stared back at the screen. 'God,' he said softly.

Gitz lingered in the living room. 'Eddie, he's a good guy. This is a story, man, a story . . .'

Mulcahy stared at the television. 'Gitz?'

'Yeah?'

'Not a chance.'

Gitz shook his head. 'What use are you? What use are you?' he asked himself, as he walked off towards his bedroom.

In the weeks before the indictment, Mulcahy had finished his report. It was a desultory piece of work: larger events had overtaken it. Of course, the report now had to address the death of Sam Whitaker. Dutifully, Mulcahy had posited several hypotheses, arraying the evidence for and against each. The report considered the possibility that Sam Whitaker had himself sabotaged the mortgage document, as a spiteful parting shot at the firm which had abandoned him. It considered alternatively the possibility that Shepard had planted the error, as payback for the firm's partnership decision. Last, it discussed the possibility that somehow Whitaker and Shepard had worked in concert. But the report reached no firm conclusions.

The fact that continued to vex Ed Mulcahy was George Creel's disappearance. After Creel had been gone for several weeks, Mulcahy called personnel. 'What do we have for next-of-kin on Creel's employment app?' he asked.

Mitzie called him back when she found it. 'Mr L. B. Johnson,' she said. 'I don't have an address for him.'

'Relax,' said Mulcahy, 'you don't need one. Lyndon Johnson is no longer with us.'

Nor was Creel's landlord any help. One day in June the building super and a patrolman took the elevator to the third floor of Creel's building. The apartment had been ransacked. Someone had smashed the computer terminals. No computer printouts or floppies were found. Other than that the most noticeable thing was the overpowering odour of souring milk. The closets and bureau were full of clothing. Two empty suitcases were in the bedroom closet. The police officer looked for a wheelchair answering the description supplied by Creel's office,

121

but it was not there. The one wheelchair in the apartment was standard hospital issue.

Later that day a detective arrived and interviewed the landlord. 'Don't look like he was planning a trip,' he said.

When Mulcahy learned of this from the landlord, he telephoned the Area G precinct. The detective had prepared a missing person's report.

'What will you do with your report?' Mulcahy asked.

'File it,' the detective said.

'And?'

'Keep it,' he said. 'In the file.'

'I see,' said Mulcahy.

George Creel never returned to Freer Motley, never wrote seeking after the two weeks' pay he was due. A month later, Creel's landlord cleaned out the apartment and readvertised.

'Mike, if you want to run the case, run the fucking case. Give it to someone else. Or run it yourself.'

First Assistant DA Paul O'Hanlon sat stiffly on the brown leather chair pulled up before the great desktop. A big man – years ago, he had anchored the offensive line at Boston College – tall, broad, he seemed to sit unnaturally high in the chair. It was dark in the District Attorney's office that evening, the mahogany panelling lit dimly by the lamps on the table and desk, and it was quiet outside the door. Most of the staff had cleared away.

'No,' said the District Attorney, leaning back in his chair, a pair of patent leather shoes resting on the desk top. He was dressed in a tux, having returned from a fundraiser somewhere. The jacket had been thrown across a chair, and his tie, unlike O'Hanlon's, was unknotted. 'It's your case. You will not fuck it up. You will not lose it. No Lon Din Baos, not before election day.'

At the sound of the name, the First Assistant shifted suddenly and demanded, 'How long do I wear Lon Din Bao? How long?'

'Long as I do,' said Connell.

O'Hanlon glowered at his boss. It was utterly unfair to saddle him with the Din Bao fiasco.

'Mike, in four years I have tried twenty-one felonies. Twenty were convicted. I got you twenty hooks, Mike, twenty bad guys, twenty press conferences.'

'And one Lon Din Bao.'

'I am goddamn tired of hearing about Lon Din Bao. And I am goddamn tired of his name hanging out there unspoken, any time you need to bust me.'

'You're tired of Lon Din Bao?' Connell's smile had vanished, and he sprang from the chair and leaned across the deak. 'You *will* be tired of hearing about him when Reising is done! Goddamn tired is right. Din Bao might as well be Reising's running mate for this job. Do you think Reising's got you in mind for his First Assistant?'

'Assign it to Ehlberg, Mike.'

'Paul . . .'

'No, Mike, I'm tired of this. Assign it to Ehlberg or Flood. I'm sick of this. You don't think I'm up to pulling your shit out of the fire for you, you assign it to one of them.'

'Paul, you listen to me . . .'

'No, Mike, you listen to *me*.' Now O'Hanlon was close to shouting at his boss, and Connell knew he was going to get a speech. So he settled back in the chair in silence. 'I get a call at 2.30 in the morning, I'm in Roxbury twenty minutes later, and I got a man in blue who's down. I got a cop killer loose, I got a man down, I got the entire fuckin' Area D third shift ready to blast anything that moves, I got a hot summer night with three dozen illegal aliens in and out of the fire escapes, and yeah, I sent them in. You are goddamn right. I had a police officer down, Mike!'

'Paul . . .'

'You are goddamn right I sent them in to search the place. Let the SJC look me in the eye and say otherwise. Let them stand up and make the call! The SJC. They've never been to Roxbury, none of the bastards. You know, and I know, and everybody who has ever been near that town knows, that I go and wake up a fuckin' magistrate to get a warrant, and that evidence is gone. Gone! The fuckin' phony passport, the gun, the coke, the projectiles, are gone. Gone, Mike! And if the SJC didn't see that, I can't help it. I don't send them in, right then, you don't have a conviction either. You don't have a goddamn indictment 'cause you got no confession, you got no witness without a motive and a rap sheet, and you got no weapon!'

'Paul . . .'

'No, Mike, don't give me that shit. Not here, not just you and me. You are out there on the street 11 July 1990 and you do the same thing.'

'Paul, Ernie Brodsky was a friend of mine, too.'

124

O'Hanlon caught himself and stopped, for he knew there was no ready answer to the rebuke. Every prosecutor in the county had had a soft spot for Ernie Brodsky, the incorruptible detective who was gunned down on that hot summer night back in 1990. O'Hanlon was no different. And so the inference was there. For a brief moment on a sultry night in 1990, standing in the road in the projects, with cops and Vietnamese screaming at him, and with the walkie-talkies squawking, the blue lights in his eyes and Ernie Brodsky down, Paul O'Hanlon surrendered his judgment. O'Hanlon, who had tried dozens of felonies to conviction, the First Assistant, the best in the office – Paul O'Hanlon stumbled.

He had tried the case, and tried it brilliantly, but his hands, and the Commonwealth's were tied by that split second in July. 'Fuck it!' he had screamed at them there on the street. 'Do it! Secure it and do it! Scour it! I don't want a goddamn speck of dust missed!!'

O'Hanlon had issued the order. He sent them in without a warrant.

Detective Brodsky was killed when he interrupted a drug deal in a second-floor apartment at the front. He was shot at the threshold, and bled to death after he had staggered into the living room. The killer grabbed the shell casing and fled upstairs to a fourth-floor apartment in the rear, which was shared, among other illegals, by Din Bao's girlfriend. It was one of the places where Din Bao liked to rest between felonies. It also had a fire escape, but that was of no moment to Sy Belsky, who found in the girlfriend's ownership enough of a privacy interest to justify almost two weeks of suppression hearings.

As he sat in the darkened office, thinking of Belsky, O'Hanlon's jaw clenched involuntarily. He hated the man. It seemed to the prosecutors, sometimes that Judge Belsky would not be content until every rapist, every thug, every killer, every drug trafficker, was stalking the streets. In a twenty-five-page opinion castigating the police department and the District Attorney's office, he had suppressed the evidence.

The office waged a desperate battle in the SJC to reverse Belsky, but the sly old liberal had beaten them with fifteen pages of findings, all of them alluding to witness demeanour, credibility, even the allegedly halting manner in which trifling questions were answered – the kind of detail which Belsky knew the SJC couldn't take away from him.

'Paul, the day before yesterday doesn't matter in my job,' Connell was saying. 'Only yesterday matters. We got an election coming up. You've got to get me a new yesterday. We lose this case, and you and I can talk as long as we want about what's fair in life, and what ain't, but the fact of the matter is, you and I are on the street.'

O'Hanlon knew it was true. Belsky's suppression order stuck, and Paul O'Hanlon was left to try the Din Bao case almost without evidence. He tried it like a man possessed. Demonic, single-minded, he drove the police department, drove them to ferret out every witness, and he pounded the defence, pounded and rammed and shouted. In closing argument he begged that jury to revenge Ernie Brodsky. He had put a little bit of his heart in his hands, and offered it to them in exchange for a verdict. The jury was out for almost two weeks. During the last week, rumours of a mistrial circulated through the courthouse, and there were daily bulletins of shouts and sobbing from behind the door. When it was over they came back to the courtroom with tears in their eyes, and they looked only at the floor. The jury could find no refuge except one, and so they clung to, and took to heart, the instruction on reasonable doubt. They stood in a Suffolk session, and their verdict was read, and then they rushed from the place, unable to look at anyone, not the prosecutor, not the victim's family, and least of all Lon Din Bao.

The next day the newspapers pictured him, walking out into the sunshine of Pemberton Square, the cop killer a free man, wearing a smirk from ear to ear. And Paul O'Hanlon, rising after a sleepless night, looked in the mirror and saw that, in the space of three weeks, he had started to go grey.

Mike Connell had run unopposed in 1988. But Mel Reising's campaign for District Attorney began to gather steam soon after the Din Bao acquittal.

On 10 June, in a small courtroom in Colorado, John Shepard waived challenge to rendition, and they delivered him to the custody of the sheriffs, for transport to Massachusetts. There he was, on 12 June on the front of the *World*, still looking cocksure as he was led from the rear of a Boston police cruiser in handcuffs. The headline screamed 'Like *this* Deal, Counselor?' That night Frannie Dillard chortled on the television news: the high-flying legal eagle had hired R. Felix Parisi. Felix Parisi! A legendary criminal defence lawyer. The reporters could hardly wait for the show.

Ed Mulcahy sat in his shorts, spreadeagled on the couch, with a beer in his lap. There was Parisi on the news. Ed laughed at the carnival. Parisi had met his client – what, two hours ago? Already he had the speech going. 'This case is an abuse, a transparent, vainglorious, sneaking effort to make headlines by a prosecutor notorious for pandering to the media,' he whined.

'It fits,' Mulcahy said, to no one in particular.

Parisi always tried his cases in the press. Time was when most of them were big enough to excite some interest. He hadn't been heard from in a while on a case this celebrated. But the old formula hadn't changed. Like every other case, *Commonwealth* v. *Shepard* would become a trial of the prosecutor, a drumbeat of whiny charges from Parisi that the DA was conducting the most unethical, the most unscrupulous prosecution ever heard of. In fact, Felix Parisi was never more than a hair's breadth from sanction himself. His grandiloquent speeches were never burdened by the issues, and when they stumbled over a fact, that fact usually wasn't relevant.

Parisi had become so famous among petty criminals that, in large measure, his cachet was his utter unavailability. Whenever a case involving Felix Parisi was called to trial, invariably an associate raced into the courtroom to advise the judge that Attorney Parisi was on trial in the Essex Superior Court or the Hampden Superior Court or the Peabody District Court, or any court but that court. Attorney Parisi was always 'on trial' somewhere else. He was good for a year of continuances, usually.

And in most small cases, a year of continuances is a win. One more year out of jail. One more year for witnesses to forget, leave town, lose interest.

The summer passed, and the case slipped for a time from public notice. Life at Freer Motley returned to a somewhat normal pace. In late June, Ed Mulcahy was assigned to Pressco, a large fraudulent conveyance case. Soon he was buried in depositions of financiers.

One Tuesday evening in August, Mulcahy found himself at the Delta terminal at New York's LaGuardia Airport. He had twenty minutes to kill before boarding the shuttle for Boston. He was tired. He'd just finished a long, surpassingly dull deposition. For almost ten hours spread over two days, he'd listened to an investment banker – a man who'd made $6 million on the deal Mulcahy was litigating – testify that he couldn't remember. That he didn't have notes. That he didn't know. What in the hell did those people do all day? he wondered. Well, he was going to catch a commuter from Logan to the Vineyard, and spend the day Wednesday catching fish. Big fish, and lots of them.

If he hadn't had so much time to kill that night, he might not have glanced across the terminal at the bank of telephones against the wall. He might not have decided to check his voice mail. He might have flown to Logan, and then to the Vineyard, and then it would have been Thursday before he checked his messages. And that might have been too much delay. Maybe the whole thing would have gone away.

But that night, he had the fifteen minutes. And so, a moment later, he was stooping at a telephone, one hand over an ear, straining to hear the second voice message. The connection was poor and the voice was soft and distant – he had never heard it subdued before. But there was no mistaking it. It was John Shepard's.

13

At 10.10 a.m. Wednesday 24 August, Ed Mulcahy sat on a badly sprung office chair in the attorneys' room at the Charles Street jail, staring through the wire mesh. On his side of the screen was a dreary metal shelf. Overhead a fluorescent light flickered. There were no windows. Nothing relieved the monotony of the mustard yellow brick walls. Mulcahy shuddered. He had not been in one of these places for a long time.

On the other side of the screen the lock rattled loudly and the door opened. John Shepard walked in, followed by a corrections officer.

'Fifteen minutes, gentlemen,' the officer said as he left. He swung the door shut behind him, and it slammed with a crash.

They stared at each other for the first few moments of their small allotment. Ed Mulcahy had not seen John Shepard for a long time. He remembered him, as he always did, carving precise telemark turns through deep snow, bobbing slowly away from sight.

But that had been a long time ago. Shepard didn't appear so graceful now, but his mouth still wore that ironic grin.

'How're you doin', man?' he asked.

'I'm okay. How about you?'

'I'm about what you'd expect.'

'I'll bet.' A door crashed in the distance, and there was the vague racket of a loud argument.

'Welcome to my home,' said Shepard.

Mulcahy chuckled.

'You know, Ed, the thing about jail is the noise. You just can't describe the noise. There isn't a damn quiet thing in a jail. Not a quiet door, not a quiet television set, and for damn sure not a quiet human being. It's the noisiest goddamn place I've ever been.'

'I can imagine.'

'Well, probably you can't. That's the thing.'

'Well, I guess not,' said Mulcahy.

The men small-talked for a few minutes. It was easier. Mulcahy found it difficult to look at Shepard, for the fluorescent lights cast an ugly yellow glow on the prisoner, but his eyes were dark and burned with anger. Mulcahy was conscious of time. 'John,' he said at length, 'why am I here?'

'I need your help, man.'

'What is it? What can I do?'

'How about an acquittal?'

'I'm serious,' said Mulcahy.

'So am I,' Shepard said. And the narrow gaze bored in on Mulcahy through the darker side of the wire mesh.

The men looked at each other in silence. Away somewhere the racket had recommenced. 'Dafuck

132

you doin'! Dafuck you doin', man!' someone was yelling. And then more noise, indistinguishable.

'You want me to try the case?' Mulcahy said.

'Yeah,' said Shepard, 'that's the general idea.'

'You have a lawyer.'

'Yeah.'

'Felix Parisi.'

'Yeah.'

'I mean, Felix Parisi, the most experienced criminal defence guy in . . .'

'He's a stiff. And he's lazy.'

'How would you know? You're a corporate lawyer.'

'I know. He's past it.'

'You don't know,' Mulcahy said. 'You don't know. Every defendant goes through this. You have all day to sit here and think about it. So you think, "Do I have the right guy?" "Should I get somebody better?" You don't know what he's doing on your file. And you begin to panic. It's . . .'

'Ed, has he called you?'

'Who?'

'My experienced criminal defence guy. Has he called you?'

'No.'

'It's only a murder case. Why call the guy who did the in-house investigation on Idlewild?'

He was negotiating now, and he was still the best negotiator Mulcahy had ever met. 'What does Idlewild have to do with it?' Mulcahy asked.

Shepard was silent. Mulcahy went on, 'John, what makes you think I'm any better?'

'You don't quit until you're dying.'

It took him aback, the reference, for it was something they had never talked of. 'I don't quit,' he repeated. 'I don't quit because I've got no talent. I plug away because my instincts are wrong. I'm a schlep. I'm a civil schlep, too. I do interrogatories. "Judge," I say, "I move for further answers. These answers are non-responsive." Heavy, heavy stuff, motions to compel further answers to interrogatories. That's what I do, John. I haven't tried a felony in five years.'

'Look, Ed,' said Shepard, 'you work. You work and you're good. This guy Parisi, maybe he was good once. Maybe he has some knack. But all he does is talk. He's all talk. He comes in here to interview me. He's got a half hour. A half hour to gather information, right? For that half hour, who talks for twenty-eight minutes? Him! For twenty-eight minutes! "I am going to do this," he says. "The jury will never believe that," he says. "I will tell the jury this other thing." Well, lemme tell you something. If I'm on the jury, I vote against Methuselah and any fool who hired him.'

Mulcahy frowned.

'Look,' said Shepard, 'I made a bad mistake. A bad mistake . . .'

Mulcahy felt his throat go dry. He wasn't sure he wanted to hear what might come next. But he had misjudged the moment, for Shepard was referring to his lawyer.

'I never in my professional life respected my elders, right?' he went on. 'And pretty quick I was better than them, better than all of 'em. Come to this most important decision of my life, and I do what every other pissant does, and throw in my lot with a grown-

134

up. Fuck 'im. He's past whatever he had, and I'm not sure what the hell that was, beyond self-promotion.'

And even in that palace of noise, it was almost silent for a moment. The only sound was the buzz of the overhead lighting.

'So what's the defence?'

'The defence is suicide, isn't it?'

There was another pause as Mulcahy weighed matters, looking through the screen at Shepard's darkened features. It was hard to make him out.

'But you can't sell suicide without explaining what was going on in his head,' Shepard went on. 'Somebody has to dig into Sam Whitaker. I mean, I'm frankly as confused as anybody else why that miserable tightass Yankee sonofabitch would off himself. But I don't see work outa this guy. I don't see it! This old fool Parisi hasn't put damn all together. You got to help me, Ed.'

There was a rap at the door and it opened suddenly, scraping across the linoleum with a rude clatter. 'Time's up,' the guard said. In the distance someone was shouting again. 'Son of a bitch!' the voice said, and there was a crash of metal on metal.

'Officer,' said Mulcahy, 'this is important. Five minutes, please.'

The guard frowned. 'Just five, Counsellor, that's it. Cell check in ten minutes.' He swung the door to.

'Has he done any of his own forensics?' Mulcahy asked.

'Forensics?'

'His own fingerprint analysis? Hair, blood sample analysis? Has he hired a shrink on whether the

135

evidence adds up to a predisposition of suicidal tendency in Whitaker, stuff like that?'

'If he has, it's a miracle. No, I'm sure he hasn't. Done any of that.'

'That costs a lot. How are you fixed?'

'I'm done. He cleaned us out.'

'What's he into you for?' Mulcahy asked.

'A hundred.'

'Jesus.'

'Yeah, right. Like to see the motherfucker's time sheet, too. Reckon I'm paying him five grand an hour. Maybe more. I had sixty. He's got all of that. He's got forty from Mom. She's about broke. And he wants another seventy-five to try it.'

It was quiet again, almost, but for the buzz of the failing fluorescent light. 'Hell, John, the firm wouldn't let me take it anyway.'

Shepard looked at him. 'I need you, man. It's my turn.' His voice softened. All the bravado was gone, and he sounded far away. 'I can do a lot of things,' he said quietly, 'but I can't stay in a place like this.'

Mulcahy nodded. He knew the chip was due, and he'd known for several minutes he'd pay it in with or without a call. 'Jesus,' was all he said.

'You know I can't pay you.'

'You just made that pretty clear. Any helpful ideas about your former employer?'

Shepard smiled. 'Hey, if they can't take a joke . . .'

They rose together. Mulcahy knocked on the door, and the guard returned. Shepard was at the doorway, and a thick-necked officer in a crew cut was hustling him out when Mulcahy asked, 'Have you got a trial date?'

'A week Tuesday.'

'You're kidding.'

'No.'

'That's thirteen days!'

But the guard hauled John Shepard through the door. As it clanged shut, Mulcahy heard him call out, 'I closed Idlewild in eight!' And then he was alone with the sprung chair and the wire mesh and the flickering light.

Somehow, that was not a consoling thought.

It is almost a mile from the corner of Charles and Cambridge Streets to the financial district and the Freer Motley office, but it was a pleasant day in late-summer. Mulcahy needed to think. He began to walk up Cambridge Street, trying to organise his thoughts. They wouldn't fall into place. Emotions played at him. He felt liberated: he felt desperate. He wasn't sure how he could finesse the management's committee on this client. He had no idea how to defend the case. Thirteen days! But still, he felt that this was what he was supposed to do, what he had been prepared for doing. He felt right.

As Ed Mulcahy walked up Cambridge Street for Government Centre on that day in August, his mind travelled back to the longest conversation he'd ever had with Shepard. It had been at 11,000 feet, under a clear Colorado night sky, as the two men lay out on the deck at Uncle Bud's Hut in the mountains above Leadville, under a riot of stars, talking long into the night. It had been a perfect gem, an uncut, unspoiled day, from the first bite of eggs at the Golden Burro in Leadville, to the warm sensation of the bourbon rolled across the tongue as he sat watching the stars from the hut's deck. In that world, John Shepard was as close to peace as his nature permitted. In his life the only challenges of moment were physical, and the only transcendence he knew was to meet a physical test. He had many skills, and a great intellect. But these were celebrated by others, and gave him no comfort.

'Now that you've had a day on tellies,' Mulcahy remembered Shepard saying, 'are you ready to leave all that line-waitin', candy-ass wearin', cement-footed shit behind?' There was an easy drawl in the voice, and the eyes twinkled.

'Maybe,' Mulcahy laughed. 'But there's two parts I haven't got yet.'

'What are they?'

'The uphill part. And the downhill part.'

Shepard chuckled. 'Give it time,' he said. 'Give it time.' After a while, he went on. 'Time – I wish I'd given a few more things time. Like this place. Whenever I'm here, I wonder how I let myself get away.'

Mulcahy stared up at the sky. The stars, numberless, beamed out from every quadrant. 'Your people out here?' he asked.

'My mom, yeah,' Shepard said.

They sat on for a while, passing the bourbon flask back and forth.

'What's she do?' Mulcahy asked.

Shepard laughed. 'She's a surgical nurse in Denver. That's some of what she does. But mainly, she praises the Lord Jesus. She's a Pentecostal.'

'That explains it,' said Mulcahy.

'What?'

'Why half the time I feel like I'm talking to an Old Testament prophet.'

'I might just be, you know?' said Shepard, and laughed again. 'One of those old motherfuckers covered in boils and hollering hellfire. Teethed and whelped on the Good Book, I was. You can't slip a verse by me.'

After a while, Mulcahy asked, 'Your father a Pentecostal too?'

'Not hardly. You might say my dad was the kind of man gave Pentecostals a reason for being Pentecostals. Not your temperate kind of man. He's dead now.'

It didn't seem a subject which Shepard wished to pursue.

'And you?' Mulcahy asked after a while.

'Me?' Shepard was refilling his cup from the flask. 'I'm a sinner,' he said. 'Don't see much use in church bound religion, I can tell you. Lot of fat old gals in polyester whoopin' and praisin' the Lord, and a lot of skinny men looking sideways at you. Not for me.'

He took another sip of bourbon, and rolled it around his tongue. 'If there is a God, this is His temple. And I don't suppose he'd begrudge a man a snort on a night like this.'

They looked out on the snow fields glimmering in starlight. 'You got to respect the Christian faith for one thing,' Shepard said, after a moment.

'What's that?'

'They take sinners. The real Christians, I mean, not the phonies. They even like 'em. I like 'em too.'

139

They sat in silence, two small mortals on the side of a vast mountain, stupefied by the splendid starlight.

'Why did you move east?' Mulcahy asked.

'Now there's a question.' Shepard shook his head and took a hit from the tea cup. 'Jesus, but you litigators ask a lot of questions.' He was silent for a while. 'My problem is,' he went on, softly, 'everywhere except here, I want to kick a thing's ass. You know? I get to Freer, and figure out how to kick the ass of corporate law practice, and then I want to do it. It drives me crazy until I *do* do it. And once I've done it, then . . .'

'Yeah?'

'Then I can go, I guess.'

Shepard went on. It was not cold, and there was no wind. The sound of his voice was a gentle murmur in the night. 'The mountains, though, the mountains give you peace. Maybe it's because I know they can kick *my* ass anytime they take a notion. And ain't a thing I can do about it. And then every once in a while, they relax, like today, and say, "Come on up here, enjoy." I like that.' He took another sip from his cup, and sat for a while. Then he rose and stretched. Mulcahy could remember, even with the remove of years, the starlight so bright that he could see Shepard grinning.

'Mr Mulcahy,' Shepard said, 'I'd say you're much improved by my society.'

At the corner of State and Congress, Mulcahy caught sight of himself in a floor-length window panel, and it brought him out of his reverie. A silly smile was on his face. I am a fool, he thought.

When he returned to the office, he had time for precisely two acts before the fury of the management committee descended. He instructed his secretary to open a file. This meant notifying the billing department of the new case and obtaining a billing number. Normally, the gnomes in client accounting wouldn't crack a smile if a lawyer opened a case for Joan of Arc. Probably, they'd misspell it. But John Shepard was a name even they reacted to, and, just as Mulcahy figured, no one waited for the case opening sheet to notify the management committee.

The other thing Mulcahy had time to do was place a call to Parisi.

'I have just been engaged by John Shepard,' he said, leaving a message. 'Please call immediately to arrange for transferring the file and for a return of the balance of the retainer.' He left his number.

Ten minutes later he had a call. A woman identified herself as 'Attorney Parisi's assistant'.

'Attorney Parisi is in court,' she said.

'Well, get this message to him,' said Mulcahy. I need to talk to him ASAP.' He left his home number, and the call ended.

Moments later, Estella came in. Did Mulcahy remember those interrogatory answers due in Pressco? He rolled his eyes, as if to say, 'Somehow it'll keep.' She went on. Mr Shanklin wanted to see him. 'Now. I'm afraid it may have to do with the John

Shepard thing. Someone in client accounting said they thought the management committee would have to approve and so they left a message.'

He smiled.

But when Mulcahy met the Count in Shanklin's corner office, no one was smiling. It was all over very quickly. The Count decreed that Mulcahy was not to represent Shepard. Mulcahy replied that he already represented Shepard. He would withdraw, immediately, the Count said.

'I won't, Al. I'm going to take this case.'

'You can't possibly take the case. There's an obvious conflict.'

'What conflict? Sam Whitaker is not a party to this litigation. I have no first-hand knowledge and so couldn't be called as a witness – '

'Ed,' said the managing partner, cutting him off, 'go back into your office, close the door, and think about what I am about to say to you. No Freer Motley attorney will defend John Shepard in the murder of Samuel Whitaker.'

'I don't need to go back to my office,' Mulcahy said. 'John Shepard is my client.'

'Then you will have to resign from the firm,' the Count snapped.

The men stared at each other. The office was like a tomb: dimly lit, curtains pulled, the grim granite slab of a desk bare of any ornament save its telephone and the 25-watt lamp. For some reason, all that Mulcahy could think of was how extraordinarily ugly the Count was, as the shadows fell across his crooked face. He remained behind his altar, glaring. Mulcahy turned and left.

One thing was certain. Nothing good ever happened in that office.

14

Mulcahy had a headache. This was all happening too fast. He returned to his office, shut the door, popped a couple of aspirins, and tried to think, but it was too much, too fast, too confusing. Finally he pressed the intercom. 'Estella,' he said, 'cancel whatever I've got.' He rang off and picked up the telephone to call his father. A few moments later, he left for the bus terminal.

As Mulcahy approached the Falmouth Quay that evening at 6.45, there was the old man, in the *Ethel B*, his beloved Brownell, bobbing gently at the dock. It was a lovely summer evening, and the elder Mulcahy was seated aft with a pipe and the *Oak Bluffs Standard*, when Ed, still dressed in his suit, walked up. The Captain looked up from his paper and smiled. 'Guess you don't aim to catch fish.'

'The hell I don't.'

'I won't clean 'em for you.'

'Did you ever?'

'Did I ever, hell. How are you, boy?'

They embraced. Mulcahy took off his shoes and socks, jacket and tie. Barefoot, he loosed the bow line and cast the fishing boat off. His father guided the craft slowly out of the Falmouth channel into Vineyard Sound. Once free of the shore, the Captain opened up the throttle, and the engine noise forced the men to shout.

'Gonna redredge the saltwater ponds.'

His son nodded.

'Scallopers are bullshit about it. Same old thing, though. Can't reason with the goddamn state.'

'Blues running?' Mulcahy asked.

'They were. Slowed down some recently.'

'What are they hitting?'

'Hit a sneaker two weeks ago. Kinda quiet now.'

'Want to fish some?' the son asked.

'I reckon. Not often I see you on a weekday.'

'No, I'm kind of confused. Thought I'd talk to you about it.'

'My hourly rate's pretty expensive,' the old man said. 'Up to a dollar and a half.' He was quiet for a moment as they passed astern of a big ocean-going Donzi.

'Tell you what,' the older man continued. 'Been some bonito by Dog Fish Bar, over to Menemsha. We'll head over there and drift a while. I've got some fly rigs in the cabin. Bonito's a helluva fight on a fly rod.'

'If you hook one.'

'Hell,' his father snorted. He made his bearing southwest and they rode in silence for quite a while. When they reached Menemsha, he picked his spot a little east of the other boats, and cut the engine. The

145

old wooden-hulled fishing boat began to bob on the gentle tide. The early evening sun twinkled on the water.

The old man liked to tie a number 10 with doll's eyes and a feather – he got the eyes in bulk somewhere. The mechanics and the old salts at the marina docks laughed at him until he landed a 42-inch bass in the salt water fly-fishing derby three years earlier. Now a lot of guys fished doll's eyes. He had rigged the fly rods with them.

The surf remained gentle. Hardly a breath of breeze came off the bigger water to the east. The two men began flipping their flies out. The son's cast was more flamboyant, with warm-up strokes sounding a windshield-wiper whoosh overhead before the cast. The father's was simply direct. With a sharp salute of the forearm, he sent the tippet on a line for the point he'd chosen. He looked at his son and squinted in the setting sun. 'Not too many flying fish round here,' he said. 'You ought to try dropping it into the water every now and again.'

'Gotta dry it,' Mulcahy said lamely.

'Mmm hmm,' his father said. 'Bonito hate like hell to take their dinner wet.'

They fished awhile in silence. No one had any strikes. At length the son said, 'I got asked to take a murder case today.'

'Mmm hmm. Thought you were out of that business.'

'Thought so too.'

'And?' The old man squinted at him.

'I took it.'

'Mmm hmm.'

'Dad, did you read about the Sam Whitaker murder? You know, the senior partner at our firm?'

His father nodded.

'I guess I should say, Sam Whitaker *suicide*. Anyway, do you remember they charged a guy named John Shepard, who had been an associate there, guy who worked for Whitaker?'

'I remember something about that.' His father had set his flyrod in the rack and was packing his pipe.

'Yeah. We were acquaintances. And he was the guy who, on the skiing trip . . .'

'Oh, yes, I remember him. Your mother and I met him at your office one time.'

'Yeah. I'd forgotten that.' Mulcahy put a cast out to leeward. They were quiet for a few minutes. The doll's eye twinkled on a gentle swell and was swallowed up by early-evening surface sparkle.

'So they charged him with the murder? I'll be damned.' The old man worked the pipe. 'He seemed like a good man. Well, you never know about people. Surprising.' He tamped the tobacco and pulled again. 'He your new client?'

'Yes. He's my new client. Couple of little problems though. The case goes in thirteen days. I've forgotten how to try a criminal case. Oh, and I got fired for taking it.'

'What's that?'

'Yeah. When they found out I took the case, they told me to drop it. I said no. So the managing partner hauled my ass in and said I'd have to resign.'

'Mmm hmm.' His father pulled on the pipe. He took his seat astern, and sat smoking on his pipe.

147

Between pulls, he asked his son, 'Think you've done the right thing?'

'I don't know.'

Mulcahy continued to cast. It was quiet, with just the lapping of the little swells against the hull. The sun was setting away over Cutty Hunk. His father smoked the pipe.

'Your man – did he do it?'

'I don't know.'

'Why don't you ask him?'

'It's not that simple.'

'Mmm hmm.'

The old man sat for a while. Then he said, 'Look, son, I don't know anything about your business.' He shook his head. 'Gettin' a man off who murdered someone, why, I just don't understand that.' He pulled on the pipe. His lips worked the stem. He beckoned. 'Jig that line some. Strip a little in.'

Ed played the line, but there were no strikes. His father said, 'On the other hand, if he didn't do it, well then. Sometimes a guy has to get fired just to keep his self-respect. Jobs come and go.' He was silent again, and they both looked way out west where the sun was setting. The boat rocked gently, lulling them. 'There's another thing,' the older man said, as it began to grow dark. 'Maybe you feel like you owe him this. Kind of a symmetry to it, I guess. And I know one thing. That's the kind of debt you don't get but one chance to pay. You don't want to be an old broken down sonofabitch like me with him an old broken down sonofabitch sitting in a jail. You don't want that. And if your law firm doesn't understand it, why, maybe you best not be with those people anyway.' He puffed on his pipe, turned back, and looked toward Menemsha's darkening shore.

'So you think I'm doing the right thing?'

'Hell if I know.'

They fished on well past dusk. Ben Mulcahy had a couple of strikes, but they didn't catch fish that night. After dark he put his running lights on and ran his son back to Falmouth in time for the last bus.

As Mulcahy disembarked at the public dock at Falmouth, and prepared to cast off, he said, 'You know, he can't pay me, either.'

'Hell,' said his father, shouting over the rumble of the engine, 'if I'd a worried about that, there'd a been a lot of boats never got fixed!'

Mulcahy cast off and watched as the *Ethel B*'s running lights disappeared into the summer night.

15

Back in his office in Boston, Mulcahy had been mildly surprised to discover that his pass still worked. It was midnight when he retrieved the call from Attorney Parisi on his voice mail. It left a home number. Here goes nothing, he thought.

The phone rang several times before a sleepy voice answered. But the speaker was soon awake.

'Hello. This is Ed Mulcahy.'

'And this,' said the voice dramatically, 'is Attorney Felix Parisi.' It was that high-pitched voice, all right. You couldn't mistake it. Mulcahy imagined the withered old advocate in a bathrobe, addressing his wife. 'My dear,' he might say, 'you will now be made love to by Attorney Felix Parisi!' But Mulcahy soon snapped back to reality.

'What do you mean by calling me at this hour?' Parisi was saying.

'I apologise,' said Mulcahy. 'There isn't much time.'

'What is this message you have left me?'

'I met with John Shepard yesterday. He has retained me as defence counsel. You will be withdrawing from the case. I need the . . .'

'What makes you think I will be withdrawing from the case?'

Mulcahy paused. 'What makes me think you'll be . . . well, for starters, you've been instructed to.'

'I haven't spoken to my client.'

'I suggest you do so. Look, don't take this personally. I've been hired. That's it. Let's be pros about this. I need your file tomorrow morning.'

'I'm in court tomorrow morning.'

'I'll see your assistant.'

'I'll have to speak to Mr Shepard first.'

'Well, please do so, and do so immediately.'

'Mr Mulcahy, do you have any idea what you're doing?'

Good question, thought Mulcahy, after he had hung up the phone, with only the sounds of a vacuum cleaner off in the distance.

But he still had one more assignment for himself that night. So he sat in the darkened office, studying the Freer Motley partnership agreement under the solitary glow of his desk lamp. He had never read it very closely before. He smiled as he found what he needed, and then wrote out a memo to Shanklin. 'I decline to resign from the firm, and I stand upon my rights under Article 17 of the partnership agreement,' his note said. He folded it, placed it in one of the blue 'Deliver' envelopes, and, at last, headed for home.

Article 17 bought Mulcahy a little time. He could be terminated for cause only by the affirmative vote of sixty-seven per cent of the partnership. A partnership meeting could not be convened on less than twenty-four hours' notice. He would be a partner for another day at least. Maybe two. At least he'd have his pass. Maybe that was all that really mattered.

Morning dawned sunny and clear again, and Mulcahy, though tired and not exactly confident, was at least resolute. It was a serenity touched by fear: in short, the feeling of a trial lawyer. Estella had that wide-eyed look as he walked in from the elevators. He smiled.

'Anything for me?'

'Anything for . . . are you kidding?' she returned. 'You would not believe how this phone . . .' But his hand was up, waving it off. 'Come on into the office.

'Hold any calls, except for Parisi,' he said, taking off his jacket. Then he rattled off a concise list of assignments: she was to load up the ten banker's boxes of Idlewild documents, his criminal rules, three volumes he identified of the annotated criminal statutes, *Liacos on Evidence*, and his lawyer's diary. Throw in two boxes of pens, four dozen yellow pads, a dozen wallets and a box of manila files. Some plain bond paper. No letterhead. And a laptop. Oh, they better send some instructions with the laptop. And a home printer and fax. With three or four reams of paper.

She looked at him quizzically.

'Going to be working out of my home for a couple of days.'

She nodded, but seemed unconvinced.

'Maybe a number of days,' he said under his breath.

'What?' she asked.

'Nothing. Estella, gotta get this stuff out immediately. Big new case. Have a messenger here at noon, get one of the mailroom guys on this now. I want the boxes out the door at noon.'

'Yes,' she said. 'How do I bill this?'

Mulcahy stopped. He reached into his desk drawer for the firm's client printout and flipped through it. '207826,' he said, smiling to himself. If the Count was going to expel him from the partnership, the least Mulcahy could do, he thought, was to have the bill for moving expenses show up on one of the Count's cases.

Estella left.

At 11.30, Mulcahy watched as the last of the boxes disappeared into the elevator. The message light on his phone was flashing, and the spindle on Estella's desk was full of pink slips. Estella told him that Shanklin had called again and insisted that Ed come to his office at once.

Mulcahy handed her the blue envelope. 'Give him this,' he said. He gave her one instruction more, and left for Parisi's office in Commercial Wharf.

Not your usual day at the office, Ed Mulcahy said to himself as he stepped into the elevator. He thought ruefully of the half-dozen friends he had not even talked with about this. And then it occurred to him that although many must have heard, not one of his colleagues had come by to see him. Funny places, law firms.

The elevator seemed to stop at every floor. 'What's up?' one of his partners hailed him, cheerily, as they headed for the ground floor. Mulcahy smiled. The elevator door opened.

'Oh, not much, you know. Termination for cause, that kind of thing.' Mulcahy smiled and winked as he left the elevator.

The man behind him laughed. He hadn't known Mulcahy to have a sense of humour.

16

Across town, Parisi's assistant met Mulcahy in the reception area of one of those second-floor rehabbed suites in the waterfront warehouse developments. As soon as he entered the reception area, Mulcahy could see that the address was tonier than the establishment. The furniture was a little frayed around the armrests, the grey carpet gone dirty at the door. The room was cramped, and the veneer was peeling away ever so slightly from the corner of the receptionist's desk. No one was there as he entered.

Mulcahy looked around. Dominating everything was a full-length colour photograph of Parisi, the old fellow looking somewhat jaundiced as he smiled woodenly before an American flag in what appeared to be a courtroom. Around the vast photograph were dozens of small ones of Parisi shaking the hands of various wheelers or arm in arm with minor pols. Most had a thin layer of dust on the frames. Mulcahy looked around himself, wondering whether he was in a law office or a Greek restaurant.

He heard footsteps and looked up to see Attorney Parisi's assistant. She had big hair, which was red that day, and might have been the day before, or might not. He noticed that she wore her clothing tight. In her circle, perhaps that was an advantage. In Mulcahy's, it was merely an incentive to keep the meeting short. She looked at him coldly. 'I'm Lisa Rubo,' she said, 'Attorney Parisi's assistant. Please sign here.' She handed him a receipt, and one rust-coloured file wallet.

He looked at it. 'This is it?' he asked.

'That is the file, yes.'

The file wallet was about three inches thick. There were no subfiles except one headed 'billing'. Everything was jumbled in the wallet. He leafed through it. 'This is everything? Police reports, witness statements, legal research, motions, interview notes, everything? This?'

'That is the file,' she replied.

He was silent for a moment as he paged through it. Then he said, 'I want to get this straight. Experts, government forensics, analysis, witness outlines . . . it's all in here?'

'That is it.'

'Did you hire any experts?'

'How Attorney Parisi conducted the defence of this matter is none of your business.'

'I see,' he said. 'Well, I guess we're going to need the balance of that retainer, then. Do you have a final bill and the rest of his money?'

'The retainer has been fully applied,' she said. 'In fact, Mr Shepard owes this office in excess of twenty thousand dollars.' She stood with her hands on hips.

'You're kidding me.'

'I assure you, Mr whatever your name is, I am not kidding you. Attorney Parisi has devoted enormous resources to the defence of this man, and this is the thanks . . .'

Mulcahy had heard enough. Normally he was slow to anger, but too many buttons had been pushed, and he'd had too little sleep. 'Ma'am,' he interrupted, 'a three-inch file is not enormous resources. It's not any resources. It sure isn't a hundred grand. And, ma'am, please tell Attorney Parisi from me as follows. I want to see that final bill. I want it itemised. And if my client hears one word about another twenty thousand to Attorney Parisi on this case, I'll subpoena his time records. Looking at this file, I'll probably subpeona them anyway.'

It was a good moment for snapping a briefcase shut, and he tried. But the hinge had been akimbo for about six months, and he had to lever it down and jiggle the clasp. She stood with her hands on her hips, watching him as he reached the door. 'I'm *sure* that Attorney Felix Parisi keeps detailed time records,' Mulcahy said, and left.

Standing in Commercial Street, outside Parisi's building, Ed Mulcahy felt truly alone. But there was much to do. He went to the bank and cashed in a twenty for a roll of quarters. From there he walked to Pemberton Square.

Pemberton Square houses the Suffolk Superior Courthouse. Beneath its vast mansard roof, and within its archways, its garrets, its massive stone, lawyers have tried cases for almost a century in dowdy courtrooms

157

which stand cheek by jowl with back offices, hidden corridors, afterthought stairwells. In Suffolk, the file clerks are trained in the art of avoiding a glance, and remain steadfast in their absolute refusal to know or communicate information. An Old Testament patriarch, if he happened to come to the desk looking for a docket, might wait there many hours before being noticed. As to actually finding anything, all bets are usually off. Generations of yellowing files litter the cabinets in the courthouse's rabbit warren of back offices. Outside, the building is tired, now. It bears insult to every side, standing propped up by a Depression-era annex. In its time, the courthouse gazed haughtily over Scollay Square, and the annex towered over the skyline, visible from the docks. But Scollay Square is gone now, and the remaining pair of buildings seem to have limped into the latter years of this century, like a squat dowager aunt leaning on a disappointing nephew. Opposite the courthouse a nondescript office tower has sprouted up, and before it a perspective-robbing hemisphere of puny office space, set off by a moat of windswept brick. The old courthouse deserves broad lawns and perspective. Now it is hemmed in on all sides.

Mulcahy stepped briskly across the plaza, his shoes falling upon the flagstones commemorating the Bill of Rights. He was careful not to tread on the Seventh Amendment. He was going to need that one. Maybe the Fifth as well, he thought ruefully.

'Sir?'

It was the guard, looking impatiently at Mulcahy. When you're not a player, they remind you at the door. He fumbled for his bar card.

In the courthouse's central atrium, he looked up at the bronzed glower of Rufus Choate, as footfalls on the terrazzo echoed around him. Choate, he knew, was one of the last century's legendary trial lawyers. His expression seemed to find fault.

Mulcahy headed to the clerk's office. After signing an appearance form, he pushed quarters into the machine to make the copies, and filed the original. He then walked to the new courthouse annexe, took the elevator to the 5th floor, and dropped a copy with the secretary for service on the District Attorney's office.

'I'd like to see someone on the *Shepard* matter,' he said.

He waited for a while in the lobby, until one of Paul O'Hanlon's flunkies, a young lawyer named Gleason, came to see him. The man looked at him in puzzlement. Mulcahy noticed he was chewing gum.

'I've just appeared for the defence,' Mulcahy said. 'I have Felix Parisi's file with his discovery material. The last batch you sent was dated 28 July. Is there anything else?'

'Parisi's withdrawing?' the young man asked.

'Yes.'

'Isn't that a damn' shame? Wow.' The gum clicked and popped.

Mulcahy looked at him. 'The discovery material?' he said, again.

'Gee,' Gleason said, 'I'll have to check.'

'I'll wait while you check now,' said Mulcahy.

'Well, I'm kind of tied up right now,' the young man said. He smiled, chewing the gum.

'This case is scheduled to go to trial in twelve days.

159

I will be filing a motion to continue. Would you like me to include in my motion that the District Attorney's office was kind of tied up right now and couldn't check whether all of the discovery material had been provided? What did you say your name was?'

The man stared back at him. 'Maybe we're going to miss Parisi. Wait if you want to,' he said, turning on his heel.

Mulcahy waited. From behind the glass, the receptionist looked at him fearfully. She had stopped chewing her gum. He smiled at her. She smiled back, tentatively.

Twenty minutes went by. Then thirty. Finally the young man returned. He had a three-inch file of photocopied material. 'There were some additional forensic reports,' he said, 'and witness statements. I'm not sure these were asked for . . .'

Mulcahy glared at him. 'They don't have to be *asked* for,' he said, taking the wallet.

But they should be, he thought to himself on the elevator down. Maybe Shepard was right.

At home, rounding the corner from the elevator to his apartment door, they were there to greet him: the heap of boxes from Freer Motley. One by one he carried them in, stacking everything by the refrigerator.

'Oh my God!' said Gitz, appearing from the kitchen in sweats. 'Home before 9 p.m.! Home in the day time! Call the copy desk!'

Mulcahy shook his head. 'What are you doing here?'

'Got a night game,' he explained. 'You?'

'I got a long story.'

'I got time for a long story.'

'I don't,' said Mulcahy, without humour. He felt Gitz's eyes on him as he settled at the kitchen table. 'Look,' he said at last, 'will you keep this quiet?'

Gitz couldn't stand a secret kept from him. 'Sure,' he said, nodding vigorously up and down.

'Confidential, Gitz, means you don't talk to the yellow fellowship.'

'Silent,' said Gitz, 'as a tomb.'

'Even the so-called "good guys".'

'A pharaoh's tomb. A really old pharaoh's tomb covered with a half mile of sand that nobody's discovered yet.'

'I have a new client.'

'Yeah?'

'It's a murder case.'

'Murder case? Cool. I thought you downtown guys didn't get your hands dirty.'

'It's not cool. And I'm not a downtown guy. Not anymore.'

Gitz mouthed the words. 'Not a downtown guy any . . . I'm not getting this.'

'Well, I have a client whom my former partners found disagreeable.'

'Former partners?' asked Gitz.

'Yeah?'

'They . . .?'

'Yeah.'

'Holy shit,' Gitz said. He was silent for a moment, digesting this. 'So who's the client?'

'Confidential?'

'Like my mother's diary.'

'You would *sell* your mother's diary. For cheap!'

'More secret than my mother's diary, then,' said Gitz. 'Come to Papa. Whaddaya got?'

'John Shepard.'

'Holy shit. Holy shit.' He stopped. 'Did I mention "holy shit"?'

'You did.'

'Holy shit.'

Gitz left the kitchen to gather his things for the Sox game. 'Ed,' he shouted, 'you might have to let me off that promise. This is big.'

'You are not released.'

'Think of the public interest, Ed. The public has a right to know. Think of it!'

'You are not released.'

Gitz popped into the kitchen with his satchel. 'Wow,' he said. 'All I can say is, "Holy shit".'

'You always did turn a neat phrase.' Mulcahy heard the door slam, and Gitz's footsteps on the stairs. Opening a yellow pad, a beer, and the top file on the kitchen table, he sat down to read.

Ed Mulcahy could lose himself in a file. It was several hours before he came up for air. But when he did he felt lonelier than ever. He was going to need help, and lots of it.

Leaving out the evidence of motive, the disappointment over Shepard's failed partnership bid, it looked – well, it looked bad.

The coroner had concluded that Samuel Whitaker had been killed by a single shot to the right side of the head. Examining the deceased for lividity and colour, he estimated the time of death as some time after 4 p.m. and before midnight on 16 May 1992. The projectile and the shell casing had been recovered, and the deceased was found holding his Navy-issued sidearm in his right hand, slumped on the floor of his study, at the east end of his farmhouse in Sheringham. The weapon had been fired once. It appeared that the projectile had come from the weapon, and it appeared certain to have caused the death. The body was discovered by a housekeeper, who let herself in at approximately 8.20 the following morning, and discovered the body in the study at approximately 8.25. A suicide note had been found. The victim had not, however, recently consulted a psychiatrist or a doctor. No one had observed depression in the victim, although various witnesses had observed the signs of a hostile relationship with the new powers at Freer Motley.

The note was simple. It read:

It was a lapse in judgment. At my age! This is the best way. Anna, Beth, Em, I love you. Remember me otherwise, in better days. I love you always.

It had not been signed.

At 6.15 p.m. on 16 May, a twenty-three-minute telephone call had been placed from a phone booth on Joy Street to Whitaker's Sheringham house. The telephone booth was a block from Shepard's door, and the closest telephone booth to his apartment on Beacon Hill. On the evening of the death, at 7.32 p.m., a short call had been placed from Whitaker's home to Shepard's exchange: one minute.

No eye or ear witness had been found. The house

sat on almost one hundred acres and was a working farm, with fifty Guernsey cows, about a dozen sheep, and chickens. The house was about fifty yards from the road, and the nearest neighbour's home was almost a half mile away. At the time of death, only Whitaker was home. His wife Anna was visiting a daughter and granddaughter in Connecticut. The housekeeper had left for the evening. No one had heard a shot.

When he was arrested in Estes Park, Colorado on 8 June, Shepard had given a short statement. He said that he had left Boston on 16 May, the night of the shooting, at about 8 p.m., driving west on the turnpike. He had stayed in a motel in New York State near Elmira during the early-morning hours of 17 May. He stayed at a motel outside Clifton, Missouri that night, and arrived at a friend's house in Boulder, Colorado, late on the night of 18 May. He couldn't remember the names of the motels and had paid cash.

Shortly after noon on 17 May, state police found a tan suit jacket in a waste bin at the Massachusetts Turnpike's Framingham rest area, on the westbound side, about twenty miles west of Boston. Fibres consistent with the jacket were found on a chair in Whitaker's study, and on the carpet near the body. Three fibres consistent with the carpet had been found on the jacket. On the right sleeve and lapel of the jacket were extensive bloodstains. The blood was found to be A-negative: Samuel Whitaker's blood type.

Mulcahy looked at his watch. Time for the news. He put the file down, grabbed another beer, and flicked on the television.

Ten minutes later, there it was, the teaser. 'A late development in the John Shepard case,' said the announcer, 'when we come back.'

'Great,' said Mulcahy to himself. 'More things the press knows that I don't.'

There was Fran Dillard after the commercials. 'News in the John Shepard case today, Jim,' he said. It was a live shot, in front of the courthouse. 'Prominent defence attorney Felix Parisi today abruptly resigned from the defence of John Shepard, whose murder trial is scheduled to start after Labour Day. Attorney Parisi issued a statement . . .'

'A statement?' Mulcahy said aloud.

The report continued. '". . . I regret that Mr Shepard would not take my advice in this matter," Parisi said. Citing "ethical reasons which must remain confidential", the criminal defence veteran told reporters that he had been forced to withdraw from the case.'

'What the . . .?' Mulcahy said again. He was fumbling through his notes for Parisi's home number. 'He's lost his mind . . .'

But it got worse as Dillard hammered on. 'According to Professor Jeffrey Stillman at the Harvard Law School, the rules of ethics require an attorney to withdraw from a case if he believes that his client wishes to take the stand and testify falsely. Confidentiality rules forbid the lawyer from identifying the actual reason . . .'

'The son of a . . .' Mulcahy was saying as he fumbled through his notes for the number. It rang for a while at the office. No answer. He got a home listing from information.

'That's right, Attorney Felix Parisi. Swampscott? Sure.'

He picked up the phone on the second ring.

'Mr Parisi, this is Ed Mulcahy.'

'What is it?'

'I am watching my television and not believing what I am seeing.' He heard the nasal Parisi whine start to kick in, and raised his voice, cutting him off. 'I think you have lost your mind. Parisi, call them back, tell them you lied about this, or tomorrow I go to the board and ask to have your ticket pulled. Call them back. I'm going to be in the Board of Bar Overseers in the morning. Are we clear about that? Do you hear me? *Do you hear me?*'

He shook his head as Parisi launched into a whiny soliloquy, and, closing his eyes, held the receiver away from his ear. At length, sighing, he hung up.

Again Mulcahy picked up the phone. A moment later, he had the number. 'Get me Frannie Dillard, please,' he said, when the WFBA receptionist answered.

'I'm afraid he's on the air.'

'I'll hold. Tell him it's John Shepard's new lawyer. He just went with the Shepard story and I have a comment. He may have time to get it in before 6.30.'

But it took them five minutes to get Dillard, and the newscast was already in sports when he answered.

'Frannie Dillard?' Mulcahy asked.

'Yes?'

'Please listen very closely. My name is Edward Mulcahy. Do you have a copy of my appearance?'

'Sure do.'

'Then you know I represent Mr Shepard.'

'Yes,' he said.

'I have a statement. Will it make this report?'

'No, sorry. But it may make the eleven o'clock. Listen, where are you? I can get there in an hour and we'll . . .'

'No. I'm doing it by phone. You can tape it. Are you ready?'

'No, wait.' There was a short delay before Dillard said, 'Okay, shoot.'

'My name is Edward Mulcahy. I represent John Shepard. I understand from a news account that Mr Shepard's former attorney, Felix Parisi, issued a statement to the press today. In that statement, I understand that Mr Parisi claims he was forced to withdraw from the defence for ethical reasons. The statement is not true. Mr Parisi was fired. For incompetence. Further, his statement to the press was unethical itself, and a breach of the attorney-client privilege. We intend to report that statement to the Boston Board of Bar Overseers in the morning. That is all.'

He hung up the phone, now shaking with anger. 'I need this?' he asked aloud. The phone rang again, almost instantly, but he let it go. What the hell? he thought. Might as well get sued by Parisi, while I'm at it.

17

It was the next afternoon before Ed Mulcahy returned to the file. He spent the morning drafting a Board of Bar Overseers complaint, which he filed with an affidavit just before lunch.

The last thing he or his client needed was this distraction. But all litigation seems to go that way. Ancillary disputes arise. The two sides become emotional; lawyers sprint to court and positions are hardened over issues which, fundamentally, have nothing to do with the case.

Just after one, he was back in his apartment, at the kitchen table, trying to force his mind back into the investigation. Outside the window, a pair of chicka-dees perched on the feeder, chiding him for letting a second day go by without filling it. Peering in, they scolded at the man bent over the file. But it was useless. They flew off.

Mulcahy came back to the jacket: a 43 long with a Brooks Brothers label. Stapled to the jacket sleeve had been a laundry ticket. The laundry which issued the ticket had been positively identified as the Beacon Hill Cleaners, on Cambridge Street, two blocks from Shepard's apartment. Police had found in Shepard's clothes box, which he had shipped on May 16, ten suits. Three were from Brooks Brothers. Nine were 43 longs.

In Whitaker's Sheringham home, off the study where Whitaker was found, was a lavatory. A bar of soap had been recovered by detectives. It bore one partial left thumb print and complete right thumb and middle fingerprints. According to a fingerprint expert, the right thumb and middle prints were too badly smudged to be identifiable, but the partial print from the left thumbprint appeared to be Shepard's. On the back of the couch, on the tile floor of the bathroom, and on the carpet, human hairs had been found and catalogued: a total of seventeen. In the opinion of the forensic expert, three were hairs of the deceased. Fourteen were consistent with Shepard's hair.

'Jesus,' Mulcahy said softly as he read the next report, from Colorado State Police. They had impounded Shepard's Subaru Wagon on 8 June. From the driver's well – where the driver's feet engage the pedals – and from a tyre tread on the right rear wheel, a detective had removed a total of four pebbles. These had been bagged and hand-delivered by a Sheriff's detective to Massachusetts. In the State Police crime lab, they had been examined by a geologist, and compared with a sample of one hundred pebbles taken from Whitaker's drive. According to the expert, the pebbles found in Shepard's car and embedded in its tyre were consistent in content (approximately 15 per cent pyrite-flecked granite), size, and colour.

He read on. A credit card record indicated that on 16 May Shepard had purchased $5.38 of gasoline from the Lamartine Sunoco Station at the corner of Maple Street and Route 135 in Natick. The service station lay on the direct route from Whitaker's home to the Massachusetts Turnpike.

Two hours had gone by as Mulcahy read the file. There was plenty more. Almost two dozen statements from Freer Motley attorneys, some describing loud arguments between Shepard and Whitaker, six directed to the questions which Mulcahy had himself investigated: whether Shepard had been involved in the Idlewild mortgage error.

At length, Mulcahy put down the files, and sighed. It had been a long time since he'd spoken to Stevie George. He found the number in his address book, and smiled when he heard that voice. 'You have reached the offices of Steven A. George and Associates,' it began. Ed chuckled. He rather doubted there were any associates. When the tone sounded, he left a message.

His eyes wandered back to the files. Unconsciously, he sorted the jumble of notes in a pile and began going through them. Three telephone calls disturbed his reverie before he got the one he wanted. He listened, chuckling, to his machine as Shanklin left two messages. The third call was from Estella. 'Ed, if you don't mind my asking, what's going on? Mr Shanklin has been down twice to see you, he seems very angry. I told him like you said, I didn't know where you were.'

'Anything from John Shepard, Parisi, or the DA's office?' he asked.

'No.'

'Anything else?'

'There's a partnership meeting at 9 tomorrow morning. Mr Shanklin said to be sure to tell you if you called.'

'I didn't call.'

'Okay, Ed, I heard about the late news last night. I missed it but the girls were saying that you were on, about Mr Parisi. What is going on?'

'I'll tell you later.'

'I don't like this.'

'I don't either, Estella. It will be all right.'

He hung up. Sure it will be all right, he thought. I just lost my practice and I'll probably be sued for slander. And for nicking a computer. Then I'll lose the damn case, get sued for malpractice, and be audited by the IRS for underpayment of my estimated taxes. It'll be fanfuckingtastic.

The call he wanted came at 6. He arranged to meet Stevie at 2 the next afternoon, after he filed his motion for a continuance with the court, and after he'd met again with Shepard, to begin going over the Commonwealth's case.

18

Stevie George had a two-room office on the second
floor over a watch-repair shop on Bromfield Street,
five blocks from the Suffolk County Courthouse, and
eight blocks from the Charles Street jail. Form
counted for little in Stevie's office. The linoleum was
peeling. His battered metal desk, a cast-off, stood by
the window next to a green file cabinet, another
orphan. Across the room was an ancient brown
couch. In the middle was a large grey table, with
rubber stripping along the edges and on the surface.
The street noise from Downtown Crossing pierced
his windows easily, and a fair-sized truck pounding
uphill on Washington Street could rattle the window
panes. Engraved in a semicircle in the glass was the
legend 'Stephen George, Investigator'. The seal of the
Boston Police Department, covered with signatures,
was framed and hung over his desk.

A former Boston Police detective, Stevie had gone
out on his own when his independent streak ran him
through the last of many lives. He stood five foot five

in his stockinged feet, and gained two or three more inches with a foppish set of platform shoes. He had gone completely bald, and wore a brown toupée that listed comically to one side or the other of his head. He was a man of impressive girth, with a habit of buttoning his jacket round his middle and then unbuttoning it again. On his left cheekbone was a most extraordinary, nipple-thick wart, protruding a half inch or so from his face. For years, friends had urged him to see a dermatologist about it. But Stevie had grown, in some bizarre way, fond of it. 'Get it cut off?' he'd say. 'Think a the scah!' And he would stroke it between thumb and forefinger like a waxed mustachio.

Stevie had a nose for where he might find a witness, almost as keen as for where he might find a good deal on a pastrami sandwich.

'Eddie!' he said, as Mulcahy entered his office at two. 'Howahyuh!'

'I'm good. I'm good, Stevie. It's good to see you.' The two men shook hands, Mulcahy's smaller hand disappearing between the bulbous fingers of Stevie's. Looking about him, Mulcahy noticed the tell-tale wax-paper crumpled on the table. He had surprised Stevie in the midst of his afternoon snack.

'Bullshit. Inna big time now, aren't ya?' said Stevie. 'Freeuh Motley. Jaysus. Big time pahtnuh. No more cokeheads, no more SSI fraud. Dafuck are ya doin' heah? Ya wanna Danish?' He beckoned Mulcahy toward the table.

'Stevie, it's a long story. But the short version is that I just filed an appearance for John Shepard. Case is going a week Tuesday, and I don't have anything.

And by the end of today, Freer will probably kick me out of the partnership.'

Stevie raised his hand to signal a pause as he came to that point where his full attention must be absorbed by the Danish. Mulcahy waited, watching, as Stevie worked a great mound of pastry into his cheek. He levered his jaws open. 'Whattaya, shittin' me?'

'No. I've told them I'm going to take Shepard's case, and they've told me no one from Freer Motley will take the case. Kind of makes the decision.'

'Shepid? The Widdukuh murder? Whattaya, crazy? Ya gunna fuck up a Freeuh pahtnuhship to take that maggot's defence? Eddie, ya not even a criminal guy anymoah, are ya?'

'Not really.'

'Shepid? I heard aboudim.' He paused again, working the wad of Danish back into his mouth, then gulping it down. 'It's a hook, Eddie,' he said. 'Heuh, have some Danish.'

'No, thanks,' Mulcahy said, declining the wax-paper pressed towards him again. For a moment, Stevie's face betrayed his relief. He began to work his jaws around the second Danish as Mulcahy explained. At length, Mulcahy got to the issue of money.

'Ah, puhfect,' Stevie said between mouthfuls. 'The maggot cahnt pay. You are crazy, Eddie, to be puhfectly honest witcha. You're gonna take this case and lose ya pahtnuhship, and the maggot cahn't pay ya?'

Mulcahy smiled. He had forgotten that, in the argot of the professional prosecutors, all defendants are maggots. 'That's about it, Stevie.'

'No, Eddie, that ain't about it, is it? Because the rest of it is you want Stevie to be Florence Nightingale too, ain't *that* about it? I gotta help you help this maggot, and he don't have a dime?'

'Right,' said Mulcahy.

'Shit.'

Stevie pondered the strangeness of the world. Smart guys, guys who graduated from Holy Cross and got law degrees, give up Freer Motley partnerships to defend some maggot who can't pay. There were things he would never understand. 'You callin' it in?' he asked.

'What?'

'Dah's will.'

Mulcahy was silent. Three years earlier, when Stevie's father was diagnosed with terminal cancer, Mulcahy had arranged to have one of his colleagues draw up the old man's will. It was a simple thing. The man had little to leave. But it had given a frail and failing old Irishman the sense that his affairs were in order. He died in peace. The bill was approximately four dollars. For photocopying.

'You ah. Shit!'

Stevie came close to Mulcahy, who had perched on the corner of the big table in the middle of the one-room office. 'Look, this maggot was a big corporate lawyuh, right? I'll do it. I'll take it on the come. If they hook him, I lose. But if we acquit the maggot, I get paid. If it takes two, tree yeahs, I get paid. I ain't doin' it free for some maggot who's gonna be loaded some day.'

'Can't charge contingency fees in criminal work, Stevie, it's . . .'

'Unethical. Ya, fuck you too. That's the deal.'

'All right.' They shook hands.

For the next hour, they sat at Stevie's desk, as he worked slowly through the file and an extra-large meatball sub. 'Hmmm,' he'd say from time to time. 'Hmmm.' When he came to the fingerprint report, he said, 'Evans, shit!'

'What?' asked Mulcahy.

'They got Evans. He's the best.' He read on in silence. 'Pebbles! They got pebbles in this case? Never seen a case wit' *pebbles* before.'

He read on. 'Shit,' he said again.

'What?'

'Our guy bought *gas* on the way out?'

'He says it wasn't him,' said Mulcahy.

'Sure he does,' said Stevie, reading on. After a while he said, 'Gimme the fibuhs.' Mulcahy handed him a manila file. 'Doctuh Hemp! Good old Doctuh Hemp! He's all right. Gets rattled onna stand sometimes.' He read the report. 'You got pathology theyuh?' Mulcahy handed him another file. 'I dunno this guy. Doctuh Goldman. Hmmm.' He read in silence. 'What else we got?'

Mulcahy went through the remainder of the file with him. 'Don't look too good for ouwah guy,' said Stevie. 'But, hey, no eye witnesses.'

'There's one guy we need to find,' said Mulcahy. And then he told Stevie about his strange interviews with Creel, and Creel's abrupt disappearance. Stevie took notes. 'Awright,' he said, 'I'll start on Creel in the morning. Look, I gotta go now. Do me a favuh. Copy the whole file. There's a machine in the back. Might need some paper. I got it from Dick Kiley in

Middlesex, ya knowim? Good guy. Lets me buy out the lease. Any copy machine that ain't good enough for a clerk's office, gotta be pretty shitty, heh? I gotta go, it's almost six. Copy this shit, leave it heah. Gimme ya numbuh. I'll call yah. I gotta go.'

'Where are you headed, just out of curiosity?' asked Mulcahy.

'Dinnuh time,' he said. 'Gotta get somethin' to eat.'

Stevie had donned his fedora. He turned from the door. 'Pull the doah shut when you leave, okay?'

'Okay.'

'Heh, Eddie, you picked a great fuckin' case not to get paid on.'

They were in the cage again. Mulcahy had read the files now, read the indictment and the forensics and the witness list, the grand jury testimony and the police reports.

'Look, I read the interviews in Parisi's file. I get the picture, I think. But I want to go through that last day, 16 May, again.'

'Sure,' said Shepard. On his side of the cage, he was pacing, back and forth, back and forth, one wall to the next, two steps, about face, two steps back to the first, about face.

Mulcahy looked down at his notes, and began to recite the day. 'Up around 9, out to do some errands.'

'Earlier than that, probably. Seven-thirty, eight.'

Mulcahy made a note. 'Okay. Bank, garage, pharmacy. Returned about 11. At home all day packing. The movers came around 2, left around 4. You packed the Subaru. You left the apartment about 8,

177

drove down to Storrow Drive, exited for the Mass. Pike, and drove straight west for about six hours. You stopped at a Days' Inn outside Elmira.

'That's right.'

'Who saw you during that time?'

'Who saw me?'

'Right. Who helped you carry boxes to the car, or chatted with you on the sidewalk? Did you see any of your neighbours?'

Shepard thought for a moment. 'No one,' he said.

'No one,' Mulcahy repeated. 'You packed up a car on a Beacon Hill street, you carried boxes down the stairs, tramped back up the stairs, and never saw anyone?'

'No.'

'And you were home for, what, from 11 until about 8?'

'Yeah.'

'Alone?'

'Right.'

'You didn't leave the apartment, except to ferry stuff down to your car?'

'No. Well, I think I went for a run, but, you know, other than that, no.'

'All right, then. You left about 8. When you were driving, did you stop anywhere for gas, coffee, a bite to eat, something like that? Strike up a conversation with anyone?'

Shepard shook his head.

'Any calls? Anybody talked to you by phone?'

'My mom, I think.'

'When?'

He thought about it. 'It was pretty early that evening – 6, 6.30, something like that?'

Mulcahy nodded. 'Any others?'

He shook his head. 'Can't remember any.'

'And you didn't stop at Sam Whitaker's house?'

Shepard had his back to the screen. 'I did not stop,' he said, 'until I got to Elmira.'

'When was the last time you talked to Whitaker?'

Shepard turned around and peered through the screen at Mulcahy. His face was in shadow. 'On 31 March,' he said. 'At about 5 o'clock.'

'John,' said Ed, 'they've got the phone records. He called you on 16 May, at about 7.30. You spoke for, looks less than a minute. And, at a phone booth up the hill from your apartment, someone placed a call to Whitaker that afternoon. They spoke for over twenty minutes.'

'Is there a record of me ever calling him? From my apartment?'

'No. Not that they've shown me.'

Shepard sat pondering for a moment. 'He didn't call me,' he said.

'And how do we explain the 16 May record?'

'I don't know. He didn't call me. Look, Ed,' he said, 'you're going to teach these people on the jury why he killed himself, right? 'Cause that's what they're going to want to know. All this other stuff is very interesting, but that's what they're going to want to know.'

Shepard had stopped pacing now. 'Whenever you want to bring somebody round to your position, you have to figure out what he wants to know.'

*

179

In a lawyer's office on Freer Motley's 20th floor, a young woman – her age indeterminate, actually, but still somewhere in the twenties – sat before a computer terminal on a side table, staring intently at the prose she scrolled through. The office was littered with banker's boxes full of photocopies, folders, manila files, copies of court decisions, advance sheets, legal periodicals. Her desk groaned under stacks of paper. There was, in fact, no obvious place to write anything. In a corner of the room, a waist-high heap of newspapers, First Circuit advance sheets, and back numbers of the *Massachusetts Law Weekly* teetered precariously over a forlorn Norfolk Pine. On the credenza, the terminal competed for square inches with more stacks of papers: papers heaped upon spavined volumes of the *Federal Reporter* heaped upon advance sheets stacked over more papers. Buried beneath it all somewhere there was apparently a CD player of some kind, for Mozart's Horn Concerto emanated softly out.

And in the centre of all of these heaps of paper sat Kate Maher, her shoes kicked off and her legs curled beneath her blue cotton skirt, shocks of curly red hair spraying this way and that, her nose inches from the terminal and her forehead drawn tightly in a frown.

Kate was cute. It infuriated her, that word, but it was what they had always said about her, and what they always would say. Not that she was beautiful, certainly not, and not even that she was pretty. (You would not deny that she was pretty, it was just that the word was not quite apt.) Nor yet that she was petite, for Kate was on the tall side, a little angular, inclined to hunch over. Yet cute was the right word.

Her hair shot off in wild directions, her figure got lost under anything heftier than a camisole, and she was resigned to the fact that freckles were with her for life. But she had a buoyancy, a feistiness, and a cleverness about her.

She approached most things analytically. Take the matter of dress, for example. Not for Kate that boxy women's garb seen on so many of her contemporaries, the stiff outfits which looked as though someone had sewn the trouser legs together on a man's suit. After law school, when she contemplated so many of her friends rushing to uniform themselves that way, she analysed the problem. Who is it, she thought, whom we have to placate? In the main, the answer was, men: forty-five- and fifty-year-old men, the ones running the firm, men with thinning hair and Coke-bottle glasses, and belts lost beneath a growing waistline, men all dressed in the same grey uniform. And what do these men know about how a woman should dress? Almost nothing. A middle-aged man in a suit, she reasoned, might sooner diagram the female reproductive organs than announce, with any confidence, standards of feminine attire.

Her syllogism complete, Kate wore skirts. She owned no suits, no necktie equivalents, no starched Victorian blouses buttoning up the throat. She wrapped her angles in long, comfortable, somewhat bohemian skirts, and wore sweaters and flat heels. And while some sniffed that her mode of dress was not quite appropriate – it looked far too ... too *comfortable* – those critics tended to be women. And they tended to wear boxy suits.

Thus Kate, with one leg curled beneath her

cornflower cotton skirt, sitting comfortably before the computer screen. Should a bomb have gone off at that moment, only the interruption in the computer service would have brought the event to her notice. For Kate was gone, lost on a legal side-road, and engrossed by the scenery. On that evening, the subject was liability of corporate directors for clean-up of their corporation's hazardous spills. Her mind was running in several directions at once: identifying the cases arrayed for one rule or another, cataloguing the relevant facts in her client's situation, playing through decision trees on a tortuous series of possible mischances. This was her great gift: the ability to analyse a tree down to the deepest taproot and up to the highest leaf bud. It was also her curse. It was why her CD player was covered with advance sheets, why her Monet poster had disappeared under dust, why she was there at all at that hour.

The telephone rang, and she was surprised to hear Ed Mulcahy's voice. That sound banished Mozart. Shivers of the doctrine of indirect operator liability scattered from her consciousness as she returned suddenly to the dusty reality of her office. *Ed Mulcahy?* Ed Mulcahy had been, for four days, the subject of a furious rumour mill at Freer Motley. These days at Freer Motley, the question was: what or who next? Sam Whitaker, John Shepard, now Ed Mulcahy, of all people. The rumours took on a sort of surreal cast because they were so at odds with the straight-ahead, plodding Mulcahy whom everyone thought they knew. It was like the soft-spoken librarian turning out to be a bigamist. Talk at the office had been of little else. Anonymous bulletins had been

182

delivered with breathless confidence: Mulcahy had quit; Mulcahy had been fired – fired for representing Shepard – fired for theft of firm property – fired for clobbering Shanklin – fired for suspicion of complicity in the Whitaker murder – fired for other misdeeds only speculated at. And rumours had gained momentum with bits and scraps volunteered with ersatz authority by acquaintances. The more distant the acquaintance, the more assured the bulletin. Such a one confirmed that he often spoke on the phone with his door shut – well, then. And the way he kept to himself even after Mr Whitaker's murder . . .

So it had gone for four days. Disgusted, Kate had stayed apart. There was just no constancy in people.

Kate had been Mulcahy's lieutenant on several cases, and they had become friends. She was, in fact, his most reliable associate, the one he called when he had to have an answer by the morning. She was the only associate who had earned his absolute faith. Time and again she had proved her ability to get done whatever job needed doing; to analyse the problem, to take the deposition, to find the right expert, to get a witness subpoenaed. And what she had liked about him was his utter lack of ornamentation or artifice. He was just a hard-working, thoughtful man who came to work in the morning and worked hard all day, who thought through legal problems analytically, as she did, who eschewed showiness. She liked that.

Their relationship had grown into one of those office friendships between men and women which fit no ready category. The pace of a few of their cases had thrown them together in emergencies. They had known long, tense nights together at the office preparing responses to dawn raid injunction motions; they had together horse-shed arrogant client executives for the witness stand; and together been through more than one trial before unfriendly judges. He had absolute faith in her loyalty and intelligence, the toughness of mind she would bring to the task of solving a difficult problem. And she had faith, too: faith in his judgment, faith in his want of ego or façade. Of this kind of relationship was born a close friendship, and when such things happen to people, it is – and was here – so often evident in a glance that their closeness might move beyond its peculiar constraints.

Might do, but thus far had not done.

She heard him ask her how she was, and heard herself respond conversationally, but it hardly seemed real. 'I'd like to see you,' he said then. 'I guess I can't meet you there.'

'No,' she laughed, 'not a good idea.'

So they agreed to meet at a bar, and in a half hour she arrived at the Oyster House to find him already there. He rose when she came in, and met her at the horseshoe bar where there was an awkward moment of greeting before the lobster tank, as each stood uncomfortably, not sure whether to exchange a formal Gallic kiss, or a handshake. They settled on a sort of clumsy compromise of handshaking and shoulder pats. Each was relieved when that was over. They returned to Mulcahy's booth, sat on opposite sides of the table, and ordered. The crowd in the old side of the Oyster House bar had thinned, and the booth was quiet.

'So you're really representing John?' she said, when he told her of the trial preparation upon which he had embarked four days earlier.

'I really am.'

'Is that why they fired you? They did fire you, didn't they?'

He took a sip. 'They did. You have the honour to be having a beer with the first ever Freer Motley partner terminated for cause. It took them eighty-three years to come up with a mistake as big as my election. Yeah,' he said, 'that's why. When the Count heard I was going to take the case, he – well, he was a man with a mission. Must have called me fourteen times. Got me in his office and told me to drop it. I said I wouldn't. He said I'd have to resign. I said I wouldn't do that either.'

'That's why they had that partnership meeting,' she said. 'You can't have a sudden, unplanned meeting of nearly a hundred partners, some of them flying in from the Washington office, others showing up in shirtsleeves from vacation, without every associate in the office wondering why.'

'That's why,' he said. 'They had to vote a finding of cause. They needed sixty-three votes, and twenty-four hours' notice. I hear they had Harold Mooney there.'

'I heard that too,' she said. Mooney was chairman of the litigation department at Adams and Sherman, one of the largest old-line firms in town.

'I guess they must be scared of me, huh?' He laughed. 'I don't seem so scary to myself.'

She took a sip from her tonic water. Kate was one of those women who always seem – and for no obvious reason – to be waging a heroic struggle against weight: nibbling carrots, drinking seltzer water, the sort of woman continually mortified by some physical detail which escapes the rest of the world's notice. She hadn't a model's figure, but was slimmer than Mulcahy. Taller, too.

'What is all this with Parisi?'

'Mars,' he said. 'The man is on Mars. I mean.' He shook his head. 'Now I have to move for a change of venue! Which I'll never get.' He shook his head again.

'The *Transcript* said he was going to sue you for slander . . .'

'No doubt. No doubt.' He drained the glass and called for another.

'Wow,' she said, thinking about it. 'Why did you do it?'

It was a hard question. He didn't tell her the whole of it. But what he told her was some of the truth. First he sipped his beer for a moment, thinking. 'When I met him in jail,' he said, 'it was clear he needed help. And he asked me to do it, really wanted me to do it. So I'm saying, here's this friend in trouble, who needs my help, and what shall I do about it? I said I would. I guess I'm a knucklehead. Someone says, "I'm desperate, I need you, please," and I do it. Wasn't really thinking about what would happen at the office. I mean, I knew it would be a problem. Didn't know it would be *that* kind of a problem.'

He paused, thinking out loud now. 'I don't know what I would have told him if I'd known it would have meant being fired. I'd like to think I would have done the same thing, but I don't know. Anyway, once

I'd told the guy I'd do it, it being thirteen days until the trial was supposed to begin, for the Count to sit in his corner office and tell me that "no partner of Freer Motley will appear for the defendant in this case", it just – I don't know. I just suddenly thought, "The hell with it. I represent Shepard. I'm going to do it, and they can do what they want about it." It felt kind of liberating, actually.'

She found herself staring at him with a silly grin on her face, and turned away. 'Did you talk to Tony?' she asked. Tony Alberti was *de facto* deputy of the litigation department and had been a kind of mentor to Mulcahy. He was a gifted trial lawyer and a shrewd firm politician.

'Not before,' he answered. 'He was out of town at depositions. He called me at home when he found out. Actually he was very good about it. Said he understood. He said he was hearing they'd terminate for cause, but that he'd vote against it.'

'Did he?'

'Don't know. Probably. I'd want to check the ballot.'

They talked on, as the crowd in the bar dwindled. At length he revealed from under the table the laptop computer. He unpacked it from its case. 'Kate, this thing's beating me. I can't make it format in the page numbers and footnotes and stuff like that, and I can't make it print. I also can't seem to activate the modem to get in Westlaw. You're the world's leading expert on these things, aren't you? I was hoping maybe . . .'

But he hadn't finished speaking before she had the computer unpacked and was starting it up and working through the windows. For about ten minutes, he laboured to take notes while she explained how to access the functions. Then she looked up and said, 'This is ridiculous. You don't have time for this.'

'Well, you're right,' he said, 'but I don't have a choice.'

She shook her head and her eyes opened wide to him. 'You have a choice,' she said softly.

He understood her. 'No,' he said. 'I *don't* have a choice. Kate, I'm grateful to you, but that's not why I called you. Just teach me how to work the thing.'

'No. I don't do lessons.' She smiled.

'Kate, be serious. One act of ritual suicide for John Shepard is enough.'

'Ed,' she said, 'you will not be serving your client very well if you spend the remaining hours before his murder trial learning how to operate a computer modem. I'll help you out. I'll work only at night or before the working day. It'll be a snap, actually. I'm kind of intrigued.'

He reddened as she began to take charge, calling the waitress for another round, eliciting from Mulcahy what filings he would need first, what motions *in limine* he was planning on, what file memos on difficult points of evidence. Kate had no experience in criminal work, but she had the cheerful confidence of an experienced lawyer that one legal problem couldn't be that different from another. When she was finished he didn't know what to do or say, but the prospect of having even someone to talk to was irresistible. So he took her hand between his own – again, with a certain ambiguity, for it was not the handshake of business people and it was not the caress of a lover. He said, 'I'm very grateful to you.'

Each of them was a little unnerved by this. Perhaps each of them felt, and was surprised to find, that the other's touch was warm and welcome. Perhaps they clasped hands for just a moment longer than was quite proper, but it was ambiguous.

As they were leaving the Oyster House, they passed by the horseshoe bar, and Mulcahy came face to face with the Daniel Webster portrait. The painting is hung by the window to Union Street, behind great soapstone sinks brimming with oysters. Webster is drawn as though leaning up against the same deeply polished semicircular bar which is there today. He stands by a plate of oysters and a tankard of brandy, no doubt pausing on his way home from another victory at court. Perhaps the oysters disagree with him: he looks stern. Rufus Choate, Daniel Webster. Lately Mulcahy could not avoid the disapproval of dead trial lawyers.

They walked along Union Street, and up the steps to Government Centre. 'Is it true what they say?' she asked. 'About you and John?'

'What do they say?'

'About the accident, I mean. In Colorado. That he saved your life.'

'It's true,' he said, and then fell silent. They walked on towards Tremont Street, and along Tremont to the Old Granary burial ground. He stopped by the wrought-iron grille and they looked in together at the monuments – at the prominent obelisk Benjamin Franklin erected for his father, and at the darkened stones beyond. It is an eerie place – an ancient cemetery in the heart of the city, its colonial grave markers worn smooth by the years, standing in the shadow of the surrounding office buildings.

'Yeah, it's true,' he said again, as she stood by him. 'But saving my life wasn't enough for John. First he had to come within two hours of killing me.'

Her eyes asked him to go on, but he shook his head and they turned towards Park Street. He paused at the corner, and motioned towards the now-darkened lane of jewellery shops, third-rate stereo outlets, delicatessens.

'What's that?' she asked.

'Our new address,' he said.

19

He watched Kate vanish into the station. Mulcahy stood by the stairway, thinking that he ought to go down himself and catch the Green line. But there was no dodging it now, no more evading the memory he so hated to relive. He looked down at the laptop case, and in his mind's eye the strap on the case became a packstrap, the case a blue Lowe mountaineering backpack.

He sighed, caving in, conceding that he'd have to go back through it now, or surrender to its distraction for weeks. So he set off through the Common. Tonight, he would make the six-mile trip to his apartment on foot. As he began his walk along the darkened pathway, Mulcahy's mind returned to Colorado.

It had begun on the second day of what was to have been a week-long telemark trip three years before. Shepard's taunts, and his stories of back bowls of unblemished powder, had finally lured Mulcahy, an alpine skier, to try a hut trip. A narrower cousin of the downhill ski, the telemark is usually equipped with a three-pin toe clip or a cable binding, so that the skier's heel can come up off the ski. With its metal edges, the ski is sturdy enough for downhill turns. But with the skier's heel free, the skis adapt to back-country climbing, particularly when wrapped with poly 'skins', whose fabric mimics the quality of the animal skins that French Canadian trappers of long ago had used for this purpose. Fur would lie flat and sleek on the snow as the ski moved forward. As the ski slipped back on an incline, it would ruffle and bite, giving traction.

One of the superbly-situated high mountain huts of the Tenth Mountain Division system in the Colorado Rockies, Uncle Bud's had been a welcome sight to Mulcahy that March afternoon when they finished their first day's climb out of Leadville. Sprawled on the deck, he sucked down the thin air and marvelled at the setting. Ringed by peaks, the hut sat in a high meadow, surrounded by snowfields dotted here and there with stands of spruce.

That first day had been a gorgeous one, a whisperless, sun-splashed March day. But in the pink and grey of the mountain dawn as the two men emerged on to the deck that second morning, each knew that the second day would be different. The sky was roiled with strato-cumulus clouds, racing low across the peaks, as the sun winked in from the eastern horizon only in occasional bursts. It was colder than the day before. The wind had shifted to the northwest. Shepard frowned. 'Looks like a storm. Well, you don't come by all this gorgeous snow by sunshine, right? We'll just have to find Jesus with our goggles on.'

'I never thought of you as one of His anointed, exactly,' Mulcahy answered.

'He moves in mysterious ways, motherfucker.' Shepard smiled, but only for a moment, before his voice returned to business. 'Keep your compass and Topo map in a jacket pocket.'

Mulcahy nodded.

'Then, as the Good Book says, get thee up into the high mountain.'

Moments after they took their first steps up the trail, Mulcahy turned to get a last look at Uncle Bud's, with its sunny cosiness, its well-fired wood stove and steaming snow kettle. But it had already disappeared. He turned back to see Shepard vanishing up around a bend.

The climb out of the high meadow was steep. Ahead of Mulcahy, Shepard moved with economic speed. He wasted no motion, his strides never faltering or slipping. His skins gave good purchase, and though the way was steep, most of it could be managed without herringbone. Mulcahy struggled to keep up. He felt his thighs burning.

Shepard quickly pulled away from him up the trail. That was like him, too. He always had to beat you.

Mulcahy's heart rate had begun to quicken. Why was he lugging all of this clobber into avalanche country on skinny skis, huffing and puffing to keep up with a certifiable nut? Because he could never say no to Shepard? Partly. Hardly anyone could. (He chuckled to himself, between gulps of thin air, thinking of that Monday morning when he got into his office to find a scarred pair of old Karhu telemarks on his desk, the wax still on them and messing the papers beneath, with a note attached, in Shepard's rude scrawl: 'Do a Hut Trip, Fathead!')

Was it because Shepard had found the thing in Mulcahy to challenge? That he had fixed him with that laser glance over a desk strewn with beer bottles and dared him to say no? Partly that too. That was the secret of his brilliance, after all. And partly it was because Mulcahy had seen the guy ski the headwall at Tuckerman's Ravine on a spring morning a year earlier, and been bitten by the bug. Shepard had beaten him down the headwall, rising in and out of the telemarker's tuck, his skis hugging the fall line, racing, plunging for the run out far below. Later, beneath the sunbathing rocks, as they leaned on their poles gasping for breath, Shepard had winked at him, and said, 'Free the heel, man. The mind will follow.'

In the forest, Mulcahy drank in the scent of Douglas fir, and listened to the sound of his own breathing. He pictured Shepard, up ahead on the trail, driving himself, sensing the pulse in his carotid artery, urging on the thump of his heart. Mulcahy knew that nothing could so consume Shepard as the chance to drive his body – built for work as it was – beyond its limits.

The trail continued up. Despite the cold, beads of sweat appeared on Mulcahy's forehead and dripped past the leather barriers of his glasses into the corners of his eyes. Sweat dampened the scapulae beneath his rucksack and appeared darkly around his pack straps. He felt his gluteus muscles as tight as split wood, and his thighs burning with fatigue. The only sounds were the swoosh, swoosh of the ski-steps, the deep gasp of mountain air, occasionally the twangy rattle of a ski thrust sideways for grip.

Two hours into the climb, Mulcahy came into a meadow. Shepard was waiting for him there. Mulcahy could see his impatience. Gusts of wind came and went, and the cold had taken on a bite.

'Feet okay?' Shepard asked. 'No blisters? If you feel a blister comin' on, fix it now. We got a long day today.'

Mulcahy nodded. 'I'm okay,' he said, still wheezing as he struggled for air.

The meadow was ringed by spruce, with a stand of aspens to one side. Through a break in the trees, far to the south, the tips of the Sangre de Cristos swam in and out of the gathering morning cloud cover. But Shepard didn't wait long.

'Think I'll take a lift pass, man,' Mulcahy said, wheezing, as he hoisted his pack back to his shoulders.

'Easier for a camel to pass through the eye of the needle than a fathead to enter the Kingdom of Pow Pow,' Shepard said.

Mulcahy sucked at the thin air as he hoisted his pack again. The Kingdom of Pow Pow was all right, he thought. Just a little short on oxygen.

The trail gained a crest with a southern exposure, but the clouds had thickened and so there was little view. Low cloud cover continued to race in from the northwest. The pair moved on. The trail followed the ridge for what seemed another mile or so, now a gradual climb but still uphill. Then they emerged on to an exposed spur. The grade was steadier, and Mulcahy was able to keep up.

'Look at this, man,' said Shepard. Mulcahy's gaze had been fixed on the taller man's ski-tails. He looked up and watched Shepard sideslip off the ridge and ease ever so slowly to a stop. 'Now check this out,' he said, looking at something in the snow. Mulcahy skied down to him. There it was, just an inch or so across, traversing the slope about twenty feet below Shepard's downhill ski, like a crack in plaster. It stretched out of sight in either direction. You didn't have to be a mountain man to know what it was. Mulcahy felt his throat go dry. 'Not a good idea to ski below it?' he asked.

'Roger that,' said Shepard. As they clambered back to the ridge they spoke quietly. 'I was in an avalanche once,' Shepard said. 'Senior year in high school.'

'Seriously?'

''At's about as serious as I care to get.'

'How'd it happen?'

'We traversed the glacier on the northside of Peak Five, out by Breckenridge. Early morning, wasn't sunny or nothin'. Thing of it was, I had a "Peips", had a shovel, I'd read the books, was with a pretty good group, all that, and it didn't matter. Took them two hours just to find me, probably another twenty minutes to dig me out of snow like day-old mashed potatoes. Only reason I made it is that when the slide come to rest I had this bubble of space around my head. Turned out my head was only about nine inches from the top, and I managed to work an arm up so I could breathe. Pure dumbass luck.

'I still dream about that sometimes, about being trapped like that. You know, it was a noisy bastard, too.'

By mid-morning they reached the crest where the trail turned west and dropped down a chute into the valley. Fingers of spruce poked up the ridge from the drainage below. In between was powder, steep and open. They stopped for water and gorp. It had grown colder, and each man put a shell over his fleece jacket. They finished a few handfuls of the trail mix, then knelt to clip back in.

Mulcahy eyed the chute. A steep field of snow dropped into an alley between a rock outcropping and a file of spruce. Far below it fed into the green treetops of the forest. 'Any suggestions?' he asked.

Shepard smiled. 'Ed, my man, at times like this, a motherfucker should do two things.'

'What's that?'

'Well, first, genuflect. Catholic, ain't you?'

Mulcahy nodded, his eyes still fixed on the plunge below.

'Right. You know about genuflecting, then. Bend your knees. Can't ski in tellies unless you drop that back knee right down on the ski. Get it right down there. Gives you a platform.'

Shepard fixed his goggles. 'And as for the rest,' he said, 'take counsel from the prophet Micah.'

Mulcahy looked across. 'Micah?'

'Not up on your Old Testament?'

Mulcahy shook his head.

'We Pentecostals are partial to the Old Testament, man,' said Shepard. 'Lots of good hell fire there. Look him up, you Romish heathen!' In an instant, the brilliant red parka was into the chute. And as Shepard jumped into his first turn, he sang out, 'Do

197

justice! (a turn), Love mercy! (another turn), and ski humbly before (another turn) thy God!'

Mulcahy stood for several minutes at the lip, watching Shepard form hard, fall-line turns through unbroken powder, the boot soles popping up behind the rooster tails of soft snow. A minute or so later he was a blue and red figurine far below.

Mulcahy had not mastered the telemark turn, even without a forty-pound pack. At length he shoved off, alternately dropping his tips towards the fall line, and checking them uphill. Thus he picked his way clumsily down the chute. Near the bottom he fell, the weight of his pack catapulting over his shoulders and pulling him forward over his ski tips into the deep snow.

His skis, which were free to rotate through almost any axis, plunged crazily into the powder. He came to rest, gasping for air, listening to the laughter thundering up from below. His goggles, hat, and poles littered the chute. 'Yard sale!' Shepard roared.

With a great strain Mulcahy freed a ski. The other was immobile, and he had to dig round it with his mitts. It was almost ten minutes before he had gained his footing again. He reached the woods at the bottom rubber-legged and hyperventilating.

They stopped for lunch soon after. It was a cheerless meal. They had still ten miles ahead on this too-ambitious day, and six of them would be in climb. Mulcahy felt tired and dejected.

As they were finishing their lunch of tuna fish and Snickers bars, it began to snow. First a few flakes fell, but then the snowfall thickened. By the time they had repacked, their packs had a dusting of white, like powdered sugar on doughnuts. They donned ski goggles and shouldered the packs. In only a few minutes, the snow squall had become a snow storm, and a stiff wind began driving more snow from the north.

'Goddamn it,' said Shepard, as he held his compass before him and tried to draw a bearing. The compass was instantly opaque in snow, and, in any case, there was nothing upon which to bear beyond the thirty or forty feet of visibility. Now they were breaking trail uphill, as well. Quickly it became hard work, and even the skins gave but poor purchase.

The snow fell heavily, and the temperature began to drop. With frequent stops to check the compass against the USGS map, and to hurl blasphemies against the storm, Shepard led the way across a valley and began the slow climb to Hunston's Saddle, between Lower Goat's Ear and Lyons Peak.

Slowly, unrelievedly, steadily, up went the trail, with nothing visible, nothing even sensible except whiteness and wind, cold and stinging snow. They began the climb at 10,000 feet, with another 2,500 feet to gain. Halfway up, the snowstorm seemed to redouble in vigour. Mulcahy felt his thighs quiver. He sucked at the air, unable to fill his lungs. His head spun lightly and he stumbled often.

Beneath Mulcahy's skis, the snow began to work its way between the duct tape and the skins, and, as the tack of the skins began to loosen from the p-tex of the skis, between the skis and the skins. The gap between Shepard's red parka and Mulcahy lengthened to the utmost point of visibility within minutes of each trifling rest stop. On came the snow.

Late in the afternoon, in a chowder broth of snow and cloud, the skiers felt the grade fall away from their strides. Exhausted, Mulcahy realised that they had gained the saddle.

They stopped, grateful for rest but aware that any lengthy break would be a mistake in that weather. It was now bitterly cold. The wind had picked up, and was driving snow horizontally. Mulcahy gasped for breath. He pushed his parka sleeve back clumsily with a leather mitt to see his watch. Four 'clock. It is often around four o'clock when things go wrong in the mountains.

'How'r ya doing, man?' Shepard was hollering to be heard over the wind.

Mulcahy just looked at him, his head bobbing. The wind was roaring outside his hood.

'This does suck, don't it?' Shepard shouted, grinning like the devil's messsenger – and in that driving wind and snow, with his parka zipped up and his goggles on, the grin was the only thing visible about the man.

Mulcahy nodded again.

'Listen, man,' Shepard hollered, 'only five miles to Wilderness from here, three of 'em down. You've done the worst part . . .'

Shepard paused to catch his own breath. He fished a chocolate bar from a pocket and offered Mulcahy half. It was rock hard. Mulcahy thought his teeth would break. They each took water.

'Got a nice bowl down through here for about a half mile,' he resumed, still shouting to be heard. 'Then it drops into easy trees, wide stuff for another mile or so. It runs off to the bottom at the left where a cliff comes in offa Lyons. Let's go. We gotta get out of this wind.'

Mulcahy stared towards the slope. He could see about twenty feet. It was all white.

Shepard was tired. Not thinking as clearly as he usually did, wasn't as observant as he should have been. He was bored and frustrated with the climb and the day, and the poor weather. He didn't see that Mulcahy was, in fact, all done; that he had no more spring in his legs, no more recovery.

'Don't say I don't take you to nice places!' he shouted. 'Only fun you'll have all day is right here!' He tucked the map into his breast pocket and fixed his goggles. Mulcahy watched him drop into a wide, stylish telemark turn, carving smoothly through the deep snow. Then as the red parka with the blue backpack rose for the next turn, driving snow turned it grey. Shepard was lost to view.

Mulcahy dropped into the bowl. But there was no bounce left in his thighs. He fell into deep deep snow. With an effort, he righted himself, rose, began to ski – and fell again. He was breathing hard when he gained his feet the third time. He had lost Shepard's tracks. Snow filled his ears and nostrils. It caked his goggles, gathered in iceballs around his collar and shot up his wristbands. He couldn't see a thing. He began to ski scared. His weight got back on him. Again he fell. And yet again.

He got into the trees only after a half-dozen falls. His legs were quivering and he was breathing hard. He was doing everything wrong on skis: with no confidence left, he was not trusting his weight to guide the skis, but forcing them, muscling through the deep powder. This had him off balance and sorely taxing the little strength he had left. Down he went. He tried to make his way left, but he seemed to have dropped into a gully. He saw no cliff, no runoff. The trees grew thicker, roaring out of the white soup of the blizzard, then thickening around him.

Dusk was falling, although he could see only that the white which destroyed perspective on all sides was greying swiftly. Mulcahy stopped. He struggled to get command of his breathing, and stood for perhaps a full minute in the deepening cold, hearing only the gasping of his own lungs. The only other sound was the relentless shrieking of the wind. He pulled on the thin air. He had lost Shepard. He was still miles from his destination.

His mind began to jump this way and that. This was not good. This was definitely not good. Little snippets of thought competed with panic for his attention. Shepard would have missed him by now. Even if Shepard climbed back out of the bowl, Mulcahy's tracks would be covered by the time he reached the point of separation. And it would be night then anyway.

He stamped his feet in the snow, shaking powder from his legs and arms. Something, difficult to place, felt wrong, and he looked down. He stared stupidly for a moment, aware only that in the noise of the wind and through the obscuring snowfall, something appeared asymmetrical, but uncertain what. He shook snow off his downhill ski. 'Oh, God,' he said.

One of his skins was gone.

He must have lost it in one of the falls. How did he miss it? 'Jesus,' he said, involuntarily. Without skins, in deep snow, it is impossible to go uphill. With one skin? He looked about him and picked a line for an uphill traverse. He fixed his eye on a spruce about twenty feet distant, as far as he could see in the now darkening storm. The wind was howling around him.

He struggled for a few minutes, staggering and slipping backward. He could barely manage even a slight uphill grade.

Thoughts now raced, one after the other. He could not return to try to follow Shepard's track. He would never make Wilderness Hut tonight.

Ed Mulcahy knew little about wilderness survival, but his instincts, even in their numbed state as that afternoon slipped into dusk, were not poor. Don't panic, he thought. Don't panic. He looked about him on the steep mountainside, selecting a large spruce where he side slipped and then dropped his pack. Using his skis, he packed down a six-foot-square downhill from the tree. After some time he had produced a surface upon which he could stand. He unclipped his skis, set them off to one side in the snow, and, with his mitts, began to shovel a snow cave to one side of the tree. It took a half hour to carve a man-sized space out of the snow bank. Tired and perspiring, he removed his sleeping bag from his pack, unwrapped the space blanket, lined the cave with it, and pushed the down sack into the cave. The only clothing he paused to remove before easing into the sleeping bag were his mitts and his gaiters. He left his thick leather Merrill boots on. When he had slid into the cave he pulled the pack in underneath him. He watched the snowflakes drive sideways across the slope for a few minutes more, and while any visibility remained, stared at the USGS map. He ate a Snickers bar and some gorp.

Night came on quickly. Wide-eyed, Mulcahy lay staring out from his cave. All of his senses were disjointed. The storm obliterated any starlight, any moonlight, any light at all. It was impenetrable blackness. The wind continued unabated, a steady screaming in the spruces. He could just make out, within himself, the sound of his heartbeat in his ears. He lay wide awake for many hours, but his thoughts would work in no logical direction. Finally, fatigue overtook him and he drifted into a restless sleep.

When he awoke, cold and shivering, the wind had increased, and it was driving snow against the few square inches of his face which were exposed. Condensation had formed on the inside of his space blanket. In the bitter cold of that night, it had frozen against his sleeping bag. It was still dark when he awoke. He lay quivering in the cave, waiting for morning.

It was a long time coming.

Thank you, John, he thought, staring out from the cave. That swagger, that cockiness sure was charming when the sun shone. Shepard had lured him here with tales of telly heaven in the steep and deep. They were wonderful stories. And now Shepard had simply gone. He was the world champion talker, all right.

The events of the afternoon and night had had the virtue, at least, of such immediacy that he'd had time only to think in half-hour intervals. In a half hour the tracks would be obliterated. In a half hour it would get dark. And so on. Now in this dark interlude before dawn he had too much time to think. Because now he had only morning to wait for and not an idea in the world as to what he should do when it came.

It was in that surreal time that Ed Mulcahy first wondered whether he might die. That he might actually die, because he had tagged along after John Shepard. He was immobile. It was cold, and the storm showed no signs of abating. He knew that people often died in the mountains. It occurred to him that it would take a while to die out here. Death by cold would be lonesome. And then he thought of himself being dug out in the late-spring some time, by men who would shake their heads over the foolishness of easterners, flatlanders, tourists. It would be an embarrassing epitaph.

His muscles were stiff and cold, and the fatigue had not passed. He felt himself thinking a little more clearly than before. His instinct was for going: for trying. How long would he stay here? How would anyone find him? This storm seemed like it might go on for ever. Gradually he became aware of tree trunks taking shape. When the grey suffused to off-white, he could see that snowfall had covered the entrance to his cave. The end of his pack which poked out was indistinguishable. He was cold. He needed to get moving. But this instinct met with his professional scepticism. He stared at the topo map. He found Hunston's Saddle, Lower Goat's Ear, and Lyons Peak. He could see the southeast spur from Lyons. He must be north of that. But where?

It was all academic. He could not manage an uphill grade on one skin even if he could see where he was going. This argued for waiting. As did the voice which said, simply, 'Stay put. Let them find you. You can last a while out here. You have a sleeping bag. You have good clothing. You have matches . . .'

He had matches. And he thought about those matches while the grey pre-dawn took an eternity lightening to morning.

Mulcahy rooted through his pack for the gorp. The beginnings of a plan took shape as he took inventory: besides his clothing, he had four apples, the breakfast oatmeal, instant coffee, two packages of freeze-dried macaroni and three or four other items. He had a compass, a Peips (a radio transmitter for use in finding avalanche victims), a head lamp, a Swiss Army knife, a waterproof match container, and his space blanket. He ate some of the dehydrated oatmeal with snow. The sugar tasted good. He decided as he ate the oatmeal that he would pack up his sleeping bag and ski a ways downhill, looking for a fallen tree. If he could find something with dead wood, he might be able to get a fire going. And then . . . well, there was no 'and then'. For the moment, he was content with a thirty-minute plan.

The fallen tree took some finding, but he found it, about a half-mile downhill from his first encampment. It took more than an hour to pack down a circle and gather dead limbs from the spruce. He left until last the breaking of the finest twigs to use as tinder. He tried to build a frame for them, laying them delicately across the two largest branches he'd been able to break with his boot. The fuel was good, and in better weather it might have worked. But heavy snowfall wet the twigs as soon as they were laid. For one breathless instant, as he huddled over the tinder, it seemed as though the match flame might catch. But the wind whistled through and snuffed it out. When he was down to his last match, he quit trying.

Still it snowed and the wind blew out of the north. Would there be no end to this storm? He could think of nothing else, so he dug another snow cave, and passed the rest of the day restlessly. By nightfall he was genuinely cold. His toes, his fingers, his lips were numb. His cheek responded only dully to contact. With an effort, he ate an apple. He'd had to warm it between his thighs to be able to get his teeth through it. Then there was the macaroni. He wasn't sure if he could eat that, so he saved it 'til morning.

The driving snowstorm quickly obliterated any sign of a skier. Mulcahy's first snow cave, and his tracks down the mountain, were covered within an hour, and quite invisible when, in mid-afternoon, John Shepard skied a traverse one hundred yards above them.

Before dawn, Mulcahy drifted out of half-sleep to a numbness in his extremities. Thoughts came one upon the next, in flashes. There was no order to them. Logic still said to stay put. The storm could not last forever. But fear was for moving on. For doing something. Where or why seemed to matter less now. The snow had obliterated the last stick from his firewood of yesterday. It seemed to him intuitive that he must move on, for if he stayed there he would be interred with the fire.

The human skin is the body's largest organ. It is, among other things, a massive radiator, subject to the same laws of physics which govern an automobile. When exposed to cold, it conducts heat from its interior to its exterior. High wind, in subzero temperatures, is particularly effective. With that exposure, the skin radiates heat with deadly efficiency.

The body is resourceful. It will burn calories furiously to try to counteract heat loss, even cannibalise itself to do so. But it cannot long escape the first law of thermodynamics. That is why death by hypothermia comes with such astonishing rapidity. It begins with the body's usual warning klaxon: pain. Numbness and shivering follow, and give way to disorientation. And then, as its core temperature falls even by modest degrees, the body sets off a rapid, sequential shutdown of all but essential functions. Not long after that, it simply fails.

However strong, however well nourished, however courageous, no man is a match for acute hypothermia. He must be restored to shelter or he will die. And on this third day of the blizzard, Ed Mulcahy had begun the process. He was dying.

Even the map had frozen. It was brittle and tore in Mulcahy's shaking hands. He studied it again, the contour lines swimming in and out of focus. Wilderness Hut lay west of Hunston's Saddle. From the runoff of the bowl he had missed, which must lie, as he looked downhill, to the left, the trail followed some sort of river drainage gently up a valley. He would head south, hoping to find the cliff Shepard had spoken of, and then west. And he would pray.

A thought came to him as he readied himself. Finding his Swiss Army knife, he cut a half dozen heavily needled spruce boughs. With the duct tape Shepard had wrapped around his poles, he fixed the boughs to the underside of his left ski. His fingers moved like the fingers of a marionette. He could grasp the tape only by mashing his thumb against his palm. The taping job was sloppy, but after half an hour he had a makeshift snowshoe for a left ski. Then he brushed as much of the ice and snow from his remaining skin as he could manage. The ice clung to the skin's fibres like cockleburs on a dog. It had caked both the surface of the skin and the gap between skin and ski. With the last of the duct tape, he tried to secure the remaining skin. Again, the wrapping was clumsy and the tape seemed to have lost its tack in the cold anyway. He knew the duct tape would not last long. The gaiters were frozen solid. He folded them like roofing shingles until the ice cracked, trying to get them round his boots. But his lifeless hands could not manage it. He could barely manipulate the three-pin binding latch to engage the toe of his boots.

His fingers were now beyond pain, and he moved his hands clumsily, clublike, as he shouldered the pack and fixed his goggles. He drew a bearing for due south, the compass shaking in his hands. The path lay steeply uphill. The hill fell off a little to the west. He'd try southwest.

And, with one ski for traction, he began to stagger his way out.

Hypothermia was now seriously impairing Mulcahy's function. His gait was spastic. His balance was poor, and he fell often. He made progress, but barely, legs splaying as he misplaced his weight, tumbling backward just when he had gained a foothold. He stuck gamely to his southwest bearing. Odd, it seemed to him, how the woods played tricks on him: how his guess of the bearing was always slightly off, and how the tendency was to doubt the compass. He had to school himself not to. But it was difficult, for his concentration, like his balance, was weak and unfocused. There was no feeling in his feet now: the sensation was as though he were walking on blocks of wood. Greased blocks of wood.

He staggered on through the day, growing weaker, colder, dizzier. The grade dropped downhill for a mile or so, and then resumed a steady uphill climb. The makeshift snowshoe deteriorated over time. By midday, the last of the boughs had dropped off. He stumbled more, losing vision now. His body was beginning to shut down.

The trees seemed to thin and he came, here and there, on a clearing, but nothing that he could make out, in the snowfall at any rate, as a west-bearing drainage. The dizziness became so acute that he stopped to clutch his temples. When he tried to take a compass reading, the figures swam in his eyes, and odd bits and scraps of memory would chase the compass face from his consciousness. The definition between present and past began to blur.

He thought of John Shepard, briefly, but the image quickly faded. He was past anger then.

More images came, and still more, and no logic to them, one crowding upon the next, pebbles falling into dark water, visible briefly, then gone. As his mind loosened, the compass bounced against his chest and he forgot to take bearings. He thought of his brother Tommy, and of the time when, as boys, they had spent an afternoon stringing a knotted rope from on overhanging tree at the gorge near Grandfather's, and how they had swung it out, out, out and dropped into the pool, until late in the evening, and how his father came and pretended to scold. And he felt that warm evening sun again. He swung down and out, now skimming within hand's reach of the pool, now rocketing up into the sky, now pausing exquisitely at the apogee of the rope swing, and then dropped into the icy chill of the pool and, and – he felt the cold, again, and again saw his compass banging about on his chest. Tommy is not here, he thought, realising that he wanted his brother there above all others. But it was just for a moment. His mind was vague, and now it held thoughts only briefly.

All day he had stumbled, and fallen, and staggered to his feet, and moved on. But then there came the last stumble, the one from which he would not have risen again. He felt the cold powder on his cheek, and saw that it had caked his goggle. No matter. The inside had fogged up some time ago.

He heard a rasping for breath. It sounded like some ancient, tubercular panhandler. Was that himself? Well, it was good to rest. He thought he might just rest a while there, just catch his breath before going on. He tried to recollect where it was he was going, but he couldn't, and thought he'd worry about it later. After he'd caught his breath. He was so numb and tired, and it would be so pleasant just to rest a bit.

He moved his tongue and felt the cold thrill of the

powder. He thought he should sit up, but the thought passed. For a while, he listened to his breathing. It was like a mother's lullaby, the only sound in his ears. It faded softly away. He faded in and out, in a stupor, but dimly contented.

Perhaps a long time passed. Maybe it was only moments. But Ed Mulcahy swam into consciousness again, sensible of the cold, and the whiteness all around.

'Ed!'

With a mild curiosity, he recognised that word. He heard it again, and again, sometimes a long way away, sometimes very near. His name, wasn't it? He groped to take his bearings. He became dimly aware of a darkening forest, that he was in it, that he was weak with cold, in the fading afternoon, slumped beneath a stand of aspen, breathing heavily, dimly conscious of the wind. Something was in his field of vision. Something was happening about his head. He realised slowly that he was staring at a familiar pair of mountaineering goggles, a familiar beard, and a red parka he had seen before somewhere.

'Goddamn it, Ed,' Shepard said, 'come on, man, don't fuckin' give up on me, don't do it. Ed!'

John Shepard's fiery eyes bore down at the slumped skier. He willed him back to consciousness. 'Come on, come on!' he urged, as he rubbed the man's face. 'Come on.'

The eyes were fixed. His skin was pale. Then Shepard saw the dried, whitened lips part, and heard Mulcahy whisper, 'I'm cold.'

'Oh, man,' said Shepard. 'Oh, Jesus Lord. Okay, we're going to do it. We are going to do it.'

'I'm cold,' Mulcahy whispered again.

'It's all right, man. Wilderness is only two miles from here. Two miles. You can do the motherfucker in your sleep!' Shepard was pulling and tugging and he got the shoulder straps of the downed man's pack free. Then he had Mulcahy on his feet again, but tottering, like an infant dandled from its father's arms. A flask was at his lips and he drank something which burned his throat. And then a canteen, with water.

Mulcahy blinked. It had stopped snowing.

Shepard strapped Mulcahy's pack around a tree limb. 'I'm getting this in the morning, all right? We'll just get you to Wilderness now, get that fire going, and you're going to be okay. Okay?'

'John,' he said softly, 'John.'

Shepard studied him again. The disorientation was grave. 'It's all right, man, I brought you fresh skis and skins. I figured you might have a broke one, so I got some from a gal at Wilderness. You don't mind chic skis, do you, man? You are going to make it. You are going to make it.' He didn't say, didn't need to say, that although he'd been able to borrow a pair of skis, none but he had been fool enough to strike out from Wilderness Hut into that storm. Shepard unclipped Mulcahy's skis, and clipped him into the new skis, with the fresh skins, and fussed at him, and dusted snow off, chattering like an infielder. He removed Mulcahy's gloves and rubbed furiously at his fingers. Then he traded mitts, pushing Mulcahy's hands into his own warm, dry pair. 'Can you walk?' he asked.

Mulcahy didn't answer. Shepard peered at his face,

213

rubbed hard at his cheekbones, frowning. 'All right, we're going to be okay,' he said, perhaps, this time, more to himself. He hung up his own pack, and clipped Mulcahy back out of the skis. Then, aided only by adrenaline and a furious determination to succeed, he hoisted Mulcahy in a fireman's carry. 'We are in the hut in an hour. An hour, Ed, you got that?'

'Yes.'

'This fucking hike is a promenade. A walk!'

And, with a 165-pound man on his back, John Shepard began a three-mile journey up the drainage.

Later, he confessed that it had happened just when he had lost hope of finding Mulcahy alive. He had slept at Wilderness Hut for two nights, and hunted for his companion through the driving snow during the days. At the end of the third afternoon, when the storm broke, he could think of nothing else to do, and turned back for the hut. He was wondering where the hell the nearest road might be, figuring he'd have to ski out early in the morning and get hold of Mountain Rescue, skiing slowly up the drainage, when he saw them: a set of tracks that traversed the drainage and disappeared into the forest. With heart racing, he turned and followed them. They were crazy tracks, the left ski splaying out to the side and a half-dozen disturbed patches where the skier had stumbled. He found Mulcahy a half mile later, lying awkwardly in the snow, just as he must have fallen.

Ed Mulcahy spent three days in Wilderness Hut. Of the first, he could later recall only a murmur of hushed voices and darkness, and the gentle steam from tea and bullion broth. But Mulcahy remembered the third night at Wilderness Hut clearly, as though it had happened only days before, remembered how they sat at the picnic table by the cast-iron stove, drinking coffee. And he remembered how, out beyond the window, the Colorado night was clear and peaceful, with a stunning field of stars arrayed above, and a still, moonlit snowfield below.

In the dark, the open woodstove cast firelight into the room, throwing the faces of the two men in and out of shadow. 'John,' Mulcahy had said to him, 'no one else could have done this.'

'Don't worry about it,' Shepard replied, missing the nuance in the remark.

They sat silently for a few minutes. 'I owe my life to you,' Mulcahy said, blankly.

'Your life is pretty good collateral,' was what Shepard had said. 'I'll take a mortgage in it.'

Mulcahy looked up to see the lights in Cleveland Circle. He had walked for nearly two hours, following Commonwealth from its terminus at the park in Boston's Back Bay through its windings and turnings west to Boston College. He was finished with the memory now, and he wouldn't have to relive it again soon. It was like that for him – building pressure for weeks, sometimes months, at the periphery of his consciousness, building like steam, until he purged it by reliving it, step by step, minute by minute. And then he would be free of it again, for a little while.

He didn't like to be reminded of his helplessness in

that wilderness. He least of all liked to dwell on his debt to John Shepard. Over the three years since it had happened, he had tried his best to avoid reminders of it. He had given up skiing. Life had gone on.

Mulcahy turned from Commonwealth, and followed a side street the last three blocks to his apartment building, walking in and out of the pale illumination of the streetlights.

Now, in the darkness, he had arrived home, and cleared his mind of all but the ultimate question. It would have been convenient to content himself with a plausible fiction, that he was repaying a debt, which is how Ben Mulcahy would see it. Or it could be that Ed was simply a professional, ready, as a professional should be, to take on an unpopular case, whatever the consequence – how Kate might look at it. But neither of them would be right.

He came to the building and unlocked the door. The lobby was empty, as was his mailbox. He waited for the elevator to come creaking to the ground. It took almost as long to travel four floors as the streamlined elevators of the downtown office towers spent racing up twenty. In the elevator was an old mirror, framed in oak trim. As the old elevator laboured upward, Mulcahy stared at himself, looking in vain for the smile he'd seen in the windowglass at the corner of State and Congress.

There was enough vanity in Mulcahy to leave uncorrected those others who might imagine the best of him, even when the best was not true. But Mulcahy's insistence on worrying a matter down to its facts never let him rest with himself. Why was he turning his back on a career for this case? He knew it wasn't quite the debt. And he knew it wasn't an exemplary commitment to the profession. He was in this case for another reason. And it was the same reason he'd followed the man to Colorado in the first place, those three years ago.

Ed Mulcahy was in the main a logical man, and so this was something in himself he could never rationalise, whose source remained mysterious to him. It was the simplest of things. He craved something he never felt he had been granted. He wanted John Shepard's respect.

20

The wall clock showed five minutes past nine. Outside the plate glass, it was dark in Bromfield Street. Kate sat nervously on Stevie George's brown couch, a sprawling, dilapidated affair which presented two options: perch precariously on the edge, or surrender to a recumbent, Roman disarray.

Kate perched. Stevie had his feet up on the desk and his nose in a file. A slice of pizza was in his left hand, its acute angle hanging limply towards the floor. Across the room, Mulcahy read through the cases Kate had found to support motions for change of venue and continuance. She had found two good ones.

'Thank you,' he said, still somewhat abashed by his failure to refuse her. 'This is great.'

'I'll do the motions and the briefs,' she said. 'I think, though, I'd better not do any drafting on Freer's system. If you know what I mean. We can set up the laptop here.'

'How do we print things out?' Mulcahy asked.

She reached into her satchel and withdrew a large, white plastic box. 'I brought a printer.'

Five minutes later, she had set up a workstation on the table. 'And, Stevie,' she said, 'if you'll let me borrow the phone line, we can access Westlaw.'

Stevie's mouth was full of pizza. He rolled his eyes. 'Sure. Why not. Take my office. Take my phone too. Take me, Katie Kate. I'm yours!'

Mulcahy had spent three more hours in the gerbil cage with a truculent Shepard. He stuck by his story: he said he had got into his Subaru at about eight on May 16, and headed west on the Mass. Pike. He stayed at a motel somewhere near Elmira. And that's all he knew. He hadn't been to Sheringham. He had never been to Sheringham. Mulcahy kept waiting for help as his client stalked back and forth in the attorneys' room, rattling off the answers. It seemed practised, somehow, too facile.

Facile, except for the problems. Shepard did admit to the shouting match with Whitaker. 'I just lost it, man, I just totally lost it,' he said, shaking his head. 'What can I say?'

'And Idlewild?'

'I told him I'd see it through. And I did.'

'There was a time when I wanted to ask you more about that,' Mulcahy had said.

'Go ahead, ask.'

'The mortgage?'

Shepard turned towards him, and his eyes crinkled into that ironic smile, that way he had where you couldn't be sure if he was laughing at you or just at life. 'Damned if I can say for sure how that number got there,' he said.

'How about your best guess?'

'Ed, you told me it was done on Whitaker's terminal. The old man had lost his clout in the office and decided it was payback time. You caught it, and he decided to check out, rather than face up to it. That's what this goddamn thing is about, not some day in the life of John Shepard.'

Mulcahy sighed. 'Look, are you trying this thing, or am I?'

'Aw, don't whimper, for Chrissakes, it doesn't suit you.'

That was when he had lost his temper. 'Whimper?' he had blurted out, 'Whimper! This *pro bono* case cost me a job, John!'

A challenge was something Shepard could never back down from. He flew at the screen, and his face was jammed against it so that Mulcahy could see his teeth against the steel mesh. 'And what do you think it's costing me, Ed? What? Answer me!' Had the screen not been there, his hands would surely have been on Mulcahy's throat. He shoved his palm savagely at the mesh, once, and then as quickly pulled back, rubbing his temples.

Then they retreated, for neither of them wanted, or could afford, this. For a moment, there was only the sound of men struggling to regain their breath.

'I'm sorry,' Shepard had said.

Mulcahy had decided to press ahead as though it hadn't happened. 'Let's say he put it there,' he asked, after a few moments. 'How come no one found it?'

'It was an eight-day closing of a billion-dollar deal. There was a lot to do. Whitaker stuck it to them and somebody missed it. That's all.'

220

'They'll say that it's not your style to miss anything, John.'

But Shepard just shook his head. 'They'll say a lot of goddamn things.'

There was one more thing. Shepard had thought of what might have explained the call. He said that he was humping his stuff down to the car, in and out of the apartment. The phone still worked, and the answering machine was still connected. One of the last things he did was to unplug it and toss it in a box. Maybe there was a message on it he didn't listen to.

In the office on Bromfield Street, Mulcahy had finished recounting the interview.

'Yah, right,' said Stevie, 'and maybe I'm the Prince a Wales. Look, Eddie,' he said, 'tell 'im to stop fuckin' around, okay?'

Mulcahy nodded.

Stevie was pondering, working it through. 'Awright, Eddie,' he went on, 'forget the case for a second, okay? I need a better feel for this guy Shepard. Tell me more about him.'

'What do you want to know?'

'I wanna know what makes him tick.'

He thought about it. 'Hell if I know. A time-bomb, maybe.'

'Think it went off?' Stevie asked.

'Why don't you tell him about Apex,' Kate suggested, quietly.

Mulcahy nodded. 'Yeah, that's a good idea. You want to know what makes him tick? Maybe you should ask Alan Fredericks.'

For it was Fredericks, a pudgy, pleasant, and

ineffectual corporate partner at Freer Motley, who had gathered a younger Shepard in tow one morning years before for a meeting across town at the old-line firm of Daley & Hoar. The story had passed quickly into the firm's oral tradition and had regularly been retold. Kate did the honours.

Apex Technologies, an entrepreneurial client of Freer Motley, had set up its corporate office in Londonderry, New Hampshire. A manufacturer of high resolution lenses, it financed itself through FirstBanc Massachusetts, and promptly fell victim to Department of Defence cutbacks.

Fredericks and Shepard stepped into the office tower at the corner of State and Assembly, and rode the elevator to Daley & Hoar's offices. They were set at idle in a lush conference room for half an hour before a gruff Daley & Hoar partner named Thomas Hill arrived. He sat impassively looking only at his watch, barely listening to Fredericks's rather plaintive recitation. Shepard, dutiful for as long as he could manage, which was not long, interrupted Fredericks. 'Let's you and I talk, Mr Thomas P. Hill.'

Those were his words, as reported later by Fredericks. Hill glowered at the upstart. Fredericks reddened. But before he could say anything to his mutinous lieutenant, Shepard had forged ahead. 'You and I, *Mr* Thomas P. Hill.'

Hill glared at Fredericks with amazement. He'd as soon have lunch with the janitor, who, at Daley & Hoar, would at least be clean shaven.

'All right,' Shepard said, 'where's the men's room? I can pull my pud there in peace, which is sure all we're doing here.'

He didn't wait for directions. Fredericks by now had his head in his hands. He tried to resurrect the meeting but it went badly, and soon he was on the receiving end of a lecture about his choice in associates, and composing in his mind a blistering memo to personnel.

What happened while this was going on, Fredericks had to piece together afterwards. Apparently Shepard did not head to the men's room. He walked to the receptionist, who must have given him a floor directory, for he then found his way to Hill's floor. There he would have walked past a brace of guppy-jawed associates (Shepard having long ago learned that an attitude and a constant 'How'r you doing' would get him past most people in any medium-to-large city office), and, in a moment, found what he was looking for. The corner office of Thomas P. Hill.

'Excuse me, sir! Sir . . . you can't!' Arms windmilling, Hill's secretary had bolted from her carrel and pursued him into the office. 'What are you . . .?'

Shepard, to all appearances unaware of her presence, sat down in the partner's deep oxblood leather chair, and leaned back.

'You come away from there at once!'

'Mr Hill's in your 28th-floor conference room,' he said. 'The one with the view of the airport and the godawful framed portrait of paint drops. Would you call him up and tell him I really did want to talk with him? Thank you, ma'am. And bring me some coffee, would you?'

But the secretary, now certain that a psychopath was loose in the office, fled from the room before he'd finished, and a moment later could be heard shrieking into a telephone. It wasn't long before a furious Hill burst into the room, with Fredericks close behind.

'What do you think . . .!' he demanded, then interrupted himself with, 'Fredericks, what in the hell is going on here? Get this pillock out of my chair!'

'Shepard, goddamn it . . .' said Fredericks, cheeks quivering.

Three secretaries hovered outside. Associates were gathering. Someone was dialling for building security.

'*Mr* Thomas P. Hill, would you please sit your ass down?' asked Shepard, almost in a whisper. 'Here,' he said, 'have your chair back. Helluva chair, though. Now, make yourself comfortable and read this.'

He dropped on the immaculate desktop two documents, and walked over to look at one of the many plaques on the wall.

'What is this?' Hill demanded.

'It's a UCC-1 and a copy of my client's articles of incorporation.'

'I can see that.'

'I figured you could.'

'Well, what is the point?'

'The point is that *this* is the UCC your associate filed for Apex, and *there* are the articles. Why don't you read them?' asked Shepard. He turned back to studying something on the wall. 'Well, I'll be . . .' he said, in a pastiche of his own drawl. 'Damned if it ain't in Latin!'

'Fredericks, take this cretin out of my office. Now!'

'*Mr* Thomas P. Hill, for a guy with a problem, you are awful grouchy,' said Shepard. 'But before you kick me out of your sanctuary, tell me something. What county was the UCC-1 filed in?'

Hill was silent. Shepard continued, 'Let me help. Rockingham. Where is Apex's principal place of business today? Londonderry. Which is in Rockingham. Everything according to Hoyle, right? Well, no. You see, where was Apex incorporated? At its lawyer's office. And where is that lawyer's office? Manchester. Which is across the county line, in Hillsborough.'

Hill stared at the papers. 'Apex's principal place of business is in Londonderry, in Rockingham County. That's where this was filed.'

'It is now,' Shepard said, 'but not when the loan was made. When the loan was made the company's principal place of business was in Hillsborough. When the loan was made, the company was two guys, three patents, a contract or two, and a ground lease in Rockingham County. As of then, Apex's documents list the lawyer's office as the principal place of business – across the county line in Hillsborough County. Look at the articles. Hell, look at the address shown on the UCC itself. I mean, how embarrassing is that?' Now Hill did read. The UCC-1 form indeed listed the lawyer's office in Manchester, which was indeed in Hillsborough County, as the company's address.

The form, a routine filing, had more than routine consequences. If filed in the right office, it would make the bank a secured creditor, and make Apex's assets the bank's collateral. This would give the bank security for payment of the debt, and leverage in negotiations. But if filed in the wrong place, it would

225

make the bank just another somebody to whom Apex owed money.

Shepard went on. 'Your associate assumed Rockingham because that's where the ground lease was. Good assumption most times. But he didn't check the documents. So you wound up in the wrong county. Are we communicating yet? *Mr* Thomas P. Hill, you have made those filings which you ought not to have made, and not made those filings which you ought to have made, and there is no health in your closing documents. You filed this in the wrong county. I believe the word for that is "unsecured".'

Hill had whitened. 'I'm sure we filed in both counties.'

'That's what I said when I saw this,' said Shepard. 'I'm sure they filed in both counties. Simple as putting sugar on your Wheaties. But damned if I could find anything in Hillsborough County with y'alls name on it. If you want to pick up the phone and call my secretary, she'll be glad to fax the search results right over.'

Hill glowered at him. He had no intention of telephoning the man's secretary. 'We'll make a corrective filing.'

'Oh, that's good,' said Shepard. 'The Trumpet shall Sound, and the Dead shall be Raised! You'll make a corrective filing. That's good. You'll make a corrective filing! Now doggone it, why didn't I think of that? Only, *Mr* Thomas P. Hill, have you ever heard of chapter 11?'

Shepard was referring to bankruptcy. Hill could repair the oversight with a new UCC filing, but Apex

226

could file a bankruptcy, and the filing would nullify the repair. Shepard was right. He knew it. Fredericks knew it. And Hill knew it.

'We'll litigate it.'

But Shepard just shook his head. 'Oh, that's great. You'll litigate it. In the bankruptcy. For, what do you think, two years or so? And we take you up, or you take us up, to the District Court, and maybe the First Circuit. And everybody will publish opinions. And the opinions will recite the facts, about how Daley & fucking Hoar filed in the wrong county. About how they didn't even bother with a protective filing. Meanwhile your client is saying to you "Eh, Tommy, 'splain to me why *we* should pay for this screw-up? Why we should send you the next case?" And he sees his boys on oversight, and they say, "What gives with this?" And he says – well, what do you think he says, Mr Hill? Does he say, "I fucked up," or does he say, "Daley & fucking Hoar fucked up?" Tell you what my guess is. Oh, sure, litigate away. Gird up those loins. Litigation makes a lot of damn sense.'

Hill was silent. 'Mr Shepard, have you anything else to say?'

'Well, yes, damn it,' he said. 'Where the hell is that woman with my coffee?'

Things continued to go very badly for Mr Thomas P. Hill, as Fredericks liked to tell it – and all of them at Freer loved to tell this part, too, for the two firms were, shall we say, *competitive*. Hill had forgotten, or at least swallowed, the indignities of the afternoon. An hour or more went by as Shepard wheedled and cajoled and cooed and whispered and stormed. He had more moods than a summer afternoon. Fredericks stood dumbstruck, off to one side. The part he loved to tell about later was the last act of Shepard's bravado.

They had broken Hill. He had given them everything they came for. The time, the terms, all subject to a client's blessing, but junior loan officers would do Hill's bidding, that much even Fredericks knew. In fact, Fredericks could think only of escaping quickly, before something went wrong, as the meeting dragged to a lingering close. Shepard was saying, 'Well, we've enjoyed working with you.' He said it several times, almost stupidly, until finally Hill said, 'What do you mean?'

'We've enjoyed working with you. You're a good guy. We'd like to work with you again.'

'What does that mean?' asked Hill, looking at Fredericks. 'What does that mean?' Hill probably hadn't been called a 'good guy' by someone in his twenties for, well, thirty years. Fredericks shrugged, as if to say, 'Like I have any idea of what the hell is going on here today?'

'Just that we'd like to work with you again.' This from Shepard.

'I don't understand what you're talking about.'

'Well, you do a lot of work for FirstBanc. Right? I mean, a lot of work. And you boys have a lot of corporate clients. So you must bump into conflicts. All the time. Maybe you even have one now. You might need to refer cases now and again. To someone like us.'

228

'You're not serious?' He looked at Fredericks. 'He's not serious. Is he?'

'Why not? Mr Hill, think about it. Not so crazy as it sounds. What have you learned about me today? That I'm an asshole, and that I do my homework. Those are the job descriptions for a workout guy, right? And, I mean, hell, you've had a hideous day. Two creeps from Freer show up, one of 'em barges into your office, and they've found some screw-up your associate made. So you're riding back to Wellesley tonight, and you're thinking, "Who the hell else knows about these UCCs?" Right? I mean, that's what I'd be thinking. And hell, there aren't many things I wouldn't do, right? And I do know about the UCCs. Problems, problems. Anyway, it's a helluva way to wind up, like this, when in fact you're a nationally recognised lawyer, on the advisory committee on Article 3, and all of that. There's a happy ending here, I think. Anyway . . .' On and on it went. Shepard sidled and wheedled and coiled.

When he and Fredericks left Daley & Hoar that afternoon, Shepard had a two-year forbearance for the client, and a $10 million FirstBanc letter of credit deal for the office.

As they walked back, Fredericks asked, 'How'd you know he was on the Article 3 advisory committee?'

'I checked *Martindale's*. I always check *Martindale's*, man. Begin with the people. The people are the key. The paper is negotiable, but the people, you're stuck with them, they are what they are.'

A little further down Congress Street, Fredericks

asked, somewhat plaintively now, 'Why didn't you tell me about the UCC?'

'Well, hell,' said Shepard, 'a guy's gotta have some fun, don't he? Besides, you'd a wrote the sonofabitch a letter, he'd have had six associates research it, and everybody would have drawn lines in the sand. We might have actually had to *file* bankruptcy, which is the last goddamn thing Apex would stand for. We only had one crack at the bluff, I figured, which was the meeting, and we couldn't get that except by going in naked. Without the meeting, I never would have got near the guy with the only argument that matters: which is what happens to the name of Thomas P. Hill, Lord and Master of a corner office at Daley & Hoar.'

It was silent again in the Bromfield Street office, as Stevie rubbed his chin, still leaning back in his chair, the heels on the ends of the shoes on the ends of the stubby legs just barely clinging to the desktop. But Ed could tell that, perhaps for the first time in this affair, his investigator had heard something about his client which he kind of liked. He would get over it.

After a while, the only sound was a gentle tapping from Kate's computer. Mulcahy sighed. 'Stevie,' he said, 'what do we have? What are our options?'

Stevie's chair creaked as he rocked forward, and then back. Outside a cabbie leaned on his horn. Then it was quiet again. 'Well,' he began, 'we gotta cowboy, I guess. Whattawe got? We got a guy who's alone, who leaves town alone, and who gets to Elmira alone. Owah friendly ain't-gotta-dime-for-investiga-tuhs-or-lawyuhs client, while he's driving alone, just happens to pass the exit for Sheringham, and happens to get off and buy some gas there. And a whole buncha his shit ends up scattered all over the study. And he gets a call from the victim two hours before his death, which he now cahn't remembuh. So fah, what we got don't sing opera, you know what I mean?'

Mulcahy nodded.

'We need a story to tell,' Stevie said.

'I think so, too,' Mulcahy said. 'So what's the story?'

'That depends. That depends.' Absentmindedly, Stevie fondled his wart between thumb and fore-finger. 'That depends on the forensics. Can you beat the forensics?'

'I don't know,' said Mulcahy.

'Let's say you can beat the forensics. Okay? Then, who the hell knows? We got takin' hemlock, just like it looks. I mean, either Whittakuh planted this thing and got caught, or at least was on watch when some fuckup about near killed his pahtnuhship. And if it ain't suicide, we got hell hath no fury, client wit' an attitude, lots a shit. The double life, the Sheringham Stalker, maids wit' blades, I dunno, anything.'

'Maids with blades?' Kate interrupted, looking up from the computer screen.

'Inside job. The help.'

She shook her head. This world *was* different from civil practice. Mulcahy said, 'Okay, you're saying, it could have been his wife, it could have been the help, it could have been, what, an ex-client?'

'Sure.'

'And what is, what is it, the double life?'

231

'He's in the drug game, he's borrowin' lotsa cabbage from people who ah not nice, he's got something goin' on. Somethin' like that.'

'Samuel *Whitaker*?' Kate asked.

'Look, he asked for the possibilities.'

Mulcahy was making notes. 'Somehow he doesn't strike me as a drug trafficker,' he said. 'Okay, suppose I can't beat the forensics.'

'You cahn't beat the forensics? Well, three possibilities. One, Shepid's lying – he was there, paid a visit on his way to Rocky Mountain High, but it wasn't him, and now he's afraid. That's one I'd dig into, personally. Or, two, he was framed, I suppose.' Stevie frowned.

'Framed?'

'I suppose. I'm just giving you the possibilities, okay?'

'Right,' said Mulcahy. 'What's the third one?'

'Eddie,' said Stevie, shaking his head. 'Eddie, what planet ah you on? What's the third one? Ask Paul O'Hanlon what the third one is.'

'All right,' said Mulcahy. 'Look, Stevie, assume we can beat the forensics. Find out what you can on those possibilities, or at least the first two, okay? And look at the people on Idlewild, too. Ruggerio was the real estate guy. Look at him, Weiner, Russell, the other Fletcher Daye people, anyone else who jumps out of my report.

'Kate,' he said, turning to her, 'I'd like you to look at suicide. That's yours. We'll need a complete psychological profile of Samuel Whitaker. What was the motive? What were the signs? What was the behaviour which marked this coming on?'

'Sure,' she said.

'Don't say sure so fast. Are you up to interviewing his wife? His kids?'

Her face fell. 'Sure,' she said again, but this time with less conviction. 'I'll try.'

'Good,' said Mulcahy. 'Thanks. I'll meet again tomorrow with Shepard, to see if, on reflection, it now occurs to him he stopped in for a drink. Or if he had any enemies in the CIA,' he added ironically, smiling at the round little investigator with the listing toupee.

'You might want to check about a plea, too,' Stevie said.

'Thanks a lot.'

'Hey, I'm kidding. But ya gotta be real in these things, Eddie, or they'll kill ya. Believe me.'

Before they broke up for the night, Mulcahy brought up one more thing, something which still nagged at him: Creel. Stevie nodded. 'Lemme see what I can do.'

A half hour later, Kate was at her terminal and Stevie was in a bar in Eastie, talking to a retired cop he knew. Stevie bought a number of drinks. Then he headed to Maverick Square.

21

The two men stood at the window, looking down at a darkened Bromfield Street. As a late-summer storm pounded the pavement with rain, a panhandler huddled in the entry to a bagel shop, thrusting his paper cup out towards the pedestrians hurrying by on the sidewalk. The rain drops roared on the awning below Stevie's office window. 'Look at him,' said Stevie. 'He ain't doin' too good.'

'Okay, Stevie, initial take on this?' asked Mulcahy.

'Well, I got an hour with Freds yesterday, got some more help this morning.'

'Freds?'

'Freddie Salvo. A state cop. Freds. He's a good guy. Confidential now, right?'

'Of course.'

'They checked it out, Eddie. Freds ain't no slouch. The wife, the family, the help, the friends. Eddie, fuggedabout it. Wife and daughters, staff, all accounted for.'

'How about the estate plan?'

'Checks out. Shit's all been in trust for a long time. Nothing changed in her estate plan, or his, for five years. All for the kids and grandkids. He's gotta lifetime beneficial interest. So does she. Nothing changes when either of 'em dies. She still got the life estate, and she can't do nothin' to change that the kids got the remainder.'

'Insurance?'

'Nothing new since 1985. It all checks out, Eddie. The maid who finds him? Twenty-one years she's been with the family.'

Mulcahy paused, looking out at the bustle below him. 'How about, what did you call it, the "Double Life?"'

'If he had one, he kept it a secret. Marriage kinda rocky, I guess, but no girlfriends that he showed off, anyway. Guy didn't owe nobody no dough, didn't have no flim-flam real estate deals. Didn't own nothing except the fahm, a monster sail boat, a lotta blue chip stock and a few acres of pine trees on an island in Maine. No close corporations, nonna that. And they ain't found no whisper of heavy shit – no frauds, no drugs, nothing.'

'So, what does that leave?'

'Well, what's ouwah maggot have to say?'

Mulcahy stared out the window. He wasn't sure he wanted Stevie to hear it. 'He doesn't know of any enemies, and he wasn't there.'

The rain gushed in rivers down the gutters of Bromfield Street. Mulcahy stood by the glass, recalling the morning in the attorneys' room. Once again, Shepard had paced back and forth from wall to wall. It reminded Mulcahy of a visit to the zoo,

235

watching the Bengal tiger pace the length of a cage, and then back again, barely containing itself, pacing too quickly. 'Look, Ed,' he had said, 'do you want me to tell you I was there? Do you want me to stop in Sheringham on the way west, have a drink with the old tightass sonofabitch, shake his hand, give him a hug, let bygones be bygones, and then drive off? I mean, the object of this exercise is to get me the hell out of here. Is that what you want?'

Mulcahy had measured his words. 'That's what I want, if it's the truth.'

'The truth! The truth isn't settin' me free right now! The truth is, I didn't kill the sonofabitch, and that's the only truth that matters. The rest is mechanics. Don't be a boy scout on me, Ed. You've seen the Commonwealth's shit now, right? Is that what you want?'

'I want the truth.'

'Look, Ed, let's understand something. Let's focus. Like I said, the object of this exercise is to get me out of here. I'll tell you why I don't think I want that story. Because it happens to be inconsistent with that bag of details you litigators *think of* as the truth. And I know that the story will trip over those details, and O'Hanlon would make me out a liar. And that could croak me. Am I right? That's why I don't think I want it. But you're the trial man! If it works, I want it. So tell me.'

The eyes gripped in on Mulcahy fiercely.

'No.'

'Look, Ed, if we say that we have no sin, we deceive ourselves, and the truth is not in us. First Epistle of John. I have plenty of sins, but not that one. The truth is bigger than details. This, this,' he said looking at the cinder block walls on either side, 'this is fucking details, Ed.'

Mulcahy wanted to change the subject. 'What about the call, John? He called you. They know he was home that night and they know his Sheringham phone placed a call to your Beacon Hill phone. Twelve out of twelve jurors will believe that. Isn't it about time for you to tell me what is really going on here?'

'Ed,' said Shepard, 'I've been worried about that. I know you're right. Everyone will believe that.' He spoke almost philosophically now. 'But he didn't call me. At least, he didn't speak to me.'

'Where's the machine?'

'The machine?'

'Where's the answering machine? The tape?'

Shepard nodded. 'Oh. Estes Park. Reliable Storage, I think it's called. You can call Frank Merchant in Estes Park, Colorado. In a white box, I think.'

Mulcahy made notes.

'John, do you have enemies?' he asked, changing the subject again.

'Enemies? Hell, yeah. A hundred Freer Motley partners, for one. Another hundred ADAs, for two.'

'No, I mean someone who may have had a motive to set you up?'

Shepard paused. 'To set me up?'

'Yeah, I don't know. You keep bad company?'

He laughed. 'I do now.' He thought about it for a moment. 'Set me up? Hmmm. Some guy in a trench coat to go around creating clues and faking a crime scene? Is that what you mean? Ed, I don't think so. Really.

'It is kind of weird, though,' he went on. 'You say they got my fingerprint, right? The fact is, I was never there.'

'It's a partial.'

'It might be wrong?'

'Yeah. Apparently. I don't know a helluva lot about fingerprints.'

'Well, Ed, don't take this the wrong way, but how about you find out a helluva lot about fingerprints? In a hurry, okay? Because these fingers,' he went on, holding up his hands to the mesh, 'weren't there.'

Mulcahy awoke from his reflections. In Bromfield Street, the two men stared out at the rain. The afternoon had grown darker.

'Let's look hard at the suicide then,' Stevie was saying. 'And let's get that message machine. What else can we do, huh? It's like that guy down there,' he said, indicating the panhandler, still huddled in the gangway to the bagel shop, thrusting the cup out into the storm. 'Ya gotta keep trying. Maybe, ya keep at it long enough, somebody drops a buck in your cup, ya know?'

Mulcahy looked out the window at the dark figure for a few moments more. As far as he could see, nothing fell into his cup but rain. Yet it lingered there, as the darkness deepened, a sodden white paper cup, suspended pitifully in the storm.

They walked down South Street towards the abutment. It was a bright, hot, humid August morning. A moving van was parked a few yards down the street, and two broad-shouldered young men were rolling furniture on dollies out into the sidewalk. In Boston, someone is always moving in, someone always moving out. At nine, they had already stripped to the waist. The air out across the harbour was thick with moisture.

Stevie George pulled at his wart and stood watching the grey-green water. It shimmered in the morning heat as, away in the distance, beyond the rusting piers and derrick, the harbour taxi made for Rowe's Wharf. Stevie's back and armpits were damp with sweat. 'This is the place,' he said. 'The kid says the guy was shootin' at him, and the last he saw, Creel goes sailin' over the concrete.'

Ed Mulcahy peered over the abutment. Below, the water lapped against the harbour wall, a skin of flotsam bobbing on it.

'Wheelchair?'

'They found it here.' Stevie beckoned at the rusted concrete moulding bar protruding from the slab.

'Blood on it?' Mulcahy asked.

'No.'

'Did the kid say he was hit?' he asked.

'Kid don't know.'

'Creel's body was never found, right?'

'Nope.'

'Did you see the reports?'

'Had 'em read to me. Not much. Coupla calls about the shots. They never talked to the kids.'

'The bullets?'

Stevie raised an eyebrow and smiled. 'The *bullets*, counselluh?'

'Yeah. The bullets.'

'Eddie, I guess you were a federal prosecutor, huh? Lottsa public corruption, lottsa drugs. Not too much with guns. Am I right?'

'All right.' Mulcahy felt the colour coming to his neck.

'Ya. Anyway, Eddie, before you get into the court-room on this one, you gotta learn something about fireahms. Now, you got your projectiles, and your casings. Your projectiles do the damage. Casings eject from the weapon as it is fired. "Bullets" are what they got in movies, okay?'

'Fine, the projectiles, then.'

'Ya gonna do a gun case, Eddie, ya don't wanna sound like a No-Nukes protestuh, ya know? Projectiles.'

'Okay, boss, sign me up for the NRA. Projectiles. Did they find any?'

'Negative.'

They looked out at the water. 'Eddie,' Stevie said after a moment, 'you ain't asked the right question.'

As Mulcahy turned to ask it, Stevie anticipated him. 'They did find two casings.'

Ed turned back to face the harbour. 'So this isn't just bullshit,' he said.

'Well. This isn't *just* bullshit anyway,' Stevie corrected. 'Plenty a bullshit in this thing, just not *all* of it bullshit.'

They placed their hands on the abutment and looked out towards the channel together, shielding their eyes from the bright light reflecting off the water.

'They would have found him,' said Stevie.

'Unless . . .' said Mulcahy, looking past the water

to the office towers glimmering a mile and a half off, behind Commercial Wharf and the Aquarium, just as the two boys had three months before.

'Nah,' said Stevie. 'Guy had no legs.'

The two men stood squinting into the hot, murky, overpowering haze. It would have been a long swim. And the harbour is still cold in mid-May.

Mulcahy turned and looked at Stevie. 'He's out there,' he said. 'I don't know why, but I'd sure like to find him.'

Stevie frowned, but he knew Mulcahy was right. They would have found the body.

'Jeez,' he said, unbuttoning his jacket and pushing his hair piece back on his head. 'Finding swimmuz, not my usual thing, Eddie.'

'Swimmers with no legs,' said Mulcahy. 'For that I should get a discount.'

'Ya. A discount on nuthin' is still nuthin', counsel-luh.' He looked out at the water for a moment, then asked, 'Does he help? Ya know, Eddie, sometimes ya work like hell to find a guy, latuh you wish he'd stayed lost. Ya know?'

'Yeah. I don't know if he helps. Probably not. So far, not too much helps this case.'

The morning was getting hotter. They stood for only a few moments more, and then walked back up the street.

'George Creel is some guy wit' no legs who works in a computuh room all day, right? In a law firm? Far as anyone can tell, he ain't into drugs, am I right?' Stevie huffed, with a last glance over his shoulder at the harbour.

'Right,' said Mulcahy.

'So how come, on 14 May, somebody wants to kill him?'

'That's why he helps. Maybe.'

Shaking their heads, the two men walked on.

Tuesday night, the last hot Tuesday of a sweltering August. 'Katie,' shouted Stevie. She had appeared at the doorway, labouring up the stairs under the weight of a large trial bag. They had a week left.

'Katie baby! I gotta BLT for ya!'

She grimaced as Stevie waved a sack at her.

'Wit extra mayo!' he said. 'Wha? Katie . . . Wha?' He shook his head, and his left hand played across his face.

Mulcahy looked up and smiled. 'Stevie, a carrot sandwich she might eat. If you hold the mayo.' He smiled at her. 'Hey,' he said. 'I hope you did better than we did today.'

She looked puzzled, and he explained. 'Final pre-trial. Defence motion to continue denied. Motion for change of venue denied. Denied, denied, denied. Judge Grosso will sanction Parisi. As if that helps. He'll give us a question or two in *voir dire* on pretrial publicity. But *he'll* read them. We go Tuesday.'

She whistled. He helped her unload the trial bag on to Stevie's table, spreading out files full of clips, photocopies, and notes. 'Wow,' he said. 'Before we get to him, Stevie, let's do the Idlewild people.'

'A buncha shit don't go anywhere, I think,' the investigator said. 'Nothin' obvious. No criminal rec-ords, board sanctions, bankruptcies – well, Weiner's had some properties been through bankruptcies, but

I guess that ain't unusual in his business. Nothin' that really grabs me.'

Stevie pulled his notepad from a stack of papers on his desk, and began summarising. They talked for a while about Sid Weiner. According to Freds, the prosecutors had been interested in him, too. They'd done some digging, but come up dry.

While Weiner's deals usually involved one party who made a lot of money, and one party who didn't, and while he was almost never the one who didn't, he had made his money in perfectly honest real estate development, so far as anyone could tell. Which is to say, he'd made it by betting other people's money and charging extortionate fees for managing his own investment. Thirty years ago, he started with small commercial buildings in his Brooklyn neighbourhood. He was a lot bigger now, and had long ago become a rich man, even though a number of his properties had been through bankruptcies and work-outs. He knew how to fight with banks, and wasn't afraid to do it.

'I ain't got anything substantial, though,' said Stevie. 'He's a fifty-six-year-old rich guy with a shoht unit, that's what I figure.'

'Excuse me?'

'Ya know the type, Eddie. Lots of toys. Cars. Apartments. The spread in East Hampton, the trips to the islands, the condo in Aspen. Keeps up the tan, trades in a wife every seven years or so, has one flunky to come in and exuhcise him, another to measure him for a new suit. Ya know, a rich guy. I ain't got much on him, except envy.'

Kate shook her head and laughed. Mulcahy smiled. 'So what do you think?'

Stevie shook his head. 'Naaa,' he said. 'Sure it didn't break his haht to stick it to DeFi. But set it all up? This guy is a shrewd businessman. He don't need to take huge chances at this point in his life. He likes toys, but he's got enough toys. He just did the biggest fuckin' deal ever in New England, got it all with somebody else's money. Why get greedy and complicated and risk blowing what you got? You're fifty-six. You got enough. That's what I figure.'

Mulcahy nodded, looking down his notes. He yawned. It was going to be a long night. 'Ruggerio?' he said.

Ruggerio had been the real estate lawyer. Stevie flipped over his pad and told him about the bridge player from Lexington with the three daughters in grade school. But Mulcahy was only half listening. He reckoned he knew Ruggerio well enough. 'Hmm,' he said, when Stevie had finished. He turned back to the table.

'So, Kate,' he said, 'what do we have on Whitaker?'

She sighed, opening her first file.

'Samuel Boylston Whitaker,' she began, 'aka "Sir Sam", though never to his face. To the manor born. If ever there was a senior partner, it was Mr Whitaker. He was sixty-six when he died. Six foot two, trim, probably not much above or below his weight of 187 in the Navy. Bore himself straight-backed, and still had enough hair to wear the brush cut he had worn since he shipped out. Eyes blue and clear, although he wore bifocals at the time of his death. Always wore a bow tie. The sight of Sir Sam peering out over bifocals was known to embarrass even senior lawyers, when they came to report.'

'Junior lawyers, too,' Mulcahy said.

Kate went on. 'Pull out Volume Six of Freer's *Martindale's* set,' she said, 'and set it on a table. It will fall open to Mr Whitaker's page. I checked. Born 1926, in Muttontown, New York, the son of a wealthy investment banker, he graduated first in his class from Phillips Exeter Academy in 1943. Not second. First. He served in the United States Navy in 1943–45, where he received a combat promotion to Lieutenant Commander and was decorated for bravery for service in Bataan. He matriculated at Yale University, where he graduated Phi Beta Kappa and *summa* in American Studies in 1950. He pulled the five oar on the 1950 boat which won the Eastern Sprints, the Harvard Boat race, and the Grand Challenge Cup at Henley. He attended Jesus College, Oxford, in 1951–52, where he took a degree in Politics, Philosophy, and Economics, matriculated at the Harvard Law School in 1953, and became president – *president*, guys, that's Editor in Chief everywhere else – of the Harvard Law Review in 1956. He clerked for Fisher Hamilton, then chief judge of the First Circuit Court of Appeals.'

Stevie whistled.

'You're right,' she said. 'It goes on. He had joined Emerson, Freer & Motley in 1958, left soon after to join the United States Attorney's office, and, before his return to what had become Freer, Motley & Stone in 1963, had become Chief of the Civil Division. He returned to Freer, soon became partner, and, beginning in 1970, became the head of its corporate department. From 1976 through 1990, he was managing partner of the firm.

'By 1970, he had become one of the two or three most influential lawyers in the city. At the firm, no major client was taken on without his blessing; no change in firm governance instituted over his dissent. Firm profits were distributed under a nominally democratic committee, but the firm was more accurately a dictatorship.'

She paused. 'Some would say a benevolent one.'

'How'd you find *that* out – about the distributions?' asked Mulcahy.

She smiled. 'Nobody can't keep a secret like law firm partners.'

She went on.

'In 1955, Sam Whitaker married Anna Lee Sturtevant, a quiet and by all accounts attractive young woman from an old Marblehead family who had graduated from Smith in 1952. The couple bought a sprawling farmhouse near the Charles River in Sheringham in 1963. Look.' She rooted through one of the files and produced photocopies of several photographs. One was a wedding picture. The young man was unusually handsome, fair and clear-eyed with a strong chin. Obviously confidence there. His bride, on that day, even through the rather unfortunate coiffing and styles of make-up prevalent in the mid-fifties, was a young woman of great loveliness.

The second photograph might have been a Currier and Ives print. There was the home that Mulcahy had gazed at in awe on that May morning.

'The farmhouse?' Stevie asked.

Kate nodded.

'Jeez,' he said. 'Bet he didn't cut the grass.' He walked to the window, and looked out at a line of taxi cabs snarled below on Bromfield Street.

Kate continued. 'Samuel and Anna had two daughters: Beth, born in 1959, and Emma, born 1961. During this period, there were a lot of local clips of Boston and Sheringham events. They were very active socially.

'It looks like Anna Whitaker did what any good wife to a prosperous man was in those days expected to do. She entertained. She accompanied her husband to fundraisers and openings, endured, indeed hosted, countless cocktail parties, raised the girls, ferried them to dressage and swimming meets.

'I tracked down a family friend who talked to me. I think she didn't quite understand which side I was on. Anyway, it appears that Beth, like her mother, was dutiful, intelligent, quiet. She seemed destined for a sort of uneasy compromise: more akin to her mother in temperament, but duty-bound to act out the part that the absence of a son had decreed. She graduated from Yale in 1980, I think it was, attended its law school, hated it, and had a brief couple of years in private practice. She got married and has a couple of children. She lives in Connecticut.

'Emma was different. She rebelled from the outset. She found ways to be sent down from prep school, ran with boys in the town, flirted with an acting career. By the mid-1980s, she was running a folk and coffee house in Vineyard Haven. However, after the most prickly years of adolescence had passed, a closeness between her and her mother began to arise. According to this friend, Anna once said that her entire life had been an imprisonment in a man's shrine. Maybe she came to admire her daughter's adventurous spirit. As adults, this friend said, the two women found a closeness they had not known before and had not expected.'

It was quiet in the office. Kate said, 'As to the last ten years or so of Samuel Whitaker's professional life, except for the external stuff, there isn't much I could find out without raising a lot of questions.'

Mulcahy nodded. But probably there was little she should have discovered about the later years that he would not already have heard. In fact, in the late-1980s, Sam Whitaker's star passed its apogee. The frantic pace of dealmaking in the financial community was something for which he had been unprepared. It was, first, against every conservative instinct. And it was generational. Scarcely an investment banker was even forty, and the entrepreneurs seemed barely to be shaving. The bankers were kids: children. Men and women with no inkling of the value of money and the risk of its loss were approving $100 million financing commitments. The 1980s saw a generational revolution in the financial community so vast that the experience and caution of a lawyer of fifty was no longer seen as an asset. It became a liability. And through the mid-80s a new breed of successful lawyer was seen at Freer Motley; younger, louder, less deferential, less seasoned.

Whitaker's law practice began to slip from him. In 1987, he brought in fewer billings than the year before, something which had never happened in his career in private practice and which was, for its time, unusual. His productivity seemed to decline just at the time the efficiency experts arrived. Suddenly there were high-priced consultants on every floor, it seemed, and a spreadsheet in his in-box every third day. By 1990, his 'productivity' placed the old bull in the middle of the pack.

Luckily, Mulcahy had thought to bring his final report with him on the day he left Freer Motley. He fished it out of his Whitaker file and read aloud: ' "In 1980, Whitaker's word in a partnership meeting was law. In 1987, dissent might be heard, although usually he prevailed. By 1989, the firm was being run without him. Then on 31 May 1990 his term as managing partner expired, and he was not re-elected."

'There was something else, too, that I had a sense the Count wasn't telling me. There was some kind of a deal there, I don't know what. But I couldn't get it out of him at the time.'

The Count *had* been only too willing to share with Mulcahy a certain amount of Whitaker gossip. The family had not been sympathetic. The running of Sam Whitaker's life at home had long ago been ceded to his wife, and it could be and was run largely without his input. Beth he never saw. Connecticut was within reach, but she was constantly pressed for time with her own children and husband. He visited Emma more frequently, but the old scars had never quite mended, and he felt an intruder when Anna and Emma were together.

Kate interrupted. 'I did find this. In 1988, Anna

249

checked herself into MacLean Hospital with a bout of severe depression. Some friends speculated that the awakening sense of self prompted by the maturing relationship with Emma drove her to this crisis point. The price of a new sense of self was her realisation of a lifetime misdirected. She slipped further from the man to whom she had served, almost all of her adult life, as a lieutenant, and deeper into herself.

'Anna made short, infrequent returns to MacLean over the next four years, three in total. Largely, however, routines in the family were undisturbed. But Anna had grown colder, more distant.

'By mid-1991, it seems like Sir Sam was alone.' Kate looked up. She had finished.

Sam Whitaker was the man with the Golden Resumé, the man with all the commendations, the tributes, the plaques, the man of luncheon addresses and committee chairmanships, the man of a thousand acquaintances. And it had come to this? It was hard to fathom.

They put the files down, and Stevie rooted through his fridge for beer. It had grown cooler.

'Suppose,' Mulcahy said, 'Whitaker got so angry with Shanklin and the rest of them over the severance that he plugged this thing in there, thinking, you know, this will just be an embarrassment for them – with their biggest client. And then things got out of hand?'

No one responded. 'Well,' Mulcahy went on, 'we'd better get some subpoenas out. Kate, thanks, that was great work. I've had some more thoughts on research. I've been wondering whether we can attack the admissibility of the print. They had to take a photo of it. Can you do some research on that, see if you can come up with anything? Also, that credit card slip. See if we can keep it out.'

'Business record, isn't it?'

'I don't know. If the theory is that he signed it, maybe he's the only custodian, and since they can't call him, it stays out.

'But if he signed it, it comes in as an admission.'

'Only if someone can identify the signature. Which you can't. See what you can find, anyway.'

'Okay,' she said, 'I'll get on Westlaw.' She unlatched the laptop on Stevie's table, and in a moment had it up and running. Using its internal modem, she accessed the legal research service, and began her work. Mulcahy's nose disappeared into a file.

Stevie sat looking at the two lawyers who had commandeered his office. 'Eddie, I dunno about this,' he said quietly.

Wednesday came. For over a week they had been looking for George Creel, and Mulcahy was growing nervous. His instinct told him that the guest book, whatever it was, was important. There'd been something about Creel's self-satisfaction when he referred to it, the way his mouth worked, as though he were fighting back the urge to laugh out loud at his own cleverness.

But the messages left with Creel's former landlord had turned up nothing. The information from the armed forces records service in St Louis had been scanty. They had found only three men from Creel's

251

old unit. One had arrived two months before Creel was wounded. He didn't remember him. The other two hadn't heard from him since the war.

'Anything else you can tell me about him?' Stevie asked one.

'Two purple hearts, and, if I remember right, one distinguished service cross. He was quite a soldier,' the man had said.

Kate had come up with Freer Motley's personnel records. But they had been of no use. No next-of-kin was listed other than Lyndon Johnson.

Stevie had pulled some strings, and managed to get a year of Creel's phone records. There were three New York exchanges shown in the year before his disappearance. Two were commercial listings for computer peripheral suppliers. One had been disconnected. They had been unable to get a forwarding address or name.

But Kate found something, a tiny something. Among the files Mulcahy had taken from Creel's desk at the end of his investigation, she had found a ream of computer printouts.

'Ed,' she asked him that day, 'do you know what these are?'

He shrugged, looking at what looked like a series of messages.

'He printed out his E-mail forums.'

'His what?'

'The forums he registered for on E-mail, or at least some of them anyway.'

'Yeah? So what did he subscribe for?'

'Something called Jarhead Jaw, a Vietnam vet

forum by the looks of it, and Lawnet, which looks like a thing for law firm MIS people.'

'So?'

'So maybe he's resubscribed,' she said.

'How do we find out?'

'Don't know. Might get it from the sysop.'

'The who?'

'The sysop. The person in charge. I don't know. Worth a try.'

That night, stripped to his shorts, Mulcahy sat on his couch between piles of unopened mail, a cold beer in his lap, watching the TV.

'Next on the A-Team, the lawyer whose client has cost him a job – stick with us,' the television announcer was saying. A commerical came on.

'Don't tell me,' Mulcahy said to himself. In a moment he saw his own face return to the screen. It looked like the photo they'd used the only other time he had ever been on television – five years before when he tried the Delano drug cases. He had more hair then.

'Goddamn it, Gitz!' shouted Mulcahy. 'You promised me.'

'It wasn't me! It wasn't me! I swear it!' said Gitz, who could hear the television.

'You're a lying hound.'

'Eddie,' he interrupted, coming into the room, his droopy eyes welling as he pointed to the screen, 'would I blow you for that asshole?'

'As the A-Team reported last week, Boston attorney Edward Mulcahy filed notice that he will defend John Shepard at his murder trial, which led to a fire storm of accusations between Mulcahy and previous counsel, Felix Parisi,' said Frannie Dillard. 'The trial gets underway next week.' Now a still shot of John Shepard flashed on the screen. The reporter continued. 'Shepard will stand trial for the murder of Samuel Whitaker.

'While Shepard had been represented by Attorney Parisi, Mulcahy, like Shepard and his alleged victim, Samuel Whitaker, also worked at the prestigious downtown firm of Freer, Motley & Stone.

'WFBA has learned that late last week Freer Motley fired Mulcahy, apparently, according to sources, for his decision to take the case. A spokesman for the firm declined any comment, although she did confirm that Mulcahy no longer works there.

'WFBA has also learned that Parisi has sued Mulcahy for defamation. When Parisi charged that he withdrew for ethical reasons, Mulcahy countered with the charge that Parisi had been fired for incompetence. Tonight, Mulcahy was unavailable for comment. Jim?'

'Who asked for a comment?' asked Mulcahy. Then he noticed the red light flashing on the answering machine in the kitchen.

The voice cut back in. 'For the WFBA Team, this is reporter Fran Dillard, reporting from Suffolk Superior Courthouse.'

Mulcahy cut off the rest of the news. The phone rang. 'For you,' Gitz shouted.

He looked up quizzically.

'Hey, it's out,' said Gitz, 'you gotta expect . . .'

'Ahh, take a message,' said Mulcahy. He rose and padded down the hall to his bedroom, his midriff hanging over the elastic on his jockey shorts. He was muttering to himself, but Gitz couldn't make it out. A few minutes later the phone was ringing again, but Ed Mulcahy was asleep.

22

Thursday morning. By noon the following day, the city would begin emptying, and the highways to Cape Cod would be clogged. The banks and the court-houses and the shops would shut down for the Labour Day Weekend. And when they all reopened, reluctantly, the following Tuesday, a clerk in the Suffolk Superior Court would be calling the case of *Commonwealth* v. *John Shepard*.

For the defence team on the John Shepard case, there would be no end-of-summer weekend. That morning Stevie had caught a break, and now he was in Dorchester, taking notes. He had found the cab driver.

He was slim, his face black as jet, voice soft and musical. 'Never in my life such a thing,' the man was saying. 'Never in my life. This man, he crawls out from the darkness, soaked to the skin, pulling himself along by his hands!'

They sat in the cab dispatcher's office, on either side of a battered wooden desk, littered with papers.

The squawk of the dispatch broke in and out over Martin Bako's voice. Stevie took notes. Bako described that extraordinary night in May when the man with no legs had crawled to his cab.

'By his hands!' His eyes widened as he recalled the unreality of that moment last spring. He shook his head.

'What happened then?' asked Stevie.

Martin Bako nodded and went on. 'First, he says, take me to Veteran's Hospital. I must have a wheelchair. And so I am taking him there. We pull into the emergency bay, and this man, he does all the talking. He talks to an orderly. And then a doctor comes, and he knows this man . . .'

'Did he say his name? Creel?'

Martin Bako thought. It was last spring. He shrugged. 'I am sorry. I cannot remember.'

He returned to his story. 'It took some time, but after many minutes they returned with a wheelchair. I helped them fold it and place it in the trunk.'

'Then what?' asked Stevie.

'Then this man is saying, can you call your dispatcher for the train times to New York? Which I am doing. It was in the evening, and I recall that there was such a train, leaving in about one hour. So I take him to a BayBank machine, and then to South Station. Only, the man is not getting out of the cab until it is time for the train to come. We sit there for a long time, this man and me. Then, it is time for the train to go, and I help him into the wheelchair, and he insists that he be wrapped up in my coat, and that I push him to the platform.'

'What time? What time was this train?'

257

Martin Bako shrugged again. 'I don't know,' he said.

'It was in the night, a Saturday night?'

'Yes.'

'How long before you got off that evening?'

Martin Bako mused for a time. 'My shift is ending at midnight. I do not recall when I picked him up, but I think, after I left him at South Station, perhaps one fare more. I think. I cannot be sure.'

'Thanks,' said Stevie. 'Thanks a lot. Here's my cahd.' He picked up his hat and left, his little legs pumping for a telephone booth.

Kate, who had snuck off to Bromfield Street, replaced the telephone in the cradle. Amtrak. That meant Providence, New York, Philadelphia, Washington, Atlanta, at least on the first trip.

She looked at her watch, realising she would be missed at the office if she were not back there in twenty minutes. She switched on the laptop and plugged in the modem. On Wednesday night, she had sent E-mails to the sysops for the two Natlink forums. She was desperately seeking an old friend, she had said, and needed the listing of all new registrants since 15 May. Now she saw responses from each. The message from Jarhead Jaw's sysop was about what she expected. If she wanted to post a public notice, it would get to all registrants, it said. End of message. She frowned, and flipped to the other one. Here she'd caught a break. It gave a telephone number and suggested that she call Pete during office hours, eastern time. That was an opening, but what would she say to the guy? He was going to ask her what this was all about.

She sat for several minutes, thinking. It was hot, and she brushed the hair from her forehead, frowning as she compared the air conditioning in Stevie's office to what was available downtown. She concentrated for a few more minutes. Pacing to the window, she looked out and down towards the crossing, noticing the camera shop at the bottom of the street. As she stood there, an idea began to take shape. 'Okay, Kate,' she said to herself, 'let's see just how cute you are.'

She was in luck, for Pete was at his desk. After several minutes, he had let her know that the request was against the regs, against the rules, and he didn't get it. If she wanted to find somebody named George, why not just post a notice?

'Look, Pete,' she said, 'this is *really* embarrassing, but, well, would you mind keeping this to yourself?'

'Sure.'

'You promise? You're not taping this call or anything, are you?'

'No.'

'Okay,' she said. 'George ... George was my boyfriend, okay, and he ... I can't believe I'm telling a stranger this, but I don't know what else to do. So, anyway, George was my boyfriend, and we broke up, okay?'

'Miss, look, I don't ...'

'No, Pete, I'm not going to get stupid, okay? Just listen. I know this is weird. Anyway, George and I, when things were cool, he liked to do movies. Okay?'

'George liked to go to movies?'

'No. George liked to *make* movies.'

'To make movies?'

'Yes. Of us.'

Now Pete was silent, and she let him fantasise for a moment. 'Okay?' she asked.

'Okay,' he said.

'Okay, well, when we broke up, I'm like, George, I can't believe you're doing this, I mean, I really loved him, the bastard – God, it's so pathetic – but, I said, like, what about the videos? And he's like, what about them? And I'm like, "*Give me the videos, George.*" But he wouldn't. He took them! The snake! And so he's got these videos of me. I've never done anything so stupid in my life as when I let him, well, you know. Anyway, I'm sorry to lay this on you, you probably can't believe there's like this totally weird chick on your phone talking about dirty movies, but that's it. George split, I can't find him. I've been calling everywhere for weeks, nobody knows where he is, and I'm desperate. Pete, I'm desperate! Can you understand! And the only thing I *know* is that George is on this forum. I mean, he's on it, somewhere. He used to download it every morning.'

'I see,' said the voice, after a considerable pause, and Kate, grinning to herself, imagined that Pete was trying to work out a result which would include seeing the videos. 'He'll use a different name, I know, he always did before,' she said.

'Ah . . . this is pretty weird,' he said.

'Pretty weird! Imagine how *I* feel, talking to you about it! Pete, did you ever, like, have a nightmare girlfriend?'

'Ah, well . . .'

260

'Okay, so imagine, like, she's out there, somewhere, and she's got this movie of you, with your thing . . . I'm sorry, but just imagine it, okay? And imagine I could give you that list that might help you find this woman. How would you feel? How would you *feel*?'

All it takes, really, is for a woman to mention a man's genitals. Pete surrendered instantly. 'So what do I do?' he asked, quietly.

'If I had all the names and addresses of new people on this forum, I might be able to figure something out from a pseudonym, or just the address. George would do something clever, he was always *so* clever. The *bastard!* I don't need everybody on it. Just people who have signed up since we broke up in the middle of May.'

It took another fifteen minutes to work out how Pete would download the two thousand or so names he estimated would have registered over the three months, and how they could be copied, and the copies paid for, and sent to Kate, and all done so that Pete wouldn't catch it from his boss. For Pete, bless his cotton socks, the mere opportunity to share information was tempting enough, but to do it with the sultry-voiced siren of someone's VCR, why that was too much for poor Pete to bear.

'All right!' Kate sang out, when she'd hung up the phone, 'All right!' She looked around at the file cabinet and the window glass, the trash can next to Stevie's desk overflowing with brown paper bags, the grey table littered with files. She banged on the desk. 'Yes! Yes!!'

*

261

It felt even hotter across the hill in the Charles Street jail, where two state police officers and an ADA had accompanied the box of evidence packages to a visitors room. It was the first time Mulcahy and Shepard had met there without the screen between them, and it was the first time they had shaken hands since the affair began. They went through the materials quickly, the evidence bags containing hairs and fibres, the weapon, the blood-stained jacket. They cast looks back and forth, Mulcahy's pen scratching across his yellow pad.

'What about the soap?' he asked.

'Still at 1010 Commonwealth,' Gleason said, referring to the state police lab.

'I asked for it.'

'So sue me,' Gleason said. 'It's a bar of soap, for Chrissakes. What are you going to do, wash up?' He glared out the window, chewing gum. For a kid, he was pretty arrogant. He was learning how to be an Assistant DA.

The cops packed up the evidence and left.

When they were alone, Shepard looked shaken. The volume of physical evidence must have seemed a powerful confrontation. 'How're you guys doin'? Really?' he asked.

'We've got some stuff. Lost our motions, you know.'

'Yeah, well, I figured you'd lose those. But Whitaker, how's that? What have we got on the guy?'

Mulcahy took him through his results to date of the investigation.

When he was done, Shepard said, 'You're not thrillin' me with this, Ed. For Jesus's sake, man, we go next week! There's gotta be more. Gotta be. Have you called all of the old Freer partners? The retired guys? Run the clip files at the library, dug into his pals in Sheringham? There's got to be more to this than, what was his name, Fellstein?'

'Fellbright.'

'Fine. He's okay. But there's more, man, there's more. Keep on it!'

Shepard was staring at him. Quietly, Mulcahy said, 'There's something else I should tell you about.'

'What's that?'

'The computers. We may have some angle on the computers. Remember George Creel?'

'Crazy fucker in MIS, guy in the chair?'

'Yeah. We're trying to run him down. He told us something about a guest book when I was doing the Idlewild investigation, and . . .'

'Ed,' Shepard interrupted, 'that's all fine. But we don't have a lot of time for sniffing the roses, you know?' He was silent for a moment, and stared at Mulcahy. When he spoke again his voice had hardened. 'Suicide's the defence, right? Like you said. Keep the spotlight on Sir Sam, okay?'

'Sure,' Mulcahy said. 'Sure, John. I need to ask you a few things.'

'Shoot away,' Shepard said.

'What about the Sunoco charge?'

'Wasn't me, man. I've never been there.'

'Well, what about your card?'

'To be honest, I never missed it until Parisi asked me about that. I paid for my gas with cash on the way out west. When Parisi found out about the charge, I checked my wallet, which the police had confiscated. The Sunoco card was missing.'

'John,' said Mulcahy, with some embarrassment, 'people are going to have trouble believing it's a coincidence.'

'I know,' he said. 'But I don't know what else to tell you. I didn't buy gas there. I've never been to Natick.'

'The jacket, then?'

Shepard shook his head and looked away. Mulcahy's mind recalled the hour before. Under the glare of the overhead lamp and the even hotter impatience of the two corrections officers, the state cops, and the ADA, they had removed the jacket from the evidence pouch, displaying it before them with the rubber gloves.

'Not mine,' he said.

'How do we . . . ?' Mulcahy began.

'I don't know,' Shepard said. 'I suppose there's a lot of khaki jackets.'

Mulcahy frowned. There might be a lot of khaki jackets. But how many of them are 43 longs cleaned at the Beacon Hill Cleaners? Shepard's lips tightened as he stared across the table. Mulcahy looked back, and tried to do it blankly, tried to suppress his own doubts. But Shepard was a better reader of men's eyes than that.

Friday night came. Mulcahy had nodded off at Stevie's table. Around him were eight volumes on fingerprint analysis, every book he'd been able to beg, borrow or steal on the subject.

Stevie said, 'Everybody but us is down the Cape, ya know.'

'Everybody but us and O'Hanlon. And Shepard.'

'Ah, fuck 'em all,' Stevie said. He was frustrated. This loser of a case was earning him no fees and keeping him off the Cape Labour Day weekend. And, except for one break with a cab driver, he'd been blanked by Creel.

'Ya know,' he said, ''cept for Katie's break with the computer people, I am coming up with nothing on this guy. He ain't got no legs, but he sure disappeared.'

'All I have is a directory coming in the mail. No promises he's on it,' she said.

Stevie muttered on about the worthlessness of the federal government, the Marine Corps, the Veterans Administration, the Armed Forces Information Service, and the rest of them. 'Cahn't even find one of their own guys,' he said.

After a while, he asked, 'How's owah maggot?'

Mulcahy sniffed and rubbed his neck. 'He's getting kind of grouchy. You know, he wants to be in the middle of everything, wants to control it all, direct it all, and he can't. He's stuck out there at Charles Street in a cage. It's driving him crazy. He's driving *me* crazy. Calls a lot.'

'Collect?' Stevie asked.

'How else do you call someone from jail?'

'A free phone bill I am not. You take a collect call, you pay for it, Counselluh.'

'Believe me, I'm not pining for the calls.'

Kate was sipping coffee and staring at the laptop screen. 'I'm losing my mind,' she said.

'What?' said Mulcahy.

She squinted at the letters. 'This brief. I worked on it last night at 1.34 a.m. This morning, I guess I should say. I can't even remember that.'

'I don't follow,' Ed said.

'When you go to the master directory, it tells you when the document was last opened. See?' She beckoned at the screen, with its list of documents, each followed by a date and time.

'This brief, the one I'm writing on keeping the Sunoco note out. The file was saved last night at 1.34 a.m. Unless it was you, Ed?'

He chuckled. 'Yeah, we know how handy I am with the damn thing.'

'Writin' briefs in your sleep, Kate?'

'Looks like it,' she said, frowning.

'I gotta go,' Stevie said, yawning. He took his hat and picked up a satchel. 'Katie,' he said, 'you need a boyfriend, know what I mean?'

'No, I can't imagine what you mean, Mr George. Good night.'

Mulcahy chuckled as the heavy footfalls banged away down the stairs. 'Kate, you have been working pretty hard,' he said.

'Ed,' she said, playfully, 'can you imagine me in a porno movie?'

He reddened, and his jaw hung slack.

'Can you?'

'Ah,' he said, 'there is no safe answer to that question.'

'Well,' she said, with a mischievous smile, 'somebody can.'

*

And so they came down to their last weekend. Stevie George attended to sustenance, if not good dietary habits, bursting in with more food than evidence, arms clutching grease-stained brown paper bags. 'I got pastrami, I got tuna fish,' he was saying the Saturday afternoon before trial. 'I gotta Reuben, I got a roast beef special. Whaddaya have?'

He emptied the two greasy sacks of sandwiches wrapped in wax-paper on the table. He unbuttoned his jacket. Then buttoned it again.

Mulcahy was lost in thought in *Lewis on Fingerprint Analysis*. 'Not just at the moment, Stevie . . .'

'Whaddaya mean, not just at the moment? At what pahticulah moment ah ya gonna get some lunch? It's one o'clock almost. Ya wanna stahve?'

'I'll get one in a bit,' he said, 'thanks.'

'I'm tellin' ya, Ed, they gonna find ya with ya ahms and legs curled up, lying on ya back from stahvation. We're talkin' good stuff here. I got pastrami. I got tuna fish. Well, the tuna fish ain't so good. But I gotta Reuben, I gotta roast beef . . .'

'Stevie, I know. Thanks.'

He looked at Kate. She declined politely. 'Ah, ya both fulla shit. I'm gonna eat the Reuben.'

'Eddie, listen to me,' Stevie said, between bites. 'I been thinking. I got problems with this suicide. It don't feel solid enough.' He munched away at his sandwich.

It was hot in the office. Sweat clung to the upper lip. A shirt stuck to a man's back. Outside the only glimpse of sky was a murky white, of summer haze baked in heat.

Mulcahy had been outlining his cross-examination

of Evans, the fingerprint expert. He put down the book.

'Listen to me, you guys,' he said. There was authority in his voice, and some exasperation, too. 'The defence is reasonable doubt. Reasonable doubt based, among other things, on the suggestion of suicide. We've been through this, and we've picked the defence and *we . . . are . . . going with it.*'

'Eddie,' said Stevie. 'It come in the mail.'

He held up the answering machine, a black plastic box, dusty, with the cords wrapped around it.

'And,' he said, his mouth still full of sandwich, 'there ain't no message from Samuel Whitakuh on it.'

They all fell silent. Mulcahy paused and looked around the room. 'We have three days before trial,' he said, after a moment's thought. 'We don't have time to change course now. We've got to focus.

'Remember something else. We don't have to prove this case. If everybody walks into that jury room confused, we win. Reasonable doubt. O'Hanlon needs answers, but I only need questions. Maybe he did call, and Shepard's now afraid to admit it. Maybe it was his fingerprint, maybe it wasn't. Maybe it was his jacket, maybe it wasn't. Nobody saw him there. Pebbles could have been any damn pebbles. And so on. *I only need questions!* Just keep the *focus.*'

Stevie shrugged, mopping up the mayonnaise from the wax-paper with the last of his Reuben. 'Sure,' he said.

'Stevie?' Mulcahy asked, some time later.

'Yah?'

'Why did you get six sandwiches?'

He took a bite out of the roast beef: a large bite. He worked his jaws round a mouthful of food. 'Tree of us, ain't theah?'

Mulcahy nodded.

'Well then.'

Mulcahy turned to Kate. 'Anything on Creel?'

'Pete's list hasn't come yet, but it should be here next week.'

'We're on trial next week.'

She shrugged. 'I've tried everything. Nothing else has worked.'

'Keep at it, Kate.'

Monday night, 5 September, Labour Day. It was the night before the case would go to trial. Most of America was within fifteen feet of a barbecue, but Ed Mulcahy stood alone in his fourth-floor kitchen, where he had just finished his opening. He'd practised it there, leaning on the sink, watching his face in the window. Was it a convincing face, with its dark curls receding from the forehead, and maybe a little too much pudginess in the cheeks? Was it persuasive, as it recited the life story of Samuel Whitaker: the causes of depression, the loss of control, the suicide? His mind wandered from the window and the text, and he reopened his files – but not his forensic files, not his Shepard files. He reopened the Whitaker file. He heard Stevie's voice, over and over again. *It don't feel solid enough*.

His gaze fell upon the telephone. What the hell? he thought. She didn't mind any indignity. Only after Kate's line was ringing did it occur to him that he

269

hoped no male voice would answer, although he had no business having an opinion.

None did. She had been asleep, though. He apologised, and she assured him that it was all right. 'Kate, what do you think about this suicide, really?'

'I don't know,' she said, and then there was a long pause as she came fully awake. 'He was an alpha male, you know? And they force him aside in his professional life, while at the same time his wife falls apart . . . this Idlewild thing happens. He reached a breaking point. Maybe.'

'He was also shot at in the South Pacific, and marched through jungles. Is this a guy who just gives up?'

'You had told him that the mortgage was opened on his computer. After that stainless professional career, was he just not able to take the shame of exposure?'

Now it was Mulcahy's turn to confess he didn't know. He told her about Sir Sam's speech at the May partnership meeting. 'It was weird,' he said. 'One moment he's standing alone against a tide of fear, talking to us about courage, the next he's saying he's outlived his usefulness.'

'He said he'd outlived his usefulness?'

'Not exactly,' Mulcahy said. 'It wasn't quite clear what he was saying. Kate, did you know any rowers in college?'

'Yeah,' she said, 'I dated one for a while.'

'What kind of people are they?'

She paused. 'Boring,' she said with a laugh.

He asked her what she meant.

'Well,' she said, 'with Dave, it was just crew and the library, crew and the library. On and on and on.'

'Right,' he said. 'That's what I remember. One of the guys in my frat rowed crew. Same kind of guy.'

'Rowing and studying?'

'That's one way to put it. But another would be, he was the type of guy who didn't have any notion of giving up. He couldn't give up. He'd *die* on an ergometer before he'd stop pulling the thing. It just wasn't in his nature to do anything else.'

At the other end of the line, she was silent. They were both thinking that Samuel Whitaker hadn't simply rowed. He'd been on the winning boat at Henley.

'Kate,' said Mulcahy, 'there were eighty, maybe ninety partners in the partnership meeting at the Faulkner that night. And Sam Whitaker was the only one of them who wanted to fight.'

She wished him good luck.

Part III

23

It was 6 September: Suffolk Superior Courthouse, Pemberton Square. Judge David Grosso's session, Room 8b at 9.30 a.m. on a steaming Tuesday, the day after Labour Day. Outside the session, a rabble of criminal lawyers, news reporters, family, idlers, cops, and court officers milled about, the hallway noise growing with each passing minute. A man with a blue folder poked his head in and just as quickly, vanished. An old man with a cane walked in and took a seat. Was he lost? Who knew?

Outside there was no breath of life, no hint of autumn, only the pale white cast of a suffocating heat. It was a day for trudging grimly to the office. The streets around Pemberton Square were full of sullen passers-by. Summer's attitude had gone, and left behind only its stale humidity, reeking like a sweat-soaked gym bag.

In the lobby and in the session, the air was still and muggy. The air conditioning was malfunctioning again. Two large fans buzzed furiously, with no measurable effect. A court officer, for whom no case was sensational enough to divert attention from the *World*, paged through the newspaper.

The bench was of oak, dark, musty, a relic of a 1930s project long since past any pretence of elegance, a joyless, faded brown. On the floor was imitation cork linoleum, innocent of wax and deeply embedded with grime. Light penetrated the dusty panes in the square window frames poorly. The heat penetrated better than the light. And the air penetrated least of all.

Paul O'Hanlon had already arrived. He cut a wide path in the courtroom. The searching eyes in his jowly face had lit upon each newsperson he'd seen since stepping off the elevator. He had endured no end of pressure from Connell on this one, but he had finished his preparation, and at last he was out of the office and the library and in the place he understood, the place he liked to be. And he didn't mean to lose. So he stood in the gallery, declining, at some length, and with careful explanation, to comment on the heinous crime committed by the defendant and the overwhelming evidence against him. Dressed in a dark grey chalk-stripe suit (apparently indifferent to the heat), an Egyptian cotton shirt with spread collar, and a shimmering silk tie, O'Hanlon looked more like an investment banker than a public prosecutor. As they say in the DA's offices, Paul had put on the aftershave for this one.

O'Hanlon's ham hands played circles in the air. A junior ADA and an investigator attended and provided knowing shakes of the head. The pencils raced across the reporters' notepads.

At 9.45 a.m., Ed Mulcahy stepped out of the elevator with a banker's box, sidled through the mob, and entered the session. Wordlessly, he nodded at O'Hanlon, and walked straight to the defence table where he placed the box. He returned for a perfunctory handshake, and then sat, staring forward.

'Mr Mulcahy, do you have a moment?' A reporter approached. But Mulcahy did not turn, and did not answer. She shrugged and returned to O'Hanlon.

By 9.55, the session had filled. Kelly, the clerk, entered from the lobby, athwart the bench. They all seem to be named Kelly. 'He'll see counsel,' he said sourly, with the time-honoured gruffness of a Suffolk clerk. The crowd grew quieter, watching. O'Hanlon rose and, attended grandly, marched to the lobby. Mulcahy followed alone.

'Good morning, Counsel.'

'Good morning, Your Honour,' said the lawyers in unison. Judge Grosso indicated the two chairs before his desk. Mulcahy and O'Hanlon sat, the latter flanked by his aides de camp. The judges' lobbies in the Suffolk sessions are spare indeed. The walls were a dingy lime colour, the desk purely institutional. Apart from three wooden chairs, the only other things in the room were a telephone, a bookcase, and a milkcrate full of files.

'Have you gentlemen had adequate time to discuss this case?' Grosso asked. The silver-haired judge regarded the lawyers over the tops of his bifocals.

'I believe we have, Your Honour,' said O'Hanlon.

'There will be no change of plea,' said Mulcahy.

Judge Grosso fixed him with a stare. His eyes were a pale blue, and the gaze was a piercing one. He was a large man, as tall as John Shepard, but broader. His face betrayed no expression except an intent concentration.

'Very well,' he said. 'Are both sides ready for trial?'

'The Commonwealth is ready,' said O'Hanlon.

'The defendant renews his motion for a change of venue.'

'The motion is denied.'

'We renew our motion for a continuance,' said Mulcahy softly.

'Mr Mulcahy, are there any new grounds?' asked the judge.

'The grounds are the same, Your Honour.'

'The motion is denied.'

'On this one, I need to make a record, Your Honour.'

'Of course. Paul, please ask Mrs Lewis to come in.'

Kelly left to fetch the stenographer. When she had been seated, at the ready, Judge Grosso said, 'The defence has a motion?'

Mulcahy softly repeated the grounds for his request. He had just been retained. He lacked time adequately to prepare. It appeared that prior counsel had failed to undertake certain tests which might lead to evidence probative for the defence. Discretion would suggest that, in a murder case, some solicitude be given to the rights of a defendant.

O'Hanlon began to respond, but the judge cut him off. 'The Commonwealth's objection is noted,' he began. And then he, too, in fluid prose, dictated an order denying the motion: noting that the defendant had been represented by able and experienced defence counsel, had attended previous hearings in the case,

278

had not identified any particular witness who was unavailable today, and could not, by switching counsel on the eve of trial, delay matters at such high inconvenience to the Court, the witnesses, and the orderly process of justice. 'And so the Court exercises its discretion to deny the motion,' he finished. 'Any further motions?'

'We move for leave to conduct our own *voir dire*, Your Honour.'

'Denied, except for the questions on pretrial publicity, which I will ask. I believe you know the practice here, Mr Mulcahy.'

'May I be heard?' the lawyer asked.

Judge Grosso frowned. 'Certainly,' he said. 'Mrs Lewis, please place this on the record as well.'

Mulcahy smiled. He knew this was a pantomime. On a hot September morning, there was not a chance in a thousand Judge Grosso would allow him to muck around with *voir dire*. But there was a deeper purpose to this fencing. Mulcahy had been absent from criminal practice for too long. He needed to re-establish a presence: polite, deferential, but firm and persistent. Half of what you do in a trial is by the rules. The other half is what you get away with because it looks to everybody like you know what you're doing. He needed to start educating the judge that he knew what he was doing. Even if he didn't.

He also needed to lose a couple of rounds now: establish some sympathy. Something told him he might need a close call or two in the coming days.

'Your Honour,' Mulcahy began, again softly, '*voir dire* conducted by the Court is never very effective, with all due respect. Let me give the Court an example. The Court will ask a question, looking out from the bench, a position of authority and strength, a position reinforced, if I might make the observation, by Your Honour's somewhat striking physical presence, and the Court says, "Is there anyone here who feels that he is subject to bias such that he would not be able to render a fair verdict?" Well, the Court is asking for a confession of weakness from a group which already feels somewhat intimidated. I submit that the person in the group who does suffer from such a bias would be intimidated from revealing it in those circumstances. By contrast, one on one questioning from the lawyer is, in my limited experience, much more likely to bring out the kind of bias which might disable a juror. Judge, I am not asking for a lot of time . . .'

'The motion is denied. Anything further?'

Mulcahy paused. One of the unusual job requirements of a trial lawyer is the ability to drop a point in mid-sentence and veer off in another direction, like a hound which suddenly catches a new scent. 'Defendant,' he said with perfect equanimity, 'has moved that he be permitted to sit at counsel table.'

'That motion,' said Judge Grosso, 'is allowed. Anything else?'

There was nothing. 'All right, gentlemen,' said Grosso, 'let's go pick a jury.'

When Mulcahy returned to the courtroom, Shepard had been brought in, flanked by two court officers. His suit hung loosely on him, flapping at his chest. The bravado was there – he had his chest puffed out – but his eyes were a little nervous.

Mulcahy came to him and they shook hands. 'How're we doin', man?' Shepard asked.

'One for four. Don't worry. It's just batting practice. Buck up!' Mulcahy tried to invest his infield chatter with some of the pluck he remembered from Shepard. But his client merely nodded, eyes glancing about the room. Mulcahy returned to his seat. In a moment, the court officer led Shepard to the adjoining chair, then stepped a few feet to the side. But not far.

The *venire* was brought in, a room full of uncertain citizens. They filled the gallery. Jury selection began. Mulcahy felt, as he always did, the futility of trying to keep up with the clerk, racing through the handwritten forms, stealing a glance at each juror, as Kelly rattled out the names. Kelly saw *voir dire* as he saw most aspects of trials: a pointless and malicious conspiracy to keep him from the newspaper.

'Comm'wealth content?' he demanded at the first sidebar, pronouncing the word, as all clerks do, with two syllables. His tone dared the prosecution to be anything but content. But Paul O'Hanlon was not content. He looked down at Kelly with a frown. 'When I am content, Mr Kelly, I will be sure to let you know,' he said.

Back and forth they went. As the morning went on the box filled by fits and starts, those jurors who passed the test shrugging as if to say 'Sorry' to those who had walked the gauntlet of lawyers, only to be excused a moment later.

At one-thirty, Mulcahy struck his last juror, a secretary in an engineering firm. She seemed all right on paper, but he hadn't liked the way she refused to

281

look at the other jurors when she took her seat in the box. He needed them to work together, to be persuaded by each other. So he struck her.

But what followed was worse. A housewife from Roslindale. As she stepped briskly to the box, Mulcahy's eyes caught the asterisk on the page and the fine script at the bottom, which described her son's death in the Northeastern University mugging two years before. No, no, no, he thought.

'Defence strikes Juror 31,' he said, when they reached the sidebar.

Kelly smiled at him. 'Yer outta per-emptories, Counselluh. You assertin' cause?'

Mulcahy's heart sank. He looked at his notes. He had run through his peremptory challenges – the allotted number of times he could reject a juror without giving a reason. Now he was left only with 'cause'. And, unless the juror knows a party, or blurts out a confession of bias, cause is infrequently found. *Never* strike a juror without checking who's coming next. Never. He knew that. He looked up. Grosso leaned down from the bench.

'Your Honour, she's a crime victim,' he began. 'We move to strike for cause.'

'Denied. Is the Commonwealth content?'

O'Hanlon beamed. 'The Commonwealth is content, Your Honour.'

'Very well,' said Grosso. 'Mr Kelly, swear the panel.' It was 2.45 p.m. Sixteen citizens of the Commonwealth, twelve jurors and four alternates, rose self-consciously to their feet. Making shift to look somewhere other than into the eyes of any other human being in the room, they repeated the oath after

Clerk Kelly, in that anonymity-craving unison of jurors everywhere. When they sat again, none of them looked at John Shepard. At that point, they rarely do.

The trial of John V. Shepard, accused of committing murder in the first degree by deliberately premeditated malice aforethought, in violation of chapter 265, section one, of the General Laws of the Commonwealth of Massachusetts, was underway.

Kate Maher had not been in the courtroom for the empanelling. In the morning she'd had a couple of meetings, one with a client, another with a partner who had called to chew her out for a delay on his project. It wasn't until three that she had slipped off to the office on Bromfield Street. Finding it empty, she let herself in and sat down at the laptop. The heat was stifling. It seemed indifferent to the air conditioner, for all the machine's racket.

Kate flipped on the switch, plugged the phone jack into the modem, and waited for the menu screen to appear. It was slow. One hand brushed her hair out of her face.

Perhaps it was the heat, but the delay did seem interminable. When at last the menu screen came up, she placed the cursor over her file name, 'CCslpbrf', and pressed the 'enter' key. The machine beeped back at her, and in little grey letters this legend appeared:

Document not available.

'What?' she asked the screen. It stared back at her. She tried again. The computer gave her the same response.

Kate was pretty handy with computers, but even those who are handy do what the world does when the machine acts up. They switch the machine off, hope the elves vanish, utter an incantation, and try again.

When she did that, again tapping in 'CCslpbrf' and pressing the 'enter' key, the document appeared on the screen. Strange.

Kate got to work.

They weren't anonymous, but they were largely blank. Mulcahy had the names from the juror questionnaires, but the information was limited and *voir dire* merely an exercise. Over the coming weeks, each would acquire an identity. Mr Brody, he remembered, and Ms DeVito. Then there was Tie Pin man. He wore a tie pin and a pocket protector and his sideburns were a little long for the fashion. An engineer, according to his form. In the corner was the Ancient Mariner, a skinny old gent with a golf shirt buttoned to the top button, and flowing white hair. Then the retired contractor. Then Mrs Watts, dressed primly in a suit, holding a handbag, one of only two blacks on the jury. And there were the others. The schoolteacher. The mechanic. The graduate student. The minister's wife. Mulcahy thought he'd lucked out on her. O'Hanlon had used his last per-emptory on another student. She'd been next in the *venire*. And then there was the lady from Roslindale. She was frowning already.

It is a bizarre system. A man's life is in their hands. You can talk to them, but they can't talk back. You can put the evidence before them, but only once.

They can't ask to have that witness back on the stand. Nor will they get to see those exhibits everyone is talking about until the end. They can't say, 'Yes, we understand about that point, get on with it.' They can't say, 'Please tell us about such and such.'

And you never really know who they are. Things are different in other states. In California, the litigants will spend a king's ransom empanelling a jury, and at the end of the trial the lawyers will know more about the jurors than the jurors know about the evidence. And in Texas? Texas jury trials grew out of a time when there wasn't nuthin' else to do for diversion but set in on a trial. In Texas, you can do almost anything you want in jury selection short of bribing a juror. Actually, that's not quite correct, according to some out-of-towners who've ventured into the Lone Star State. They say that it appeared to them that you *can* bribe a juror, just so long as you and he are from Texas and the medium of exchange is not cash.

Not so in the Commonwealth, where the criminal trial dates to the time of the Puritan, and where all of that would have seemed like too much fun. A Commonwealth jury is austere and even somewhat mysterious, from the empanelling until the verdict.

At the end of the first day, Mulcahy was left almost alone. The courtroom emptied fast, and O'Hanlon's people had cleared out quickly. Mulcahy was packing his boxes when he noticed an elderly woman waiting uncertainly by the rail.

'Ma'am?' he said.

'Mr Mulcahy?' she asked. Her voice was soft, but firm.

285

'Yes, ma'am?'

'I just wanted to bless you for all you have done.'

He examined her more closely. She was a frail woman, hair gone completely white, not above five foot three in height, wearing a pale blue dress. Her cheeks were sunken, and her skin lined and pale. It seemed to be stretched too thin across her forehead. He recognised the resemblance in the eyes.

'Mrs Shepard?' he asked.

'Yes, sir.'

He shook her hand, and she took his in both of her hands. And then she embraced him. He was surprised – she was such a small woman, to have given birth to such a large man. Her ribs quivered like autumn leaves beneath his hands.

'You'll do your best, I know you will,' she said, her voice quaking.

'Yes, ma'am,' he said, 'I will.'

'And the Lord Jesus will provide,' she said. 'Mr Mulcahy, I'm sorry to carry on so.' She took a deep breath. 'I just wanted to say thank you.'

'I'll do my best,' he said.

'Thank you. Thank you,' she said. 'Thank you so much.'

She turned and made for the door.

And then she stopped, and asked, 'Mr Mulcahy, may I ask whether you believe that the Lord Jesus Christ is your saviour?'

He stared at her, stunned, and then his eyes fell. 'I, I –' he said. 'I try to. It's difficult sometimes.'

The little woman was silent. She stood clasping a handbag with both hands, and her eyes burned on him, just as her son's could do. Mulcahy could see that he had that of her.

Then he tried to make light of it, for the tension was powerful. 'I think it may be more important to put my faith in the presumption of innocence,' he said. But he knew instantly it was the wrong thing to say.

'Oh, no, Mr Mulcahy,' she said. 'Oh, no. No, sir, I am very grateful to you, and I know that it is your job to think about these legal matters. Please do not take this the wrong way, but it is more important that you put your faith in the Lord Jesus Christ. I would rather you do that, sir.'

He felt the colour in his cheeks and didn't answer. He couldn't return her gaze, and merely nodded when she said again, 'Please.'

The doors swung open, and closed, and he was alone.

Paul O'Hanlon stood in the District Attorney's office, two floors below, glowering at his boss. Connell had offered him a seat, but he wouldn't take it. 'Mike, for Christ's sake . . .'

'Right. I should bet the election on this trial instead.'

'You should have a little faith in your people, Mike.'

The DA shook his head. 'You've got no eye-witness.'

'You don't care if I've got ten eyewitnesses.'

Connell smiled. O'Hanlon was right. 'Paul,' he said, 'one knucklehead juror beats ten eyewitnesses, and one knucklehead verdict beats a hundred thousand votes.' The DA was shaking his head. 'I want him to plead,' he said. 'Plead him out to a second and wrap this up.'

'A second!'

'It's a life sentence, Paul, for Christ's sake.'

'Yeah. That's what the newspapers will say. And the parole board gets him the street in fifteen.'

'Paul. Do it. Get that kid Mulcahy in here.'

24

At the outset of a criminal trial, what is defence counsel but a spectator with a better seat? It is the prosecutor's case to put on. He must prove the elements through admissible evidence. In a circumstantial case, such as the case against John Shepard, there are many traps. Chains of custody must be unbroken. Expert reports must be tight. Ordinary citizens – 'civilian' witnesses, the prosecutors call them – must be counted on not to fail. A laundry clerk who identifies a jacket ticket three times in preparation may flinch on the witness stand, or become confused. The records keeper for the credit card company must do his job correctly.

No such burden rests on the defence. Counsel can lie back silently for days, watching, waiting to hammer at the one link in the chain which may fail. Mulcahy knew the prosecutor's evidence thoroughly, of course. He had had all of the discovery material for a week. It was the theatre of the thing, the themes which Paul O'Hanlon would work, his manner, which would be new. He settled in to watch and wait.

Always more at home in the session than in the DA's corner office, Paul O'Hanlon was an instinctive courtroom lawyer with a string of felony convictions broken only that once in four years. He worked without notes and used the room easily, ranging about the well comfortably but respecting the jury box, keeping away from it in the early going, only venturing to touch it late in a trial, when he felt a rapport had been built. He had a rich voice, an actor's voice.

What he loved best was cross-examination. When the defendant was a young tough so bold or foolish as to venture to the witness stand – and defendants usually are young toughs – O'Hanlon had the knack of making it visceral. He called them out. In questioning he often seemed but a hair's breadth from a fistfight, as though, worsted suit and all, he might leap into the box and pummel the defendant. His jowls shook, he leered, he rolled his eyes. He strained to find a way to push the witness towards humiliation. He squared off against them and challenged their intelligence, their manhood, whatever they took for honour in their own topsy-turvy world. It often had the trick of bringing the defendant to surrender his guard, to lay aside his affected humility and show the jury a flash of the meanness which, O'Hanlon would later argue, led him to the crime.

And he was a storyteller. He would not simply drop a pile of evidence on the jury room table. He would sift it, weave it, hang it like ornaments around a tree, bearing in mind always the tree's own symmetry. And for long moments at a time, Mulcahy was himself rapt at O'Hanlon's opening, at the story of the ambitious, vengeful corporate associate, betrayed by his mentor, a slave to his own arrogance, who, to spite the man he thought had betrayed him, had sabotaged his transaction, and then murdered him in cold blood. He listened to the description of how Shepard's anger had boiled within him, how he had, at length, seized on the vicious plan to stage a false suicide. How he had littered the crime scene with evidence of his presence – how he had carried that evidence away with him on his jacket and even lodged in the tyres of his car on his mad flight westward.

It was mid-afternoon when O'Hanlon finished. The jurors looked disturbed. Perhaps their discomfiture was due, in part, to the unrelenting heat that day, for it continued stifling in the session. The buzz of the fans brought more annoyance than relief. Lying before Mulcahy on the oaken table was the yellow pad containing his outline, with its carefully regimented argument headings and numbered subheadings, the cogent, ordered narrative of the collapse and self-destruction of Samuel Whitaker, so painstakingly drafted over so many nights.

He rose, awkwardly, looking down at it. And then he remembered a wise old prosecutor who'd said to him once, 'Never make a jury a promise you're not sure you can keep.'

He looked once more at the yellow pad and then left it there as he walked over to the box.

'Ladies and gentlemen,' he said, 'the man seated at counsel table, John Shepard, is guilty of a lot of things. He's guilty of having a temper, he's guilty of having a mouth like a stevedore. He's guilty of a fair degree of ego. He is a sinner. As all of us are.

'But the evidence will not show that he is guilty of this charge. A terrible mistake has been made here. A cruel mistake. A mistake caused by the Commonwealth's desperate need to take what appears to be a tragic suicide, and transform it into some headline-grabbing murder. We do not pretend to know Samuel Whitaker's mind: his fears, his emotions, whatever it was that led him . . . that led to the events of 16 May. The evidence, the credible evidence, will not bear out Mr O'Hanlon's wild speculations. When the evidence is in, the prosecution will not have proved beyond a reasonable doubt that John Shepard had anything to do with this terrible event. The evidence will show that John Shepard is an innocent man.

'I will return to ask for your verdict of acquittal.'

And he sat. Well then. He wondered if anyone had noticed that he hadn't any earthly idea of his defence.

That morning the printout of LawNet registrants had arrived. Meeting after court in Stevie's office, the defence team opened the envelope excitedly, but their enthusiasm soon cooled as they looked at the row upon closely spaced row of names and addresses. George Creel had not opened a new account, not in his own name, but almost two thousand other people had.

'Figure three minutes a name, to call information and the person,' Stevie said, 'and you got six thousand minutes.'

'A hundred hours,' Ed muttered.

'Two man weeks,' said Stevie. 'Not to mention the phone bill.'

So they sat in silence for a while longer. Then Stevie said, 'Suppose you're Creel. Someone tries to kill you, you're scared, ya leave town in the dead of night. Ya move to a different city and start using a pseudonym. One thing ya might do is keep your real first name. Ya don't want to have someone call you Phil, and then have to remember that your new name is Phil. So maybe he's still George.'

It was a slim reed, but no one had a better idea. They divided up the twenty-four pages, and after half an hour had highlighted fifty possible accounts: eighteen Georges, and another thirty-two with the initial G.

'What the hell?' said Ed. 'Might as well try.'

Of the fifty possibles, forty-two had listed phone numbers. Stevie theorised that Creel would likely *not* have a listed phone. There were eight of those. Stevie rattled them off. 'George Fiske in East Barrington, R.I., George Johansen in Madison, Wisconsin, G. Goldman in Berkeley, Cal., G. Seal in Lincoln, Nebraska, George Salidis in N.Y.C., G. Newman in Bethesda, George Tasker in Fort Worth.'

'East Barrington,' Stevie said. 'Providence. First stop on the Amtrak. Kate, I need phone numbers for the twenty largest law firms in Providence, Madison, Wisconsin, Lincoln, Nebraska, Dallas-Fort Worth, and D.C. For D.C., better give me the fifty largest. Hell, better copy the *Martindale* entries, since we may need a lawyer's name.' It would mean a lot of cumbersome copying of *Martindale-Hubbell*, the legal directory, and an unexplained whopper on Kate's 'administration' copy charge, but she could do it.

25

Paul O'Hanlon had almost a cinematographer's theory of trial work. He began with a snapshot to tease them. Then he moved to motive, to lay the groundwork for persuasion. He'd leave to last the physical evidence – giving the jury the tools they needed to follow their emotions. Paul O'Hanlon knew juries.

But John Shepard didn't, and during that first day of trial testimony Mulcahy wondered if he was going to need a seatbelt to keep the big man still. Shepard would shift in the chair, lean over to whisper, write a note, wring his hands together, take his lawyer by the shoulder. It got even the court officers nervous.

'You can get her on such and such,' he'd whisper, and would write a note, pointing at it. Or he'd whisper a question. Or be at Mulcahy's ear, saying, 'Object, can't you object to that?' No doubt trial work would be easier without clients. There's enough to do in listening to the direct, cataloguing the important points for cross, trying to stay on top of the reactions of judge and jury, and making objections.'

'John,' Ed whispered, 'put a lid on it.'

'There ain't a lid big enough, Ed,' he shot back.

O'Hanlon had begun that Thursday morning with Angelica Biali, the maid, who took the stand meekly, and answered each question like a startled animal. She would set the scene for him, and wept as she described the horror in Mr Whitaker's study on the morning of 17 May. When they brought them to her, she turned away from the photographs and wept again.

Over in the Bromfield Street office, the telethon was underway. Stevie would dial the law firm and ask for George Fiske or George Seal or whomever. The operator would say that there was no George Fiske. Stevie would ask her to check – he was a new employee. She would assure him that there was no such employee. Stevie would hang up the phone and check the law firm off his list.

On that first day, they eliminated Providence, Madison and Lincoln. By nightfall, there were no leads.

Friday came. In 8b, O'Hanlon began the sketch of Shepard. Poor Hester DeSantis was one of the first witnesses he called for this purpose. The witness stand was the very last place on earth the old, somewhat stooped lady with the white hair done in a bun wanted to be. It was plain to every eye in the room that even after three months, she had not recovered from the shock of the death of her employer of almost thirty years. She barely whispered, and every juror, full of sympathy, craned forward to hear her.

'Mrs DeSantis,' said O'Hanlon, 'I want to draw your attention to a meeting that took place in Mr

Whitaker's office between Mr Whitaker and the defendant one afternoon in mid-March. Do you recall such a meeting?'

And he had to beckon her when she nodded gamely, too shy to speak, reminding her to answer audibly. 'Yes, sir,' she said.

'Your desk is just outside Mr Whitaker's door, is it not?'

'Yes, sir,' she said.

'And do you, would you, see people as they entered and left his office?'

'Yes, sir.'

'On the afternoon of 18 March, I think it was, tell the jury what you saw and heard.'

She nodded. 'Yes, sir,' she said. 'He – Mr Shepard, I mean – came in to see Mr Whitaker. He didn't ask or knock. He just burst in, sir. Then there was a lot of shouting and . . . he left.'

Shepard was at Mulcahy's ear, but he brushed him away. 'John,' he whispered, 'sit still and shut up.'

Up at the front the questioning proceeded. 'Mrs DeSantis, what did you hear the defendant say?'

She looked uncertain. 'Should I say the, the words . . . here?' she inquired of the judge. He smiled back at her kindly.

'Yes, Mrs DeSantis,' Judge Grosso said gently. 'You should say the words.'

'He said Mr Whitaker was a gutless . . .' She began to whisper. Mulcahy cringed. This kind of witness is deadly. 'A . . . gutless prick. I'm sorry. That was what he said. And he used other foul language of that kind, sir.' She reddened and looked up apologetically at the judge again. It was clear to Mulcahy that everyone in the room was sure she was telling the truth. She went on, under questioning, to describe Shepard's yelling about a partnership vote, and Whitaker's betrayal.

'Mrs DeSantis?' asked O'Hanlon. 'Please describe the tone of voice.'

'Oh, yes. He was shouting. Shouting at Mr Whitaker. All the girls heard him.'

The dutiful student in Mulcahy thought of objecting to what all the girls heard. But there really was no point. The prosecutor went on, 'Did he say anything else?'

'Yes,' she said, with gathered conviction. 'He said, "I won't ever forget this, Sam," and then he walked out and slammed the door.'

'I won't ever forget this?' O'Hanlon asked. He never was quite able to hear the answers he liked the first time through.

'Yes, sir. "I won't ever forget this, Sam." That was what he said.'

O'Hanlon nodded. Then, as though it was an afterthought, he said, 'Oh, Mrs DeSantis, did he say anything to you?'

She blushed again. 'Yes,' she said. 'He walked by me as he slammed the door. And I was looking at him, I suppose. And he said to me, "And fuck you too, you scabby witch."'

'I see,' said O'Hanlon. Mrs Watts turned to her neighbour. The lady from Roslindale didn't look happy, either. O'Hanlon went on.

'Did Mr Whitaker have a computer terminal in his office?'

'Yes, sir, he did.'

'Did you ever see him use it?'

'Oh, no.'

'Never?'

'No, sir. You see, everyone got one when the new management came in. But he never used it. He never went to the training.' She shook her head and the jurors smiled, picturing the dear old secretary's bootless reminders to her boss to go to the training.

'One more thing, Mrs DeSantis. Were you familiar with Mr Whitaker's handwriting?'

'Oh, yes, sir, for thirty years.'

'Was he right- or left-handed?'

'Left-handed, sir.'

'Your witness,' said O'Hanlon, returning to his chair.

Mulcahy hesitated before rising to cross examine. Left-handed? he wondered, as he strode to the lectern.

'Good morning, Mrs DeSantis.'

'Good morning, Mr Mulcahy,' she said, trying to smile at him.

'Actually, I have only a few questions for you. I want to ask you about the months before Mr Whitaker's death. Had he acted strangely in any way? Out of character, anything odd or unusual about his routines?'

She pondered for a moment, and said, 'No, sir, I don't think so.'

'I see. Well, in the week before he died, he was in the office, was he not?'

'Yes, he was.'

'Did he have any visitors out of the ordinary?'

'No, not that I can recall.'

'Any unusual calls?'

'I can't think of any.'

That was when it struck him, in the middle of his cross-examination of Hester DeSantis. He stopped, swaying lightly on his feet, as the full import of O'Hanlon's throwaway question rose up like a wall before him.

'Mr Mulcahy?'

It was Judge Grosso, looking down over the top of his bifocals.

'Excuse me, Your Honour.' He threw one up for grabs. 'Do you remember who was the last person he talked to?'

She thought for a moment. 'That was Attorney Russell, I think.'

'He called her?'

'No, I think he asked me to arrange to have her meet him for lunch at the Bay on that last Friday before ... before it happened. That was his club.' She dabbed at her eyes with a handkerchief, and tried to smile.

'I understand. And who was Attorney Russell?'

'She was the attorney for the buyer in the Idlewild transaction, I believe.'

'I see. Did you arrange for the lunch?'

'Yes, I remember that I did. I called her office and they said that she would join him at twelve-thirty. It was a Friday and Mr Whitaker said he wouldn't be back after lunch. And I set it up.'

'Thank you, Mrs DeSantis.' Mulcahy returned to his seat.

They had barely time for a sandwich at Bromfield Street, for Mulcahy had seen the Count in the gallery, and wanted to study his notes before the afternoon session. But he knew.

'Still like suicide, Eddie?' Stevie asked.

'Let's deal with that tonight. Jesus, what an idiot I am!'

'Look, don't kill yourself,' he said. 'Shit happens. Where are ya gonna find out he's left-handed? We got a lotta time. Lotta time.'

Ed asked them how they were doing on Creel, but the news was not good. They had eliminated all of the 'Gs' but Salidis and Goldman.

'Kate,' Stevie said, 'I don't like either one a them guys. Berkeley might be a student. And owah pasty-faced hacker probably don't pretend to be Jewish. So Goldman I doubt. Same thing on Salidis. Owah guy don't pretend he's a Greek, probably. Besides, better hope it ain't New York, God knows how many law firms they got there. We'll never find him.'

Kate frowned. 'Washington isn't much better on that last point, but I think we should keep on the DC firms.'

'Kate, we've done forty. We're down to firms of a hundred or so.'

'Big enough for MIS departments,' she said, 'and Washington is only an Amtrak away from the Hub. Besides, what would Creel be in Washington?'

And when no one responded, she answered the question herself. 'He'd be a new man.'

Stevie began telephoning the next twenty-five firms, and asking for George Newman.

After lunch in 8b, O'Hanlon put the Count on the stand, and though the afternoon was hot and the jury seemed sleepy, he took a while with the preliminaries. Mulcahy looked to his left. Shepard shrugged.

'Did you and the members of the management committee have negotiations with Mr Whitaker in February 1992?'

'We did,' said the Count.

'What was the nature of that negotiation?'

The Count cleared his throat, and took a sip from the water glass. 'Sam Whitaker,' he said, 'was one of the great lawyers in this city for many years. For many years, he ran our law firm. Everyone had the highest regard for him, and we, as a firm, are greatly indebted to him.

'But we felt he had reached an age where he had passed his effectiveness in management. And, like many great men, he was unwilling to let go.'

Shepard was scribbling a note. Mulcahy looked down. 'The serpent was more subtle than any beast of the field,' he read, and put the note in his pocket.

Shanklin went on. 'So we had, Mr O'Hanlon, an unpleasant negotiation that ended in February.'

'What were the specific subjects of that negotiation?'

'Well, mainly, we wanted to arrange a retirement figure for Mr Whitaker. And we offered him what I think was a generous package. But it required him to step down from his practice in eighteen months.'

'Did the subject of John Shepard arise in this conversation?'

'Yes,' said the Count. 'Mr Whitaker asked what would happen if he did not accept. He was advised that, of course, he could not be forced to retire, and that if he did not do so, he would continue to practise,

301

with his compensation governed by the management committee, like everyone else's. And in the course of that discussion he also mentioned that he had planned to put up John Shepard for partner the following month.'

'What response did you make?'

'We told him that would no longer be possible.'

'And did he make a decision?'

'Yes. He elected the severance package.'

'And Mr Shepard?'

'He was not nominated for partnership.'

'Mr Shanklin, did Mr Whitaker contact you several days later regarding Mr Shepard?'

'Yes, he did.'

'What did he say?'

'He upbraided me for having disclosed our discussion. He said that Shepard had stormed into his office and shouted at him. He said Shepard described the entire arrangement.'

'Your witness, Mr Mulcahy,' said O'Hanlon, and sat. Mulcahy wanted to get into the mortgage. It had been edited on the victim's terminal. Had something passed between the Count and Whitaker? Could the Count's testimony help with the suicide theory?

'Mr Shanklin,' he began, 'Mr Whitaker was the lawyer in charge of Freer Motley's team, representing Depositors' Fidelity in the Idlewild LBO, was he not?'

'He was.'

'In May of this year, did it come to your attention that there was an error in one of the mortgage documents in that deal?'

'Yes.'

'Claims for malpractice were made, informally, against Freer Motley, by the bank?'

Shanklin stared at him angrily, but other than speak to a dozen managing partners and ensure that this man never again practised in a first-class firm in the city, he knew he had no alternative but to answer. 'They were,' he said.

'You ended up settling those claims?'

'We did.'

'On what terms?'

'You very well know that the terms of that settlement are confidential, Mr Mulcahy.'

Judge Grosso was peering over his bifocals. 'Is this germane, Counsel?'

'Let me lay some foundation, Your Honour. Were the terms of the settlement known to Mr Whitaker?'

'I assume so,' said the Count.

'Well, you and he were present at a partners' meeting in which the terms were explained, were you not?'

'Yes.'

'Those terms imposed financial hardship on all of the partners?'

'I don't know if I'd call it . . .'

'Financial disadvantage, then?'

'Yes, certainly.'

'And this financial disadvantage was the direct result of a transaction for which he had been the lead lawyer?'

'Yes. That is true.'

'What were the terms?'

O'Hanlon rose to object, but Judge Grosso nodded him off. It was going to come in now. And so the jury listened as the Count explained the $140 million contingent guaranty. But none listened so aptly as the reporters, who knew they had tonight's evening news lead and tomorrow's headline.

When the Count had finished his answer, Ed studied the sallow witness, with the dark eyes, the widow's peak, the sunken cheeks, the impassive thin lips. It is tempting to prod an angry witness: he may say something foolish. There was so much more that Mulcahy might ask him, so much about the Freer Motley coup, the changing of the guard, the slipping of power from Sam Whitaker's hands. But the Count was too smart to take chances with. A cross-examination in which you make a successful sortie and suffer no casualties is a good cross-examination. Better to be satisfied with little, than risk much. This evidence would help the suicide theory. Mulcahy studied the Count's face for a moment more, feeling regret: there was much more to mine there, and this would undoubtedly be the only chance he'd have, on this earth anyway, to control the questioning of Albert Shanklin. But he didn't know the answers. If you don't know the answers, don't ask the questions.

He sat down.

Shepard and Mulcahy had only five minutes in the lock-up before guards hustled the prisoners off to the van.

'John, two things. First, you got to sit still and shut up in there. Every time you flinch, stir, write a note, whisper, or scratch your balls, that jury thinks O'Hanlon's scored a point.'

'Yeah, I know. I'm sorry. I'm used to running the meeting, that's all. I'll try to be better, man.'

'We got another major problem, John.'

'Hell, I thought you scored some points on the Count,' Shepard said.

'Not Shanklin, DeSantis. Whitaker being left-handed.'

'Well, what the hell can we do?'

'John, are you giving me all the help you can give me?'

'What's that mean?'

'I don't like the story. That's a problem for our suicide theory, and I don't like the story. That call isn't on your machine. And he was left-handed.'

'Don't lose your nerve on me, Ed. Not now. And I'll be a better boy, I promise. No more whispering. I won't even scratch my balls any more, okay? Except when they itch.' He winked. Mulcahy couldn't fathom that face. We're not communicating, he thought, as the guards arrived to escort his client downstairs to the van.

When he returned to the session, Mulcahy found O'Hanlon waiting there for him. He stood uncomfortably. With the exhibits locked up and the judge and jury gone, the attorney's files all carried off, and the gallery empty, and yet standing there in his pinstripe suit, with the cufflinks just peeking out from the suit jacket, he looked like an actor left in costume on stage even after the props have been removed. But the source of his discomfort was otherwise: he didn't like being a messenger.

Mulcahy's first thought, as he pulled his two-wheeler into the corner office on the 6th floor, was that the District Attorney was shorter than he expected. But the handsome face was familiar to everyone with a television set, with its broad smile and the deeply set blue eyes under his sandy hair, with just the trace of white speckling the sideburns. He bounded up from behind his desk and across the office carpet to pump Ed's hand.

'This the guy, Paul?' he asked, as they came in, and then interrupted his own question with, 'Sit down, sit down, fellas.'

They took seats at a conference table across the carpeted office from his desk. 'Ed, I gotta tell you, it's great to see some new kid from nowhere giving Paul fits. I mean, you got him here, with a team of people every night, every weekend.' He winked at O'Hanlon, who sat stiffly.

'So I had to meet the kid who's doing it. Word is this case cost you your partnership. And a Harp to boot! I got to meet that kid. That shows some moxie.'

Mulcahy didn't know what to say. He hadn't expected accolades from the corner office, and hadn't heard any, from any source, in a while. So he didn't say anything. He stared down at the table.

'I hear you're working with Stevie George?'

'Yeah.'

'Give him my best. Been a long time,' Connell said.

'I will.'

'Ed, I gave up trial work a long time ago. I'm a politician, and a smart enough one to leave trials to the experts. But I do get a laugh seeing Paul have to bust his ass. He gets so used to winning, sometimes I worry he starts to get a little lazy.'

'Bullshit,' O'Hanlon said.

'Ah, lighten up, Paulie.' Now Connell was winking at Mulcahy. 'Where'd you go, the Cross?'

'Yes,' Ed said, 'class of 'seventy-nine.'

'Class of 'sixty-seven,' Connell said. And then he was off on the topic of the Holy Cross football team for another ten minutes. Ed began to wonder what his real agenda was. Connell, sensing this, came to the point.

He leaned forward in his chair, with just that look of a caring priest. 'Look, Ed, like I said, I'm no trial lawyer any more, but I've seen a lot of cases. Let me tell you something, because I think you're a good and decent guy. I think you're going to lose this one. You *might* win it. You're working your ass off, and you might pull it off, but I think that in the end, the jury will go out, and sweat a little, but then take a deep breath and do the right thing, and they'll come back and they'll all kind of give you that half-smile, you know the one, Paul, where it's like they are saying, "Sorry, Ed, we really liked you, but the evidence is the evidence," and kind of shrug at you. I think they'll convict. What do you think, Paul?'

'They'll convict,' he said.

'Look at him,' Connell said, grinning and shaking his head, 'he's one arrogant mick, isn't he? He always says that. But I got to admit, he's usually right. I think he's right this time, Ed. I think they'll convict. Maybe not. But probably. What do you think?'

It was a strange question to ask defence counsel. Ed shrugged, and looked back at him. 'Talk is cheap,' he said.

'Now,' Connell said, and the playfulness seemed to leave his voice, 'let me tell you what isn't cheap. Let me tell you about what I do know. If they convict, here's what will happen. People – not just lay people, but lawyers, Ed – will say, one, Shepard did it. Two, Mulcahy threw dirt on Sam Whitaker's grave to get him off. Three, he lost.

'That's what they'll say, and that's what they'll think. The criminal brethren will breathe easier they ain't competing with one more hotshot, and let the word get around to the drug dealers and pimps and such that you're an amateur. Downtown, the white shoes will be bullshit at you. And none of 'em will give a rat's ass about how hard you tried, or how well you did with a few witnesses. You'll be 0 and 1, lifetime, Ed. That much I know.'

He shrugged his shoulders, half smiling at Ed as at a wayward child.

'Why are you telling me this, Ms Connell?'

'Call me Mike, for Chrissakes, Ed. I am telling you this mostly for your own good, and a little bit for mine. Let me paint you two pictures. The first one is what I think is happening. You try the case. You lose it. You hang around the back of the Roxbury District Court, looking for court-appointed work. For a long time. Paulie, what do they get?'

'Sixty-five.'

'Sixty-five dollars an hour, Ed. Got any law school loans left to pay?

'Anyway, that's picture number one. Now picture number two. You plead him to second degree murder. Shepard does some time, a lot of time, fifteen years at least, but not his whole life, and if he's a good boy, there's a light at the end of the tunnel. I call Tim Cain at Freer, and I say, "Tim, this kid

Mulcahy's a helluva trial lawyer, and I think you guys screwed him, and it would mean something to the Governor's office to know that its bond counsel made it up to a friend of mine." I got a little juice with the Governor, you know, and your old friends at Freer do a lot of bond work. I could help you. This thing blows over, you get back to work at Freer where you belong. And let's be honest, I get something too. I get a bad guy guaranteed to go away for a long time. Everybody wins.'

Connell smiled beatifically. In truth, it was his favoured outcome: an outcome where everybody wins. Even if some win a little more than others. 'A little juice with the Governor' was becoming modesty, for everyone knew that Mike Connell was in the Governor's kitchen cabinet. It was widely bruited that Connell would announce for his office when the Govenor ran for Senate in 1994.

Mulcahy nodded slowly. 'Everyone except Shepard,' he said.

'Shepard wins too. He doesn't go away for ever. And let me tell you something else. There's talk around, lots of it, that the Governor is itching to move on to a Senate seat. Some people think I might run for Governor some day. Let's say I do. Let's say I do and I win, and I appoint the parole board. If I'm right about this trial, there's only one ticket out for Mr Shepard and that's commutation. Who do you think gets to sign the petition?'

Again, the beatific smile. 'Plead him out, Ed. Plead him to a second and get on with your life.'

They looked at him, not for an answer, for they knew he would not give one there, but for a hint, a

309

suggestion as to whether this young lawyer liked the heat or wanted a way out, a way out with face saved. Ed strove to mask his expression, remaining silent.

'Ed,' said the District Attorney after a moment, 'tell me something. You think he's innocent?'

He felt his face redden.

'Come on, Ed, we're off the fuckin' record, just a couple of Harps talking about cases. Tell me you think he's innocent. I just want to hear you say it. I want to hear your voice.'

'That's for the jury to say.'

'No, Ed, forgive me, the jury only says whether we proved it. Whether he is innocent, that's for you and me. And him. Bet you've asked yourself the same question. But I wonder if you've asked *him*.'

Now the District Attorney's eyes were all atwinkle again. 'Huh?' He was grinning at him, an infuriating grin. 'Huh? Think it over, Ed,' he said. 'Don't let me think the Cross graduated a knucklehead. All right?' And he smiled again and slapped him on the back, and said good-naturedly, 'Paul, get him the hell out of here, I gotta go meet some of our constituents.'

When they were at the door, he called out to them. 'Ed,' he said, 'I still didn't hear you say it!' And then he grinned at him, and went back to his desk.

Mulcahy walked uneasily to the lobby, where O'Hanlon left him by the door. 'What do you think, Counsellor?' the big prosecutor asked.

'I think,' said Ed, 'that I've just been offered a bribe.'

'Don't be a Boy Scout, Ed,' he said, just as John Shepard had done. 'Your client wouldn't.'

*

310

And so the first week of trial was over. It had not been a good one for the defence, and that Friday evening they clung to each other's company in the Bromfield Street office long after night had fallen. Like students after an exam gone badly, they went back through the questions, over and over again.

'Stevie, why do you think he'd offer a plea to murder two?'

'Who knows?' he shrugged. 'Don't start thinking O'Hanlon's too worried about his case, though. Ya know, Connell's a politician. He needs convictions and pleas. Alls it takes is one wild card on the jury, and that can happen in any case. Election's in two months, and Reising is killing him with that Din Bao bullshit. Fuckin' SJC. Look Sheila Brodsky in the eye and do that shit to the case.' Stevie shook his head. 'And that snake Reising, he don't care, fuckin' catnip to him. So Mike's playing the odds. If you plead him, Mike gets his scalp, and he's long gone from the prosecutor's office by the time Shepid gets out.'

Ed nodded. He replayed Connell's offer in his mind, particularly the portions concerning himself, which he had not related to Stevie and Kate. The conversation turned back to the evidence.

'What's to stop Mr Whitaker using his right hand?' Kate asked. She looked up hopefully from the laptop.

Mulcahy walked to the window and looked out at Bromfield Street. Stevie was still out on his tail. There was a huge throng milling in and out of Downtown Crossing. Must be a concert somewhere. The college kids were back in town.

'No, Kate. I don't think so.'

'It doesn't have to be perfect,' she said. 'Reasonable doubt, remember? We don't need answers. We need questions.'

'Right now I'd prefer a few answers. I don't know. I don't have time to think about it. He's into the forensics Monday morning, I'll bet.' He looked mournfully at the stacks of files on the table. 'I've got a lot of work to do.'

For the next hour Kate sat at the laptop. He reread his notes on the jacket.

'What on earth?' she muttered.

He looked up. She was staring at the screen.

'Kate?'

'Ed, come here, look at this.'

Mulcahy stood by Kate's side and squinted at the terminal. He couldn't see anything. It was the last page of the brief, the page with the signature block. Other than the fact that the block was out of alignment, nothing was out of the ordinary.

'Look at that signature block,' she said.

'Yeah?'

'I didn't type it that way.'

'Well, I sure as hell didn't,' he said to her.

'I know you didn't. I didn't. Stevie didn't. You didn't.'

'Whattayou two talking about?' Stevie asked.

'Ed, I call a document, it says it isn't there. Then it *is* there. I log on, and the machine says I saved a document at 1.34 a.m. Only I didn't. Now there's a formatting glitch I didn't put in.'

'We'll upgrade our computer on our next case, Kate, soon as we get a paying client . . .'

She wasn't listening to him. 'When you move a

document, sometimes you get these formatting glitches.' She looked at him, and now fear covered her face. 'It's not the laptop. I think – I think someone is getting into our files. Reading them. Copying them, maybe.'

Mulcahy felt a knot in his throat. 'Stevie, anyone else got a key to this place?'

'No, Ed, someone's *accessing* the files. By computer.'

'How?'

'The modem, I guess. I don't know. A week ago I called up a brief and it was unavailable. I didn't even think of it at the time, since I got it right back. But somebody else was in it – that's why it was unavailable. That's why it shows things opened when I didn't open them! Somebody must have copied this brief too, and the formatting was messed up.' She unplugged the modem, staring angrily at the traitorous phone line.

'That sonofabitch O'Hanlon,' Stevie said. 'Didn't think he had it in him.'

Mulcahy had gone to the window, and was staring out at the street. 'I don't think so either,' he said after a moment. And when he wheeled and looked at them, he was smiling. 'My guess is Paul O'Hanlon wouldn't know how to copy his *own* computer document. You sure about this, Kate?'

'I am sure about this,' she said.

He nodded. 'Okay,' he said, 'keep going. Ignore it.'

'What are you saying?'

'We can't find George. But maybe George can find us.'

*

313

Once again they were in the hot attorneys' room, with its grimy wire mesh, the flickering yellow light, the sounds of distant racket. Ed calculated the minutes he would have to be in this place, the time before he could return to the open air, and then looked up guiltily at the two eyes which read his thoughts.

'They're offering second degree murder.'

'Today's special!' Shepard laughed sourly. 'What's it cost?'

'Life. With possibility of parole, after fifteen years.'

Shepard nodded and sighed. 'Fifteen years, and then I get to say, "Mother May I?" When I'm almost fifty. Where, at Cedar Junction?'

Ed nodded, acknowledging that any sentence would be served at one of the roughest prisons in the Commonwealth.

'And you want me to take it?'

'John, I have to report any offer.'

'But you want me to take it?'

He didn't answer.

'Ed, let me ask you. Should I take it?'

Mulcahy searched his expression, but could not tell whether Shepard wanted his advice or wanted simply to test him.

'I can't say.'

'Jesus. They offer life, and you can't say?'

'Life with parole. If they convict on the indictment, you never come home.'

'Are we going to win?'

'I don't know.'

'Gut, Ed, pure gut. Pure instinct, pure sixth sense. What's it saying to you?'

He shook his head. 'Don't trust my instincts, John,' he said.

'Well,' said Shepard, as he rose to leave, 'thanks for the visit. But I'll tell you something, Ed. Three months of this place is enough for me. They'll drag me kicking and screaming into anything longer. And hell, if their case is so good, why's he offering?'

'I don't know. I wonder about that.'

Later, as he trudged up the stairs to the subway platform and replayed the conversation in his mind, Mulcahy tried to rationalise it. Shepard was a negotiator, and he was a lawyer. He was about business. As John had said himself, the only thing that mattered was getting out. So it was probably nothing. Still, the thought nagged at Ed Mulcahy. Maybe Connell had scored his point, because it nagged at him, what Shepard hadn't said, how he had not remonstrated, not once. The conversation had been about time. Not innocence.

Late that night, as he lay awake in bed, trying to will himself to sleep, Mulcahy heard Gitz come in.

'They win?' he hollered.

'Naw,' he heard Gitz reply from the living room.

'You write a story?'

'Sure.'

'What was the score?'

Gitz's head appeared at Ed's bedroom door. 'The score?' he scoffed. 'The score? Philistine! This is the *Transcript* we're talking about, Mr Mulcahy! If you want the *score*, get the *World*.'

Gitz disappeared. Mulcahy heard the tramp of his shoes. 'But if it's art you want! If it's prose! If it's a fine phrase exquisitely turned! If it's mordant wit! If it's . . .' The voice faded into the kitchen.

'I'd just like to know there was something going on where I know the score, that's all,' Mulcahy said to himself.

26

'So, you know what today is?' John Shepard asked, when Mulcahy appeared in the lock-up behind 8b on Monday morning. He was, of course, wearing yet again the one tired grey suit he'd been permitted for the trial.

'No, what?'

'My anniversary, 12 September. Three months in jail today. Ain't that right, Freddie!'

Freddie, passing through the corridor towards the session, shrugged. 'Tell it to the judge,' he said.

'Well, if Falstaff ever sits his ass down and lets us put on a defence, I'll invite Mr Mulcahy here to do just that! Jesus, Freddie, how many trials have you had to sit through with that motherfucker!'

Freddie had to laugh. 'He's a pretty good lawyuh, you know.'

'Yeah, Freddie, but so's my guy.'

Freddie disappeared into the session, and John's mood seemed to disappear with him. He turned back towards Mulcahy and rubbed his temples. His eyes were red from lack of sleep. 'Three months, Ed. Three months in the cage. Fuck O'Hanlon's offer. I've had about all the fun I can have with this. You've got to get me out. Okay?'

Court is a little like church. The congregation is supposed to have its mind on loftier matters, but sometimes, as you look around the pews, you'd think their thoughts were mainly on their wardrobes. And so Mulcahy wondered, as the young state trooper rose from the gallery on Monday morning and walked to the witness stand, whether he had polished the boots which he wore up his calves. He must have. They shone like mirrors, and their soles made a squeegee sound as the beardless witness crossed the courtroom. He was so starched and shiny and squeaky that Mulcahy idly wondered whether he'd manage the articulation necessary for sitting. But he gained the witness stand well enough. Another thought stole into Mulcahy's mind. Just what is it about being the state police that makes them want to dress like the S.S.? He'd gotten to know a few of them as a government prosecutor, and they were good people. Definitely good people. So why the knee-high boots? Why are they 'troopers', rather than patrolmen or officers? There wasn't time to think about it.

O'Hanlon took Trooper Thomas Gowan quickly through the preliminaries. Then the plastic evidence bag, the one containing the tan suit jacket with the bloody breast and sleeve, emerged from the prosecutor's evidence box, was handed like a relic to the prosecutor, who carried it to the clerk's bench. All eyes were on it as Kelly fixed the Exhibit sticker to it. The room was quiet.

'Trooper Gowan,' said O'Hanlon, 'I show you what has been marked as Commonwealth's Exhibit 8. Do you recognise it?'

Gowan held the polyethylene evidence bag in his hands, turning it over carefully. All eyes in the jury box remained on the bag. The officer unfastened the pouch.

'Yes, sir,' he said.

'What is it?'

He removed the khaki jacket from the plastic, and turned it over carefully on the shelf before him. 'This is a men's suit jacket, which I observed in a dumpster at the Natick rest area off the westbound lane of the Massachusetts Turnpike on 17 May 1992.'

'How can you identify it, Trooper?'

'I fastened a tag on which I had printed my initials and the date to the jacket before I placed it in the evidence bag. I see that tag here. I also placed my initials and the date on the bag itself, which are,' he continued, turning the pouch over again in his hands, 'here.'

O'Hanlon nodded. 'What observations did you make about the suit jacket at that time you found it, Trooper?'

Trooper Gowan described, in the formal copspeak universally adopted by police officers on trial, the colour, size, appearance of the garment, and the 'brownish stain' which he 'observed' on the right lapel, breast, and forearm of the jacket.

'What time did you find the jacket, trooper?'

'Approximately 12.20 p.m., sir.'

'And the rest area where it was found, where does this lie in relation to Sheringham, Massachusetts?'

'The rest area is approximately ten miles west of Exit 17, which serves Natick and Sheringham.'

'What is the most direct route west on the Turnpike from the centre of Sheringham, Trooper Gowan?'

'The most direct access would be via Maple Street to the Massachusetts Turnpike, and then westbound on the Turnpike. The first rest area a driver would reach would be the one where we found the jacket.'

A moment later, the jacket was offered in evidence. Mulcahy objected. There was no direct link to Shepard. Yet. He knew the jacket would be admitted, as it was. The objection was solely to preserve an issue for appeal. If he could think of one later.

The jacket was admitted. Kelly marked the evidence pouch, and it was returned to the witness. 'Trooper Gowan,' asked O'Hanlon, 'what, if anything, did you find in the left pocket?'

The pocket? Mulcahy didn't remember anything on the Commonwealth's list. He started to reach for his evidence file, but the witness was about to answer.

'Objection!' said Mulcahy, rising to his feet, and trying to flip through the evidence file at the same time.

A moment later they were at sidebar. Mulcahy had the file open. 'Judge,' he said, 'I don't know what this witness is about to identify, but whatever it is, it wasn't on the Commonwealth's exhibit list.'

'Your Honour, the Commonwealth would offer a note found in the jacket pocket, apparently in the defendant's handwriting. The note may not have been separately identified, but has remained in the evidence pouch and was available for inspection by the defence. Indeed,' O'Hanlon continued, looking over to his table, where his assistant was rifling through a box of files, 'I think there is a record that Mr Mulcahy inspected the jacket prior to trial.' Gleason returned with a copy of the list, and several other documents.

'Where is the exhibit list?' asked the judge as the lawyers huddled around him. A copy was handed up and he shook his head as he read. There it was. Commonwealth 8: Men's tan suit jacket. No reference to a note.

Judge Grosso frowned. 'We'll excuse the jury,' he said.

Mulcahy explained that while the jacket had been shown to him, the examination had been brief, there had been no forensics ordered, and since he was not aware of a note in the pocket, he had examined only those aspects of the jacket which he understood to be in the case, including its style, size and make, and the nature of the stain. Judge Grosso nodded throughout the explanation. He well knew how these inspections could go, with the state police breathing down defence counsel's neck, and an assistant DA drumming his fingers on the tabletop.

Mulcahy sat and listened while O'Hanlon briefly tried to back and fill. It was a clerical mistake. The evidence was tendered for inspection and, according to State Police records, *had* been inspected by the defence. O'Hanlon's deputy had been there for the inspection. 'These things happen, Judge,' he said.

'What was the theory of relevance?' Grosso asked. O'Hanlon said that the note contained a telephone number which the Commonwealth expected to link to Shepard. Through the note, they expected to provide further evidence linking the jacket to the defendant.

David Grosso was frowning. He was no friend of sloppiness. And this was, at best, sloppy. He nodded his head when Mulcahy rose again. He did not need to be reminded that failure to identify the note might have deprived the *defence* of a chance to perform the very kinds of forensic tests upon which the prosecution now wanted to rely.

'I think Mr Mulcahy is right,' Grosso said, after listening for a few moments to the argument. 'Doesn't the link through a phone number demonstrate that this is an independent piece of evidence, with independent probative value? That seems to me to be its relevance, if any, and that seems to me to be the reason that it should be within the rule which requires disclosure of Commonwealth exhibits.'

O'Hanlon didn't answer. The judge went on: 'No reason has been proffered for nondisclosure, other than clerical mistake. I will sustain the objection. The note will not be admitted.'

Mulcahy felt a charge of excitement. A small battle won! Elated, he returned to his seat. When the jury had been brought back in, the examination of Gowan moved swiftly on to other matters. O'Hanlon pounded ahead, setting the chain of custody for the blood laboratory evidence which would link the jacket to Whitaker, laying the foundation for identifying the laundry ticket stapled to the jacket's lining as consistent with tickets used at Shepard's laundry.

Marcus Hemp took the stand. He held a Master's degree in chemistry, and was employed by the Crime

Laboratory of the Department of Public Safety. A short, middle-aged man, perfectly bald, he had testified many times and was comfortable on the witness stand. He spoke slowly, deliberately, in a professorial manner. His demeanour was quiet, non-adversarial.

O'Hanlon worked the witness slowly round to his opinions. He walked him through a laborious inspection of the Sheringham farmhouse study by the forensic unit. His gathering of fibres evidence from the carpet in the front hall, living room, and on the lower staircase, and from the couch in the living room. He spoke in detail as to how these fibres were compared with certain clothing upon which he was asked to perform an analysis, how a spectrographic and microscopic analysis was prepared.

He was shown several exhibits. He identified the suit as one upon which he had been asked to perform a comparative analysis, and an evidence pouch containing the fibres which had positively matched the suit.

O'Hanlon wound on to the point. Over the whirring of the fans, he asked whether, on the basis of his examination of the fibres evidence and his expertise in fibres analysis, Dr Hemp had formed an opinion, based on a reasonable degree of certainty in the field of fibres analysis, as to the source of the fibres in the pouches marked Commonwealth exhibits 28, 29, 30, and 31 for identification.

'I have.'

'And what is that opinion?'

'In my opinion, it is highly likely that the fibres contained in Commonwealth exhibits 29, 30 and 31, came from Commonwealth exhibit 8.'

The fans whirred on. O'Hanlon took Hemp through the bases for his opinions: the microscopes, the textures, the fibre content, the woof and weave. Hemp proceeded matter-of-factly. The bottom line of his testimony: the suit jacket had been in Whitaker's study.

Mulcahy rose to cross examine late in the afternoon. It was insufferably hot. The jury seemed on edge. It wanted no more of woof and weave. Mulcahy began with the suit.

'This is a tan, khaki, Brooks Brothers suit jacket?'

'Yes.'

'It was bought off the rack there?'

'I have no way of knowing.'

'Well, there are khaki suits like this one on every Boston street corner, are there not?'

'No, not in my judgment, sir. There are not.'

A voice was trumpeting in Mulcahy's brain. Leave it! He didn't leave it. 'There are not?' he heard himself ask out loud, as the voice inside his brain shouted, 'Idiot!'

'No, sir. Would you like me to explain?' Hemp smiled at him. He had testified often enough to know that defence counsel never wants an explanation. But Mulcahy was trapped between two rules of trial practice. Never let a witness explain. And never appear to avoid a subject. It can only be done through control, and he had lost it. Well, he would brass it out. There was no choice. 'Please, Dr Hemp,' he said. He turned, affecting nonchalance.

'Every yard of woven cloth is different. They are

324

similar in the way fingerprints are similar. Thus, four khaki suits viewed across Downtown Crossing may look similar, just as four fingerprints viewed from a distance of a couple of feet look similar. But to one who is trained, examining them closely, they are all different.'

It went on like this, but got worse, a gentle, learned explanation of fibres which left the jury believing that Shepard's suit was as unique and important as the Rosetta Stone and had been in Whitaker's study as certainly as Whitaker himself.

Now the jury was frowning. The closeness was stifling. It was late. What was the point of this? Hadn't they heard it once? They seemed to stare with one gaze at Mulcahy, lips pursed.

'Dr Hemp, in your examination of the study, did you find other fibres, inconsistent with Commonwealth 8?'

'Oh, certainly, one always does.'

'I didn't ask you about other cases, Dr Hemp.'

'I'm sorry. I thought the jury would want to know.' The last slipped out so genuinely, and so artfully, that Mulcahy was again caught unaware, and fumbled for his next question.

'Those fibres could have been accounted for by persons other than Mr Shepard?'

'Certainly.'

'So other people must have been in the study.'

'Yes. That is usually the case with such a room.'

'And you can't say that Mr Shepard is the only one who could have been in that room other than the deceased.'

'Certainly not. I can say only that it is likely that

his jacket was there. Whether it got there some other way than on his back, I have no way of knowing.'

It was four o'clock. Mulcahy was folding his files together, and repacking the banker's boxes, when it occurred to him. Even at the very moment of Grosso's ruling, something should have told Mulcahy that all was not right. O'Hanlon let it go. No rejoinder. No request to brief the issue overnight, take a run at it tomorrow. *A phone number* – a direct link. And the beefy prosecutor just dropped it. Suddenly a feeling of nausea struck him, rising from the pit of his stomach. Mulcahy had not even thought to *look at* the note.

He set off to find Kelly. A moment later he was peering down at the pink telephone slip while the clerk hovered impatiently by the lobby door, his fingers drumming against the sill. There Mulcahy read a single line of pencilled print:

T.M.D.–669–0241

'Jesus, did we have our ass kicked today,' Mulcahy said, shaking his head. He had telephoned the number as soon as he got back to Bromfield Street. It was a Dorchester listing: one Antonio Caesar Chavez. No, Mr Chavez had never heard of John Shepard. There was no one there by the initials, T.M.D. He had lived there since the early '70s. Mulcahy stared into the darkness. The Commonwealth *couldn't* link the note to Shepard – that was just the point. Yet the note was in the pocket of the jacket – it was in fact evidence that the jacket was *not* Shepard's. The *Brady*

326

rule obligated the prosecutor to disclose to the defence evidence which might tend to raise a reasonable doubt. So what had they done? They had contrived a way to dupe *Mulcahy* into keeping the note out of evidence. It was brilliant. He couldn't claim unfair surprise – the evidence had been kept out. He couldn't complain about the prosecution failing to disclose evidence – they had offered the note, hadn't they? How could anyone complain on appeal?

'Heh, lemme tell ya somethin', okay?' said Stevie, his portly legs propped up on the desk. 'O'Hanlon's a smaht guy. He's gonna score some points. Don't worry about it. But the fuckin' *fibuhs* guy – him we don't need to shoot owahselves in the foot on. Jaysus.' He pulled on his wart, twisting it between his fingers.

Mulcahy shook his head. 'Kate,' he said, anxiously, 'think Creel's reading?'

'I don't know. No hints.'

Their heads were together as they peered at the computer screen. Mulcahy could feel a coil of her hair against his ear, but it seemed not to distract her at all. 'You know, Kate,' he said, as they scrolled disappointedly through the files, turning nothing up, 'I've figured it out.'

'What out?'

'Creel. He's really God. And Shepard is really the devil.'

'What about me?' chirped up Stevie.

Mulcahy considered the question. 'Doubting Thomas,' he said.

Kate asked, 'And you?'

Mulcahy shut his eyes. 'Job,' he said quietly. 'I am Job.'

327

'Who's Joe?' asked Stevie.

'Not Joe, Stevie. Job. Just when he thought things couldn't get worse, they did. His troubles were numberless.'

'But his faith was abiding,' Kate said softly, and winked at him.

In a darkened office, O'Hanlon was on the telephone to Connell. He had tracked him down at a state representative's fundraiser in a Newton restaurant and was relaying his conversation with Mulcahy, over the background din and the occasionally distinct, 'Mike, howarya!' and the punctuation of Connell saying, 'Good to see you. Good to see you.'

'They want a not guilty, Mike,' O'Hanlon said.

'Don't we all?' Connell answered, and then was quiet for a moment. O'Hanlon could hear the noises of the party continuing behind him. 'All right, Paul,' he said, softly and distantly, 'throw everything you've got at him. Everything. Maybe he just needs a little pressure.'

Paul O'Hanlon knew what had happened when he heard the line disengage. The DA had disengaged as well. He would have nothing else to do with this case. He would leave it to O'Hanlon, and would return only to slap his back and be one of the fellas once the verdict was in.

If it were a conviction. If it were acquittal, he wouldn't be back. But that was all right with Paul O'Hanlon. He had been there before, and so he was smiling when he replaced the receiver in its cradle.

*

Late in the evening, Mulcahy sat in his kitchen, with June bugs crashing into the screen as the heat continued unabated. Mercifully, Denise had finally seen something in Gitz, and so he wasn't around. That was a blessing. Mulcahy was in no mood for Gitz.

They kicked my ass today, he thought again. It had been the one consuming thought in his consciousness since he had left the courthouse. Outfoxed by O'Hanlon on the note, and plain stupid with Hemp, a witness he didn't need to beat, a witness he could have left alone, he had done everything wrong, losing control, magnifying his importance, re-emphasising points for the jury. It was a disaster. Beads of condensation flecked the beer bottle. His mind returned again and again to that painful examination, a civil lawyer's examination, a thing devoid of instinct, of control.

He lingered sleepless and confused. The case seemed so clear when he took it that summer day at the Charles Street jail. Now nothing was clear: not the facts, not his own abilities. He was a hack lawyer trying a murder case.

And his client? Who was John Shepard, anyway? This case needed the cynicism of a Stevie George. Shepard needed a lawyer who knew he'd done it. Instead of one who wanted to believe that he hadn't. He got up to go to bed.

Just then it happened. As Mulcahy stepped barefoot on to the cold black and white tile of the bathroom, the last synapse clicked, and the ancient thought, which had been struggling since May to make the journey, burst into his consciousness. Mulcahy stood stock still for a moment. Then he turned,

329

and went to the bookshelf in his bedroom. Why he'd kept them he didn't know, but there they were, lined up on the bottom shelf: his first-year casebooks. Sandwiched between Gorjance's *Property* and Holzinger's *Torts*, was Rando on *Contracts*. He opened it. Twelve-year-old highlighter and notes jumped from every page. The old spine was long broken.

He sat on his bed, and it took a while to find. But he did find it, in the chapter on the Parol Evidence Rule. *Swartout Shipping Company* v. *Liberty Bank and Trust*. *Swartout*, the old chestnut.

He read the case again, fascinated as he had been the first time he read it twelve years before. Like so many opinions, it was dry, its facts arrayed only in summary fashion, so that the judge could state the legal rule and the holding of the case. But even the law students had seen that there must have been an enormous human story there.

The case involved a ship financing. A bank financed the purchase of a container ship, and had obtained a security interest in the ship through a standard form of ship mortgage. The price of the ship was $70 million, and the bank had loaned $68 million. But through a typographical error, the ship mortgage document had stated the mortgage amount as $68 *thousand*.

He remembered now how they had discussed it in class. He could recall Rodman, the professor, asking them all to think about how it could have happened to anyone. The financing had been closed over several days, someone had typed the wrong figure, someone else had failed to proofread. Had the associate been fired? The partner? Had the firm been sued for malpractice? The opinion didn't say.

It did say, however, that the language of the mortgage was plain and unambiguous, that there was no evidence of fraud (the error having allegedly been the fault of the bank's lawyers), and therefore, that under the Parol Evidence Rule, no evidence could be admitted from the lender to the effect that the deal really was intended to be for $68 million. And so it was a case for the casebooks: a case where application of an ordinarily sensible rule of human commerce produces a result where rules matter more than truth. Summary judgment had been granted to the ship purchaser by a federal judge. No appeal was reported – the case must have settled.

'Ladies and gentlemen,' Mulcahy could still remember Rodman saying from the well of the lecture hall, 'if you don't think proofreading will be a part of your job, remember *Swartout*. And when you are up late proofing documents for a closing, and you are sick of it, remember *Swartout*.'

Remember *Swartout*. That's what Rodman had said to the class. 'Damn him. Damn him,' said Mulcahy, slamming the case book shut.

For he didn't need to ask. Every law student in America learned contracts from Dean Rando's casebook. If you studied contracts, you owned a copy, and if you opened the fourth edition to page 312, you found *Swartout*.

The knot in his stomach tightened. In trial work, most of the preparation can be sustained on cognitive skill and hard work. But the actual trial taps the gut, and that is a different resource. That deep sense of

331

despair, the sense of the case being utterly, desperately real, and of its getting away from him with blinding speed, struck him hard. He lay awake almost all night, his mind racing.

He had no partnership. He had no defence that gave him confidence. And what little defence he had, O'Hanlon was beating him on. Ed Mulcahy was in steep powder, and the snow was falling.

In 8b, O'Hanlon marched forward, witness after remorseless witness. He had mapped his campaign carefully. Now he was building his mountains of physical evidence. And it all followed a trail. The trooper led to the jacket, the jacket to the bloodstains, the bloodstains to the victim. The bloodstains came in. The blood type was a positive match with Whitaker's blood.

The telephone records came in, slowly and laboriously. The evening of the murder, at 6.15 p.m., someone telephoned Whitaker's office and his Sheringham home from a public telephone booth at the corner of Joy and Cambridge Streets, three blocks from Shepard's apartment. The call to the home lasted twenty-three minutes. Whitaker, or someone at home, had telephoned Shepard at 7.32 p.m. for less than one minute.

Next O'Hanlon called an attendant from Lamartino's Sunoco, in Natick, David Porelli. He identified the service station copy of Shepard's Sunoco charge card slip.

'Your Honour, I offer it in evidence,' O'Hanlon said.

'Objection,' said Mulcahy.

'Grounds?'

'Hearsay, Your Honour,' Mulcahy protested.

The judge removed his glasses, as if to assure himself that there really was a lawyer on his feet objecting to the admission of this piece of paper. 'Mr Mulcahy,' he said, 'it's a business record.'

'Your Honour, if I could be heard . . .'

'No. Overruled. It will be admitted.'

'Your Honour, I have a memorandum . . .'

'Mr Mulcahy, I'm very glad you have a memorandum. But your objection is overruled. It is admitted.'

He sank to his seat. Sometimes you work for days on a legal point, and lose it in twelve seconds.

In a moment, Mulcahy was taking Porelli through the obvious points on cross-examination. He had been on duty that evening. The slip showed that $5.38 worth of gas had been purchased on 16 May. No, he could not remember Shepard, or his car, or anything about the transaction.

'I pump a lot of gas,' the young man said. And who would be surprised by that?

Mulcahy was on the point of finishing when he looked again at the exhibit, the faint scribble on the carbon of the Sunoco bill.

'You didn't write down the plate of this vehicle, did you, Mr Porelli?'

'No,' he said, 'I never do.'

Mulcahy nodded. 'So there's no record of what car was being driven by the person who presented this card, is there?'

'No, I guess not,' said Porelli.

'And you don't ask drivers for ID, as a rule, do you?'

'No, we don't,' he confessed.

'So anybody with John Shepard's Sunoco card could have purchased this gas?'

'I guess,' he said.

Mulcahy nodded again, still squinting at the slip.

'How much gasoline,' he asked, 'is five dollars and thirty-eight cents worth?'

'Depends what grade.'

'Right,' said Mulcahy. 'Let's assume it's regular unleaded.'

'I don't know, that runs about a buck twenty-nine,' said Porelli. 'How many gallons is that?'

'Four gallons or so sound about right?'

'I guess,' said the witness.

'Now, Mr Porelli,' said Mulcahy, 'do you know the capacity of the gas tank of a 1984 Subaru GL wagon?'

'Subaru wagon's a thirteen, I think,' he said.

'You'd agree with me that the buyer of this gas probably was filling his tank?'

'Objection, calls for speculation,' interjected O'Hanlon.

'No, he can have it,' said the Judge, who had guessed where Mulcahy was going.

David Porelli guessed it too. 'Yeah,' he said, 'I'd say so. You might get a guy wanting five dollars of gas, or ten dollars of gas, or twenty. But not five thirty-eight. I'd say that's a fill-up.'

'So, Mr Porelli, if the buyer of this gas was filling his tank, he must have had about nine gallons when he pulled in?'

'Sounds about right,' he said.

'And his tank would show about three-quarters?'

'Yeah, about.'

'That's all,' said Mulcahy, and he returned to his desk. He looked over at the jury box. Mr Brody, juror four, the one who usually had his eyes closed, had opened them, and was looking across the room, nodding.

'Appleby Shillinghaus. Good afternoon,' a pleasant voice said.

'May I speak to George Newman, please?'

'One minute, sir, I'll connect you.'

Stevie started so suddenly that his toupée shifted. All through the afternoon he had been lulled by the monotonous march of inquiry, failure, hang-up and redial, the early-afternoon heat, the sense that this wasn't going to work. He had been on autopilot. When he heard the extension ring, he replaced his phone in the cradle, and looked over at Kate.

'Katie Kate,' he said, 'we got a possible.'

She pulled a chair next to the investigator's desk and handed him the *Martindale's* listing. There was no George Newman for Appleby, Shillinghaus, Mitzer, and Steele. Whoever George Newman was, he was not a lawyer there. So far, so good.

'Stevie,' she said, 'remember how skittish he is. We can't call him directly. And we don't want it to get back to him that we're asking questions.'

Stevie nodded and was on the phone again. When he had the firm, he winked at her and said, 'I need to speak to your Human Resources manager. What was that name? . . . Yes. . . . Yes, could you?'

He waited for a moment while they connected him. 'Ms Levine? Yes, hello, this is Kevin Fuller from the Peterborough Agency, and ... oh, you don't? ... We're in Baltimore ... uh huh ... we don't do as many DC placements as we'd like, but I have something interesting for you, I think. Anyway, I don't want to take too much of your time, but I have an outstanding candidate for that MIS position you ... Yes? Oh, you did ... I see ... Yes, I see ... For some reason I must have an old ... yes ... When did you fill that position, if I can ask? ... Uh huh ... July? Really. Well, I'm going to have a word with my people ... yes, indeed! ... Anyway, sorry to bother you, perhaps another time ... yes ... yes, Peterborough Agency ... we're in the book. ... Yes. Yes, any time. Thank you.'

'What happened to your accent?' Kate asked.

'I can talk like you Ivy Leaguhs, every once in a while.' He grinned. 'Anyway, looks like maybe we got lucky. One more call to make sure.'

'The "Peterborough Agency"?' she asked.

Stevie nodded. 'Eh, what the hell? One more call. This next one ain't so elegant. Let's hope we got a receptionist long on reception and short on brains.'

And so he placed a third telephone call to the Appleby Shillinghaus receptionist. And this time the rotund investigator leaning back in his desk chair was Attorney Michael Millburg from New York. Attorney Millburg explained that he was counsel to one Mr Fullerton who was planning to attend the United Technology Closing next week, an august and particular personage, and, as it happened, a disabled one. Perhaps the receptionist had heard of his work for the Spinal Cord Injury Society of America? She had not. Well, in any event, Attorney Millburg explained to the receptionist that Mr Fullerton was extremely finicky about wheelchair access, table heights, hall widths, interior doors, bathrooms, firm attitudes, and other such matters. Would there be anyone in the office who was disabled, to whom he might speak about these matters? He did it all so smoothly that the receptionist never stopped to ask why, if Attorney Millburg was coming to a closing at the office, he didn't already know a lawyer there to whom he might direct the request. No, she waded right in, and told him that she knew exactly who might help, and transferred the call.

Kate craned her neck to listen when the voice answered, 'This is George.'

'Ah, is Mr Spellman there?' Stevie asked, pulling a name at random off of the *Martindale's* list.

'I'm sorry, you have the wrong number. You'll find him in the directory,' said the voice curtly, and the line went dead.

Stevie looked at Kate, and she nodded. It was he.

'Helpful prick, ain't he?' Stevie said, as he replaced the phone.

In 8b, another state trooper had followed Porelli to the stand, to walk the jury through the road map. The Commonwealth had spent a few dollars on this one: a brightly coloured foam-core enlargement, tracing the roads and streets from the Sheringham farmhouse back to the turnpike, tracing the flight of the murderer in red, of course, showing how it passed

Lamartino's on the way to the turnpike, and the rest area on the westbound side thereafter.

Next came the pebbles. A Colorado state trooper arrived to complete the chain of custody. A geologist from the University of Massachusetts testified to a reasonable certainty that the pebbles in the Subaru footwell and embedded in the tyres had come from the drive at the farmhouse.

O'Hanlon had saved the bar of soap for last. Fingerprints are always the most persuasive. It was about quarter to four. 'Your Honour,' he said, 'the Commonwealth's next series of witnesses will speak to the fingerprint evidence. I expect those examinations to be long. Perhaps we should adjourn here.'

Mulcahy was shaking his head as the jury were led out. There, he'd gone and done it again. The jury, having heard about fingerprint evidence, would have all night to work up the proper sense of suspense. They would be most attentive in the morning.

Stevie was in the gallery as Mulcahy left, a few minutes later. 'Here, lemme help you wit' dis shit,' he said. 'I got some good news.'

Half an hour later, the three had reconvened in Stevie's office. Kate had already booked her ticket for the morning.

'Eddie,' said Stevie, 'forget about Creel for a second. He may end up a wild goose chase. Okay? But what about the case. Where we goin' wit this?'

'What do you mean, Stevie?'

'The case, where we goin'? What's the defence?'

'The defence is, "I wasn't there, and he killed himself."'

'Eddie, don't take this personal, but that defence

338

don't sing opera. It don't sing folk songs. It don't even rap. What about all the shit that *was* there? All the fibuhs and the hairs and the pebbles? What about the fingerprint?'

'Well, we go after it. What else can we do? The fibres are consistent with many different jackets. Besides, O'Hanlon may not link the bloody jacket to Shepard. The pebbles might have come from somewhere else. The hair analysis leaves some margin for error. And the fingerprint is smudged, and may not . . .'

'And pigs might fly, if they had wings. But they don't. Eddie, nobody's gonna believe alladat.' Stevie sighed.

'Well, what else do we do?'

'Listen,' said Stevie, very earnest now, 'I been in and out of that courtroom when I ain't on the phone to every law firm in America. I saw some of Gowan and Hemp, anyway, and I been watchin' the jury. I think they're gonna believe the stuff is Shepid's, okay? So how'd it get there? Let's go back to that. How'd it get there? Either he was there, or somebody else put it there.'

Mulcahy sighed. 'We've been through that.'

'I know! But this other shit isn't going to work.'

Mulcahy shook his head. It was a little late to change theories.

'Look, Eddie,' said Stevie, 'just think about it tonight. You got Evans, the fingerprint guy, tomorrow. I don't know if you can shake him too much. He's good. But think about the theory. If there's anything you can get from him on that, I think you should try.'

'On a conspiracy? What do I ask him?'

'Jaysus, Eddie, you're the lawyuh!'

Having found *Swartout*, having linked the mortgage error to Shepard, Mulcahy found himself driven more and more to confront the likelihood of Shepard's guilt. Had he planted the error? On Whitaker's terminal? Had Whitaker confronted Shepard after debriefing Mulcahy – figuring that Mulcahy could or would not? He began to fall into a kind of depression, as the logician in him surveyed the mounting evidence. Something refused to surrender belief in the man, but it was unclear whether that was just emotion, or every lawyer's desire to win his case. Whatever its source, it was the side which conducted mock speeches to the jury.

'Members of the jury,' it would say, 'one other thing.' And he saw himself swagger like Shepard, with that habit of puffing his chest right up, and grinning, and he began to pick up his speech pattern. 'Shepard is arrogant and loud and he lives on the edge and doesn't give half a warm piss about the world's view, or even yours, we all know that. But Shepard, corporate scribe though he may be, is a lawyer, and he's got an idea or two about what happens when guns go off and titans are found tits up on the carpet! He knows that snoops and detectives and dusters and scoopers and pluckers and tweezer squeezers and computer sleuths fan out over the study, and they comb the phone records and the mail and the credit card accounts and the cops interview twelve dozen people in the area. Shepard ain't stupid, people! He ain't stupid!'

340

But Mulcahy was beginning to wonder.

Kate knew she was too late. Although she had caught the first shuttle out of Logan, and it was airborne punctually, by the time she had elbowed her way through National's US Air terminal and made her way by cab to number 3100 K Street, it was 9.10, and Creel was sure to be at his office already. A handsome new development at the bottom of the hill below Georgetown, 3100 K faced out over the Potomac. From a fountain in the Arcade, Kate sat in the sun and watched office workers arrive for work until about 10. She was hoping to catch him outside Appleby's office, where she supposed all sorts of things might go wrong. So she watched the office workers stream into the building until ten. But there were no wheelchairs.

She had brought work with her – she had a deposition to take the next week in Pittsburgh, and lugged her trial bag to a table near the dock. But there was too much sunshine to concentrate on an environmental insurance dispute, and she was too nervous about the Creel meeting. She ended by pacing, pacing, and asking herself how she had gotten this far into things.

In Boston, State Police Lieutenant Francis Evans from the State Police Lab began his testimony. He was, quite simply, the best in the Commonwealth. Some spark had been lit at his training at the FBI academy, for he began to publish little articles on the ins and outs of fingerprint analysis. By 1992, he had been doing it for more than fifteen years, and his CV included more than a dozen monographs on the subject. He lectured at state police academies nationwide.

His manner was everything you want in an expert witness. Dispassionate, he testified as though indifferent to whether the jury convicted or acquitted, so long as they got the facts straight on the fingerprint evidence. He always prepared well. He never lectured. He had that facility for explaining complex science in simple concepts, without condescension. And he was utterly confident.

Before 10.40, the jury had already learned that Commonwealth Exhibit 21, a bar of soap, had been recovered from the washroom adjoining the study. It was found on a soap stand next to the sink. Evans had received it at the State Police Lab for fingerprint analysis. The soap contained a positive partial match for the left thumbprint. As Evans testified, removing the green sliver from its evidence packet with a set of large tweezers, Shepard craned his neck forward. He scribbled a note to Mulcahy.

'I need to see that,' it said.

The fingerprint evidence was a physical challenge for the prosecution. Only a partial print had been recovered, and, since the medium was soap, it could not be recovered through ordinary means. The State Police Lab had made photographs of the soap, enlarged them, and run their analysis from the photographs.

O'Hanlon's direct examination went smoothly. Evans identified the soap, gave as his opinion a positive fingerprint match, and then explained to the jury the points of similarity between the print and John Shepard's booking sheet thumbprint.

Just before lunch, the exam took, for Mulcahy, an unexpected turn. 'Lieutenant,' asked O'Hanlon, 'did you examine the keys on the typewriter marked Commonwealth 30?'

'Yes.'

'Were those keys dusted for fingerprints?'

'Yes.'

'With what result?'

'We obtained clear prints of the victim, Samuel Whitaker, on sixteen typewriter keys. On the other keys, prints were smudged and impossible to match.'

'With reference to the suicide note, Lieutenant Evans, did you make any observations relative to your fingerprint analysis of the typewriter?'

What was this? Whatever it was, Mulcahy didn't like it. 'Objection,' he said, rising to his feet.

In a moment they were at sidebar.

'There was no report of prints on the note,' he said.

'But that's not the question, Your Honour,' O'Hanlon replied. 'The question is, which keys on the typewriter are smudged, and how do those keys line up with the letters of the alphabet which appear in the so-called suicide note?'

'Well, Your Honour, I still . . .'

'Your objection is overruled, Mr Mulcahy. This clearly is an important question, and the question of identifying the letters in the note against the letters on the keyboard which do and do not contain Mr Whitaker's prints, that could be done by any witness.'

Mulcahy battled to keep his face even as he

returned to counsel table, but he had been beaten again. Not just on the evidence question: that he expected to lose. But he had never even thought of this. He didn't need to hear it, now, either: the keys which matched the letters in the note were smudged – none of those contained identifiable prints. O'Hanlon would argue to the jury that someone wearing gloves typed those keys: someone other than Samuel Whitaker.

He looked up, and saw that O'Hanlon had returned to the podium. Before resuming, he turned subtly toward Mulcahy, made a mocking bow, and smiled.

'I'm here to see Mr Newman,' Kate said to the Appleby receptionist at just past 2.30. 'Catherine Guest.' There had been no sign of him through the lunch break. She had given up on surprise, and decided to make the frontal assault. It was riskier this way, confronting him in his new office, but afternoon had come and she hadn't a choice.

'Mr Newman, in MIS?' the receptionist asked.

'Yes, that's right.'

A moment later, the receptionist was explaining that Mr Newman said he had no meeting, and knew of no one named Ms Guest.

Kate looked down at her planner and said, 'Oh, no, we scheduled this meeting a week ago. I'm quite sure. From Shepard Analysis Group. Tell him I've come all the way from *Boston*.'

The receptionist spoke a few words more on the phone, and then said, 'He'll meet you in the third-floor lobby.'

The elevator door whispered open, and when she stepped out she could see him, sitting in the chair behind the glass, squinting out through a pair of round spectacles. The colour had gone from his face, and his mouth was quivering. He looked thinner than she remembered, his shirt a little more rumpled, the shirt tail out and resting untidily in his lap.

She extended a hand and said, 'Mr Newman.' He didn't take it, and it didn't put him at ease.

'My office, please,' he said, and wheeled the chair about.

He had a cubbyhole, interior office in the Appleby MIS department, and he raced the chair along the corridors for it like a refugee making for the border. It was a tiny space, and she had barely prised herself in when he had the door shut behind her.

He looked grimly at her now, as he caught his breath and said, 'Well, Miss Catherine Maher, who else knows I am here, please?'

'Ed Mulcahy and Steven George.'

'No one else?'

'No one else,' she replied.

'I see,' he said. Now she could see, behind the lenses, that his one good eye moved up and down and along her breast, her throat, her face, her hair, while the other eye stared vacantly into space. 'Is it not enough for you people nearly to have gotten me killed once?'

She sighed. 'That was not us. We're just trying to defend a murder case.'

'Very reassuring.'

'While I'm sure this must be a shock, please don't panic. No one has any intention of telling anyone about you. There are only three of us on this Shepard case. No one else is working with us, no staff, no one. We didn't figure out where you were until last night, and no one has written anything down.'

'Miss Kate, no one has to write anything down! You flew down here today, did you not? Pay by credit card? Have you telephoned anyone today? Did you people telephone this office yesterday?'

'Mr Creel, you must trust me. You have been here how many months? In all that time, no one has disturbed you. No one will find out from us. Frankly, we don't want the prosecution talking to you.' She had said too much, and wanted to change the subject. 'You know about the Shepard trial?'

'I saw something . . . something in the *Transcript* I picked up at out-of-town news. Not surprising.'

'Why do you say that?'

'Oh, nothing. Intuition. Strong personalities, machismo, that sort of thing.'

'I see,' she said, although she didn't. 'Well, we're on trial, and we need your help.'

He shook his head.

'Mr Creel. The guest book.'

But he shook his head again. 'Miss Kate, I want nothing to do with this.'

'A man's been accused of murder,' she said.

'And another man was very nearly murdered,' he answered. 'I'm sure that if your man didn't do it, he'll say so, and the jury will believe him.' He gave her the little perfunctory half smile, as if to say, 'So there.'

'Mr Creel,' she said, slowly now, choosing her words carefully, 'it is my duty to defend him. If I think that the guest book helps him, I must try to get

346

it. We think it may somehow show Mr Whitaker's involvement in the mortgage affair, which may explain the suicide. Now, we can only get this thing one of two ways. We can get it because you give it to us, explain to us what it is, tell us where we can find it, and no one ever has to know that you did so. Or we can get it by forcing you to appear in court, in public, and identify yourself, and it.'

And she withdrew from her bag the envelope containing the subpoena, unfolded it, and placed the document on the edge of his desk. She saw that his good eye went to it.

The subpoena sat on the desk. 'Mr Creel,' she said, 'I don't wish to serve this subpoena on you. I am,' she said, 'not doing so, not right now. I wish for you to remain anonymous. We don't want for this to cause you any more difficulty. But we need your help. We need that guest book.'

She withdrew her hands to her lap, and the paper remained on the desk. It was a game of chicken now, as to who would take it. He folded his arms and stared down at his lap.

'What is it, Mr Creel?' she asked, gently. 'I don't understand. If you just put us on to the guest book, we can leave you alone and you can go on with your life. What is this about?'

He sighed, shaking his head. 'Miss Kate, a man with a gun tried to kill me. I provided Mr Ed with information about this mortgage affair, I told him of the existence of the guest book, and within days a man with a gun found me, followed me, and tried to kill me. And now this charming little girl has dropped in to say she's ever so sure nothing naughty like that could ever happen again, could it, George? Oh, no. Now, Miss Kate, why am I having a little trouble with that?'

She had reddened at the reference to a 'little girl', and felt the advantage begin to shift.

'Have you ever swum the harbour, from East Boston to the Aquarium?'

'No,' she said again.

'I don't recommend it. Even if you happen to have legs.'

'Your involvement,' she said, 'can end with this meeting. Just let us have the guest book, and you can wash your hands of this.'

'Oh, that's reassuring. My involvement will end. And none of the exceedingly clever people who tracked me down before will be clever enough to do so again.'

She shook her head. 'I don't know what to say, except that I think you're being a little . . . a little sensational. I know you were shot at. I know all about that. I know a few things about that which you may not know. We think we are beginning to understand the motive. But the guest book may help with that, too.'

She could see his eyes flicker beneath the glasses while she was speaking, the one eye fixed on her and the other wandering off to space. He waited for her to go on, but she said quietly, 'The guest book, George. Please.'

It was tiny, Creel's office, with almost no room for her chair between his workspace and the door. They were only a few feet apart. He was quiet for a moment, rocking slightly, back and forth in the chair.

She could tell that he was working at it, now. And then it seemed from his face as if he had reached a conclusion, for he smiled as he caught the advantage – caught it and, in his mind, played the match to where the pieces had all been exchanged and she would have to surrender her last one.

'All right, Miss Kate, let's talk about the guest book.'

'Okay,' she exhaled slowly.

'You don't,' he said softly, 'know what it proves.'

'No. That's why I need it.'

'You think it might help show old Samuel Boylston Whitaker's complicity in a gigantic fraud.'

'It might,' she said.

'Or it might not,' he pointed out.

'Okay,' she said.

'You don't know.'

'I don't.'

'That paper,' he said, indicating the subpoena, 'does it say I have to come and testify about it?'

'Yes,' she said. 'That is what it says.'

'In the courtroom?'

'Yes.'

'Miss Kate, does the paper say I have to come and tell the lawyers what I know *before* I go to court?'

She felt the colour come to her cheeks, and her mouth quiver, and now her eyes shrank from his as his one good eye bored into them. 'No,' she said, 'it does not say that.'

He nodded. 'The guest book might prove Mr John's guilt.' He smiled.

'It might prove his innocence.'

He laughed. A pause, and a machine gun burst of laughter, and then there was silence. 'Miss Kate,' he stammered, giggling, 'what's your best guess?' And then, at the word, 'guess', he dissolved into another burst of mirth.

'Is that,' he said, going on as he calmed himself, 'is that the defence in this murder case you and Mr Ed are doing? There might be some evidence which *might* prove his innocence, a piece of paper you've never seen? Let's go get it and hope that when George comes to testify, it helps?' And he giggled again, bringing his hand to his face.

She remained silent.

'Well, Miss Kate,' he said, finally, 'it seems to me that you have two choices. You can hand me that subpoena, in which case you will learn what I know about the guest book at the moment the jury does. Or you can decide to defend this case on the basis of what you know.'

His face had now gained a measure of its usual self-contentment. Creel was fond of games, and he had only to find the game in this affair to turn it to his liking.

Kate, reddening, had no response.

'The subpoena?' he asked, extending his hand to the paper on his desk. 'Am I to understand that I have been, how did you put it, *served*?'

Kate looked at it, and looked at him, considering the smug invitation he'd made, and wanting to pull off some psychological masterstroke; wanting, for a moment, to have Shepard there. But Kate was no gambler. She folded up the subpoena and restored it to her planner, and then she tucked the planner in her bag. 'You have not been served,' she said.

*

In Boston, Mulcahy was rising to cross examine. He began by attacking the smudges on the photograph of the thumbprint. But the smudges did not obscure the points of similarity. His effort to demonstrate the statistical possibility of points of distinction being in the smudged portion went poorly. Evans had been well prepared. He clung staunchly to the accuracy of this method. The photographs were of extremely high quality and able to preserve the detail of the print. While the left side of the print was smudged, enough of the print was preserved to give Evans certainty of a match.

An hour into the cross-examination, Mulcahy looked up and caught sight of Stevie at the back of the room. The investigator was nodding his head slightly from side to side.

'Your Honour, may I have a moment?' Mulcahy asked.

He conferred briefly with Stevie. Then he saw his client beckon to him, and went to the table.

'Mr Mulcahy?' It was Judge Grosso, now growing impatient. Mulcahy returned to the podium, took a deep breath.

'Your Honour, may the defendant examine Exhibit 21?'

'Certainly. No one is to touch it, of course. Mr Kelly, please assist.'

They brought the evidence pouch to counsel table, and huddled around Shepard as it was opened. Mulcahy, George, and Shepard conferred for a moment more. Then Mulcahy returned to the podium.

'Lieutenant Evans, were any other fingerprints found on this bar of soap?'

351

'No,' he said.

'None?'

'That is correct.'

'You didn't find Mr Whitaker's fingerprints on the soap?'

'No, we didn't.'

'What kind of soap is that, Lieutenant?'

'I don't know.'

'You don't know?'

'No, I'm afraid it was a sliver, and the brand name imprint had been washed off.'

The pouch was carried to the witness stand. 'Well, please take a look at it,' Mulcahy continued. 'Would you recognise the scent of Lifebuoy soap?'

The witness examined the soap, through its plastic pouch. 'I'm afraid I wouldn't,' he said.

'Let me ask you this,' said Mulcahy. 'How many other similar bars of soap did you find in the Whitaker house?'

'Other bars of this kind of soap?'

'That shade of green, yes, that scent.'

'If memory serves, I don't think any other bars of this kind of soap were identified. I believe bars of Ivory soap were found, and some others. Would you like me to check the police report?'

'If that would refresh your memory, Lieutenant.'

'It would.' Evans paged through his file. It took a few minutes before he found it: nineteen bars of Ivory soap catalogued throughout the bathrooms, kitchens and linen closets. Four bars of Crabtree and Evelyn speciality soap in the master bath. Three bars of Lava soap in the rear washroom, kitchen cupboard and basement soapstone sink.

'No bars of Lifebuoy soap found, used or new?'

'Apparently not.'

'And no soap which matched this soap in colour or scent?'

'I believe not.'

'How about prints which you believe to be Mr Shepard's, were any more found?'

'No, sir.'

'None in the washroom, for example? None on the sink, or the faucets, or the toilet handle?'

'No, sir.'

'None on the door? The doorknob? None anywhere in the study?'

'No, sir.'

'No fingerprints anywhere else in the house? None on the front door, for example, none on the knocker?'

'None on the front door except for the housekeeper's.'

'I see, Lieutenant. Thank you.' Mulcahy looked up. Ms DeVito was frowning. So was the mother from Roslindale. Bless her after all, Mulcahy was thinking, maybe she keeps a big house. No one else on the jury registered any expression at all.

'No further questions,' Mulcahy said.

Mulcahy was trying to reassure Kate, but it didn't work. It had been a long flight, empty-handed, back from Washington.

'You did the right thing,' he said. 'You couldn't take that chance. You did all you could.'

She shook her head, biting her lip. Then she felt his hand on the side of her face, and held it there, with her eyes tightly shut, as her arm stole round him.

'You did all anyone could,' he said, softly. 'Hell,

the goddamn subpoena wasn't enforcible anyway.' A Massachusetts subpoena would have had no effect outside the Commonwealth. They hadn't time or legal basis to get a subpoena out of the Maryland courts. But they had gambled on the bluff working.

'It would have worked,' she said. 'He never guessed that.'

He felt her grip tighten on his fingers, and the coils of her hair upon his face.

'We still have a chance, I think,' he said. Her eyes asked him to explain, and so they went back through it. Yes, she was pretty sure he hadn't guessed that they knew he was getting into their computer.

'You know,' she said, 'he asked me who else knew where he was. I told him you and Steven George.'

'Yeah?'

'He never asked me who Steven George was.'

'So, what we have to do,' he said, after pondering that for a few moments, 'is drop the right hints. I think he's like a lot of us, really. He wants to know that his bogey-man has gone away. And he wants to know that he's needed.'

They discussed the plan. She would leave a memo in the computer, telling him that she'd been called off to New York, and they would communicate by leaving memos there for each other, which she could access while out of town by modem. If it wasn't too heavy-handed, it might work.

27

Thursday morning. John Shepard's defence team had gathered again in Stevie's Bromfield Street office. O'Hanlon had heaped circumstance upon circumstance, but the rumour was he would rest today, rest after calling one last witness.

'Tim Ogle?' Mulcahy was saying. 'What the hell is he going with Oggles for as his last witness?'

'I tried to call him,' Stevie said. 'Won't talk to us. Smug bahstid.'

'Kate?'

She shrugged. 'I have no idea, Ed.'

'Okay,' he said at last, 'I've got to go to court.'

The skinny lawyer with the pronounced adam's apple stepped forward and took the stand. Ogle wore a double-breasted blue suit set off by a crisp pocket handkerchief. It looked new. The soles of his newly shined black shoes squeaked as he came across the floor. He looked deferentially up at Judge Grosso, nodded to him. The judge did not nod back. This better be worth it, O'Hanlon, he was thinking. The skinny man in the snappy suit did not look, to Judge Grosso, to be worth it.

'My name is Timothy Ogle,' he began.

'Where do you live, Mr Ogle?' asked O'Hanlon.

'221 Cross Street, number 5A, Boston.'

'And how are you employed?'

'I am an associate with Freer, Motley & Stone. In the corporate department.'

'You are an attorney?'

'Yes, sir.'

'How long have you been an attorney?'

'I was admitted in 1991.'

'Did you join Freer Motley in 1991?'

'Yes.'

O'Hanlon spent about ten more minutes going through background, irrelevant stuff. Nothing new or interesting. At 10.20 Mulcahy looked impatiently at his watch. Shepard shrugged, doodling on a notepad.

'Now, Mr Ogle, did you have occasion to work with Mr Shepard on a matter known as the Barron workout?'

'Yes, sir.'

'What the hell am I about to hear?' Mulcahy whispered. He could see that Shepard had whitened a little. As he leaned over to answer, Mulcahy pointed to the notepad. Shepard started writing.

Meanwhile the story was coming out from the witness stand. Shepard, Ogle, and their client, a banker named Fitzsimmons, had gone to Florida to spend a day in fruitless negotiations with the bank's borrower, one Herman Barron. Two years before,

Barron had leveraged a series of jewellery stores with a major LBO financing, and now his companies were in deep financial trouble. At the end of a long day, they sat on wicker armchairs in the hotel lounge bar. The Windjammer, it was called.

'Was Mr Fitzsimmons with you at The Windjammer?' O'Hanlon asked.

'Well, he was at the beginning, but then he excused himself and said he was going off to bed.'

'I see. Did Mr Shepard make a request at that time?' O'Hanlon asked.

'He said the waiter should bring us a bottle of Johnny Walker.'

Ogle went on with the story. He told the jury how, in the quiet lounge, Shepard had said, 'Now, Herman, let's settle this thing.'

O'Hanlon cut in again. 'Did Mr Shepard make a proposal when the whisky came?' he asked.

'Yes,' said Ogle. 'Mr Shepard said, "I propose to you that we stop screw – ah, we stop fooling around, and get this thing done. We will talk. If we can't settle, we drink. We keep drinking this bottle until there's a deal, or we're dead."'

'That's what he said?'

'That's what he said,' said Ogle.

Ed had been staring at Shepard's notes on the yellow pad, and realised, too late, that he should have done something to try to cut this off. It was collateral. But they were so far in it that he'd pay a price with the jury if he objected now. He let it go on.

'What did Mr Barron say?' O'Hanlon asked.

'He asked, "We keep drinking until there is a deal?

That is your proposal?" And Mr Shepard said, "Yes, that's the proposal." And Mr Barron said, "And so you are trying to take advantage of me?"'

'Your Honour,' Ed said, rising to his feet.

'I'm sorry, Mr Mulcahy, it's a little late to object to this line now,' said Judge Grosso. 'We'll see where this is going, Mr O'Hanlon.'

O'Hanlon picked up the baton. 'What did Mr Shepard answer?'

'He said, "Absolutely,"' Ogle said.

'What happened next?'

'Well, they did it. I mean, Mr Shepard, he wrote up a deal on a Windjammer bar cheque, if I remember right, and they left some blanks in it, and they both signed it. And the idea was, they would fill it in when they made a deal, and if they couldn't make a deal, then the one who was left conscious would fill it in.'

'And what happened next?'

'Well, Mr Barron said, "I have a question. You are just the lawyer. How can you make the deal?" And Mr Shepard said, "Am I a man or a god – ah, a man or a mouse? If I tell you it's a deal, it's a deal. Besides, I'm their agent, they are stuck with anything I do."'

'Did they begin this drinking bout, Mr Shepard and Mr Barron?' O'Hanlon pronounced the word 'drinking' as though he were a temperance advocate.

'They did.'

'Did you participate in this affair?'

'No, sir, I was just watching.'

'And your client? Did he participate?'

'Ah, no, like I said, he had gone.'

'I see,' said O'Hanlon. 'Mr Shepard went on after his client left. Well, what happened?'

'Well,' said Ogle, 'it continued for quite a while. They got down halfway through the bottle. Mr Shepard was going on and on about what a bankruptcy would be like for Mr Barron, about how he'd have to go to court all the time, attend endless meetings and so on, and it, well, it kind of wore him down, or seemed to. After an hour, maybe two, Mr Barron began to drop hints. You know, maybe for a forbearance, he'd come up with a forbearance fee. Stuff like that. And Mr Shepard was saying he wanted half a million and the keys. Well, that the bank would want that. It went back and forth.'

'Did they appear to be intoxicated?'

'Yes. In my opinion.'

'At some point, did Mr Shepard threaten Mr Barron?'

'Well, sort of. He said, at one point, that he ought to kick Mr Barron's . . . ah, that he ought to kick his . . . he ought to beat him up. Only he said he couldn't because it was unethical. And Mr Barron, who seemed pretty drunk too, wanted to know what he meant by that, and Mr Shepard said there was a disciplinary rule which prevents a lawyer from kicking the other lawyer's client's . . . from beating him up, or else he would.'

Now Judge Grosso was shaking his head. A bad sign, for the jury were looking to him to help them sort out this bizarre testimony.

'Mr Ogle, is there such a disciplinary rule?'

'No, sir, there's nothing like that. Mr Shepard was kind of, well, kind of rhetorical sometimes, if you know what I mean.'

359

'I see,' said O'Hanlon. 'Well, did they end by striking a bargain?'

'Yes, sir, they did.'

'What were the terms?'

'If I remember correctly, Mr Barron got a release from his guarantee by paying a hundred thousand dollars, and agreeing to a foreclosure of his company. It was a pretty good deal for the bank.'

'I see,' said O'Hanlon, 'but not such a good deal for the opponent, the man whom Mr Shepard had enticed into a drinking bout?'

'Objection.'

'Sustained,' said Judge Grosso.

But O'Hanlon had made his point. It was one of those questions which lawyers ask simply for the sake of stating it, and the answer would have been superfluous. Shepard was not a man who played by any set of rules. Mulcahy was looking over Shepard's scrawl as the prosecutor turned to Idlewild.

'Now, Mr Ogle, did Freer Motley conduct an internal investigation concerning the Idlewild LBO?' O'Hanlon asked.

'Yes.'

'Who conducted that investigation?'

'Objection!'

Mulcahy and O'Hanlon came forward, and they encircled the sidebar for whispered debate. 'Your Honour,' said Mulcahy, 'I conducted the investigation. I'm sure Mr O'Hanlon knows that. But it's irrelevant. I . . .'

'Your Honour, it is directly relevant,' O'Hanlon cut him off. 'The Idlewild LBO, and the investigation of it at Freer Motley, is the key to this whole case.'

Mulcahy interrupted again. 'Your Honour, what's really going on here is that the prosecution is seeking to discredit Mr Shepard by involving me in this personally. It's an old tactic, but very prejudicial for Mr Shepard. This has nothing to do with the facts.'

'Gentlemen!' the judge silenced them. 'Mr O'Hanlon. Where are we going with this? What does this witness, Mr – who is he? – Mr Oggle ... That was all very entertaining about the drinking party in Florida, and I'm sure the Board of Bar Overseers would be interested, but I rather suspect that is the least of Mr Shepard's worries right now. What does this Oggle bring to *my* table?'

'Ogle, Your Honour,' said O'Hanlon quietly, sounding like a penitent.

'Excuse me?'

'Ogle, Your Honour. Ogle. Not Oggle. Ogle.'

'Whatever the man's name, Mr O'Hanlon. The question is, why is he in my courtroom?' The bifocals slipped to the end of the judge's nose and his eyes bored through the prosecutor.

'He apparently knows something about the internal investigation, and I think that's relevant, and ...'

'All right, gentlemen, we'll excuse the jury.'

When they had gone, Judge Grosso turned towards O'Hanlon. 'Let's hear it.'

'Mr Ogle,' O'Hanlon resumed, 'who conducted the Idlewild investigation?'

'Mr Mulcahy.'

'And, during the course of that investigation, were you present when Mr Mulcahy spoke to John Shepard?'

'Yes.'

361

'Bullshit,' Mulcahy said to Shepard, under his breath.

'Please describe the circumstances,' O'Hanlon said.

'Well, I had been on the Idlewild deal, and last May when Mr Mulcahy was doing the investigation, he called me to be interviewed one afternoon. When I got to the conference room, I heard his secretary come over the speaker phone and tell him John Shepard was holding.'

'What happened next?'

'Well, Mr Mulcahy told me to wait, and he picked up the phone, to talk to Mr Shepard.'

'So you didn't hear Mr Shepard?'

'No. Well, actually, I heard him say one thing, before Mr Mulcahy picked up the phone.'

'What was that?'

'Ah, it was the word, "motherfucker".' The Adam's apple jumped.

'Excuse me?'

'He did that sometimes,' Ogle said. 'Mr Shepard, I mean. He'd say mother – ah, he'd say that word a lot. Sort of a greeting.'

'I see,' said O'Hanlon. 'What happened next?'

'Well, I heard Mr Mulcahy talking.'

'What did he say?'

'He said he was investigating Idlewild, and then he said "I don't want to hear this, John."'

'Anything else?'

'Not that I can remember.'

Grosso looked up from the bench. 'Is that it?'

'Yes, Your Honour,' said O'Hanlon. 'On that point.'

'Cross?'

362

Mulcahy rose. 'Mr Ogle, save for the one-word epithet, you heard nothing that Mr Shepard said?'

'That is correct.'

'Your Honour,' said O'Hanlon, 'having heard the testimony, I would stipulate that the Commonwealth will not need to examine Mr Ogle on this point. Unfortunately, however, it appears that we will have to call Mr Mulcahy. This conversation clearly occurred prior to Mr Mulcahy's representation of the defendant. There is no privilege issue.'

Mulcahy shook his head. He came forward to Kelly's desk and stood beside O'Hanlon, marvelling at the mournful look on the prosecutor's face, which looked so dreadfully disappointed that the pursuit of truth would oblige him to torpedo the defence.

'Your Honour,' Mulcahy said, 'that's what this whole charade with Mr Ogle is. Look at how Mr O'Hanlon has played this. He pretends to discover that he needs me as a witness right when he's reached the end of his case. Too late for me to withdraw. What he wants is to get in a fight with me over what I said to Mr Shepard that day. Well, I can tell you that Mr Shepard said nothing incriminating. But Mr O'Hanlon doesn't care about that. He wants a chance to try to attack the credibility of Mr Shepard by damaging *my* credibility. All he wants is me on that stand. He doesn't really care what I say.'

'Your Honour, that is purely speculation, and . . .'

'Oh, come off it, Paul . . .'

'Gentlemen!' Grosso interrupted again. 'Mr Mulcahy,' he said, 'if you were examined on that conversation, what do you expect the evidence would be?'

'Well, Your Honour, best I can remember, the call

came in. Shepard told me he was leaving town, wanted to say goodbye, hoped to see me some day, something like that. And I think I told him that he probably didn't want to talk to me. And he asked why? And I told him that I had been assigned to investigate the Idlewild mortgage error. Which he told me he hadn't heard about. I believe he said something like, Why would I take that assignment, couldn't I see that the firm was trying to set him up? Something like that. And he wished me well.'

O'Hanlon was on his feet. 'Clearly that is relevant, Your Honour. I believe it expresses a consciousness of guilt.'

Grosso was frowning. 'Did you put Mr Mulcahy on your witness list?'

'No, Your Honour, it was not until now that I knew . . .'

'Well, if you'd properly interviewed Mr Ogg – Mr Ogle, you would have known.'

O'Hanlon began to respond, but the judge waved him off. 'Having examined the demeanour of Mr Ogle while testifying, and the demeanour of Mr Mulcahy who, as an officer of this court, has made to this court a representation, I find that the probative value of the testimony is slight, if any, while the prejudice to the defence of permitting Mr Mulcahy to be called as a witness would be great. I rule that Mr Ogle will not be permitted to testify concerning the Mulcahy/Shepard call, and that the prosecution will not be permitted to call Mr Mulcahy to the stand. Would the officers bring the jury back, please?'

'Anything further with this witness?' Judge Grosso asked, when the jury had resumed their seats.

'Yes, Your Honour, there is additional evidence,' said O'Hanlon, as he moved back to the podium.

'Mr Ogle,' he said, 'was the defendant employed as an associate at Freer Motley when you joined the firm?'

'Yes.'

'What was your general relationship with Mr Shepard?'

Shepard wrote a note on his yellow pad and passed it to Mulcahy. 'Purely physical' it read. Mulcahy chuckled.

'We worked together on some deals,' the bantam witness said. 'I mainly worked for him.'

'When was the last time you worked for the defendant?'

'Last March. I was on the Idlewild team.'

'You worked on the Freer Motley team which represented Depositors' Fidelity on the Idlewild transaction?'

'Yes.'

'Did you report to Mr Shepard on that transaction?'

'Yes.'

'With reference to the Idlewild closing, what were your responsibilities?'

'To jump when he said jump.' There were chuckles from the jury box.

O'Hanlon moved to the back of the box. 'Directing your attention to 23 March of this year,' he began, as the jury perked up. Here we go, thought Mulcahy. O'Hanlon continued, 'Did you have a private conversation with Mr Shepard?'

'Yes.'

365

'Where did that conversation take place?'

'In the elevator.'

'In an elevator at the offices of Freer Motley?'

'Yes, sir.'

'Who was present?'

'Mr Shepard and myself.'

'Was anyone else present?'

'No.'

'How is it you are able to recall the date of this conversation?'

'Mr Shepard and I had just come from the first meeting of the Idlewild team. In Mr Whitaker's office. We left the meeting together and were in the same elevator afterwards. I remember that day very clearly.'

'I see,' said O'Hanlon, who had a knack of feigning just to have learned a point he had coached his witnesses on. 'What did Mr Shepard say to you in the elevator?'

'He said that he was going to kill Samuel Whitaker.'

O'Hanlon paused with mock-heroic seriousness. 'Mr Ogle, this is very important. What . . .'

Mulcahy was on his feet. 'Objection to the commentary, Judge. This is not important at all.'

Grosso, who had been a fair trial lawyer in his own day, had to suppress a smile. 'The objection is sustained. *Both* counsel are admonished to avoid commentary on the evidence. Proceed, Mr O'Hanlon.'

'Yes, Your Honour. Mr Ogle, what were the defendant's exact words?'

'As best I can remember, his words were, "Call me a pussy if I don't kill that Episcopal pissant."'

The effect was somewhat dampened by suppressed laughter from the gallery, but sixteen jurors had sat up and taken notice.

'No further questions,' said O'Hanlon, and sat down.

The jury watched the larger man take his seat, and then looked for Mulcahy to rise. But he sat for a moment, shaking his head. He got to his feet slowly, still carrying on, to all appearances, some kind of ironical conversation with himself. He walked slowly to the witness box, head still shaking. Half a minute went by. Ogle removed his glasses and began to polish them with his handkerchief.

Mulcahy stopped at the witness stand, staring past Ogle at the windows above the bench. The jury looked at the two men, beginning to grow uncomfortable with the silence. Ogle shifted in his seat. Mulcahy turned to look at the little man in the new suit. They were separated by about two feet. Softly, almost in a whisper, he asked, 'That's it?'

'I don't understand.'

'That's it, Mr Ogle, that's your testimony?'

'I've answered the questions, yes.'

Mulcahy nodded. Still moving slowly, he walked back to the rear of the jury box, now separated from the witness by the sixteen observers. He turned. 'Mr Ogle,' he said, 'you came all the way across town to tell us that?'

'Objection,' said O'Hanlon, and although Judge Grosso sustained it, he was thinking much the same thing to himself.

'Mr Ogle, did you consider yourself a close friend of Mr Shepard?'

'No, not really.'

'Did you ever go to his apartment?'

'No.'

'Did he ever go to yours?'

'No.'

'Did you ever socialise together?'

'No.'

'But Mr Shepard betrayed a secret plot of *murder* to *you*, is that your testimony?'

Ogle was rattled. His long morning in Court was only beginning. 'I can only testify as to what he said.'

'In an elevator, Mr Ogle?'

'Excuse me?'

'Mr Shepard confessed a secret plot of murder to you in an *elevator*, on your return trip from an office meeting?'

'He – well, he said what he said,' said Ogle. He removed his glasses and began to polish them again.

'You reported this conversation to the police, of course,' Mulcahy continued.

'No, actually, I didn't.'

'Mr Ogle, you didn't report to the police that you had information concerning a murder that was about to occur?'

'No, I didn't, at the time, realise . . .'

'You didn't realise that you had heard a confession of murder?'

Ogle was silent.

'The District Attorney, then? You straightaway telephoned Mr Connell's office?'

'No.'

'You are an attorney, Mr Ogle, aren't you?'

'Yes.'

'Don't you know the importance of reporting criminal activity to the authorities?'

Ogle looked helpless. 'Yes.'

'Well, I'm sure that, at the very least, you dictated a file memo to preserve your memory of this *important* conversation, didn't you?' He looked over at O'Hanlon and smiled as he laid stress on the word. A cross-examination like this doesn't come up every day. You have to milk it a little.

'No, I didn't.'

'Mr Ogle, you have a dictaphone at your office, don't you?'

'Yes.'

'You use it all the time to dictate memos, don't you?'

'Yes, I suppose.'

'And yet you didn't pick up your dictaphone to record this confession of murder, did you?'

'No, I didn't, but . . .'

Mulcahy cut him off. He had noticed Shepard beckoning, and he returned to counsel table. 'A moment please, Your Honour.'

'Certainly, Mr Mulcahy.'

Half a minute later he returned to the lectern. 'Do you know Elizabeth Sterling, Mr Ogle?'

'If you mean Elizabeth Beckett-Sterling, yes. She's a lawyer at Freer Motley.'

'Right, just the one,' said Mulcahy. 'Were you present on an occasion when Mr Shepard said to Ms Sterling that he would string her by her tits from the top of Ten Post Office Square? Members of the jury,

I apologise, but Mr Ogle, those were Mr Shepard's words, were they not?'

'I think he said "sagging tits", but, yes, to the best of my memory.' Now there was outright laughter from the gallery. Ogle's glasses began to mist again. He removed them and wiped furiously.

'I see. "Sagging tits".' A juror coughed. Mulcahy looked up and saw that a couple of the men were looking away, their hands obscuring their mouths. Not Mrs Watts, however. Her expression was one of pure disgust. At the table in front, O'Hanlon was holding his head in his hands. Mulcahy continued, 'Mr Shepard is a profane man, isn't he?'

'Yes.'

'He often speaks crudely?'

'Yes.'

Mulcahy paused. Now he turned back and began to walk slowly back to the witness box. Ogle's Adam's apple rose and fell. He shifted in place. Mulcahy came up to the box, leaned on it with his left hand, and said, ever so slowly, 'Well?'

Ogle looked back at him. 'What?'

'Did he?'

Ogle was looking around himself now. 'Did he what?' he asked, timidly.

'Did he string Elizabeth Beckett-Sterling by her sagging tits from the top of Ten Post Office Square?' He threw the question at him, and saw Mrs Watts flinch in the box. But it was the moment to turn the tone of the examination from the comic to the contemptuous.

'Your Honour,' O'Hanlon was rising to his feet, 'I object.'

'Overruled, Mr O'Hanlon, the Commonwealth called this witness.'

'Mr Ogle?' said Mulcahy.

'No,' he said, 'as far as I know, he did not.'

'He didn't string her from the top of Ten Post Office Square by any part of her anatomy, did he?'

'No.'

'Sometimes Mr Shepard's language is what we might call "colourful", right, Mr Ogle?'

'Yes, I suppose that's true.'

'Mr Ogle,' said Mulcahy, 'how old are you?'

'I'm twenty-five. Be twenty-six in October.'

'Good. The age of discretion is not so very far off. Now, in your twenty-five years, have you ever heard anyone say, "I'll kill him", "I'm going to kill so-and-so", words to that effect?'

'Yes.'

'People sometimes say that to express exasperation, don't they?'

'I suppose so.'

'When they have no intention of committing murder?'

Ogle looked up pitifully, his eyes like saucers behind the eyeglasses. 'Yes,' he said.

'Before this elevator confession you have come here to share with us, you and Mr Shepard had just come from a meeting with Mr Whitaker, right?'

'Right.'

'And Mr Whitaker had just announced that you would all be working essentially straight out for eight days, right?'

'Yes, that's true.'

'Mr Shepard had a ski trip planned, didn't he?'

'He did say something about skiing,' said Ogle.

'And you and Mr Shepard had just been told by Mr Whitaker that the Idlewild deal would have to be closed, correct?'

'Yes.'

'Mr Shepard would have to cancel his vacation plans, right?'

'I guess so.'

Mulcahy walked back to defence table. He paged through a yellow pad slowly. 'Now, Mr Ogle, about your little trip to Florida. Did you report any misconduct of Mr Shepard to the Board of Bar Overseers?'

'No,' he said.

'You *didn't*?'

'No, I, I uh, I didn't,' he admitted, the embarrassment plain to all in the box. Mulcahy knew exactly what was happening in the young associate's mind. Like most lawyers, Ogle didn't know the fine points of the Rules of Professional Conduct as well as he should. He probably did know that in many jurisdictions there is a duty to report misconduct. He was wondering, now, whether Massachusetts was one. Later that afternoon he would pull out his rule book and find that there is not. But by then it would be too late.

'Mr Ogle, Mr Herman Barron's lawyer was a man named Abraham Finestein, is that correct?'

'Yes.'

'You described a negotiation in a Florida bar in which Mr Shepard and Mr Barron were drinking, do you recall that testimony?'

'Yes.'

'Isn't it a fact that Mr Finestein was present at all times during that negotiation?'

'Well, he . . .'

'Yes or no, Mr Ogle!' It was the first time in the trial that he had shouted, and Ogle was silenced instantly.

'Just answer my question, Mr Ogle. Is it true that Mr Finestein was present at all times during that negotiation, yes or no?'

'Yes, it's true he was present,' Ogle said. 'But, Your Honour, if I . . .'

Now Judge Grosso, who had heard enough himself, cut him off. 'There is no question before you, Mr Ogle.'

'And he offered no objection of any kind to the settlement agreement, did he? Yes or no, Mr Ogle?'

Ogle looked about the room for help – to O'Hanlon, to Grosso – but there was none. 'No,' he said.

'Mr Ogle,' Mulcahy said, softly now, 'have you got any work to do back at the office?'

Ogle said, 'Yes, a lot, actually.'

'Good,' said Mulcahy. 'Why don't you go back and do it?' And he sat down.

O'Hanlon looked quickly at the box and made his decision. In his preparation sessions with Gleason, Ogle had left Finestein out, thinking to improve the story just a little bit, and now it was Paul O'Hanlon who didn't know the whole account, and whose trial instincts told him to get a disastrous witness off the stand, and do so double quick. Sometimes you catch a break, and the break which Mulcahy caught then was that Paul O'Hanlon had never been a civil lawyer. He hadn't known, as any civil lawyer would have known, that however bizarrely the Florida evening might have ended, it must have begun with Barron's lawyer present. So O'Hanlon didn't redirect. And Timothy Ogle never got his chance to tell the jury that the lawyer Finestein, like all of them on that hot and humid Florida night, ate and drank too much, and that Finestein was indeed *present* in the Windjammer lounge, and that, while it was literally true that Shepard had waved the scrawled agreement before Finestein's misty eyeglasses as his head lolled on the wicker chair, and equally true that Finestein had offered no objection, the fact of the matter was that Abraham Finestein had offered nothing at all, except the gentle, rhythmic, rumble of his snores.

But Paul O'Hanlon didn't know that. And when Ogle had scuttled from the courtroom, O'Hanlon spoke the words which a defence lawyer loves and hates to hear. 'The Commonwealth rests, Your Honour,' he said. They are comforting words for a defence lawyer because, as bad as it may have been, it might not get worse. He begins to think, maybe it won't get worse. But the comfort is short-lived, particularly if his client has that expectant gleam in his eye which arises from the foolish desire to testify. Then it can get worse.

Court adjourned for lunch. It couldn't have ended on a lower note for the prosecution, Mulcahy thought. He'd have at least half an hour to enjoy the feeling. After lunch, and after the judge denied his motion for directed verdict, he'd have to put on a defence.

28

The courtroom was full that afternoon, for they came to see the defence and there was hope of a thrill. Mulcahy noticed Frannie Dillard in front. Well, they wouldn't get it. The defence rose to call its first witness, the first of a series of witnesses through whom to build the life story of Sam Whitaker, and the story of his suicide. And even as the balding gentleman in the brown tweed jacket was taking the stand, and Mulcahy was reaching for his notes, his gut was telling him that it didn't add up.

After the preliminaries, he came swiftly to the conversation he wanted to put before the jury. 'Where was the meeting, Mr Fellbright?'

'At the Two Mallets Tavern in Sheringham. I was having a drink there with Treat Higgins and Sam.'

'When was that?'

'Some time in April, I think.'

'Did Mr Whitaker say anything to you about the "meaning of life", anything like that?'

'Yes.' Fellbright paused before answering, and his

eyes assumed the remoteness of a man who is actually seeing and hearing the event again. ' "We're long past it, Martin," he said. "We're long past it, long past the stage where you wonder what the point is, and come to the realisation that there is none." '

'Did he say anything else?'

'Well, yes. He told us this terribly affecting story about a comrade in the Philippines, some fellow from Brooklyn called Izzy. A fellow who could not have been more different than Samuel. All he wanted, Sam said, was to marry his girl and start a bakery. And of course Sam was destined for great things, Yale, Oxford, his career. But I guess they became great friends. Izzy was killed.

'Sam became very misty-eyed in the Tavern. It was quite unlike him. And he said, "Izzy was as brave as any man I ever met. And he was cut down at nineteen by a machine gun nest. He never got the girl. Never got the bakery. And now, our sworn enemies the Japanese? Our soulmates, our soulmates!"

'And he said to me, "Martin, there really is no point. No point to thirty years in the law firm, and sometimes I think, as I look about my empty nest, there was no point to the nest." '

Resuming his seat, Mulcahy thought the testimony had been powerful. But Paul O'Hanlon knew juries.

'Mr Fellbright,' he began, 'Sam Whitaker admired Izzy for courage, didn't he?'

'Yes, I think that's right,' said Fellbright.

'I see. Now, Mr Fellbright, you knew Samuel Whitaker for more than thirty years, didn't you?'

'I did.'

'Your families grew up together?'

'Yes.'

'On many occasions, you shared laughter with Sam Whitaker?'

'I did, yes.'

'And occasionally, sadness?'

'Yes, that's true.'

'When your wife died six years ago, didn't you and Mr Whitaker go off together, fishing, for a week?'

'We did, yes, in Florida.'

'Did you talk then, talk deeply, about your lives – their successes, their mischances, good times, bad times?'

'We did, yes.'

'Did Mr Whitaker, on that occasion, speak philosophically to you?'

'Yes. Yes, I'm sure he did.'

'Thank you, Mr Fellbright, I know this must be difficult. But tell me one thing. Did Samuel Whitaker ever say to you that he could not bear it, that he considered taking his own life?'

Martin Fellbright looked out at the room, the lawyers, the strangers in the back, the jurors, the crowd all seeking to extract from him some morsel to satisfy a selfish hunger, and he felt a sudden surge of angry loyalty. None of these people, whatever their motive, had the right to do this to Sam.

'No, Mr O'Hanlon,' he said. 'He never said anything of the kind.'

Once again the table in the Bromfield Street office was littered with wax-paper.

'All right, I admit it,' Mulcahy was saying, his back

to the room. 'Suicide is going down.' He turned on his heel and stared outside.

'What do we do?'

No one had any ideas.

'Anything else on Creel?' he asked.

'He hasn't left me any notes on the computer,' Kate said. 'At least, not that I'm smart enough to read.'

Stevie shook his head. 'Time's getting short, guys . . .'

'Short!' Mulcahy exclaimed. 'Short! We are damn out of time! Act over. Curtain down!'

'Well . . .' Kate said.

'Well, what?' Mulcahy said.

'Maybe we're not out of time.'

'Talk to me, Kate.'

'I could serve some subpoenas.'

'Huh?'

'Well,' she said, looking uncertainly about the room, 'I have a file of twenty-seven witnesses. Each one might have something to say relative to the suicide defence.'

'Suicide is going nowhere,' Mulcahy started to say.

'Naw, Eddie, that ain't what she's sayin'. Right, Katie Kate?' And Stevie smiled. 'Take a little while to get through twenty-seven witnesses. Enough of a while to give us a little more time. That's what you mean, right?'

'Well, sort of,' she said, blushing. 'Ah, there is sort of a rule about not doing things for delay's sake . . .'

'Do it,' Mulcahy said. 'Paper the goddamn city with them. And Stevie, find me something. Something. Shepard's enemies. Anything.'

*

At about 10 p.m. the cash machine on Common-wealth refused to surrender to Ed Mulcahy either cash or his card. 'Card retained. Contact branch regarding account,' the screen read.

The machine was nothing if not pithy. Mulcahy stood alone in the alcove, staring at the computer's brisk message as headlights from the avenue played across the screen. He was impotent before it. His account was not overdrawn, he didn't think, not so far as he could remember. For weeks, he hadn't bought anything except hamburgers, and pizza and beer. Photocopies. He'd bought a lot of photocopies. But that was it. And now, at 10 p.m. on a Thursday night, Ed Mulcahy was being reminded that, like so many Americans, his lifeline was a wallet-sized chip of plastic, and his lifeline could be cut in the middle of the night, by a machine.

So he left without the cash card, and walked home. He had eight dollars in his wallet. Eight dollars in his wallet, a couple of bucks worth of change on his bureau, probably twenty dollars here and there if he scoured all the jacket and raincoat pockets, another fifty hidden underneath the front seat of his car. There were some crackers left in the lower cupboard, if he remembered right. And there might be some peanut butter left, a few cans of soup. He thought there was a six-pack still in the vegetable bin. Here, he thought, we have the liquid wealth of Edward X. Mulcahy, attorney at law: eighty dollars or so; crack-ers, beer, peanut butter, soup.

The solution to the mystery was waiting for him in his mailbox: the summons, the complaint, the copy of the trustee process order. He stared at them

379

blankly in the lobby. Parisi had sued him for slander in the Chelsea District Court. The demand was $10 million. Ed saw from the papers that Parisi had obtained an order – without notice, a so-called *ex parte* order – freezing his bank accounts. The 'trustee process summons', as they are called, had been served on the bank that morning.

Judge Joseph Labiondo had granted the motion. Mulcahy squinted and called to mind, with some difficulty, a very short, very fat judge who kept interrupting a pointless construction dispute he had tried there three years ago. Yes, that was the guy. 'The deal was, Mr Ippolito,' the judge had interrupted, cutting off the direct of Ed's opponent, 'that Mr O'Brien was supposed to provide the staging. Am I right? Am I right?' And Ippolito had nodded vigorously, while Ed tried, hopelessly, to object, to confine the witnesses to what was written (nothing) and said (also nothing) about the staging which was the basis of the trifling dispute. But it was a trick they don't teach in law school. How do you object to the question when it is the judge who asks it? So the objections were all overruled, and the fat little jurist kept saying, 'Your client was supposed to supply the staging, Mr Mulcahy.' Wagging his pudgy finger, he kept saying, 'Your man, sir.'

Thus the Honourable Joseph Labiondo. That day Mulcahy's Irishman had heavy weather of it against his Italian opponent. Whenever a witness got too near the evidence, the big mop of white hair flew, and the judge cut it off. 'Mr Mulcahy, you're wasting my time,' he'd say. Judge Labiondo's time was excessively valuable, and there was nothing like evidence for wasting it.

Ed sat in his kitchen with the papers from the Chelsea District Court in his hand, studying them, feeling that sense of violation – not unlike the feeling of a burglary victim – which the recipient of a lawsuit always feels, that sense that unknown enemies and unknown plans are afoot, schemes to steal away one's property.

He stared at the papers. Two hoary principles of American jurisprudence came to his mind. The first is that litigants are not supposed to be able to do things to each other without 'notice and a hearing'. It means pretty much what it says, that they don't deprive you of your property without telling you what's going on ahead of time, and giving you a chance to speak out against it.

And the second principle is, that if Felix Parisi moved the judge's admission to the Knights of Columbus thirty years ago, then we can all ignore the first principle.

Well, that was very interesting, but the main point that Wednesday night was that he had no cash. In the darkness, Ed punched in the numbers now committed to manipular memory, and when he heard her voice, said, 'Kate, now it looks like *I* need a lawyer.'

Kate's parade would bring them only two trial days, for not all of the witnesses could be found, and most were too weak or tangential even for delay purposes. But for two wearisome trial days, the Emily Howes and the Treat Higginses and the Buster Bradleys, the

Bay Clubbers and the Cohasset Yacht Clubbers and the vestrymen, the planning board members, the bridge players, the neighbours on Dover Street, came to Room 8b, clutching their subpoenae, and waiting to be called.

Mulcahy would go dutifully through them all. From here, there, and everywhere he gathered scraps of evidence which might point to suicide: the stray depressed remark, the misfortunes, the strains on the marriage. It was uniformly unimpressive: fifteen minutes of direct testimony, identifying a tiny episode, followed by a half hour of cross, emphasising by twelve other references to Whitaker's resourcefulness and courage the utter triviality of the event in question. In 8b, the gallery thinned out.

They were tired when they met that Friday night at Bromfield Street, tired and depressed. O'Hanlon had had his way most of the week. The exultation they'd felt over Ogle's cross had swiftly passed. Time would pass inexorably as they marched through the suicide witnesses. They passed out a round of beers, but even Stevie had lost his volubility.

Ed turned to Kate and asked her, 'How's our other case look? When's the big showdown in Chelsea? I'm about out of money.'

'We're not going to Chelsea,' she said.

He looked at her uncertainly.

'LaBiondo and Parisi go way back, like you told me last night, right?'

'So what can we do about it?'

'We can get out of there.'

'What, wiggle our noses and . . .'

'No,' she said, 'removal. I removed it this morning.'

382

She referred to the right of a defendant to transfer a lawsuit from the district court in Chelsea to the jury sessions of the superior court downtown.

He shook his head. 'God, I didn't even think of that. I can't even think straight any more.' He smiled at her. 'What can I say? Good move.'

'It was no problem. Had to put up a bond, is all.'

'Great. My account grows by the day. So can we dissolve the attachment?'

'I couldn't get a hearing until next week,' she said. 'How are you fixed?'

'I've got about twenty bucks.'

'I'll cover you.'

She would cover him. This was out of hand, completely out of hand. He was in the middle of a case he couldn't handle, watching it fall apart around him, and down to loans from Kate to buy hamburgers.

She could see from his face that it was working at him, and she came to him, and put her hand on his. 'It's going to be all right,' she said.

'Yeah, it's going to be just fine. It's going to be just great! No defence. No job. No future, and no bank account.'

'Ed . . .'

'Kate,' he asked suddenly, 'do you think we should plead him?'

'Should we . . . no. No, I don't, I mean . . .'

But he was staring at her in an odd way.

' Do *you* think you should?' she asked.

He didn't answer, so she went on, 'Anyway, how are you going to do that? How are you going to get John to do anything he hasn't set his own mind to?'

'We could work at him a little.'

'Ed, for heaven's sake.'

'And what happens to me, Kate? What happens to me when this is over, and he goes down?'

'It will be all right,' she said.

'What does that mean? What does that mean, it will be all right? Kate, it won't be all right. It won't be all right at all.'

It was Kate who had the idea, that hot Saturday afternoon at Bromfield Street. Stevie had a radio tuned to the Sox afternoon game. Kate's witness string would play out sometime the following week. Mulcahy sat with a stack of witness outlines before him.

'Snow White made a name prosecuting on the Strike Force, right?' she asked.

'Who?' he asked, looking down at his notes.

'Libby Russell.'

'Oh, yeah.'

'Well, I don't know, I'm not a prosecutor, but if you're on the Strike Force, who do you know?'

'Chappelle?'

'No. Who else? You prove cases with informants, right?'

'God, I hate it when broads figure out stuff befoah me,' said Stevie, reaching for his hat. 'No offence, Katie Kate.' He almost bolted for the door, and as his footsteps crashed down the linoleum on the stairs, they heard him say, 'This woman, Eddie, this woman is a fucking genius.'

When the sound of his footfalls had faded,

Mulcahy said, 'Kate, do you realise what you're really saying?'

'Yeah,' she said. 'Yeah, I do. Pretty hard to believe.'

Stevie hadn't far to walk. He still had friends at the FBI, friends who worked Saturdays.

'Stevie, you got brass ones and I got no brains,' the agent said later that day, as he handed over the photos. 'I can't believe I'm doing this.'

Stevie took the fifteen polaroid photographs off to Joy Street and began knocking on doors.

Late that night, two men sipped Budweisers in a booth in Kyle's Tap on L Street in South Boston. A desultory few craned their necks to watch a ball-game on an overhead television. In the booth no one was paying attention. One of the men, of middle age, with short-cropped hair and wearing a windbreaker, frowned and stared at his beer. The other was Stevie. He gestured, cajoled. He spoke softly. He smiled. He pressed. It was just a hypothesis, he said, just a hypothesis. But it made sense. His guy was on trial for murder. Stevie honestly believed the sonofabitch was innocent, he said, so he'd been figuring, figuring. And he had this hypothesis.

Stevie knew something about cops, and it is true of almost all of them. They will not lie awake at night worrying about the conviction of an innocent man. But the escape of the guilty, the fact that the inno-cent's conviction may absolve the guilty, that will give a cop fits.

The man frowned and shook his head. 'Stevie, I can't believe I done what I already done, so forget about it.'

'Ten, fifteen one-on-ones, for Chrissakes,' Stevie

385

said, referring to the polaroid photographs the agent had made of the mug shots. 'It wasn't exactly the Pentagon Papers.'

'Yeah, Stevie, handing out photos of the Bureau's playmates to a gumshoe in a bad toupée, that's gonna get me a promotion.'

'Look, you give me ten, fifteen photos. Except for their names, you ain't told me nothin' about them, okay? And one of 'em, this guy Testa, whoever he is, my witness makes him. So you done the right thing, Jimmy, because she makes this guy Testa. Only my problem is, who the hell is he, know what I mean?' Stevie winked.

His companion looked at him sourly. 'Stevie,' he said, 'one whisper of this comes back to me and I'm in St Louis checking phone logs on fucking Operation Rescue, and you . . . I'll turn your ass over to six of Vinny's cousins.'

'Jimmy, come on . . .'

'Don't shit me on this, Stevie. She makes him? She makes Vinny?'

'She absolutely made him. She was sure.' He indicated the photograph on the booth table. 'She picked him right out. "This one," she said, "this one."'

'Under oath?'

'Hey, I cahn't put the broad under oath in an interview. Come on! But she was sure as hell.'

'Why didn't she tell Boston?'

'Nobody asked. Nobody knew. Shepid never reported it. He never knew it. There was no report. So O'Hanlon's guys never went asking.'

The other man sighed. 'Stevie, I don't know. I give up a Strike Force informant and I'm done. I'm a dishwasher at McDonald's. I'm serious, Stevie, how'd you like your ass audited? How'd you like six months explaining to the IRS every two hundred bucks you took to tail some Don Juan to a condominium? I can arrange it. Not a whisper of this comes back to me, the Strike Force, nothing. No motions, no affidavits based on confidential sources, none of that bullshit. You gotta get it some other way.'

'Jimmy. You know me.'

He stared at Stevie for a long cold moment. 'All right,' he said. He drained the bottle and looked at his watch. 'I gotta go, Stevie. I don't want to see you or hear from you again about this, ever, you got me?'

Stevie nodded. The man rose. '*United States of America* v. *Angelo Cerrone*,' he said, softly. In a moment the door of Kyle's Tap had swung open and closed again, and the FBI agent was gone.

Later that evening Kate stared at the laptop in the Bromfield Street office. A block away, she could hear the plaintive song of a saxophone. A lone musician was playing at Downtown Crossing.

Kate called up Westlaw and searched *Cerrone* in the District Court library. She was in luck. There was a reported decision, something from Judge Elder denying a motion to suppress a wiretap. She read down the heading, through the caption of the case, the headnotes, to the name of the Assistant United States Attorney appearing for the government. There it was. 'Golly,' was all she said, softly, as she reached for the telephone.

29

Without speaking of it directly – for indirection is everything in romance – they had developed a routine in the mornings. She would stop in at Bromfield Street at about 7.45, on her way to the Financial District. At that hour Stevie was hardly ever about, but Ed would be there, with his files scattered on the table, preparing for the day ahead, and when he heard her footfalls on the stairway, he would pretend to be engrossed in one of them. The truth of it is that, from about 6, when he rose, he would be thinking of her, looking forward to that sound outside Stevie's office door.

When she came into the room, he would be looking down, but she saw through that, and he half knew that she did. Each morning she stayed with him until 8.30, when it would be time for he to go off to court. And then they would descend the narrow staircase together, she in front, he behind with his trial bag. As they came to the street door, her scent would be all round him, the scent of her skin and hair, and of the coconut shampoo she must have used, and in the confines of the entranceway the clumsy business of getting the door opened and squeezing outside into the sunlight would be a momentary intoxication for him. Just for a moment, then, they might stand together amid the throng of officeworkers sweeping along the lane, before she turned towards the Financial District, and he in the other direction, towards Pemberton Square.

So it was that Monday morning, as they began the third week of trial. Mulcahy felt just a moment or two of escape, as he tugged his two-wheeler up Tremont, for it seemed that he had scarcely been apart from her all weekend. But the bustle and the jostle of the pedestrian traffic, and the crowds waiting to get through the electronic monitoring at the annexe doorway brought him back to reality. And today's reality was another line-up of witnesses to continue building the reasonable doubt case on suicide.

Mulcahy found them in the lock-up behind 8b again, a circle of the white-shirted court officers around John Shepard.

'So my guy's not happy,' Shepard was saying to them. 'I mean, the I Bankers sign you up for the IPO, and they're supposed to sell all this new stock, right? They make millions. And then my client has to go around on this road show with 'em, meeting every hopsack-wearin' stockbroker in East Halfwit to peddle the stock the stuffed shirts who get the commission are supposed to sell. It's a helluva swindle, these IPOs. And my guy isn't liking it too much.'

The caged door stood open and the three court

officers were gathered around him, perched on the chairs and the desk, drinking him in with that blank stare of pyjama-clad children being read to by Father. Shepard scarcely seemed to notice as Mulcahy came in.

'Sugars?' Freddie asked.

'Yeah, two, thanks, Freddie,' Shepard said.

Coffee! Freddie was fixing the prisoner his coffee! This wasn't happening.

'So here I am in the back seat of a cab with this client, and he's not happy. He does not like investment bankers. He does not like lawyers. He does not like neckties. He particularly doesn't like Harvard, anybody who went to Harvard, anybody who mentions Harvard, anybody who ever took a cab through Harvard Square, or anybody who's related to any of the foregoing motherfuckers, okay?'

'Can't blame him for that,' said one of the officers.

'No,' said Shepard, 'you absolutely got to *respect* him for that. He's Gus, right? He writes computer code. That's what he likes. And, as it happened, he's written about sixty thousand lines of pretty good goddamn code which is going to take him public.

'But tonight he's not happy. He's been on airplanes since forever, and he's been doing all the selling. And now he's bouncin' along up and down the hills of San Francisco in the back seat of a cab on his way to the fuckin' Chavot to have dinner with six nobs with *Veritas* in crimson letters on their suspenders. Last thing on earth my techie wants is dinner with six I bankers at an eight-star restaurant where you got to be a Mayflower descendant for the headwaiter even

390

to look down his nose at you. "I have had it with these guys, John," he says to me.

'So I said to him, "Leave things to John. I gotta cell phone on me, let's have some fun." I call this associate in Boston, give him the instructions, and I tell Gus what to do.'

'Yeah?' the younger court officer asked.

'John,' Mulcahy said, 'I don't mean to interrupt, but . . .'

'In a minute, Ed. The lynch mob will keep.' He turned back to the three officers.

'So I give Gus his lines, and we go to meet the six starchheads, have a drink. About eight, we go into the mausoleum for dinner. My guy sits there wearing a grin like a jackal, false as Delilah, the wonderful son-ofabitch, and he says, "Gentlemen, I want to let you know how much you mean to me and my company." And he orders the 1951 D'Orville. The wine steward gulps, and says, "*Une bouteille de Château D'Orville cinquante-et-un?*" with his little brass cup hanging around his neck, and his little notepad, and his little pencil shaking in his little hand. And my guy says, "*Non, trois bouteilles!*" "*Trois bouteilles*," the little motherfucker says. "*Trois bouteilles? Oui, monsieur. Mais oui.*" And he scurries off for the cellar. It's a three-thousand-dollar bottle of wine. My boy has ordered *three bottles*! The starchheads, they like this. They've died and gone to heaven, just thinkin' about how many motherfuckers they can tell about having *three bottles* of the 1951 D'Orville! Most expensive wine on earth. Here comes the wine steward with the three bottles. He uncorks the first one. He hovers. Six or eight waiters wander

391

by to check it out, and they hover. Our table looks like a three-card monte game, it's got so many people around it. Even in this goddamn place, it's not every decade you move some 1951 D'Orville, and nobody but nobody ever ordered *three bottles*. So, we toss back the wine, me, Gus, and the six starchheads.

'Nine o'clock, on the nose, my phone rings. "Jesus Christ," I say. "Excuse me." I click it on. "Yes," I say, "yes, he's here. Can this wait? We're at dinner, for Christ's . . . Oh, I see." And I say to the client, "They need to speak to you right away." He picks up the cell phone, and he goes all pale – Gus should have got an Oscar – and he says, "I see. All right. I'll go straight to the airport." He turns it off, and says, "Gentlemen, I'm terribly sorry. Shepard, come with me." He and I check out, and we're in a cab before the six IBs look up at the headwaiter, and the wine steward, and all the other motherfuckers leering down at them in their white ties and tails, and realise that they own the cheque for the *trois bouteilles* of 1951 D'Orville!'

'C'mon,' said Freddie.

'Don't worry, Freddie, I'm sure they lost it in a fee somewhere. But it was sort of worth it at the time. Never thought Gus would order *three* bottles of the stuff. Clients surprise you sometimes . . .'

Mulcahy interrupted. 'That they do.' He smiled at the gathering. 'John, if you don't mind, maybe we could have some story time with your lawyer?'

The court officers stirred. It was time to get to work.

'Gentlemen,' Shepard said with resignation, 'if

you'll excuse me, I need to talk to this heathen motherfucker.'

After the court officers scattered, Mulcahy conferred briefly with him about the day ahead, and then it was time to return to the session. 'John,' he said, 'a good lawyer would instruct his client never to talk to court officers.'

'And Ed, a good client would follow instructions,' Shepard laughed. 'Maybe you and I are neither.'

Mulcahy chuckled as he gathered his notes. 'I have to tell you,' he said, 'you are the first defendant in history had his coffee made for him by Freddie.'

Shepard smiled. 'Maybe I'm the first that was innocent,' he said.

'Maybe,' said Mulcahy. Or maybe you just tell a good story, he was thinking, as they returned to the courtroom.

Breaking for lunch, Shepard and Mulcahy ate tuna sandwiches in the lock-up.

'What do you think, Ed?'

In all candour, Mulcahy thought that the parade of suicide witnesses could not end soon enough, although it would end that afternoon. 'It's not enough,' he said.

Shepard nodded. His colour was drained, and it was easy to see that he'd grown greyer around the sideburns, and in the hair curling on his neck. He looked tired. Trials are fatiguing, and no one sleeps very well, least of all the defendant. 'You know what I'd like?' he asked.

'What?'

'An afternoon in the sun. With grass under my feet.'

'That all?'

'Well, if we're making a demand, throw in a melon-chested gal with her skirts around her ears, I won't object. But between you and me, I'd settle for the grass.'

'Tonight,' Mulcahy said, 'we talk about you.'

Monday night came, and Stevie was talking. 'You know, this broad Russell is an unusual broad. My theory on people is that when nobody in a person's life is loyal to them, there's a real problem, you know? I mean, I asked some of the people who knew the broad at the Strike Force, you know, the Fibbies and what not, and, not like they're tahlkin' but ya can tell, there's no loyalty there. They didn't like her. Ya know? She has this sugary kinda way to her, and would put her hand on you soft and gentle, and smile at a guy, but it was just a show. Eddie, prosecutors are a loyal bunch, but not to this broad.'

He fiddled with the wart. 'The funny thing is, she's everybody's friend, right? Ten-megawatt smile and always with her picture in the papuh at some charity ball. Everybody's friend, and nobody's friend. So I done some diggin'. She's got like thirty law school classmates in Boston, right? I called fifteen of 'em. I get twelve no comments. I get three guys who tell me a little bit of stuff, they didn't know her that well, stuff like that.'

'So what?' asked Mulcahy.

'So not one person tells me the broad is great. I done this before Eddie. You start cold callin' everybody in the world who knows someone, wit' most people you get two kinds of answers, mainly. Ya get, "Fuck off, I ain't talking ta ya," and ya get, "She's the greatest person on God's earth." Ya know? Only nobody outa fifteen people tells me that she's even on their Christmas cahd list. And we're talking Elizabeth Russell here, right. I mean, the broad has a gold-plated resumé and is on fourteen do-good committees and another hahf-dozen muck-a-muck boards. So how come she ain't got no friends? No friends at Justice, no friends at the Hahvahd Law School. Funny.'

Mulcahy shook his head. Stevie was rambling. What did it matter if Elizabeth Russell had no friends at the Harvard Law School? Was that a defence?

'Stevie, you got anything other than pop psychology?'

'Aw, okay, let's trash the investigatuh! We ain't paying him, so we might as well trash him! Pop psychology! As a matter of fact, Attorney Mulcahy, I got a lot more than pop psychology on your pal at Strike Force. Nice thing about you former AUSAs is you all hadda clear an FBI screen.'

He flipped through his notepad.

'Back Bay address, Lexus in the basement, a lotta fancy clothes. They know her on Newbury Street. Single, never married. She's a comer in her law firm, young stah pahtnuh type. A very flash broad, in my opinion. Extremely gorgeous. A dish. Snow White, they call her. A lotta charity boards and shit around town. Name's always in the papers.'

Mulcahy chuckled. 'Is "Snow White" in her FBI report?'

'Eddie, *everything* is in an FBI report. If you mastuhbated in the fifth grade, they got it in there. You should see the shit they got on you.'

Mulcahy's face fell.

'I'm kiddin', Eddie. Believe me. I'm sure you bored hell outa them guys. Don't worry about it. Anyway, Libby Russell. She worked at Albion & Moore outa law school, and then went with Hank Chappelle over to the Strike Force. She followed him to Fletcher Daye about three years ago. Does corporate law now. She's been on some pretty big deals in the last yeah and a half.

'She went to Hahvahd Law with Shepid, ya know. Same class. Econ major at Penn before that. Full scholahship to Penn. Hahd luck story.'

'Libby Russell a hard luck story?' Mulcahy assumed that she must have grown up at debutante balls.

'Yeah, ya never know about people,' Stevie went on. 'She grew up in Shakuh Heights, and it looks like they had dough for a while. Daddy was some kinda stockbroker, investment guy, something like that. Then something goes wrong. When Libby is thirteen, Daddy loses his job, they sell the house, the family splits up. Some kinda SEC thing. Anyway, mother and two daughters move to a little crossroads called Easton, Ohio, where mother works as a schoolteacher. They live in an apartment, Libby goes to public high school.

'Last the Fibbies knew, Mother still in Easton, Father who the hell knows, sister Susanna married, lives in Cincinnati.'

But Ed hadn't been listening. His mind had wandered to a night years before when he had looked up from a file to find Libby Russell standing in his doorway at the US Attorneys' office in Post Office Square. He had been working late in his cramped office. How surprised he was when she entered the little warren and took the one chair which was not being used as a file drawer.

That dark wave rolling back to her shoulders, those lagoon-blue eyes, the perfect symmetry of her forehead, the fullness of her lips – they were a shock to the ambience of Mulcahy's office – a Monet in a broom cupboard. In his agitation, he had swept a file off the desk top, and then fumbled for its contents on the floor while she sat before him. And he remembered how it was at that moment that the radiator pipes set to clanking and banging.

Everyone noticed Libby Russell. They noticed her the day she entered the Harvard Law school. It is a place, after all, where a drop dead gorgeous human being, of either gender, is as remarkable as a free parking space. And he had noticed her the day she took up her office as Chappelle's First assistant at the Strike Force. The conversation had raced around the 6th floor, blazed through the judicial chambers, bounced from table to table in the cafeteria: four years out of school and tabbed as First Assistant to the head of the Strike Force. It was the connections. It was the hair. It was – well, people talked about Chappelle. And yet it was inexplicable. What did she know about major felonies?

She had quickly proved an able administrator, skilful at public relations, canny enough to keep herself out of the courtroom, but somehow visible to the outside world as co-author of the office's success. Everyone knew of her power.

'How are things going, Ed?' she had begun that evening in his office years ago.

Ed. She called him 'Ed'. He remembered the lump in his throat. Extraordinary – she knew – had now spoken – his first name. He was Ed Mulcahy in the middle of the pack, once one of the short guys losing the floor at the gymnasium pick-up games, now a faceless AUSA curled over files full of minor drug dealers, bank robbers, drunken servicemen who'd clocked a duty officer. He had the smallest, the sloppiest office, the narrowest window, the ugliest aspect of a not-particularly-inspiring airshaft. And in that office was Libby Russell, inquiring after his well-being.

It became apparent after a few minutes that she was interviewing him.

'Ed,' he could still remember her saying, 'you have a reputation for being meticulous. We could use some help over at Strike Force. And, if you don't mind my saying so, you have to plan. Where are you going to be in three years? Whom do you know? Who can help you get there?'

He remembered how he went crimson as her pale blue eyes stared at him, and as she volleyed her questions at him – how embarrassing it was to be exposed as someone who paid no attention to his own future, his own problems, even, as he looked wryly about the squalor of his own office, his own desk.

'Chappelle is going places,' she said. Now head of the Strike Force, the former Harvard professor had brought Russell over from her firm when he took up the job. Brilliant, well-connected, smooth, Chappelle was a perfect mentor for her, and she a perfect Friday for him. People had talked, of course. But whenever a beautiful woman with a gorgeous smile is successful, people talk.

'He can walk into Fletcher Daye whenever he feels like it,' she said. 'And bring a few people with him. A person should plan ahead,' she had said, then smiled at him again with that disarming smile.

After she left, he had thought about it. She *was* bewitching. Fletcher Daye was the politically wired law firm in town, the one with its own consulting arm and the constant stream of pols plying the elevators, trolling the conference rooms for fundraisers. But its culture was not for Ed Mulcahy. He had let the job go.

That was a long time ago. Now, in the Bromfield Street office, Mulcahy took stock of what he had. Bits and scraps was all: coincidences, a habit of being around the edges of things. And *Cerrone*. She had prosecuted *Cerrone*. But Mulcahy had been a trial lawyer long enough to be afraid of precisely this situation. It is when facts are hopeless that theories start to look seductive. Theories don't wear well in the courtroom. They have a way of unravelling in your face. An identification by a witness he had never seen, a chance connection – which he couldn't prove – with an informant, wasn't much. They teach you to be afraid of your instincts. Before you call a witness, you have to know what the witness will say. You have to be able to control the witness. Even then, you hesitate. And this was a witness he didn't even understand. But it was too late for the rules.

'Let's at least get her to the party,' he said. 'We can figure out later whether to ask her to dance.'

In the Back Bay, Kate climbed the stairs at Henri's. The four-star restaurant's dining room is in the ballroom of a converted mansion on Gloucester Street. She had long day-dreamed of going there, although she had hoped that her first trip would be for the purpose of dining, not delivery. It is rumoured that the kitchen at Henri's has no can opener, since nothing at Henri's comes from a can. The food is sufficiently stunning that the rumour has become plausible. It may even be true.

Turning the corner into the room, Kate had no trouble spotting Libby at the large table by the bay window. She was with a half dozen men, all laughing, the bottles of wine being passed freely, a waiter and a wine steward fluttering about them. Evidently it was another closing dinner.

'*Mademoiselle?*'

'Excuse me, I have to meet someone.' Kate smiled sweetly at the headwaiter, hoping he wouldn't notice how decidedly underdressed she was. She threaded her way through the tables until she stood nervously at the woman's shoulder.

'Ms Russell?'

'Yes?' Libby Russell turned, surprised, and the pale blue eyes instantly appraised the nervous young woman with the extraordinary hair who stood before her.

'I have something for you.'

'Yes?'

Kate handed her the subpoena. 'It's for Wednesday,' she said. 'Suffolk. Session 8b.'

'Oh, for heaven's sake,' Russell said.

Libby Russell stared after Kate until she disappeared from the dining room, then looked down at the subpoena. Her party had fallen silent. Reminding herself that she was, as usual, on display, she recovered her composure. 'The Shepard case,' she said, looking round her table. She managed a smile. 'I guess they must be as desperate as the newspapers say.'

As the chatter around the table slowly resumed, Libby Russell lifted the curtain and looked down at the street below the window. She saw Kate walking briskly towards Commonwealth Avenue.

'The little witch,' she said softly.

At the moment the curtain was falling back into place at Henri's, Mulcahy was across town at Charles Street, back in the cage with his client. They had been there for an hour and a half, going through the direct. Ed had given up stifling his yawns: fatigue was winning the battle. His eyes were tired and red. His vision was blurring up on him. It did that when the contact lenses go too dry.

'John,' he said, 'I want 16 May again.'

'Sorry?'

'Everything. You can start with dawn. Everything that happened 16 May 1992. Starting with sunrise. Again.'

He scribbled notes. But as soon as Shepard recited, Mulcahy was there to interrupt him.

'What did you have?' he asked, when Shepard got to breakfast at the Fire House Diner.

'You want to know what I ate for breakfast?'

'Yes.'

'You want a stool sample?!'

'Yes, I want a stool sample. I want to know if you had scrambled eggs. I want to know if they were runny or hard. I want to know if you put pepper on them. I want to know which booth you sat at. If you read the *Transcript*. If the waitress had on a tight T shirt, I want to know. I want to know a few goddamn facts, John.'

Shepard squinted through the wire mesh. 'I had scrambled eggs, motherfucker. With lots of pepper.' He smiled. Mulcahy didn't smile back, so Shepard went on. He described the events of the day, in wearisome detail: the packing, the movers coming, the carting stuff to the Subaru, the driving, the Mass. Pike west, the Days' Inn.

Ed listened, interrupted, listened some more. The phone call. He wanted that, again.

'What calls did you get that day?'

'I told you. You, in the morning. My mother. Around 6.' That had, in fact, checked out. A ten-minute call, as evidenced by her phone bill.

'What else?'

'I don't remember talking to anyone else.'

'John. A call was placed to your phone from Sam Whitaker's exchange at 7.32. A minute or less. The call was made. And it's not on your message machine.'

'I didn't speak to him.'

'Did you speak to anyone at 7.32?'

'I don't think so.'

'Think harder, John.'

He shook his head. Mulcahy ignored him.

'You talk to your mom. Now it's 6.10. You carry boxes downstairs. Put them in the car. Walk back to the third floor. Carry some more boxes down. Walk back up. There's a beer in the fridge. You stop and open it up. It's dusk now, a nice evening. Think! The phone rings. Less than a minute. Come on!'

Shepard was thinking. But he shook his head.

Mulcahy went on. 'Up the stairs you come. The phone's ringing, maybe? You're on the john. It rings. Something. Think!'

There was silence, silence, and the flickering of the lights. 'Let's go back over it again,' Mulcahy said, the fatigue creeping into his voice. 'It's evening, a nice evening in May. You hang up from your mom's call. You . . .'

'Opening the door,' Shepard said, quietly.

'What?'

'Opening the door. I'm opening the door.' He moved woodenly in the cage, remembering the event. 'I had a suitcase in one hand and my skis – my tellies – in the other. I'm opening the door with this shit and the phone rings.' He looked up in wonderment. 'I do remember it.'

'When?'

'Almost before I left.'

'Who was it?'

'It was somebody selling insurance.'

'You've got to be kidding.'

'No. Life insurance or some shit. You know the motherfuckers who call you at suppertime? "Hi, I'm

403

calling from Executive Fidelity Life Assurance Co., and . . ." You know? One of those.'

'You talk to the guy?'

'Yeah. Well, it was a gal, I think. I listened for a couple of seconds, invited her to have carnal knowledge of her closest relatives, and hung up.' He shook his head. 'I remember that now.'

'And that's it? No other calls?'

'I hang up, take the suitcase and the skis to the car. I remember that.' He was still standing distractedly in the cell, his body remembering the event.

'John. Other calls? No other calls?'

Shepard shook his head.

Mulcahy let out a sigh. He crossed his arms to rub his shoulderblades. His shoulders were stiff with hunching over. He started up again.

'You came back from breakfast at about 10, 10.15 in the morning?'

'Right.'

'And you were home, then, until you left town at about 8?'

'Right.'

'Leaving only for your run?'

'Right.'

'In the afternoon when the movers came, you were there the whole time?'

'The whole time.'

'How many were there?'

He thought for a moment. 'Three, I think. Yeah.'

'Did you notice anything strange? Anybody going through your stuff, any weirdness at all?'

'No. Three big boys lugging furniture and boxes down the stairs. Didn't take 'em all that long, really.'

404

Mulcahy sighed. 'Okay, and the only time you left, then, was when you went running? And that was about noon, for about an hour?'

'Yeah, far as I can remember.'

'And that was the only time you left the apartment?'

'Right.'

'Did you see anyone on this run, talk to anyone?'

'Well,' he said, and looked away.

'Well, what?'

'Well, I went running with someone. No big . . .'

'You went running with someone? You didn't tell me this before. Who?'

He was still looking away. 'Libby Russell,' he said.

Mulcahy rocked back in his chair. He closed his eyes. 'Jesus Christ, John,' he said. 'Jesus Christ.' He rubbed the back of his neck again. It was late.

'John,' he said, after a moment, 'what other surprises do you have for me in this case? I've damn well had enough surprises.'

'Relax, Ed. It wasn't exactly important, you know? We did that Idlewild deal, and used to talk about running a lot. She's done a marathon, or half marathon, or some shit. And she'd said, let's get a run, and I'd said sure. So we got a run. No big conspiracy.'

Mulcahy sighed and took up the pencil again. 'Where did you go?'

Shepard rolled his eyes as if to say that this was one hell of a way to waste time in the middle of the night. 'Along the river. Up to the BU Boathouse, back to Mass. Ave, over to MIT, across the Pepper and Salt bridge, home. I was home about 1, I think.'

'Where did you meet her?'

'She came by my place. About noon.'

'Where did she change?'

'Where did she change?'

'Yes, John, where did she change? It was a Monday. Where did she change?'

'Hell if I know. She got to Joy Street changed, if that's what you mean.' His eyes narrowed.

'Did you shower when you got back?'

'Yes.'

'Did she?'

'Ed. It was a run, okay? No, she didn't drop in for a shower. Or anything else.'

Mulcahy looked at the yellow cinder block walls around him, and listened to the buzz of the fluorescent light. Outside it might be dark, but in here, always the same. 'John,' he said, 'anything else I should know about Libby Russell?'

'No.'

'She keeps turning up, doesn't she? When did you plan this run?'

'I didn't. She called me.'

'When?'

'That morning, I think, when I got back from breakfast.'

'That morning?'

'Yeah. That morning.'

'That morning. Monday morning. Right after you get back from the Fire House after your plate of scrambled eggs. "Hi, John, remember me from six weeks ago? Let's go running. Right away." Kind of a coincidence, don't you think? Her catching you the day you were planning to leave? The day Sam Whitaker was killed?'

406

'Yes,' he said evenly, 'I'd say it was kind of a coincidence.'

'Did you talk to her, running?'

'About what?'

'About anything.'

'Yeah, I guess. I don't remember.'

'Did you talk about the mortgage?'

'I asked her what the settlement was.'

'And?'

'She wouldn't answer.'

'How'd you know about the error, John?'

'You told me,' he said.

Mulcahy nodded. It was true. He asked whether they had talked about Whitaker.

'I don't think he came up,' Shepard said. 'Really, it was just a run, Ed.'

'Come on, John, there's more. Tell me about Libby Russell.'

'Ed, I've told you all that's productive. We've got to brass this out, all right? Let's talk about my direct testimony again. And let's keep our eye on the defence. The damn mortgage error, the error which cost Whitaker's law firm a huge settlement, went down on his own computer terminal. He killed himself, and I wasn't there. It isn't that hard.'

'Were you sleeping with her, John?'

'I've told you all that's productive. I'll see you tomorrow.'

It was late when Mulcahy got to the Charles Street Red line platform. He stood alone, waiting for the rattle and roar as the train from Cambridge would come in over the bridge – the Pepper and Salt Bridge. The train didn't come for quite some time, and he stood on the platform, turning it over in his mind. An inmate in the Charles Street jail doesn't have much to do. He almost never cuts an interview short.

Morning broke cooler. Kate waited for half an hour at Bromfield Street, but Mulcahy, distracted by events, had gone straight to the courthouse. In the minutes before the morning session, he and Shepard met again in the lock-up behind 8b. Neither had slept well.

'You sure about this?' Mulcahy asked.

'Are you? Will they acquit?' Shepard's dark gaze fixed his lawyer's, but that smile had returned to the corners of his eyes. Looking at him, Mulcahy realised that it was the sitting quietly in the courtroom that was killing him. The listening to Paul O'Hanlon was killing him. Shepard wanted to take him on.

'I don't know,' Mulcahy said.

'Well, I'm going for it then,' said Shepard, crossing his arms, as though that were as simple as that.

'All right, John, but listen very closely. I'm worried about the Russell stuff. Don't hide anything, but don't volunteer it. Remember what I told you last night. I don't have any discovery of what he's got on you. They don't have to give us that. You say something which he can impeach, something he can refute, and you will lose your credibility with the jury. It could be anything, anything at all. And, for what it's worth, I think that if the jury thinks you've lied, they'll convict you.'

'And if I testify and he doesn't tag me on cross?'

Mulcahy winced at the expression. Was this whole thing another one of Shepard's games? His negotiations? His *stories*? 'I don't know,' he said.

'And if I don't testify?'

'I don't know.'

'Helluva lot of help you are.'

Mulcahy asked, 'John, I've been thinking about that run. Was she in your apartment?'

'In my apartment?'

'Yeah. Before the run, after the run, sometime, was she in your apartment?'

'No,' he said, 'I met her on the street, and left her on the steps when we were done.'

Mulcahy nodded. 'Well, did you notice anything missing, after you'd got back?'

They both looked up. There were noises behind the session door.

Shepard shook his head negatively.

'You mean like hairs, a suit jacket? Pebbles? I . . .'

'How about soap?'

'Hmmm,' he said. But then he shook his head. 'Hell, everything was in boxes. I don't remember.'

It was time to go. 'I'm still not sure about this,' said Mulcahy.

'Let me ask you this, Ed,' said John. 'If I tell the truth, I mean, just tell it, how can I get hurt?'

'Depends what the truth is, John.'

Each man looked at the other for a long silent moment, and maybe it was only then that each became conscious that he was well and truly alone. Mulcahy heard his shoes scrape on the linoleum, became conscious he was looking down at the floor. 'I see,' said Shepard. 'I see.' He nodded his head slowly. 'I'm not going down in silence. I'm going to testify.'

They shook hands. It felt odd to Mulcahy. He had

imposed the coldness of formality on this relationship at last.

In 8b, the seats were filled again. The two men looked uneasily about them as they waited for the morning to begin. The word always seems to get around, somehow. O'Hanlon, probably. At least it was cooler this morning. The fans were off.

'Shall we proceed, Mr Mulcahy?'

He looked up to find Judge Grosso's bifocals trained on him. Mulcahy nodded as he rose to his feet. Then he leaned over to his client and whispered: 'John. Remember. It's not a conference room. It's not a deal. You can't run the thing. Don't ... don't grandstand, okay?'

Shepard said, 'Would you please call my ass to the stand?'

'Follow my lead closely. I'm not getting into Russell with you.'

'Okay.'

'Remember what you said to me once?' Mulcahy asked.

'What?'

'The prophet Micah.'

Shepard smiled and nodded, and then was off to tell the jury that he was innocent.

Mulcahy frowned as he watched him cross the room. The jurors appeared to lean back slightly as he walked past the box. At a nod from the judge, it began, and Mulcahy took him through his direct. They conceded the angry confrontation in March. Mulcahy walked him through his last days in Boston, the drive west. It was almost over in an hour and a half. Paul O'Hanlon watched hungrily from the prosecutor's table. Cross-examination of an intelligent defendant in a big-play case. That doesn't happen very often.

When he was finished with the bulk of it, Mulcahy felt unsettled. Shepard had followed the instructions too closely. He had been so dutiful, so reserved in his answers, that none of that compelling personality had come out very clearly. It might have been anyone answering the questions. At least he didn't seem like a killer.

Just before finishing, Mulcahy asked this question. 'Mr Shepard, what brand of soap do you use?'

'Lifebuoy.'

'Was that true in May 1992?'

'Yes.'

'If someone had gone into your apartment in May 1993, what kind of soap would they have found?'

'Well,' Shepard said, 'if they found any, would have been Lifebuoy.'

He said it with a self-effacing smile, and the Ancient Mariner smiled back. Mulcahy came to the stand with the evidence pouch. 'I show you Exhibit 21,' he said. 'Can you identify it?'

Shepard opened the pouch and held his nose above it. 'It's a bar of soap,' he said.

'Yours?'

'I don't know,' he said. 'But I know the smell. It is Lifebuoy.'

Mulcahy returned to the podium. 'Mr Shepard,' he said, 'did you murder Samuel Whitaker?'

Shepard's eyes flashed brightly. 'No. No, I did not.'

'Did you have anything to do with his death?'

'Nothing,' he said. 'Absolutely nothing.'

'Nothing further, Your Honour,' said Mulcahy. He returned to his table, sat, and began to hold his breath.

Cross-examination, handled properly, is good theatre, and vexing for a witness of intelligence. The process is against him. The witness may speak only when spoken to, and must confine himself to his questioner's agenda. In a good cross-examination the witness scarcely testifies at all, permitted only to venture assent or dissent from time to time as the advocate addresses the jury. The process was hopeless for Shepard. All of his discourse was built on control.

O'Hanlon began slowly, circling his prey cautiously, flicking out a prod or a jab here and there to test him. He established the motive step by step, sketching in the arduous track to partnership, the long hours, the expectations, the arrival of the appropriate time. He established the closeness of the two men: the number of deals Shepard had carried for Whitaker. And then he questioned Shepard about the quick resignation, immediately after the Idlewild closing, and the move from town three weeks later. He controlled the questioning skilfully, never permitting Shepard to do more than agree that, yes, he had left town on such and such a date, and yes, he had resigned on such and such a date. He had been a good witness on direct, but after a morning with O'Hanlon, he seemed back on his heels, defensive. The jury was rapt at the display.

In the afternoon O'Hanlon began to focus his attack. 'The Idlewild mortgage,' he said, 'that was a document you dealt with in the negotiation?'

'Yes.'

'You heard Mr Ruggerio testify that he did not insert the amount into the Idlewild mortgage?' he asked.

This is all right, Mulcahy thought, we prepared for this.

Shepard answered, 'Yes.'

'You had responsibility for that document as well, did you not?'

'I did.'

'In fact, it was you who inserted the eight hundred forty thousand number, was it not?'

'I don't remember putting it in there.'

'It went out under a cover memo from you, didn't it, Mr Shepard?'

'Yes. It went out under a cover memo from me. It . . .'

'Thank you, Mr Shepard. You've answered my question. Didn't you go into Samuel Whitaker's office to type this last change?'

'No.'

'On 31 March, you typed two sets of changes from your own office, didn't you?'

'Yes.'

'No question about that, is there?'

'No question.'

'And Sam Whitaker, he wasn't there that night, was he?'

'I don't know. I didn't see him.'

'You didn't talk to him on the phone, did you?'

'No.'

'Didn't see him at any time that night, did you?'

'No, I didn't.'

'And yet one document was called up on his terminal at 3.32 a.m.,' O'Hanlon said.

'Apparently, that's right. After I had left.'

'After you *say* you had left,' the prosecutor said.

'No, after I left.' Shepard tried to continue. 'What I mean is . . .'

'That's all right, Mr Shepard,' said O'Hanlon, 'there's no question before you.

'Did you ever know Mr Whitaker to work on a computer terminal?'

'I have no idea.'

'Did you ever see him type anything?'

'No, I didn't.'

'The figure in that mortgage did not appear until the last draft – the draft submitted only hours before the closing began, is that right?'

'That is correct, as far as I know.'

'There was hardly time for anyone to find it, was there, Mr Shepard?'

'I'd say that is right.'

Mulcahy had expected this. But he did not like the atmosphere. Shepard looked defensive. He was back in the box, and his hands kept straying to his cheek. The jury was attentive. For the first time in a week, it was cool, almost pleasant in the courtroom. The fans were silent. Not what Mulcahy would have asked for.

'And this draft, the one in which the number first appeared, was not red-lined, was it?'

The jury nodded. They knew all about red-lining. The history of the drafts had been carefully explained to them during the Commonwealth's case.

'No,' said Shepard. 'It was not.'

414

'Red-lining would have identified the error, wouldn't it, Mr Shepard?'

'Three more hours would have identified it, Mr O'Hanlon.'

It was the first point to Shepard in the match. But O'Hanlon was on his game too. He didn't whine about the non-responsiveness of the answer. He simply volleyed it back. 'And the reason that there were only three hours left to the closing was that the figure was not placed in the first eight drafts, but left out until the very morning of closing, isn't that right, Mr Shepard?'

He was silent. O'Hanlon didn't wait for an answer. 'How many years had you been practising law, Mr Shepard?'

'Nine.'

'Ever get the mortgage amount wrong before?'

'No,' he said.

'You didn't get it wrong this time either, did you?'

'Objection,' said Mulcahy.

'Sustained,' the judge said.

'What I mean is, Mr Shepard, you put the wrong figure in on purpose, didn't you?'

'No.'

'You purposefully executed what might look like a "misprint" to catch your former law firm in malpractice and your former mentor Samuel Whitaker in embarrassment, didn't you?'

'No.'

'You did this thing on Mr Whitaker's terminal in order to implicate him, didn't you?'

'No, Mr O'Hanlon. No,' he said.

'This entire thing was a product of your vengeful anger, the mortgage, the murder . . .'

'That is not right, Mr O'Hanlon.'

The big Irishman walked back to his table. 'We know it wasn't right, Mr . . .'

'Motion to strike, Your Honour!' Mulcahy was on his feet.

'It is stricken. The jury will disregard Mr O'Hanlon's last comment. And Mr O'Hanlon will regard the rules of evidence.' Judge Grosso peered out sternly over the tops of his bifocals.

O'Hanlon seemed to wave it off. He had worked Shepard well, and he had that uncomfortable look of someone who feels he must add something to what he said, but is waiting for permission. He didn't get it. O'Hanlon looked up from the prosecutor's table.

'You telephoned Mr Whitaker on the evening of 16 May, didn't you.'

'I did not.'

'You telephoned him from the corner phone booth on Joy Street, didn't you?'

'That is not true.'

O'Hanlon was simply laying out his theory. He cared nothing for the answers. 'You did this so that the call wouldn't be traced to you, didn't you?'

'That's not true, Mr O'Hanlon.'

'And then he called you back at your home at 7.32 that night, didn't he?'

'No, he did not.'

'Well, you were home at 7.32, weren't you?'

'Yes.'

'That is shortly before you say you left town for good, isn't it?'

'About a half hour, yes.'

'And about an hour before you left town for good, you . . . oh, that reminds me of something. Forgive me, Your Honour, I withdraw the question.' He smiled and began again. 'You drove to Colorado from Boston, didn't you?'

'Yes.'

'Alone.'

'Yes.'

'It took you three days?'

'Yes.'

'And, just so the jury understands this, your testimony is that you began this cross-country trip at half-past eight o'clock at *night*, is that it?'

'I like to drive at night.'

'So it would seem, Mr Shepard, so it would seem.' He paused for a moment, pretending to be hunting through his notes. He wanted the jury to think about the point for a moment. And then he looked up, with a convincing air of genuine puzzlement, to say, 'But you got in fewer than six hours of driving before you stopped at a motel at about 2 a.m. just outside of Elmira, New York, isn't that true?'

'Yes, that's true,' Shepard answered.

'I see,' said O'Hanlon, shaking his beefy head. 'Now, to return to the telephone calls, you did get a call at about 7.32, didn't you?'

'Yes, I don't remember the time, but I got a couple of calls that evening before I left.'

'And one of them was from Mr Whitaker.'

'No, sir, he didn't call me.'

'Do you have any reason to doubt the genuineness

417

of the NYNEX record that shows a call placed from his exchange at . . .'

Mulcahy was on his feet, but the judge had sustained his objection before he had made it.

'Well,' said O'Hanlon, waving it off, 'I'm sure the jury will recall the evidence of the telephone records.' He eyed his prey for a moment, and decided to break the rules a little. He was, of course, a man of considerable ego.

'So from whom did you receive calls?'

'My mother,' Shepard began. 'I got a call from my mom. And if my memory is right, I might have had one other call.'

Now O'Hanlon approached the witness stand. His instinct suggested something to him. He did not crowd Shepard. It was a little too early for a physical challenge. But he wanted to speak softly for a time.

'From whom was the other call?'

'Insurance.'

'An insurance salesman?'

'I think so. One of those people who call you at suppertime wanting to sell you something. You know, "Hi, this is so and so, from the such and such company."'

'What was the company?'

'I don't recall.'

'So you admit a call, but you can remember nothing about the caller, is that it?' O'Hanlon asked in a contemptuous tone.

'No,' said Shepard, 'I remember it was a woman. Southern accent.'

The deep Irish voice came softly, now. 'Mr Shepard,' it said. 'You were angry at Mr Whitaker, weren't you? You were upset?' He asked the question gently.

Shepard shook his head affirmatively. 'Yes, I was. I thought he ditched me, dumped me to cut his own deal with management. I thought he let me down.'

Now O'Hanlon stood at the podium. He paused for a moment and then waded into a series of questions which were certain to elicit no evidence. He didn't care. He wanted the jury to hear his theory. And he was hoping for a little something extra.

'So you telephoned him and arranged a meeting for that night, didn't you?'

'I did not.'

'You drove to Sheringham in your 1984 Subaru and met Mr Whitaker at about 9 p.m., didn't you?'

'No, I didn't.'

'And you shot him dead in Mr Whitaker's study, with his Navy service weapon, by firing one shot to the head, didn't you?'

'I did not.'

'And then you washed your hands in the bathroom off the study?'

'I did not.'

'And then you left the house and drove down Dover Street to Route 37, down Route 37 to Coolidge, from Coolidge to the corner of Maple and 135?'

'No. No. I was never in Sheringham. I've never been there.'

'And you bought gas at the gas station on the corner, filling up and paying by credit card, didn't you?'

'No, that's not true.'

'You drove to the Massachusetts Turnpike from Natick and entered the westbound lane?'

'No, as I've explained, I drove on to the Mass. Pike in Boston at about 8, when I left town.'

'And at the next rest stop, you ditched your jacket in a dumpster, didn't you!'

'That's a lie,' said Shepard. The prosecutor was beginning to unnerve him.

'Mr Shepard,' O'Hanlon said, 'I show you Commonwealth 8, the jacket. That's your suit jacket, isn't it!'

John Shepard paused. He looked at the jacket, a searching look, an apologetic look. Then he looked across the room at Mulcahy, with a question in the expression. He hadn't thought of this simple thing. They would have to assume that he would deny it was his jacket, and so O'Hanlon wouldn't ask. He looked down at his hands.

What the hell? Ed Mulcahy, across the room, was thinking. What the . . .

And then Shepard said it. 'I – I don't know. It looks like one of mine.'

It was very quiet in the session then. No one moved. Mulcahy's face fell. He felt sick to his stomach. Straight face! he was thinking to himself. Show nothing! But he could feel the eyes of the jurors flashing back and forth between the witness stand and him.

The great florid prosecutor was poleaxed too. He was absolutely stunned. He strode back to his table. 'Your jacket?' he repeated.

'Looks like it.'

'Your jacket in the dumpster on the Massachusetts Turnpike?'

'Like I said, it looks like it.'

'Your jacket with the blood of Samuel Whitaker on it!'

'Objection!'

'Sustained.'

Now Paul O'Hanlon had his moment. The jury watched him expectantly, as he picked up a sheaf of papers.

'Your jacket, Mr Shepard. I see. You say you talked to your mother that night?'

'That's right.'

'Well, did you tell your dear old mom that your suit jacket was about to become covered with Samuel Whitaker's blood?!'

Then all was confusion, for Paul O'Hanlon had found the pressure point. Grosso began to say something, just as Mulcahy hollered, 'Objection!' But O'Hanlon saw that the shot had hit home, saw the flush in Shepard's complexion, and, knowing that he had his moment, plunged ahead, shouting at the witness.

'Did you!'

Shepard was on his feet and every juror heard him say, 'You son of a bitch!' This brought the court officers out of their chairs and charging across the room for the witness stand, and as Shepard said again, pointing his finger, 'You fat bastard, you leave her . . .' two court officers were arm-twisting him into his seat, and Grosso was pounding his gavel. 'Order! Order!' he shouted. 'Sit down, Mr Shepard,' he growled at the witness, and then turned on

O'Hanlon. 'Come to sidebar, Mr O'Hanlon.' O'Hanlon and Shepard stared at each other like prize fighters as Gleason pushed him off to the side.

Two court officers were on Shepard in a second. The jurors cringed, shrinking back in their seats, all save for the Ancient Mariner, who was grinning from ear to ear. Jesus, thought Stevie, as he watched astonished from the back of the session. What a circus. He strained to listen as the judge lectured the lawyers at sidebar with barely concealed whispers, so that Stevie could catch phrases: 'You will conduct yourself ...' And then more of the dumb show. 'Another outburst of this kind, gentlemen, and ...' And so on. It was all one of O'Hanlon's shows, of course, a dramatic signature to the one point he wanted the jury to remember. And he had succeeded in bringing Shepard out: no juror would doubt the man had a temper.

It took twenty minutes to settle the courtroom. Mulcahy rose to rehabilitate his client, but he hadn't the heart for it. Looks like his jacket! What on earth ... The timbre of Mulcahy's voice had risen, and the questions came quickly and defensively. He sensed the jury looking at him with disappointment. They were troubled. He stopped, praying for the day's recess. O'Hanlon waved off re-cross, as if to signal that the witness had been so thoroughly humiliated that it would be pointless to go further.

Judge Grosso excused the jury. When the court officer came, Shepard looked at Mulcahy, his eyes still smouldering. The court officer tugged on his shoulder. He stood up slowly, looking at Mulcahy, but he was looking away. 'It's not true, man, it's not true,' he said as the court officers fastened the cuffs and led him away.

'You lied to me, John,' he said, when they had been left alone in the lock-up. He had only ten minutes before the van would arrive to take Shepard back to jail.

'I know. But if I had told you that it was my jacket, would you have let me testify?'

'Well, no, but that's the point! If it's your goddamn jacket, and you testify, the jury is going to find out. Until you testify, there's a doubt. And worse, you caught me totally unaware. What the hell was I supposed to do on redirect? What about the note?'

'It was mine,' he said. 'The numbnuts. It's a *Colorado* exchange. T.M.D. is for "Tenth Mountain Division". I had called those guys some time before about a hut trip.'

Ed was silent. He felt himself struggling for air. 'Whether you testify is your own affair. I wouldn't have been able to stop you. I would have tried to talk you out of it. But at least, if I had known the truth, we could have tried to deal with it somehow . . .'

His voice trailed off. He could hear the deputy sheriffs coming in the stairwell. Then he asked, very quietly, one question. 'Why?'

But the deputy sheriffs were there, and they took him, one by each arm.

'Wait a minute. Wait a minute!' Shepard hollered, struggling with them. 'Ed, let me ask you this. Just – just let me ask you this, goddamn it! On May the fucking sixteenth do I dress up in Sunday go-to-meeting-clothes for forty hours of driving?'

They hauled him away.

Mulcahy left the courthouse alone. His footsteps carried him to Stevie's office, although there seemed no reason now. Kate and Stevie were there. Neither was talking much. Stevie wasn't even eating. Somewhere, though, he had found cold beers, and he passed them out.

Ed sat in the couch, staring at his fingernails. Outside the evening traffic honked and rattled and roared by. 'Wish I had a nickel for every time he's lied to me,' he said.

Kate was silent, but came and sat on the arm of the couch and placed her hand on his arm.

'That guy, the sonofabitch, the son – of – a – bitch!! It wasn't enough that he nearly got me killed in the Rockies! It wasn't enough that he cost me my job. Now he makes me a fool, a pissant. "Oh, yeah, come to think of it, I did happen to see Libby Russell eight hours before Sam Whitaker was killed. Yeah, maybe you'll find a call on my message machine! Insurance agent, that's it! Jacket? What jacket? Not my jacket. Oops, come to think of it, it does look like my jacket!"

'Where the hell did he come from, and what did I do to deserve him?'

Kate's arm was pressing his hand now, and she interrupted him. 'Ed,' she said, 'clients lie to lawyers. It happens all the time.' She spoke gently.

He looked at her. 'Did I deserve these lies?'

She turned and walked across the room. 'The lie he didn't tell is more interesting, though.'

'What is that?'

'Under oath,' she said, 'he admits the jacket. Think they could have tied it to him?'

'Think he knew the answer?'

She nodded. 'Maybe not. Still, under oath, he told the truth.'

'Stevie,' said Mulcahy, looking now at the balding investigator who had sat through this exchange with unwonted silence, 'reality check. Did he do it?'

Stevie looked away.

Mulcahy felt dizzy as he walked for the T, and lightheaded as he stood on the Boston College line. Night came and found him at home, sitting in his boxer shorts on the couch with another bottle of beer.

Gitz had come in quietly. 'Bad day?' he asked gently, as he looked at Mulcahy from the kitchen. Then he nodded to himself and said, 'That's a confirmation. Bad day.' He went to his room.

On the set in the living room, Frannie Dillard had his story, and Mulcahy watched with his head shaking as the reporter described the angry confrontation in 8b that day.

Mulcahy had failed. He'd committed a cardinal sin: pretended to be a criminal defence lawyer when he wasn't; to win the case when his job was not to lose it. He'd gone into court unprepared: never found out about the jacket; believed an account which would crumble on exposure to a flashlight. He had opened the door on the jacket wide for O'Hanlon to come charging right on through. He'd served up his client for the *coup de grâce*. On went his cerebral prosecutor with the bill of particulars. He'd tried this case without a plan. And he had ignored the truth

425

known to every competent lawyer: even what you know and research and worry over and check, even that is suspect and unreliable; but what you take on faith will always betray you. Like a schoolchild, he had let go of that truth. It had cost him, and his client.

And, he thought, draining the bottle, I never found out about John Shepard. I was his cheerleader, his kid brother, his altar boy. I wasn't his lawyer. I'm just another sap, another fool he found and used. And now? Mulcahy thought about it. He was just a guy in a pair of boxer shorts, a lawyer with no office to go to, no partnership, no clients, no bank account, even. Hell, he had no clean shirt to wear. I am, he thought, a chump who blew a career on a hunch.

Still later he sat at the kitchen table, staring into the window as night fell. There was Shepard's reflection, floating in the glass, shaking its head and saying, 'It's a lie, man, it's a lie.' With big droopy eyes, the son of a bitch! The image taunted him. Even in this moment it testified to his own weakness of vision. And then the image changed, and it was, as it was so often, that ice-crusted beard appearing out of the white snow mist, with those words of command. Mulcahy walked to the cabinet and withdrew a bottle of Scotch, then fished frost-covered ice from the freezer, and poured a big glass.

He hadn't heard Kate at all. Gitz must have let her in. She was standing there silently as he poured the Scotch. 'Hey,' he said weakly.

'Hey,' she said.

'You want one?'

426

'No,' she said, frowning at him. She started to say something else and stopped herself.

He looked sharply at her, then turned away.

'I'm sorry,' she said. 'I'm sorry about John today. Look, what can I do?'

He said nothing. Then: 'Take your clothes off,' in a voice bitter and mocking.

She stared at him in shock, and he could not return the glance. He looked down at the amber liquid. 'That's the first ugly thing I've ever heard you say,' she said, measuring her words. He saw that her lower lip was quivering. She turned and he heard her footsteps clip across the living room.

'Kate!'

She stopped. 'I'm really not interested in men who feel sorry for themselves.'

He felt his face go scarlet. 'I'm sorry,' he said.

'Yes, that's clear,' she replied as she walked back to the kitchen. 'Very sorry. For yourself. You are sitting there with your drink prepared to become petulant because Paul O'Hanlon out-tried you today. Again.'

He looked up.

'Oh, yes, that's it exactly,' she said. 'You and Paul O'Hanlon. That's what you think this is about, don't you? You and Paul O'Hanlon. Why don't the two of you just go into the locker room with a ruler and figure out who's the biggest *man*, Ed? Then we could dispense with the defendant altogether. And the victim.'

'Kate . . .'

'No, Ed, I think you need to hear this.' She went on, head shaking and the shocks of red hair disshevelled about her face, 'This is a trial. It is about a

427

victim and a defendant. It is not about you and Paul O'Hanlon. The jury are going to deliberate on guilt or innocence. Not on best actor. Something else. Paul O'Hanlon is a better trial lawyer than you, okay? He just is. Fact. Get used to it. Not very surprising. He's tried more cases, hasn't he? And he's good! Can we just deal with that?'

He stood before her, his eyes downcast, studying the table, his fingernails, his belly button, anything, waiting for her to finish. It seemed suddenly colder in the kitchen, sitting there in only his boxer shorts.

She glowered at him. 'But you, when you don't feel so sorry for yourself all the time, you're not so bad, you know? And you have a client. And a job to do. Okay?'

His head still hung. 'Okay,' he said.

'Look, you've got work to do. *We've* got work to do. And there isn't much time. Tomorrow morning, we untie your bank account. And then,' she said, a certain irony creeping into her voice, 'it's Snow White.'

He nodded and they settled in at the ashwood table with his Russell file. Heads together, they began to study the outline. He cast furtive, sidelong glances at her, wondering if she could ever be distracted once the file folders were opened.

'You know,' he said, after a while, 'when they were taking him back to Charles Street, he asked me something. And I think he's right.'

'What was that?'

'Would John Shepard have put his suit on, to drive to Colorado?'

She nodded. 'I've been thinking about something else,' she said. 'That call.'

'His mother?'

'No, the insurance salesman.'

'Sales*woman*, I think he said.'

'Exactly.'

30

Mulcahy could have guessed that things would go badly. Grosso had given him a break, adjourning court until Wednesday afternoon so that he could deal with the 'trustee process' in the morning. But Judge Hughes would be dispensing no favours that or any other day. He took the bench in 11a, and Ed and Kate watched him handle the motions ahead of theirs. Hughes was a law judge: he brought a breadth of learning in the common law to the bench. He was scrupulously fair; he was prepared; he had read the briefs; he was brisk. But he was cold, and one never knew what he was thinking.

Late in the morning Mulcahy's case was called. A young woman popped up from the rear to ask for a continuance. It seemed that Attorney Parisi was on trial in the Lowell District Court.

'Your Honour,' said Kate, 'my client's on trial too. In 8b. And his bank account has been frozen. He is literally without any funds at all. This case can't be continued.'

'How long is Mr Parisi's trial?' Hughes asked the associate.

'At least a week, Judge.'

'No,' said Hughes, 'Friday at 2 p.m. If he can't be here, he can submit affidavits. And, Miss Maher, I suggest you read the statute.'

Frowning, Judge Hughes motioned for his clerk to call the next case. Mulcahy and Kate looked uncertainly at each other as they filed out. What the hell did that last remark mean? Now it would be at least two more days before Ed Mulcahy even had a chance at getting his bank account back. And the chance didn't look so good.

It wasn't until after lunch that Libby Russell was called. Shepard, whom they had brought early into the session, hadn't seen her enter at the back of the room. He hadn't known anything until he heard the name. 'What the hell is this?' he whispered.

'We need her, John.'

Libby Russell was stepping up to the enclosure.

'No. I don't want her on,' he whispered, eyes blazing.

'Too late, John,' Ed whispered. 'Fix your face, please, the jury is watching.'

Finely dressed in a pale yellow suit, regal in demeanour, her hair drawn back tightly from her head, she stepped coolly from the gallery. She floated elegantly across the room, nodded politely at the judge, and then took her seat. Grosso was frowning. The men in the jury looked on attentively. The faces of the women were harder to read. After she had identified herself, Mulcahy decided to waste no time.

'Have you ever met Vincent Testa?'

Elizabeth Russell stared back at her questioner. 'I don't recall that name.'

'Well, Vinny Testa goes by a lot of names, doesn't he?'

'Objection!' Mulcahy smiled inwardly and guessed O'Hanlon was awake.

'Sustained.'

Mulcahy tried again. 'Have you ever met someone who has an alias or an aka similar to Vincent Testa?'

'I don't recall.'

'Ms Russell, you were an Assistant United States Attorney before you entered private practice?'

'Yes.'

'You were assigned to the Organised Crime Strike Force.'

'Yes, I was.'

'And you prosecuted cases against members of organised crime families in New England, did you not?'

'I did, yes.'

'Did your office use confidential informants?'

'For what?'

'For anything, Ms Russell.'

'Yes. We made use of confidential informants.'

'A lot of your cases made use of wiretap evidence, did they not?'

'Some of them did, yes.'

'And in obtaining warrants to place wiretaps, did not the government often rely on the affidavits of confidential informants?'

'Objection, Your Honour, this is totally irrel . . .'

'Overruled, Mr O'Hanlon. Please answer the question, Ms Russell.'

'Yes, that is accurate.'

'Did you personally speak with confidential informants, from time to time?'

'Yes.'

Mulcahy walked to the witness stand. 'Did you appear for the government in a case called *United States* v. *Cerrone*?'

Her face clouded, but only briefly. 'Yes.'

'Was Vinny Testa, or someone calling himself Vincent Testa, a government informant in that case?'

Russell had regained her composure. She turned to Judge Grosso and said evenly, 'Your Honour, as a former Assistant United States Attorney, I feel that I should request that the US Attorney's office be given adequate notice and an opportunity to be heard if there is to be questioning concerning confidential informants.'

Judge Grosso nodded and looked at the lawyers. 'Sidebar,' he said.

'Gentlemen,' he said when they had arrived, 'I think the witness is right. I don't know much about the law of federal informants. Mr Mulcahy, you will notify the US Attorney's office of your line of questioning and advise them that I will expect briefs from interested parties at 9 a.m. tomorrow. I will hear you at 10. We will excuse the jury, and the witness, until 11.'

'Your Honour,' Mulcahy tried to interject, 'if I might . . .'

'No, Mr Mulcahy,' said Judge Grosso. 'We'll suspend here.'

Two hours later, Mulcahy was surrounded by open

433

volumes of the *Massachusetts Reports* and the *Federal Supplement* at a table in the Social Law Library. Whether he could force disclosure of a confidential informant in Shepard's defence was proving to be a tricky question of law. The reported cases all dealt with such disclosure in the same case in which the informant had given information. But in a different case, the relevance link was more tenuous. He could find nothing directly on the question, no clear pronouncement from the Massachusetts courts which would settle the point easily for Judge Grosso. So he had to reason by analogy, placing one brick of argument on another, hoping the structure would cohere.

'The library is closing in five minutes,' a voice said. A woman smiled at Mulcahy from across the reading room. He looked around and realised he was alone there, save for the librarian, who was latching the windows with an extension pole and closing them, one by one. The law students and the attorneys had gone. Scribbling down citations and the last of his notes, he gathered his yellow pads into his satchel and headed for the elevator. A few minutes later he had found a telephone. Once again he explained the problem. Once again he apologised.

And once again Kate poured herself a cup of coffee, and settled in for a long night at the computer terminal.

Thursday morning they came to the session like a fresh battalion of reinforcements, eager, armed with briefs and motions. Mulcahy looked at them in sleepy disbelief as he entered the room, seated in a phalanx in the first bench. Jesus. Two guys from Fletcher

434

Daye, three AUSAs, including Hoskins, the chief of the Criminal Division, Russell – all of the men in pressed blue suits and crisp white shirts, all of the women sharply dressed. And a litigation partner from Freer, a miserable swine named Andrew Van Kampen. What the hell was he doing there? Mulcahy sighed. Kate hadn't made it to Stevie's. She wasn't here. Someone handed him his service copies: between the Commonwealth's motion, the United States' motions, and the witness's motion, there was about three inches. Great. Three inches of papers from the other side, and he didn't even have a brief. Not only did he not have a brief, he didn't know what the hell his argument would be. Hoskins arrived to pump his hand and heap small talk upon him, and keep him from reading the material. He felt tired, tired and irritable.

Kate was in the session before Mulcahy could break away from Hoskins. She stood dumbly in the doorway. Mulcahy turned, and then, on an instant, he realised, and she realised, and, of course, Van Kampen realised. Blankly, she drew herself back through the doorway and into the hall. Now Van Kampen looked at Mulcahy, but he did not return the glance. He followed Kate into the lobby.

They stood together before the elevators. Shocks of red hair sprayed crazily. She looked terrible. Once again, she had been up most of the night. 'I'm sorry, Kate. Jesus, I'm sorry. I didn't even think . . .'

'It's okay,' she said, 'it's okay.'

'Kate . . .'

'Here's your brief. And here are the cases. *Stingley*

and *Orosco* are the best ones. *Leblanc* is a bad case.'
She spoke without emotion.

'Look, Kate . . .'

'It's all right. I guess they had to figure it out. Read the cases, Ed. I've got to go. Read them. The hearing's in ten minutes.'

There was nothing else to say. She walked slowly to the elevator, reddening and biting her lip during what seemed an absurd delay while she waited for the car to come. When at last the door opened, there was a tear on her cheek.

Van Kampen was in the doorway as he returned to the session. 'What was she . . .?'

'Here,' said Mulcahy, handing him the service copy of the defence's papers. 'And Andy?'

'What?'

'Fuck yourself.'

But Van Kampen was walking to the telephones, and in a moment the hearing was underway.

'Unless the party shows by clear and convincing evidence a compelling need for the evidence directly related to a defence in the case . . .'

Hoskins was on his feet, swaying left to right, the phrases falling off his tongue, one after the other. Jesus, thought Mulcahy, Russell has juice. They had brought the chief of the Criminal Division. They had done a top-drawer job on the briefs. Grosso loved this – the United States Attorney's starting backfield, in his courtroom, with a set of Class A briefs prepared overnight. Grosso stared down over his bifocals, and concentrated on the advocate with his full attention.

When at last Hoskins fell silent Mulcahy came

slowly to his feet. Still speed-reading *Orosco* when the judge turned to him. He rose awkwardly, feeling tired and unfocused. His voice sounded thin to him, thin and faraway. He heard as from a distance bits of argument; sentences, ideas. But his words were unruly, like a herd of cattle which has escaped from its field, and tramples heavily this way and that. He couldn't round them up and go clearly in one direction. He heard himself talking about the defendant's right to a fair trial. And then a moment later he was arguing about the nature of the standard of proof. And then he seemed to be on to something else. Grosso was frowning.

Mulcahy looked up at the judge's eyes. Grosso was going to rule against him.

The process of persuasion is a funny thing. It follows only haphazardly the principles of argument. A judicial decision, like any human decision, is usually not a proof demonstrated by a series of logical premises. It is often an instinct, or an axiom, or an hypothesis which looks to arguments as pretext. There is a time for persuading. And when it has passed the advocate's arguments are useful only to provide the willing audience with ammunition to bolster its choice.

Grosso was going to rule against him. Mulcahy paused, ungrammatically, and the room was silent. Someone coughed. It had come to him with bitter immediacy. Judge Grosso liked this hearing because it made him feel, for one small morning, like a federal judge. The one thing he wanted and had not got, the thing he in fact deserved – a federal judgeship. And here was a close call on a point involving Elizabeth Russell.

Who sat on the Bar Association's judicial nominating committee. With Hoskins. And Van Kampen. No wonder he was here.

'Mr Mulcahy?' It was Grosso.

'Excuse me, Your Honour.' Mulcahy looked up. It was already another hot morning. Soon they would have to turn the fans on. 'Judge,' he said, 'it comes to this. My client is on trial for murder. And I need this evidence. That's all, really. That's all.'

The older man looked at him with a sort of poignancy in his eyes. Mulcahy had, with his last remark, almost broken through. Over the week the judge had grown impressed with the young lawyer's determination. But his mind was made up.

And so Judge Grosso began. The phrasing was ordered, mellifluous, punctuated by obeisance to discretion, by his observations of the demeanour and credibility of the witnesses. The US Attorney's motion would be allowed, along with the joint motion to quash. The hearing had been a dumbshow: a courtesy. He had made his decision on the papers.

Suddenly Ed Mulcahy was tired and angry. And on his feet.

'I move for reconsideration,' he said flatly.

'Denied, Mr . . .'

'I move for a stay and interlocutory report,' he interrupted.

'Denied!'

'Mistrial,' he said.

'What?' the judge asked.

'Mistrial, Judge, I move for a mistrial.'

'Denied, Mr Mulcahy,' the judge snapped. Mulcahy had gotten under his skin with the last one.

The two men stared at each other, once again, and all warmth had left the older man's voice. 'Shall we proceed with the *trial*, Mr Mulcahy?'

Mulcahy looked at his watch when Elizabeth Russell was again on the stand. An hour or so to go before lunch.

He had to kill the time. He wasn't ready for Idlewild. 'When,' he said, paging through his yellow-pad outline, 'did you first meet Mr Whitaker, Ms Russell?'

She seemed surprised by the question, and measured her response, measured it for length and for substance. More, he thought, than an idle question warranted. 'I don't recall exactly,' she said.

'Well, how long have you known him?'

'I believe I met him on one of the bench/bar subcommittees, some years ago. He was chairing a committee on ethics in the practice, and I sat on the committee. I think it was then.'

'How long ago was that?'

'I don't know,' she said, 'four years or so? Something like that, Mr Mulcahy.'

'And so at the time you were still with the US Attorney's Office?'

'Yes, I think I was.'

He asked her for other contacts over the years. There were several. Whitaker was active with the Harvard Alumni Association. She had met him at several functions. More recently they sat together on the judicial nominating committee. By lunchtime, he had elicited a regular professional relationship: meetings at seminars, bar association functions, law school alumni functions. Occasional phone calls. Charitable solicitations.

At last one o'clock came, and the jury was excused. Grosso hurried from the bench and Russell's camp rose as one, smiles on their faces as they began to edge out from the leading pew. 'Mr Hoskins,' said Mulcahy, his back turned as he faced down towards an open file at counsel table, 'as soon as we recess, I will seek relief under chapter two thirty-one section one-eighteen upstairs in the appeals court.'

'Be my guest, but I think you mean a two eleven three.'

Mulcahy felt himself going scarlet. His ignorance had burst out again. In the state courts, civil lawyers sought interlocutory appeals – prompt rulings on discrete issues, before a case had ended – in the appeals court, under chapter 231. But in a criminal trial, a murder trial, the route lay under a different statute, chapter 211, and to a different court, the Commonwealth's highest appellate tribunal: the Supreme Judicial Court.

'Let us know if you get a hearing,' said Hoskins, with just the hint of a smirk. 'Paul,' he continued, turning to O'Hanlon, 'perhaps Mr Gleason should accompany counsel, so that he takes his appeal to the right place?'

'Hoskins, you're a laugh riot, man. Why don't you try stand up?' said Mulcahy, as they filed past him with O'Hanlon.

With his dog-eared copy of the rules and a yellow pad, Mulcahy gathered up the stenographer and headed to the elevator. O'Hanlon's sidekick Gleason

440

was waiting by the elevators. Together they boarded for the 13th floor.

At the clerk's office Mulcahy was told there was no chance of a prompt hearing. Justice Johnson was the emergency judge, she told him. Wonderful, he thought. Gleason stood by as he scribbled out his motion on a sheaf of foolscap, and filed it with the trial court brief. Gleason then scribbled an objection, attaching it to his three inches of papers.

They left at 1.30.

Judge Grosso was late returning from lunch, and it was past 2.30 when the trial got underway again. Mulcahy resumed his inquiries about the extent of Libby Russell's relationship with Whitaker. He was still marking time, glancing occasionally back at the session door. There was more in this line of inquiry than he had expected, however. Had she ever telephoned him at home? Yes, she may have. Had he ever telephoned her at home? Perhaps. Had she been to his home? She couldn't recall. Had she lunched with him? Yes. It was all, of course, perfectly consistent with the number of connections between their professional lives. Mulcahy plodded on.

At 3.30, the door opened. Turning, Mulcahy recognised one of the SJC clerks at the back of the session. So, it appeared, did Judge Grosso.

'Excuse me, Ms Russell,' he said. He beckoned to the lady at the rear to pass her note to the desk. Kelly handed it up to the bench, and then Grosso signalled to O'Hanlon and Mulcahy to approach. At sidebar he showed them the SJC's order. It was a photocopy of Mulcahy's handwritten motion. It bore the notation,

It was at this moment on a warm afternoon in September that Mulcahy asked the judge for a chip. David Grosso was a good man: the surge of anger from the morning's challenge had passed as quickly as it came on. Mulcahy had earned a break, and he was now glad to give it. There was in this advocate something David Grosso admired, something stubborn and unvarnished. And when Mulcahy looked up, he didn't have to say that this process had caught him unprepared. He didn't have to say that the examination could proceed more smoothly in the morning. He didn't have to say that he was just tired. The judge sensed it all. 'Gentlemen, we're going to break here,' he said.

It was 3.40 p.m. when the last juror filed out of the session. They took Shepard off. Mulcahy sat alone at counsel table. And in a moment he had left the session and was riding the elevator – not down, to the street, but up, up to the 13th floor, where they had shot his case down with a one-word order. He hadn't a plan. There was nothing else to say to them. He was just going there.

The clerk's office for the Supreme Judicial Court is on the 13th floor, but it might be thirteen miles from the trial sessions below. No rabble loiter in the halls. Attorneys in nine-hundred dollar suits attend dignified hearings. Messengers arrive at 4 p.m. with filings. And that is pretty much it. It is a peaceful, well-ordered life – perhaps it is the very peace and order of appellate life that lead appellate justices so often to chide trial lawyers for failing to attend to details in the heat of battle.

'I filed this motion,' said Mulcahy to a desultory young woman, who, like all clerks, found nothing more irritating than the approach of a human being within an hour of closing time.

'Yes,' she said, 'yes. It was denied.'

'I want a hearing,' he said.

'I'm sorry, sir, it's been denied.'

'I want a hearing. You tell him I want a hearing.' Several heads turned from behind the counter.

'Sir, I'm afraid you will have to go. This motion has been . . .'

'Miss,' he said, 'I want you to tell Justice Johnson that I want a hearing. I have a client on trial for murder. For murder! I want you to tell him that!'

'She doesn't need to tell me,' rumbled a powerful voice, 'I can hear you hollerin' well enough myself, Counsellor.' It was a rich bass voice, a voice of command, a voice he recognised, vaguely, although he had never actually met the man, just heard the stories. He turned to the side, and in the doorway of the entrance to the judges' lobby was Raymond P. Johnson, Associate Justice of the Supreme Judicial Court.

He was still an imposing man. Though grown rather stout, he stood over six foot two, and carried his weight well. He had a fierce glower, a mean cast, white eyes gleaming like ivory in his black face, his broad dome seeming almost bald under a close-cropped haircut.

'Judge,' said Mulcahy, less passionately now, 'my name's Ed Mulcahy, Judge. I filed the two eleven three in *Commonwealth* v. *Shepard*. I have just got to have a hearing on this.' The judge stared at him in silence. Mulcahy went on, his mind racing. This was an *ex parte* communication – with an SJC justice! It was strictly, utterly, obviously, unanswerably illegal. It was crazy! But he didn't care any more. 'I'm defending a murder trial and I have got to have this evidence. I mean, it bears directly on guilt or innocence . . .'

'The Court has ruled.'

'I don't think – with respect, Judge – I don't think you've given me a chance.' He blurted out the last part.

'You had better watch yourself, young man,' said Justice Johnson. It had been a long time since anyone had given him any lip, a long time since the sixties, when as one of but two or three black lawyers who made their way through the court system, he had weathered the insolence and the pettiness of the Irish and Italian courthouse clans. Justice Johnson had since been put to pasture on the SJC, where he gave orders, wrote opinions, tasked advocates mercilessly, and ordered clerks about. It had been a long time since he'd had to dance before a hostile judge.

'Judge,' said Mulcahy, aware that at any moment he'd be found in contempt, 'you were a great trial lawyer, one of the greats, so please, remember those days for just a moment. I got into this case a couple of weeks ago. I'm all alone. I don't even have a secretary. I'm in there against O'Hanlon, three sidekicks, a half-dozen detectives, and on this motion, they throw in the starting five from the US Attorney's office just for good measure. And this is a key bit of evidence for my guy. I don't want to reverse a verdict a year from now. I'd like a shot at this now . . . I'm sorry that I've buttonholed you like this, Judge. I apologise.'

The old black jurist stared at Mulcahy. 'You think you've got a case, son? You think you've been denied *justice*?' The last word hissed out, like steam from a radiator, and he fixed the younger man in a scowl whose meaning was unmistakable. What could a white lawyer in 1992 – a mere boy! – tell Raymond Johnson about justice? The old man's eyes narrowed.

'All right,' the judge said, 'I'm goin' into chambers now. Lauren!' he hollered. A young woman rushed up. 'Get me the briefs in . . .' he turned to Mulcahy. 'What the hell case is it?'

'*Shepard*, Your Honour,' he answered, '*Commonwealth* v. *Shepard*.'

'Get me the briefs in *Shepard*. Counsellor,' he continued, turning back to Mulcahy, 'I'm goin' into my chambers now. I'm goin' t' reread those briefs. And when I'm done, I'm goin' to decide whether to order a rehearin', or sanction you. Gonna be one or the other.'

Mulcahy nodded. 'Thank you, Your Honour.'

'Don't thank me, son. Your next stop may be the Board of Bar Overseers.' The older man turned and walked through the clerk's office to his lobby door. The room was silent, all eyes on Justice Johnson. As he reached the door, he said, 'Son. You oughta know one thing. Been on this Court for fifteen years. They'll carry me out in a box, and throw a party when it happens. And I have never reversed Dave Grosso yet!' He opened the door and slammed it shut after him.

Minutes passed, and then a half hour. They had closed the clerk's office and abandoned Mulcahy to

445

the hall long since. When he asked the desk clerks, on exiting, what was going on, they shrugged. He had no idea whether everyone had gone home down a back elevator or something, but no notion of what to do if they had. So he stayed.

Forty-five minutes went by. Fifty. He made up his mind. He would leave when it had been an hour. He watched the second hand plod by. At six o'clock he pushed the elevator button, still watching the office door as the elevator came, hoping. But it remained shut fast, and the elevator door closed behind him.

Which was why, when Lauren unbolted the door and emerged at 6.15 with a single sheet of white foolscap, she found no one there to receive it.

In the evening Mulcahy sat alone in his apartment, still dazed, mind silly with the events of the day. He could not concentrate on the evidence, on the witnesses, or even on the appeal. His mind kept returning to those shocks of rebellious hair, of those blue eyes, of Kate now betrayed like everyone who came too near him for too long. He knew there was work to be done, but could not summon his mind to the task. Shepard had faded into the background, Vinny Testa, Judge Grosso, O'Hanlon – for him they all seemed pointless and small.

The buzzer sounded. It was her voice on the intercom and when he buzzed her up there she was, standing on the threshold, her weight shifting nervously from leg to leg. She was blushing. He stared at her in silence for a moment, and she stood silently too, unable to look directly at him. And then they embraced. He held her closely to him, and she sobbed softly, and clung to him tightly, and would not look up at him. The muscles of her back were tight beneath his right hand, and his left brushed softly against her hair. They stood like that for many minutes in the doorway, and when at last they separated to look at each other, still they clung tightly at the waist, in the manner of lovers.

They sat on the couch, and he held her gently. She cried softly and laughed some and told him how they had fired her that day. They had summoned her into an office with four of them, arranged so that she had to sit in their midst and could not see them all in one glance. They told her it was for cause, and Kincaid lectured her about her unethical conduct and she had to sit quietly with a lump building in her throat while the others watched. Then they escorted her, sent Shrinsky, that annoying little man, to follow her around as though she couldn't be trusted to gather her things without stealing a typewriter or something. He stood there in her office as she gathered her Rolodex and her tape player and her few pitiful books into a box.

They had been fast but, of course, not as quick-thinking as she, for she knew the instant she left the session that she would be fired, knew it as she rode the elevator down and as she walked across the bricks in Pemberton Square and as she crossed Cambridge Street and as she walked past the bustle of lawyers and bankers at the corner of State and Congress. And as she walked up Congress she was already planning. Fifteen minutes after returning to the office she had purged her computer of all her law files and printed all the useful ones, which she put into a file wallet. When it came to putting this in the box later, Shrinsky had asked her what it was, and when she said it was none of his business, he said he would have to take it. She looked at him and told him that if he tried to take it she would scream, as loudly and for as long as she could scream, and she would scream at the security guards when they came, and demand the police. She told Shrinsky this as flatly as though she were announcing her intention to walk to the washroom, and he backed down.

Mulcahy said nothing as he listened to her. She was silent for a few minutes after she told him about the day. Then he said, 'God. I'm so . . . that you were involved in this . . . I'm so sorry, Kate.'

'You know,' she said, 'I went straight to college and then straight to law school and then straight to Freer Motley, and I got to each one and I kept at each one by doing exactly what the teacher wanted. That's Kate, sitting in the front of the room with her hand in the air and the right answer on the tip of her tongue. Or Kate in the library studying for exams. Or Kate at her terminal writing a memo. And I got gold stars and then As and then top raises and glowing reviews. My whole life has been report cards.'

She went on. 'Every other thing in my life has been second to that: every human thing. No vacation ever took precedence over an assignment. But it was more than that. No family obligation ever did either. And my marriage, well, my engagement . . .' Her voice trailed off.

At that moment a key rattled in the lock and Gitz came in. 'Hey, Eddie,' he said, 'Kate.'

They greeted him and he began chattering as he headed for the fridge.

'Eddie, you get some beer?'

'Gitz, my bank account is frozen, remember?'

'Oh, yeah, well, you could steal some, or something. Geez, that doesn't affect the rent or anything, does it?' The red curls appeared at the threshold to the kitchen.

'I'm afraid it affects everything.'

'Hmmm,' he said. 'Hey, Eddie, should have seen the old buck tonight!'

'Who?'

'Elko, man, Elko. Scattered six hits, pitched into the ninth, and they beat Cleveland. He's back, I tell you. He's got his fastball back. That thing had some pop tonight, geez. Things are looking up, Eddie. They're looking up!' His voice faded away as he headed for his room.

They waited until they heard the sound of his door close. 'You were engaged?' Mulcahy whispered, and just for a moment, his grip on her arm loosened. But her grip on his did not.

'Yes. Well, I still am, technically. It's the world's longest engagement. I am betrothed to never. We are to be married just as soon as it's absolutely convenient and wouldn't interfere.'

After a time, he asked her, 'Why are you here now?'

'It wasn't convenient to go there.'

When he returned to the session Friday morning, there it was, the single slip of paper, one copy on each of the lawyers' tables, a single sheet of white paper bearing the SJC's caption. 'This Court will hear argument on the defendant's motion to reconsider its

449

order denying the motion for interlocutory relief at 9.30 a.m.,' it said. And, for the first time in days, Ed Mulcahy began to smile.

'Mr Mulcahy,' began Justice Johnson a few minutes later. He was a forbidding presence, glaring down from the bench in the ornate courtroom of the Supreme Judicial Court. But Mulcahy just felt glad to see him. 'I understand you have a motion for reconsideration?'

'Yes, Your Honour.'

'Proceed.'

This time the words came smoothly to him. He felt an effortlessness that he had not felt in quite some time. Whether the informant was called to testify in the case in which he had given information was immaterial, he said. Regardless of whether it was that case or another one, the government would have the same interest in protecting the source, while the defendant in a criminal case would have the same interest in a complete defence. The question resolved, simply, to a question of need.

Here, he went on, was a circumstantial case. If he could show the jury circumstances which pointed just as convincingly in a different direction, a reasonable doubt as to guilt would arise.

Which brought him to Vincent Testa and the witness. She had been a federal prosecutor. She also had an interest in the outcome of a high-stakes negotiation with Shepard's former employer. Testa could be linked to the apartment house where Shepard lived, and might be responsible for the theft of the credit card the Commonwealth said had been used in Natick on the night Sam Whitaker died.

'It is complicated,' he concluded. 'And circumstantial. It proves nothing, on its own. But it tends to disprove the Commonwealth's case – to show that it, too, is complicated, and circumstantial. And wrong.' Here he paused.

'Your Honour, we ask for the evidence.'

Justice Johnson nodded. For several minutes before hearing the other side, he was busy making notes.

31

Friday, mid-morning. It seemed like a long time since he had faced her on the stand. She was, again, perfectly turned out in a grey business suit, her hair, as before, drawn soberly back behind the head. But she looked slightly less assured than before.

'Good morning, Ms Russell,' he began.

'Good morning,' she answered coolly. And it was underway again. But this time, with slightly different rules. She would have to answer the questions about Testa. That would be the easy part. The rest would be tricky, the most difficult cross-examination of his life. It has been said that it takes twenty jury trials to make a competent trial lawyer. Not good – competent. He didn't have twenty jury trials. He didn't have ten.

Yes, she knew Testa. Yes, she was the prosecutor in *United States* v *Cerrone*, and yes, Testa had been a confidential informant in that case. She said she hadn't seen him for three years. But she confessed that she had known him, had had to work with him in the *Cerrone* case. As well prepared for this as she must have been, a defensiveness had crept into her voice as Mulcahy slowly mined the evidence.

The jury was interested by this, but a sense of uncertainty was palpable in the room. Nobody knew what it meant. Nor would they, until just before the end. But you have to hope they will remember, and put it together in the jury room.

When they took the morning recess, Shepard leaned over. 'Well, you got it, big guy.'

'That part I got upstairs, this morning,' he whispered back. 'That was law. The rest, I don't know . . .' He had no way to control her – no deposition, no statement – hell, he didn't even have knowledge. He had no business pressing ahead on a cross-examination like this. It would likely go badly. But he had no choice.

It resumed a moment later. 'Now, Ms Russell,' he began, 'you represented the Idlewild group in the Idlewild LBO?'

'I represented several corporations and individuals in that transaction, Mr Mulcahy, including a partnership known as Idlewild Holdings Limited Partnership.'

'Was Mr Sidney Weiner the principal of that group?'

'He was one of the principals.'

'Was he the one with the biggest stake, directly and indirectly, in the acquiring partnerships?'

'Yes.'

'Was it Weiner who hired you?'

'Yes.'

'Now, Ms Russell,' Mulcahy continued, 'you were

453

an Assistant United States Attorney, trained as a trial lawyer. How is it that you came to represent a corporate client in a complex acquisition and financing of this kind?'

'My practice changed after I returned to the private sector,' she said. 'I began to acquire corporate clients, and to be more involved in their work. They looked to me for general advice. In a transaction such as this one, I had assistance from many specialists, of course.' Libby Russell had brought aggressive marketing to a new level. Scarcely was there a Bar Association function, seminar, or other boondoggle she didn't attend. She courted print journalists assiduously, and had become an oft-quoted ready source when a story needed fleshing out with the comment of a lawyer. And it had worked. Corporate clients saw her as connected. Her telephone rang constantly.

In Idlewild, she had pulled off a near-legendary coup: a major corporate acquisition and financing – generating over $750,000 in legal fees – headed by a non-corporate specialist.

Mulcahy approached the witness with an exhibit. 'I show you Defence Exhibit 39 for identification. Do you recognise this?'

She did. It was the Grenade letter.

He asked her whether she had written it.

'Yes,' she said. 'As you know, attorneys often draft correspondence for their clients.'

'Of course,' he said. 'The enclosure to this letter purported to pay off the balance of the mortgage.'

'The enclosure *did* pay off the mortgage, Mr Mulcahy.'

He smiled. 'Well, Ms Russell, let's explain to the

jury what we're talking about. At the Idlewild closing, how much money did Depositors' Fidelity lend to your clients?'

'I believe it was eight hundred forty million dollars.'

'And your clients gave back, among other collateral security, a mortgage in Idlewild Tower?'

'That's correct.'

'Which is a large office building on Fifth Avenue in New York City?'

'Yes.'

'The amount of that mortgage, according to what the document said, was eight hundred forty *thousand* dollars?'

'Yes.'

'Now, there were negotiations about this issue between DeFi – I mean, Depositors' Fidelity – and your clients after Exhibit 39 was sent, were there not?'

'There were.'

'And DeFi took the position that the text of the mortgage contained a misprint: that the mortgage amount was supposed to be eight hundred forty *million*, not thousand, correct?'

'Yes.'

'And that dispute ultimately was settled?'

'Yes, it was.'

'Favourably for your client?'

'I'd say so.'

'Your client submitted to a mortgage on the tower, but it was less than eight hundred forty million, was it not?'

· 'I'm afraid the terms of the settlement are subject to a confidentiality agreement.'

'Well, Ms Russell, one of those terms involved the recording of a new mortgage, which is a public document, is it not?'

'It is.'

'And what is the mortgage amount shown there?'

'Six hundred million, I believe.'

'So as a result of the settlement, your client's mortgage was reduced – from what Depositors' Fidelity maintained, anyway?'

'From the bank's perspective, yes, I suppose that's right.'

'Now, Ms Russell,' Mulcahy said, 'did you call to your client's attention the fact that the mortgage was in the amount of eight hundred forty *thousand*, rather than million?'

She turned to the bench. 'Your Honour,' she said, 'I believe that is . . .'

'Privileged,' he said, finishing the sentence. 'Yes, Ms Russell, you are correct. Next question, Mr Mulcahy.'

He showed her the letter again. 'Well, soon after that conversation, you drafted Exhibit 39?'

'Yes,' she said.

'Your Honour, I offer Exhibit 39 in evidence,' he said. It was received.

While the clerk was marking it in, Ed Mulcahy recalled his cousin Hudnall Long and the skittish calf. His aunt Lucy had married a Virginian and moved away years ago. E. J. Long had been in the service, stationed at Fort Devens, and the two had met at a dance. Later he became a doctor, a country

456

gentleman who also raised pigs and beef cattle on his hillside spread outside of Danville. As boys, Tommy and Ed Mulcahy were often sent to Aunt Lucy and Uncle E. J.'s place. During one of their visits, years ago, a calf had got separated from its momma in the church pond pasture. The three boys – Ed was then about eleven – were sent to fetch the calf up out of the pasture and into the back pasture.

The church pond pasture was a long, hillside pasture of about eighteen acres, which snaked down from the road and around the farmhouse, and then further down into the valley below. The boys didn't have horses or dogs that morning, and the calf was spooked by its mother's absence. Ed had never forgotten watching Hudnall work that pasture to get the calf up to the gate at the north end. You couldn't get too close, or the calf would bolt. Stay too far away, and you couldn't get the calf moving. Hudnall used his cousins as outriders, and, with just the right combination of nonchalance and dispatch, of diffidence and command, of proximity and distance, of circling and flanking, they had worked the calf up to the north end of the field. It took about twenty minutes, and it ended with the calf seeming to notice the gate, and taking a notion of its own to go through.

The first gate was the hardest. After that they had her on the road, which was fenced, and then into the back pasture, where she would find her mother, and the herd could be driven to the barn.

That's cross-examination. You have to get a skittish calf up to the gate way up at the end of the pasture. And you have to get it to decide that it wants to go through the gate. And then, if things go well, another gate, and so on to another. But the first one is the hardest.

'Ms Russell,' Mulcahy said, 'there's something I don't understand. It was a five-year mortgage. Why did they pay it off in the first month?'

She paused and bit her lip, just for a moment. 'I don't know what their business purpose was,' she said.

'Look, Ms Russell, you've settled with the bank, right?'

'Yes.'

'Exchanged releases, it's all final, right?'

'Yes. Yes, I believe so.'

He smiled at her. Sometimes you ask questions to communicate a message to the witness. It is all right to tell me it was a misprint, he was radioing to her. Your deal with the bank is safe.

'Over the eight days before the closing, you were in a lot of negotiations, right?'

'Yes.'

'With a number of different people?'

'Yes.' He could call forty people to the stand to testify about negotiations she had been in. About how the mortgage amount had never been discussed.

'Did the amount of the mortgage ever come up in those negotiations?'

She got the point. 'In the ones I attended, I don't recall it coming up.'

'No one negotiated an eight hundred forty thousand dollar mortgage amount in your presence, right?'

'No,' she said, 'not that I recall.'

Now for some sugar. 'There were others in the deal who specialised in the real estate aspects, weren't there?' he said.

'Yes,' she said, seeing her way through it. There had been a lot of lawyers. It could still have been the actual deal, and unknown to her, if some other lawyer had handled that aspect of the transaction.

'So, at the time of the closing, did you know the amount shown in the mortgage was eight hundred forty thousand?'

'I'm not sure I did,' she said, hesitantly.

He let out a breath. She was through the first gate. Everything else he hoped to do depended on that one answer: on her concession that she had not personally known the number was there. Now to get the gate shut behind her, and move her up towards the barn. It was still a few fields away.

'Ms Russell,' he said, 'how is it that you happened to find this piece of the text?'

'I was simply reviewing the documents,' she said.

'Well, there were two hundred ninety-six documents at the closing, were there not?'

'That's about right.'

'And the deal had already closed, the money been paid, the mortgages and UCCs recorded and filed, right?'

'Yes.'

'And then at some time later you took it upon yourself to read through two hundred ninety-six documents?'

'I didn't, I didn't read all of the documents, Mr Mulcahy. I did not review all of the opinions and the corporate authority certificates and so on. I simply

459

read through the major documents to assure myself that everything was correct.'

'How many documents was that?'

'I don't know, Mr Mulcahy.' She was cutting off the ends of his questions with hurried answers, rushing a little, as though there were fences where she hadn't noticed them before – fences closing off escape routes. 'The note, the loan agreement, the mortgages – there were several other ones, as you must know – the collateral assignments, the warrant purchase agreement. I don't know ... eight, ten documents.'

'Eight or ten documents,' he repeated. 'Okay, Ms Russell, eight or ten documents. These are long documents, aren't they?'

'Some of them.'

He pressed. 'Some of them run to over a hundred pages – the loan agreement, for example?'

'That's right.'

'So how long did this review of the eight or ten documents take?'

'Mr Mulcahy, I have no idea.'

'Ten minutes?' he asked. It was a false fence, and she bolted from it.

'No, Mr Mulcahy, of course it was not ten minutes. It took a long time. Whether it was a day, half a day, I don't know.'

'I see,' he said, 'your best memory is that it was between half a day and a day?'

'As far as I can remember,' she said.

'Some time shortly before the date of the letter?'

'Right.'

'What date would that have been?' he asked. And

now she saw the gate, but saw it too late, saw that she would have to go through it.

'I don't recall.'

She could have predicted the next question herself. 'And so your time sheets would identify the day when this was done?' They both knew that most attorneys in civil practice keep daily, detailed time records of their work.

She was silent for a moment. 'Ms Russell?' he said.

'I don't know. Perhaps. If I charged for it.'

'If you charged for it? Are you suggesting to the jury that you might have spent a half day to a day reviewing loan documents and not charged for it?'

'Well, they had paid our bill at closing,' she said, but she sounded tentative.

'Ms Russell, don't you record non-billable time on your time sheet?'

'What do you mean?'

'Well, if you spend half a day at a seminar, or in an effort to develop a new client, don't you record that on your time sheets?'

She looked at him coolly. 'Yes, often,' she said.

'So you would have recorded this half day or a day prior to the letter on your time sheets?'

'It's possible,' she said.

'And if you recorded this information on your time sheets, it might refresh your memory on when you noticed the mortgage amount?'

'It might,' she said.

'Ms Russell, I ask that you look back through your time sheets at lunch and bring into court the time sheet which shows the work you did to discover the error. Your Honour,' he said, turning to the bench,

461

'perhaps this would be a good time to recess for lunch.'

'Two o'clock,' said Judge Grosso, and the session adjourned.

After Russell had left the stand and the session had begun to empty, Mulcahy looked up to see Kate in the back of the room. 'Try to get a subpoena on her firm's head billing clerk,' he said, when they were together. 'There'll be a computer printout or something where the time sheet was input. I actually don't want any of that stuff, but make a big show out of subpoenaing the clerk – and copy Russell, in case she takes a notion to draft up a new time sheet.'

Kate glanced at her watch. 'I've got Hughes at 2.30,' she said.

'Hughes?'

'Your bank account. Remember?' She smiled sweetly.

'Damn. Well, you should be back here by then, right?'

She sighed. 'The things I do for love, Mr Mulcahy. You're probably going to tell me next that you need a couple of bucks for lunch.'

'Well . . .'

She shoved a five into his jacket pocket. 'No hot dogs, okay?' Smiling again, she left.

For love? he thought. He felt himself blushing. And it inspired him to settle for a salad.

At ten minutes to two, it was evident that Kate had done her work with characteristic vigour. A whole A-men corner of Russell's partners had arrived. There was Herb Stein, who was beet red above the collar line and looked as though a vein or two might burst from his forehead. Two more attorneys surrounded Stein, each scowling grimly. At the end of the bench was a nervous fellow with a file folder of green and white computer printouts. That would be the bookkeeper, Ed thought. Well done, Kate. Russell was fuming. She was at him as soon as he entered the session.

'This is an outrage, Ed. The harassment you have been trying with me, puerile as it is, is one thing, but this goes beyond any limit. All of this material is privileged. It's not relevant. There is no purpose at all to this whole line other than to try to embarrass me. I won't forget this.'

Mulcahy nodded slowly. The room was beginning to fill. 'Did you find the time sheet?' he asked. But she turned without answering.

O'Hanlon had arrived, and now huddled with Stein. The group went to find Clerk Kelly.

Several minutes later, Judge Grosso returned to the bench. The jury had not been recalled. 'I understand we have a motion?' he said.

'Your Honour,' said O'Hanlon, 'the Commonwealth has a motion for a protective order. It is joined by the witness. This entire side show has gone completely beyond the scope of relevant issues in this case. It is an outrage. I have been advised, now, that in addition to asking Ms Russell before lunch to conduct a burdensome search of privileged records, Mr Mulcahy has, over the lunch hour, served subpoenas on a bookkeeper and the managing partner of Fletcher Daye. I mean, Judge, this has gone way beyond anything that's appropriate . . .'

As O'Hanlon worked himself into a lather, Mulcahy turned, looking to the back of the room for Kate. 'The managing partner?' he mouthed, voicelessly, when he saw her. She shrugged, pointed at her watch, and slipped out the back. He turned back to the front of the room to see Judge Grosso calling his name. The judge was not happy.

'Mr Mulcahy?'

'Your Honour, we're about done with this line. There really is only one question. When did Ms Russell discover the mistake? Has she found the time sheet that records that entry? That's all. Perhaps if we can get an answer to that, we can excuse these others.'

Grosso was still frowning. 'Gentlemen,' he said, 'we'll go one question at a time. And, Mr Mulcahy, at this rate, we won't go very far.'

I'll take it, he thought. As he returned to his table, waiting now for the jury to be brought back, it occurred to him that it might have been worth losing all of those early rounds.

'Did you find the time sheet, Ms Russell?' he asked, when she returned to the stand. He expected an objection from O'Hanlon, but there was none. Evidently there were certain positions he would take only out of the jury's earshot. From the back of the room, a tentative 'Your Honour ...' as one of Russell's team rose.

'Overruled,' said the judge.

Russell said, 'No.'

'No, Ms Russell, you didn't find it?'

'No.'

'You couldn't find any time entry of this half day or day when you examined the closing bibles?'

'No. Evidently I didn't charge for it.'

'So, you've established that you did not write the time down, correct?'

'Yes, that is correct.'

'You don't need to check any further records to know that?' he asked, beckoning at her colleagues at the back.

'No,' she said.

'All right,' said Mulcahy. 'Your Honour, the defence excuses the gentlemen who are here this afternoon under subpoena from Fletcher Daye.'

There was a scuffling noise from the back as the Fletcher Daye contingent rose and left.

'Now,' said Mulcahy, turning back to his witness, 'perhaps you didn't write the time down because it didn't take as long as a half day, Ms Russell?'

'Perhaps.'

'Perhaps it took so little time because you knew the error was in the mortgage.'

'That's not true,' she said, her tone now plainly angry.

'Your Honour, once again,' said O'Hanlon, 'I must object and inquire what this character assassination has to do with the case.'

But before the judge could comment, Mulcahy smiled and said that he was going to move on.

Three floors above, Kate was arguing the case of *Parisi* v *Mulcahy*. She had lingered in 8b for the beginning of the fallout over her subpoenas, and then, giving up on the elevators, walked up the three flights of stairs, arriving just after 2.35, out of breath, literally as the clerk was calling out the case. The irony of the continuance was that now Parisi was present, but her own client was on trial downstairs.

She stood before the bench, trying to catch her breath, while Hughes sat silently reading.

'Your Honour . . .' she ventured.

He waved her off in mid-sentence, still staring at the briefs. She watched the pages of her brief, and of Parisi's, turning slowly on the bench.

At length, he looked up coldly. While Judge Hughes was a handsome man, with good strong features beneath his thinning whitened hair, he rarely smiled, and his aspect was forbidding. When he spoke, which was seldom, the words were clipped, spoken through clenched teeth.

'Miss Maher,' he said.

She gave her argument. It was like speaking to a wall. Hughes sat impassively, never interrupting, never asking a question. And it was like that for Parisi, too, although she could see Hughes grimace, once or twice, as Parisi's argument bounced here, there, and everywhere but the statute. All that Hughes said, throughout the fifteen-minute hearing, was 'Miss Maher', and 'Mr Parisi'. And then when they were done, he said, 'Under advisement, you'll have an order next week.'

And so, knowing nothing more than she had known before the hearing, she left Judge Hughes's session, and went to the elevator.

'Now, Ms Russell,' Mulcahy was saying in 8b an hour later, 'did you go for a jog around the Charles River with John Shepard on 16 May?'

466

'If that was the date,' she said, 'I did go for a run with him.'

Shepard was signalling him. He begged a moment from the judge.

Huddling with his client, he saw Shepard's eyes were burning. 'What the hell are you doing?' he hissed.

'John, I don't have time right now . . .'

'Leave it!'

'John, I can't leave it. It's important. I'll explain . . .'

'Leave it, goddamn it! Do not . . .'

'Mr Mulcahy?' Mulcahy looked up. It was the judge. He didn't like to keep his juries waiting.

'Leave it!' Shepard hissed again.

Mulcahy stepped gingerly over to the podium.

'Your run with Mr Shepard. Do you recall that it was the last day he was in Boston?'

'Yes,' she said, 'he did say that.'

'And it was, of course, the day that Mr Whitaker died?'

'I remember hearing about his death the next day. On the radio, I think,' she said.

'Now, you ran by Mr Shepard's apartment, is that right?'

'Yes.'

'And you placed a telephone call to him before meeting him?'

'Yes.'

'From a public telephone booth?'

'Yes.'

'The booth at the corner of Joy and Mount Vernon

Streets, at the top of the hill,' he asked, fingering a NYNEX record.

She paused. 'It might have been,' she said.

'The very same booth from which the Commonwealth says Mr Shepard telephoned Mr Whitaker that night, wasn't it?'

'I wouldn't know,' said the witness.

'Of course not,' said Mulcahy, more to himself than to her. 'How would you? Well, let me ask you this,' he said. 'You met Shepard outside his apartment, and the two of you went for about a forty-minute run, right?'

'That is about right.'

'Had you ever run with him before?'

'No.'

'Ever run with him after?'

'No.'

'Did you ever speak to him again?' he asked.

Now she paused again. 'No,' she said, 'I don't believe I ever spoke to him again.'

'We'll break here,' said Judge Grosso. It was a puzzled jury which filed slowly out of the session that afternoon.

'I need a minute with you,' said Shepard, as they cuffed him in the courtroom afterwards. The court officer rolled his eyes. 'We're going to transport him in fifteen minutes, Counsellor,' he said, as he led them off to the lock-up.

When they were alone, Shepard said, 'Goddamn it, Ed! What the hell is going on! Who's in charge here?'

Mulcahy was silent.

'Where are you going with her, Ed?'

Mulcahy stared at him. 'Why?'

'I thought the defence was suicide.'

'Do you find that credible?'

Shepard was silent.

'After the jacket, do you find that credible?'

Shepard sat staring back at him.

'John,' said Mulcahy, 'you'd better tell me what's on your mind.'

He spoke softly, looking down, his hands in his lap. 'Look,' he said. 'During the closing, I was with her. Okay, you guessed it. Now explain to me how it's going to help my defence to have you handcuff me to the nightgown of the gal who wrote the Grenade letter?'

'I told you I wanted the facts. How did that one slip your mind?'

'One night we negotiated. We finished up. We did the last edits. We left. And she followed me home.'

'And you . . .'

Shepard looked at his lawyer, as if to say, 'Wouldn't you?'

'And the night of the 30th – was she with you again?'

'Affirmative.'

'Jesus,' said Mulcahy. 'It's a thrill a minute with you.'

'So, I'm a sinner. But why the hell didn't you do what I told you? Why didn't you leave it alone?'

But Mulcahy ignored the questions. 'You should know something, John. If I were to get information that your testimony the other day was not true, I might have to withdraw. Be careful about what you tell me.'

'Now just what in the hell is that supposed to

mean?' said Shepard, the colour coming to his cheeks, his voice rising. They could hear the footsteps. The guard was returning.

'You figure it out!' Mulcahy came to his feet. Shepard came to his feet. Each was tired and over-wrought. They were staring pugnaciously at each other, eye to eye, when the guard returned.

Yet another confrontation awaited Mulcahy after they had led his client off. For the session was not empty. There by the defence table in the empty room was Herb Stein, camped out and chafing for Mulcahy's return. Behind him, in the gallery, was Libby Russell.

'Where is your judgment, son, where is your judgment?' Mulcahy tried to ignore him, walking to counsel table to gather his files and pack them up in the boxes. But Stein stood by his shoulder.

'Being defence counsel does not give you a licence to savage the reputation of whoever might be handy,' the senior Fletcher Daye partner went on. 'What do you think you are doing to this young woman?'

Mulcahy closed his eyes. But he could feel his cheeks burning.

'This is a public event, you know!' Stein went on. 'And you are trashing her reputation without the slightest concern for decency. This is shameful, shameful!'

The little man stomped from the session. Mulcahy's eyes remained closed, and he heard the footsteps and the swing of the session door. But she had not left yet. It was just the two of them when he opened his eyes again, he and Libby Russell. Shimmering in her pale grey suit, lovely as before, she now looked wounded, whether really so or by contrivance.

'Ed Mulcahy, it's clear that you don't know what you're doing. You don't know what case you're in. You don't know with whom you are dealing. You're not even getting paid, according to the newspapers. I have a very long memory, and many people supporting me.'

'Like Vinny?' he asked.

She turned on her heel, and the brisk clip of her footsteps echoed in the quiet session.

When the door swung shut he was alone. They had all gone now. And they had all gone in the trial, too. Soldiers have mates, but champions are alone. Even his client had faded from the arena, leaving him a solitary advocate, solely responsible for the casualties, the collateral damage. When it was over, he would have lost the case, he would have lost the partnership, and he would have launched the attack on the rich and powerful. They would wonder why, solemnly pronounce last rites over his amateurish defence, and ponder the psychological instability which led to the premature end of a promising lawyer. Partners would speak in hushed voices around the coffee urn. No one else had taken on Libby Russell. No one would be around when the day came to account for that decision. He packed the last of the files in the boxes and slammed on the lids.

'Gotta close up,' a voice said, interrupting the silence.

Mulcahy looked up at the old court officer rattling his ring of keys in the lock-up door.

'Time to go home,' said Freddie, smiling gently. In Freddie's world, trials might come and trials might

471

go, but the 27 bus for L Street always left Government Centre at 5.19.

Mulcahy also thought it was high time to go home. But there was no particular place that felt like it.

'Freddie,' he said, as he pulled the bungee cords around the boxes, 'how'm I doing?' He tried to affect a jocularity in the question, but the old court officer could tell that Mulcahy really wanted an answer. Every trial lawyer wants to know how he's doing, and not simply to feed his ego. There are no progress reports in a jury trial.

But Freddie had seen a lot of cases. He'd seen guilty men go free and he'd seen juries convict when he had doubts himself.

'Tough case, kid. Tough case,' he said, shaking his head, as he pulled on his jacket and ushered Mulcahy out of the session.

It was the end of a long trial day, the end of a long trial week. The mind goes to jello then, unable to hold detail, unable to order the list of tasks that must be set in motion tonight if they are to mature at the proper moment. Instead, it is prone to replay the examinations, and dwell on what has already passed. His mind in a fog, Ed Mulcahy set out with his two-wheeler across the street to the Government Centre T station.

At that moment, Kate was scooping out the last of the bait for George Creel: still uncertain whether he was even following the traffic of memoranda, she nevertheless intended to see it through. It was a bogus memorandum from Ed to herself. If she could convince Creel that, with Testa now publicly exposed, he would not now risk further trouble by attempts to silence a lonely middle-aged man in a wheelchair, she might have a chance. But it had to be handled delicately. She wrote:

MEMORANDUM
TO: C.A.M.
FROM: E.X.M.
DATE: 9/24/92

With Russell's testimony today, we established the link between Russell and Testa which puts the means for murder within her reach. Testa's name will again be in the newspapers tomorrow, and all efforts to find him have been unsuccessful. Moreover, the off-the-record information Stevie has obtained from his sources links Testa to the Creel shooting. Stevie thinks we will have no chance of finding him – he will be in hiding now.

The problem is still motive. The jury are not going to find credible that she, of all people, would be involved in murder without more evidence. We still have no hard link between her and the tampering.

This is the critical item for us. Let's give maximum attention this weekend to trying to make this link – we are going to run out of witnesses, at the latest, by Tuesday.

E.X.M.

With an unsatisfied feeling, she saved the memorandum in the computer file, and left the office.

32

It was the photograph that led Emma Whitaker to place the call. She had followed, in the *Transcript*, the daily accounts of the trial. And she had been unnerved, and then enraged, to discover that the defence lawyer was trying to divert attention from the murderer by throwing dirt at her father. It was an outrage, but then, she had long since given up on lawyers as a group. Whatever the source of the rift between Samuel and his daughter in life, she remained loyal. She was blood.

But it all turned upside down in an instant. That Friday morning, as always, she padded in her flip-flops down the gravel drive to pick up the newspaper. At her kitchen counter, with a mug of tea before her, she unfolded it, hunting, as she had every morning for ten days, for the story. She found it on the lower front. There, staring out at her, was the photograph a *Transcript* sub editor had found in the photo library and set up in column six below the fold. It was the face which Emma had seen. *Her* face. It was the woman who had been at her father's funeral, when Emma had almost to tear her mother away from an ugly confrontation. And it was the woman she had seen before, those other times.

She read the story, but her eye wandered back to the photograph. She reread it, and again stared at the photograph. The woman was some kind of prominent lawyer, and she had been questioned about her relationship with some person who was supposed to have been involved. There was some acrimonious dispute over whether it was proper for the defence attorney to have called her to the stand.

Emma sat for a long time. Her thoughts were confused. She felt queasy. And then she picked up the telephone and dialled Information.

It was about 8.30 when Mulcahy's key turned in the lock. He tossed the mail on the couch with the stack of other unread mail, dropped his suit jacket on the armchair, checked, once again, the long-empty fridge to see whether by some magical process Gitz had discovered supermarkets (you never know), and, on his way to the bedroom, hit the play button on his machine.

He was just dropping off to sleep when he heard an unfamiliar voice, a woman's voice. And he distinctly heard the word 'Whitaker'.

Now he was back in the kitchen, hitting all the wrong buttons, rewinding, getting his brother's message, a salesman – Jesus – and then this: 'Hello. My name is Emma Whitaker. If this is the Edward Mulcahy who is involved with the murder trial concerning my father, Samuel Whitaker, I would like to speak with you. My number is . . .' He grabbed for a pencil and scribbled the number. A moment later he dialled. An answering machine. He got to thinking. Where was this number? He telephoned an operator.

'Chilmark,' she said.

He paced. There was no sound save the buzz of the electric clock over the stove, and shouts from the returning students below as the weekend was beginning. He walked back and forth. And then the phone rang.

A moment later, almost breathless, he telephoned his father. 'Dad, can you pick me up at Falmouth again?'

'Tomorrow? Jesus, I was going to go . . .'

'Not tomorrow. Tonight.'

'Well, for Christ's sake,' he said. When the Captain was willing to oblige, but thought you a little out of line, that's what he did. He said, 'Well, for Christ's sake.'

Mulcahy's next call was to Kate.

'Want to go to the Vineyard?' he asked.

'Sure,' she said. 'Should I bring my swimsuit?'

'No. Your subpoenas.'

Much later that evening, the Captain's old Chevy pickup turned into the gravel drive at 87 Pocasset Road in Chilmark. It eased along the drive until it had pulled up to the front step of a modest shingle-roofed house.

'She wouldn't talk to you three weeks ago,' Mulcahy said.

'Hung the phone up,' Kate agreed.

476

The entryway light was on, and the door was opened as Mulcahy and Kate alighted from the truck. A young woman, with short blonde hair, dressed in a long peasant skirt, sandals and a fleece jacket, appeared. She had pale blue eyes and a broad forehead like her father's. She was accompanied by a tall, thin man in a lumberjack shirt, with a pony tail.

'Miss Whitaker,' said Mulcahy. 'I'm sorry for the intrusion at this hour. I thank you. This is my colleague, Kate Maher.'

She didn't answer, but smiled a little before leading the two of them into the kitchen where they sat at a table next to the stove. A kettle was on the fire, and Emma set out mugs and filled a pot with tea as the others sat.

'You're the one who called last month, right?'

Kate nodded.

'I'm sorry I . . . well, I'm sorry. That was a nice note you sent my mother,' Emma Whitaker said.

Note? thought Mulcahy. He turned to look questioningly at Kate, but she was already saying, 'That must have been awful for her. She was terribly decent, your mother. I went to see her and she was firm, but so, so polite. I felt awful.'

Mulcahy was wondering what else he didn't know about. But Kate pressed ahead. 'This whole thing has been so dreadful. Your father . . . we're all so sorry about him. I'll never forget when he came and gave us a lunch talk the summer I was a summer clerk. It was a talk on "Lawyer as Counsellor". I was just floored. I thought I'd never be able to talk to a room full of people like that. He had such a presence.'

'That was Daddy,' said Emma. 'A presence.'

'When my own father died,' Kate said, 'I felt like a child again. He was a difficult man but, when he was gone, I felt as though I'd been cast adrift . . . Oh God, I'm sorry.'

She stepped around the table and placed her arm on Emma's arm. Emma's eyes were misting. 'It's okay,' she said. 'I certainly didn't expect this!'

She poured the tea. 'Mr Mulcahy,' she said, 'I only know what I read in the papers about this trial. I frankly can't believe I'm sitting in a room with the man who is trying to get my father's murderer off. Or, I know, you say he isn't. But, well . . . I wouldn't have called you if I hadn't seen this morning's paper.'

'This morning's paper?'

'Yes, here,' she said, and tossed him the *Transcript* with its below the fold picture of Libby Russell.

'The article,' she said, continuing, 'said you questioned this woman yesterday, something about a Mafia man and whether she knew him? I didn't quite follow it. But . . .'

'Yes?' It was Kate. She asked the question gently.

'I know this woman.' They looked at her quietly, seeking more. 'I think that . . . can this be confidential?'

Mulcahy stumbled on a response. But Kate said, 'Emma . . . may I call you Emma?' And when the woman nodded, she said, 'It is not confidential. Nothing you tell us can be confidential. We represent a man who is on trial for his life. We think he is innocent. And anything we can find to help him, we must use. Can you understand that?'

She nodded. Kate went on, 'So if you feel you can't reveal it, then it's better that you do not tell us. But we really do think he's a good man, caught in a terrible mistake, a terrible mistake – we're almost at the end of this trial and if you know something which could help him, we hope you will tell us.'

Emma sat in silence for a moment. She said, 'You wouldn't hurt my father – my father's memory – just for the sake of it, would you?'

'No,' said Kate, 'we would not.'

'Well, I ask you to be discreet about this. But this woman,' she said as she lifted the newspaper from the table again, and looked at the photograph, 'I've seen her. I think . . . I think that she may have had . . . that . . .' She reddened. 'That something went on with her and my father.'

There was only silence. Mulcahy, dumbstruck, was conscious of the tick-tock of the wall clock.

Kate kept the conversation going. 'Do you think . . . do you think that might have had something to do with our case?'

'I don't know. According to the newspaper, you people thought she might have been involved somehow. I thought I should tell you. Now I don't know. I shouldn't have told them. Jim?' This last was directed to the silent man. He shrugged.

'This would hurt my mother terribly,' Emma said to Kate.

'We're very grateful to you,' Mulcahy said.

Kate said, 'I confess that I saw something curious at your father's funeral. Libby Russell was there, too, and there was a frightening moment at the back of the church when her face was full of anger, your mother's face. And I thought, that could only be one thing.

479

'That was why I went to see her. I went to her home unannounced, not quite as late in the evening as this. A terrible intrusion. And of course she refused to speak to me about it. But she did it with such dignity. She was firm with me, but so, so elegant. I can't tell you how low I felt.'

Emma was smiling at her. 'That's Mother.'

There was a cold edge on the night air. The crickets were silent and the stars shone brightly outside the kitchen window in the clear island air. The moon had risen high in the sky. There was a sense of anticipation, of autumn coming. The only sounds were the clock and the propane jet beneath the kettle. Emma poured more tea. Jim declined. He stretched, yawned, and shuffled off for bed.

'Emma,' asked Kate, after a time, 'are we far from the beach?'

And so for the second time that night Mulcahy wondered what on earth was happening, as he peered through the windshield at the darkness before his father's truck. They parked it and walked through the heather to the dunes. When they emerged, somewhere nearby in the darkness the waves were crashing on the sand of South Beach. There was a silvery shimmer where the foam hit the strand. The moon was setting, and clouds had begun to come in, so that stars winked in and out here and there in the sky. Kate asked Ed if he wouldn't mind if they walked ahead. He nodded with relief. This had become her enterprise anyway.

He sat in the sand above the high water mark, listening to the roll and wash of the waves, one upon the next. It was too chilly for sleep, but he dozed off briefly. The steady rhythm of the surf was reassuring, and it felt good to be alone on the beach, far from Pemberton Square.

But he was awake when he made out, in the starlight, the two figures returning down the beach a half hour later. And in the darkness, as they walked back to the car, Emma Whitaker and Ed Mulcahy felt an odd kinship, as if they had quite by accident discovered that they both were in the charge of the same caretaker.

On the drive back to Emma's home, there was a moment when Ed might have shaken off the feeling, and said something about the case, but Kate's hand on his forearm anticipated him. 'Not just now,' she said softly.

And she retained that serene smile after they'd bid Emma Whitaker good night. When they were alone in the truck he looked at her for explanations, but she only said, 'It will be all right. It's hard for her, but I think it will be all right.' Mulcahy sighed. It was too late and too bizarre. He turned the truck for Oak Bluffs.

'I should warn you,' he said, after ten minutes or so, 'my dad snores.'

'Do you?' she asked. It was dark in the car, but he thought he could just discern the light of mischief in her eyes.

The Captain's cottage, only slightly larger than his Brownell fishing boat, was hidden among scrubby pines two blocks from the Town Forest, and surrounded by old boats and cars. The old man slept in a loft which he gained by clambering up a ladder from the galley. The cottage's one, tiny bedroom saw use only from guests, and mainly its bed was given over to boxes of marina files, stacks of old fishing and boating magazines, and books. He had cleared it off for the guests, and assigned the bedroom and the one clean towel in the household to Kate. His son was allocated the couch.

The Captain had an outdoor shower, which he used from April to October. Once a year, in October, he cleared out fungus from the bathroom and returned to using indoor facilities. But that day was still yet a month off on the September night when Ed and Kate came to visit.

It was well past 2 when the tyres crunched softly over the clamshell fragments in the drive, and the two lawyers stepped down from the truck. The setting moon now peered out from a gap in the clouds. Ed and Kate crept past the woodpile and around the old sloop's hull. 'I learned to sail in that,' he said.

Taped to the door they found a note, which read:

Have the decency to take the couch and offer the
lady the bed. There aren't any clean towels, except
the one I've left out on the bed. The outdoor shower
is cleaner. Anyone who wants to fish be up at 4.30
or leave me a note. I'll be back by 8.

Cap

Mulcahy pushed the door open and stepped in softly. Upstairs the Captain snored regularly, with now and again a lip smack punctuating the snorts. Ben Mulcahy slept only for five hours a night, but those were five hours of abandon. Ed peeled the note from the window and wrote, in reply:

If you wake me up to go fishing I will pour out all
your liquor.

Kate tiptoed round the telephone stand and into
the sitting room. 'Ed?' she whispered.

'Here,' he whispered back. Through the darkness
her silhouette appeared. Her face and auburn hair
were backlit by the dim moonlight filtering through
the curtains. She touched his hand, and slipped by
him to the bedroom, the door closing softly behind
her.

A moment later the door reopened. She shimmered
past carrying the towel, evidently clad only in a T
shirt. He lay on the couch, listening as the door
pulled to and the shower came on. He imagined the
steam rising above the pine baffles, the moonlight on
her darkened shoulders. When, a few moments later,
she came noiselessly again into the room, he no
longer had any consciousness of the snoring from the
loft. It seemed to him that the light footfall filled the
room with gentleness.

'Kate,' he whispered, 'tell me one thing.'

'Yes?' she whispered back.

She came towards him and he reached up from the
couch and took her hand in the darkness.

'What?' she asked again.

'Did you at least subpoena her?'

'Ugh,' she said, 'you are *awful*,' and she dropped
his hand. 'Awful. I am going to bed.'

'But did you?' he asked.

'No,' she said. 'She's not, she's not the kind of
person you, you *subpoena!*'

He stared across the darkened room, able only to

see her dark form against the bedroom doorway. She came back towards him. Then her face was near his, and he was intoxicated by her scent all around him, but except for the sparkle reflecting off her eyes, her face was in darkness. He felt the warmth of her lips near his.

'Some people,' she whispered, 'prefer to be asked.'

And then she was gone, and the bedroom door shut again.

He had a vague awareness, later, of noise, of annoyance, but when he finally awoke at 8 the house was empty. The Captain had, of course, risen at 4.30, to prepare for the morning's fishing. Evidently Kate had gone with him.

The Captain had business at the marina that Saturday and so, after he returned with two blues and stories of Kate having hooked a bass, Ed and Kate were left to make their own way to Falmouth on the Oak Bluffs ferry. Morning had broken clear and dry, with only a gentle offshore breeze, but fall was surely in the air. The deck was gay with brightly coloured fleece jackets. It was not until the ferry had quit its slip that the two talked again of Emma Whitaker. They had found a pair of seats at the rail, and began to talk as the ferry drew alongside East Chop.

'Can we use her?' he asked.

Kate frowned. 'No,' she said, 'we can't *use* her.'

'Well, you know what I mean. What does she have?'

'She thinks her father was having an affair with Libby Russell,' Kate said.

'I know,' he replied. 'I was there for that part. But what does "she thinks" mean?'

'She won't testify.'

'Well, hang on. What does "she thinks" mean?'

Along the rail two black children held out chunks of doughnut. Great white gulls, floating in the air currents not ten feet alongside, heads swivelling this way and that, swooped in to pluck the food away, or dived towards the water to intercept chunks which had fallen. The children giggled madly.

Kate went on, 'Mainly from one night when she showed up at her father's farmhouse unexpected and found Russell and her father there, alone. Her mother had gone to Connecticut. The two of them, Sam and Libby, were sitting down to dinner. She could see the candles had already been lit.'

'The candles?'

'Yes, on the dining-room table. Her father never set out candles on his own.'

Once again Mulcahy shook his head at the points of human proof, and how far they varied from the points of proof one might offer in a courtroom.

But Kate was rattling on. There were other occasions. Emma had run into her father with Russell on one of them, and on another, been avoided by Russell in the Common. And she had, of course, been at the rear of St John's to see Anna Whitaker's reaction.

'What did you mean, she won't testify?' Ed asked, as the Falmouth shore sharpened in view. 'Why didn't you subpoena her?'

'I told you,' said Kate. 'She's not the sort of person you subpoena.'

'Kate!'

'Ed,' she continued, 'you must trust me on this. We

485

walked the beach for a half hour or so last night. Or was it this morning?' She screwed up her nose into a frown, and then looked at him and smiled, and the sun kissed her freckles. Her hair was everywhere. 'There are people you don't demand things of. People who would never respond to a demand, but who might respond to a polite request. She is one of those people.'

She smiled again. She was right that he would have to trust her on this, because he did not understand her. 'So,' he asked, 'did you make her a polite request?'

'Yes,' she said.

'But you said she won't testify.'

'She won't.'

And then Kate explained what Emma had agreed to do, if asked.

Mulcahy shook his head. 'Kate,' he said, 'I'm not Clarence Darrow. I can't do this kind of stuff. I don't know . . .' Then they were silent for a moment. She reached across and placed her hand on his, slid her fingers between his thumb and forefinger, and stroked the back of his hand with her thumb. His fingers closed on hers.

After a while, he said, 'Kate, suppose we do not put her on the stand, and Shepard is convicted. Malpractice?'

'Maybe,' she said. 'But I gave my word.'

They sat in silence for the remainder of the crossing.

33

Kate had fallen asleep in the car, but she woke as the traffic ground to a halt by the Dorchester gas tanks, and began biting her lip, impatient to return to Bromfield Street to see whether Creel had risen to the bait.

But there they found nothing, no E-mail, no phone message, nothing. They agreed then that the time for subtlety had passed. Kate sent Creel an E-mail.

'Don't let on that we've been dropping hints,' he said. 'Just ask for his help.'

She nodded, thinking, for a moment, and then tapped out this message:

> George: please call or E-mail. New rules. No
> subpoenas, whatever you tell us. No publicity. But
> please help. Please. We are almost out of time.

It was about 4 when she sent the E-mail. They waited. There was only the one couch, and they drifted off to sleep. Kate woke, feeling the stickiness

of the salt in her hair and on her skin, and shook
Mulcahy awake. There was nothing on the terminal.
Fidgeting, restless, they decided to hunt up some
dinner.

It was about 8 when they returned, and dark
outside. Still there was no response. They snuggled
on the couch in the darkened office, and drifted off
to sleep again.

It was Kate who shook herself at 1.32 a.m. to stare
at the screen in disbelief. 'God,' she said. It read:

You have mail.

Too excited to wipe the sleep from her eyes, or even
the hair from her face, Kate had the message up in an
instant.

If you wish to pass the doors, you must ask the
proper question.

'Ed, wake up,' she said. 'He's here.' Her fingers flew
across the keys, typing out the response.

What is the guest book?

When she had sent it they peered at his message. Why
was he playing with them this way? When she called
it back up, he leaned over her and they both read:

Error. Question too broad.

Mulcahy rose, and placed his hands on her shoulders.
He leaned over her, squinting at the screen. For a
moment, she relaxed, giving way to the wonderful

sensation of his fingertips. She was so tired. He read the exchange.

'It's a game, Kate. He sets the rules. We have to play by the rules. But, hey, he's playing now. That's an improvement.'

'Okay, what are the rules?'

He stared at the screen again. 'Think of him as a sort of computer. He won't do anything he isn't programmed for. We have to ask him the right question.'

She frowned, staring at the screen.

'Ask him who the guests are,' Mulcahy said. She typed it in and sent mail. A moment later, they read:

Error: question too broad.

Mulcahy repeated it out loud. He looked at her. Shocks of red hair sprayed every which way. Her face was puffy, and under her eyes were dark circles. She desperately needed more sleep. 'This all came out of the Idlewild investigation. So maybe the guests are the guests of the Idlewild transaction?' he said.

'Fletcher Daye,' Kate said. 'The guests are Fletcher Daye. So what's the book?'

'Ask him who signed in.' She tapped it out. Five minutes later, they read the rebuke:

Error. Question too broad.

She sighed. What did they teach you in law school – to have written your closing argument before the trial began? Something like that, anyway. Whatever it was they taught you, learning the facts on the weekend before you close, by playing twenty questions with a computer freak in cyberspace, that definitely was not it.

'Too broad?' Mulcahy was musing out loud. 'It's too broad – why? Why?' He paced to the window, staring at the dim yellow coronas on the black pavement, at the bases of the street lights. 'Because, because *everyone* signs in. Where does everyone sign in?' He paced again, doing laps around the office, his mind racing. 'Ask him where they signed in, and at what time.'

Again she did so, and they waited. It was almost 2.15. Below, a car thundered by on the narrow street. Then it was quiet again.

In a moment they read this response:

Error. Question too broad.

'Goddamn it, Creel!' Mulcahy said. But the computer terminal did not answer, and the words continued to tease him from the screen.

He began pacing again. 'All right. All right. We have to play. We have to play because he's Creel and that's what he does. He plays. So we play.' He sighed. 'Where does everyone sign in everywhere all the time?'

'Ed, I don't know.' She shook her head, shutting her eyes and running her fingers across her temples.

He returned to the screen, and leaned over her in silence, staring at its infuriating scroll of messages. 'Everyone signs in everywhere all the time,' he said again. 'Where does everyone sign in everywhere all the time?'

'It has something to do with computers,' she said.

'Yes,' he said, 'but not everyone has a computer.'

His eyes wandered around the office, across the litter on Stevie's desk to the air conditioning unit, the letters on the plate glass, the battered green file cabinet, back to the nape of Kate's neck. They lingered there, then drifted back to the screen. Now they strayed back up through the list of exchanges, through the chorus of 'Error: Question too broad' messages, until they came to rest on Creel's first message. He read it out loud. 'If you wish to pass the doors . . .'

And then, very softly, he said, 'Kate, it's the doors.'

She looked puzzled.

He went on, the excitement growing in his voice. 'Everyone passes the doors, everywhere in the building, all the time. He's talking about the pass sensors in the stairs and elevators!'

And then he reached over her and typed out the last question.

Where is the record of who passed the doors?

The reply was one keystroke: an exclamation point.

'Jesus,' said Mulcahy. 'It *is* the doors.' He typed out a paragraph.

It's 2.30 a.m. In about thirty hours, we rest in the Shepard case, as I'm sure you know. He is innocent. Maybe you know that, too. But without your help, he may be convicted.

'Think he'll bite?' he asked.

'Wait,' she said, and then typed in another paragraph:

George, a lot of innocent people got hurt in Vietnam. Because of unwillingness to help, by those who could have. Please help. Please help.

She looked at him with the question in her eyes.

'A little heavy-handed?'

'It's almost 3 in the morning. I'm not at my subtlest.'

'Go for it,' he said. She hit the execute key.

Five minutes later, the telephone rang.

'That was a little melodramatic, that last, don't you think, Mr Ed?' a voice said.

Ed let out a breath. It was 2.45 exactly. 'George, it's all been a little melodramatic, don't *you* think?'

He didn't answer. The phone line crackled.

'But thank you. Thank you for calling at last,' Mulcahy went on.

'Let's make this brief.'

'Yes,' Mulcahy said. 'Of course. Is that it? Is the guest book some kind of record of the building passes in the fire stairs, the elevators?'

'Well done, Mr Ed. It is the computerised record of engagements between security passes and the pass monitors in the fire doors and elevators of Freer Motley.'

'You mean, there is a *record* kept of that?'

'There was.'

'Of who passed the various security doors at various times, there's a record of that?'

'Not exactly who. There was a record of what pass was used to activate the monitor. That's all.'

'Do you have it?'

'No. I had a printout in my apartment, but I

492

understand that was ransacked by the people who attempted to kill me.'

'I saw that,' he said.

'Oh, yes, Mr Ed, very disagreeable, I'm sure. I don't know what you and Miss Kate have got yourselves mixed up in, but it very nearly got George killed. If one of the lads who spend their days by the Maverick MBTA station had not warned me of the man in the neighbourhood, they would have succeeded.'

'I'm sorry.'

'Likewise.'

'Can it be reconstructed – the log, I mean?'

'Possibly. It depends on what has been done with my hard disc files at Freer Motley.'

'It has to be at Freer?'

'It has to be at Freer, I'm afraid.'

'You can't . . . you can't get in by phone, that sort of thing?'

He heard Creel laugh. 'Mr Ed, my good man, you can't just "get in by phone".'

'Well, you did to us.'

There was a silence. 'Well done,' he said, 'I'm impressed. But I'm afraid that is only because you have been using a Freer Motley laptop, one of my former children, which I had programmed to send me a message and invite me back in whenever an outside line is accessed. So when you people began sending E-mails to Natlink and calling up Westlaw, I was able to have a ramble. But I'm afraid Freer Motley's office computer security is a trifle more sophisticated than that of its laptops. After all, I invented it myself.'

Mulcahy let out a long sigh. They had come so far. And then the lawyer's pessimism hit him, as he remembered Creel's confrontation with Kate.

'George, why do I even want to see this guest book? Do you know that I want to see it?'

'I thought you said he was innocent, Mr Ed?'

'Is he?'

'That's not for me to say. But I have seen it. I thought it was quite interesting. And I think it might interest you, too.'

Mulcahy paused, to digest the remark again. 'Well, can you, can you go into the office? Can we check somehow?'

'Mr Ed, I don't think you heard me. This business almost got me killed once. That makes four times in my life, if you count the three in Vietnam. That's enough for me.'

'George, please.'

'I'm sorry,' he said, and was silent again. But he did not hang up, and it seemed as though he were willing to help, but only if Mulcahy should hit upon the method himself. As always, he had to ask the right question. He sat there with the phone, talking to a faceless voice, somewhere in the middle of the night. Creel waited. And then he thought of it.

'George,' he said, 'what if someone else was at your terminal. Could you walk them through it?'

'If they had the appropriate skills,' he said.

He took a deep breath. 'Okay,' he said, 'I'm going to try.' He squinted at the clock. 'It's now 2.50. Will you please call your direct line at Freer at 3.05, sharp. Please! If I do not answer, try me here.'

'Mr Ed, if I might make a suggestion, I believe that

494

Miss Kate is more proficient than you in the use of computers. If I am to be kept up all night, I'd prefer to work with someone who knows what she is doing.'

'All right,' he said, 'all right.' And then, before hanging up, he asked his one remaining question. 'You didn't want to get involved – you left town in the dead of night, and you refused to help us, before – and yet you watched the progress of this thing, reading our messages and briefs and so on. Why? Why did you bother? I'm sorry, I'm just curious.'

'Mr Ed, I told you once before,' Creel said. 'I like to keep informed about firm matters.'

Downtown Crossing was like a tomb. Ed and Kate walked hand in hand, beneath the silent department stores, past the empty turnings. They saw no one. Few lights were visible. Once a taxicab hurtled past, its shocks straining as it bounced off potholes. Other than that, all was quiet. Mulcahy left her at the corner of Summer and Hancock.

Kate heard her footsteps clip-clop along the side-walk, echoing in the silent street and against the darkened walls of the office buildings. She looked behind her, and he waved, a dim figure at the corner. And then she was alone.

Now she approached the lobby door, across the plaza. Inside, across the atrium, a pale light illuminated the security guard. She peered through the glass and breathed a sigh of relief when she saw a familiar handsome black face. Perhaps she could pull off the first part of this, anyway.

Taking a deep breath, Kate pushed the revolving door around. She walked across the lobby, forcing herself not to hurry. The guard looked up at her. She strove to keep her face expressionless.

'Evenin',' he said, recognising her.

'How are you?' she asked.

'Oh, pretty well, pretty well. Ain't seen you roun' here in a while.'

She fumbled through her handbag. 'Oh my God,' she said.

'What?'

'I can't *believe* it! Oh!'

'What is it?'

'I don't have my pass!' She shook her head and looked away as though she might cry. 'I must have left my pass . . .' She looked around. 'I'll have to go all the way back to *Cambridge* . . . I've got to get that brief written by 7.30!'

''Sall right, ma'am,' he said, slowly. 'I know you.'

'Oh, thank you so much!' she said. 'But how do I – I'm going to need to get into word processing . . .'

'Here,' he said, reaching in the drawer for a pass. 'This'll get you anywhere you need to go.' He handed her a plastic strip.

'Thank you!'

'Jes' don't forget to bring it back, now! And, ma'am, no need to mention this to the supervisors, know what I mean?'

'No, no. It'll be our secret!'

She saw no one as she exited the elevator on 17 and stepped past the pallets of photocopier paper. Inside the corridor it was silent. The lighting was dim. She walked quickly to the word processing centre, where the lights were off. Away behind the partitions she found Creel's terminal – now lonely in an unused corner. All of Creel's detritus, his stacks and reams of printouts, had been cleared away. His bulletin board had been taken down. Only the 'Gimp Surfer – Hang Stumps!' stickers on the terminal remained. She looked at her watch. It was 3.05.

The phone rang. 'I hope you have Miss Kate with you,' the voice said.

'This is Kate, Mr Creel,' she said.

'Ah. Good thinking. All right, let's turn Gertie on, can you manage that, Kate? And while she's booting up, have you a credit card?'

She gave him the number, and he hung up and telephoned back. It sounded as though he was in a public place somewhere, a railroad station, or a bus terminal, perhaps.

He gave her the password. It didn't work. 'Not a problem,' he said, giving her another. A table of multicoloured icons appeared in a blue field.

'Enter special functions,' he said.

She clicked on the icon. A menu of libraries appeared.

'How many Creelprojects?'

She looked at the screen. 'None.'

'The nasty little people. Hmm.' He thought for a moment, then gave a series of instructions. Following his lead, she threaded her way through the computer maze back to the firm's hard drive. And then, with a click, 'Ah!'

'I've got them,' she said. 'A list of Creelprojects.'

'Start with the first, then. Call them up one at a time. You'll find various things. You're looking for guest book.'

Over the next fifteen minutes, she engaged each file. But she found no guest book.

'Quite sure, are you?' he asked.

But it was not there.

'It's been deleted somehow,' he said. 'This is a problem.'

By now, Kate's ear and shoulder had grown sore from cradling the telephone. Her eyelids drooped. 'Please, George, we've got to think of something.'

'Well, we could try to reconstruct,' he said. 'But that means getting back into the Moore's hard drive. It will be difficult.'

'Moore's?'

'The security people.'

'Let's try,' she said.

For the next hour and a half, George led Kate through his computer screens like a traffic controller talking a novice down in an emergency landing. He had stowed a password to the security clearance system in an innocuous computer address book, which had not been killed. They found it. Through Internet, they accessed the computers. The password still worked, but files had been renamed. They had to search fifteen files before finding the downloaded transit information. This took another forty-five minutes.

It was 4.30 a.m. But recovering the actual data proved a great challenge, even for Creel. Someone had moved it on the hard disc, or inserted other data at gap points. With Kate typing in the code, George dictated a program to recover the data, searching for data recovered and downloaded in May 1992. The program didn't work the first time through. At 6 a.m. they had to start again.

It was light outside now, and Kate was becoming worried. She looked at her watch: 6.30. Then 6.40. At 6.50 the program clicked in, and began downloading information.

The sun was now fully up. Kate's eyelids kept dropping as she waited. Bewildered, robotic, she was about to press the 'Print' key when she heard the latch on the door. Away across from her terminal, on the other side of the partition, someone had entered the room. She heard paper rustle.

And then her terminal bleeped.

'Oh, I didn't know anyone was . . .' a man's voice started to say as he came around the corner. She looked up to see Albert Shanklin. He had entered the word processing department, apparently looking for a loan document.

She gulped. 'Oh my God,' she said to herself softly, looking away.

'What are you doing here?' the Count asked. At first he was just surprised. But then his brow furrowed as he remembered that she had been fired. He realised he might have stumbled on something fraudulent, perhaps criminal, in progress. 'Ms Maher, what are you doing here?' he demanded.

'. . . Miss Kate, what's going on?' said the voice on the phone.

'I, I – ' she stammered. Kate didn't know whether to answer Shanklin or Creel. Shanklin was crossing the room.

'Mr Shanklin, I, I just, I . . .' her voice trailed off.

'Have you printed?' Creel was saying. 'Have you printed?'

'No,' she said, this time into the phone.

'I'm calling the police,' Shanklin said. 'Exit out of that computer program at once . . .' He seized her forearm, tugging it from the terminal.

'Kate, listen to me . . .' Creel said.

'How did you get in here? Give me your pass, Miss Maher, this instant . . .'

It was his fingers on her arm that did it. For at that moment Kate let out a vigorous scream. Shanklin froze and let go. The telephone receiver was silent. 'Noooo!' Kate screamed again. And as she screamed, a bizarre idea occurred to her. She thought of Shrinsky, backing down over the wallet file.

She took a breath. 'Mr Shanklin,' she said into the telephone, 'stop it!'

'What? What are you talking about?' He was genuinely perplexed.

She covered the receiver with her palm. 'Mr Shanklin, you and I are alone in this room right now. Think about it.' And then again, to the receiver, 'Stop it! Stop it!'

'I will be back in five minutes with the police,' he said, hurrying from the room.

'What on earth was that?' It was Creel again.

'Sorry. Sorry. Look, I – oh my God, am I in trouble now. Look, hurry, George, hurry! I don't have . . . He's coming back, with the security people or the police. I haven't got time to wait for this thing to print.'

'Is there a floppy?'

'A floppy? Oh . . .' She rattled around the desk, the drawers. 'Oh, shoot. No, there isn't. I can't find one!'

'All right. Listen very carefully. Menu Print Selections. Level 3. Got it?'

She clicked on the commands, but the machine seemed lethargic in responding. 'Come on, come on!' she said.

'Do you have a printer at Bromfield Street?'

'Oh, yes. Yes!'

'Better mail it there, all right? When you have level 3, it will ask you for station change. See?'

'Yes. I have it.'

'Type in a 9, then the number for your modem. Then Application Queue Selections.'

'Damn. Oh, damn. It gives me an error!'

'Hmm. Too many windows, probably,' he said.

'Listen to me. Don't panic. Close your operating window. The down arrow is in the corner. Back out. Now reopen Application Queue Selections.'

Her fingers hit the wrong keys as she rushed. 'Hurry, hurry . . .' she said.

'See the E-mail selection in there?'

'No . . . oh, yes.'

'Good. Send it.'

'What am I doing?'

'Send.'

'I'm sending! What am I doing?'

'You are E-mailing the entire document. Have you got the icon down in the lower left?'

'Oh, God, I think I hear something . . . What? Yes, yes, it's mailing.'

'Leave the computer on, but reach round and adjust the contrast until the screen is black. May put them off. Put a post-it or something over the operating light. Don't turn it off,' he said.

'Okay,' she said. 'Okay. God, hurry! Okay, I'm going. Call me at Bromfield Street!'

Kate raced for the fire door. Eighteen staircases later, she burst into the lobby, breathing heavily.

She rounded the corner and came within view, across the lobby, of the desk. Her shoes clipped briskly on the marble. They sounded like little fire crackers. Sometimes it seemed that all of the office buildings which sprang up in the 1980s like weeds after a summer rain had overdosed on faux marble. It was everywhere: on the floors, on the walls, in the elevators. So it was at 100 Hancock.

Away across the lobby by the doors, she saw the security guard look up. It was the same man – his shift hadn't ended. Her heart was racing, and she struggled to control her breathing. Her thighs screamed from the plunge down the fire stairs. Now she could see his expression. He looked serious. He rose from the chair.

'Ma'am?' he said.

She fought to control her breathing and to stop from breaking into a run.

'Ma'am?' he said again, as she approached. She was at the desk. Thirty feet to the street door.

'I'm sorry,' she said, handing him the pass, 'I've got to . . .'

He interrupted her sternly. 'Ma'am, I'm sorry, but we've had a report of an intruder at Freer Motley.'

She stood silently, biting her lip.

'Did you see anyone suspicious?'

She looked up at the guard and exhaled slowly. 'No,' she said, 'no one at all. Sorry.'

In the distance she heard the bell of an elevator.

'I've got to go,' she said.

'Thanks, ma'am,' he said. 'Have a nice morning.'

'You too,' she said, and walked swiftly for the revolving doors. When she was through them and round the corner, she bolted as fast as she could run for Downtown Crossing.

Sunday night. In the morning they would finish the evidence. An hour, maybe two, with Libby Russell. And then the guest book. And one more witness. They sat, Kate and Ed, at Ed Mulcahy's kitchen table, with the computer printout spread before them. A large piece of white card lay propped against the fridge. On the table was a black magic marker. Both of them were past tired now.

The eleven o'clock news had come on. 'And in the John Shepard trial, the defence is expected to rest its case early this week,' Frannie Dillard was saying. 'Attorney Edward Mulcahy declined comment, but it was evident from the dramatic testimony last week that the defence strategy is to implicate others in the shooting, most notably downtown attorney Elizabeth Russell . . .'

It occurred to Ed that he hadn't seen the news all weekend. He stared at the set.

'Russell, whose cross-examination is scheduled to continue on Monday morning, would not comment for WFBA News, but her senior partner Herbert Stein had plenty to say.'

Now Stein appeared, in film which must have been shot Friday afternoon outside the session. 'What is going in this courtroom is an outrage,' he said, spitting out the words. 'A rank amateur, a man with no criminal trial experience in years, is seeking to confuse the jury by defaming my partner Elizabeth

503

Russell. Ms Russell will not stand for it. The questioning goes beyond any qualified privilege rights of the defence, and we fully intend to bring an action for slander against Mr Mulcahy when this trial is over.'

'Steiny, get behind Parisi, man,' Mulcahy said to the screen. 'I'm judgement proof!'

The news shifted to something else, and he flicked it off. 'Rank amateur. Boy, he got that right.'

'He did not get that right.' Kate looked at him defiantly. 'You watch too much TV.'

They had arranged things with Emma and Stevie. She would meet Kate in the morning. They would wait in a coffee shop until 10 a.m., and then come to the corridor on the 8th floor. Stevie would save a place in the front pew, directly opposite the witness stand.

Mulcahy studied the printout. It was a list of six-digit numerals, most beginning, as the number on his and Kate's passes had, with the numerals '60'. The right-hand column bore four-digit numbers. But the first two figures in the right-hand column invariably began with a numeral between 18 and 25. The first two digits would be followed by two more, in most cases 01, 02, 03, or 04.

They studied the last three pages of the printout for 31 March. In the midst of the figures they found these entries:

0331920327	702247	2002
0331920331	702247	1804
0331920343	702247	2601
0331920401	702247	0100

The left-hand and the right-hand columns were plain. The first was the date and time. The last was the floor, with some reference to the specific security port. 'Who do you think 702247 is? Most of these are 60 numbers.'

She said, 'Okay, look at this. At 3.27 a.m., somebody enters the 20th floor: Shepard's floor. That somebody then goes to the 18th floor: Whitaker's floor. Whoever it is gets there at 3.31. The mortgage was opened on Whitaker's computer at, what was it, 3.32, right? And it was closed about ten minutes later, something like that? Okay, so Mr 702 leaves 18, walks up to 26, gets there at 3.43.'

'Why 26?' asked Mulcahy.

She shrugged. The conference centre was on the 26th floor.

'Okay,' he said, 'what about Shepard? When did he say he left that night?'

She checked the notes. 'About 2.'

They thumbed through the transcript. 'Hmm,' he said, pointing to the reference:

    0331920152   604332   0100

'Oh one hundred, that must be the front desk,' she said.

Bingo. They stared at each other. 'So Shepard isn't Mr 702. Jesus Christ,' he said slowly. 'Now, how the hell do we get this in?'

They worked at that problem for a half hour, and came up with a plan. It was not an elegant plan, but the best that the circumstances would allow.

At last it was time for her to go. Before she left, he

505

held her close to him, and his fingers stroked softly at the back of her neck. 'Kate,' he whispered, 'what do you think, do we have enough?'

She was silent, and buried her face in his shoulder. He had no answer either.

34

Autumn arrived on Monday. The heat had lifted now, and the day broke clear and breezy. The dinghy sailors would be pounding furiously across the Basin by noon. Up over Beacon Hill, moments after the court officer opened up 8b, Stevie George arrived to set up camp on the front pew of the gallery, picking defiantly at his wart and daring all comers to challenge him for the seats. The rest of the gallery quickly filled, long before they brought the jury in. The word had gone around the courthouse reporters. The defence would probably rest today.

As Kate and Stevie had to co-ordinate the witnesses that morning, Mulcahy was left to be the mule. At about 8.30, he struggled up the stairs to Centre Plaza. It had been a battle, towing the two-wheeler with one hand, trying to balance the posterboard sketches under the other arm. When the wind blew, he whirled, and the sketches popped passers-by or dinged themselves on storefronts. The two-wheeler tipped and spilled.

Now he faced his goal, across the plaza to the right, beyond the dark swirl of suits and brogues streaming past for the courthouse and the surrounding offices. But just as he lurched out into the mainstream, a gust of wind snapped one of the posterboards into the air. He spun to grab it, spilling the boxes from the bungee cords. File folders slid to the pavement. He whirled and slapped the posterboard to the ground, and leaped desperately after the flapping files. The papers skittered loose and he crawled after them in a forest of briskly stepping legs.

Still on his knees, he had gathered the mess together and got the files back into the boxes, when he noticed before him a pair of ankles, and, above that, a pair of legs: a very compelling pair of slim ankles, affixed to equally arresting calves.

When he looked up, he found that he was on his knees before Libby Russell. She looked down at him, and his face went crimson. In getting up, he stumbled, dropping one of the charts again.

'Oh,' he said. 'Good morning, Ms Russell.'

'For heaven's sake, Ed, we were in the US Attorney's office together. Call me Libby.'

He sighed. 'I know. It's better for me if I stick with Ms Russell.'

'Well, fine, but will you at least have a cup of coffee with me?' Now she smiled at him. Her eyes were the palest blue, and, when he saw the smile, he felt glad she hadn't simply thought of smiling at him Friday on the witness stand.

He considered it for a moment. 'Thank you,' he said, 'but no.'

She shook her head. 'May I speak with you at least?'

'Yes,' he said, 'certainly.'

And so they had a conversation, there in the middle of Centre Plaza, with passers-by hurrying this way and that around them. She wore a pale grey suit, and stood an inch taller than he. He wavered awkwardly, trying to balance the charts on his shoes and leaning on the two-wheeler.

'I'll be brief,' she said, and the smile was gone. 'This is very damaging to me. Very hurtful. My face is all over every newspaper. Because of John Shepard. John Shepard grasping at straws. That's not fair.'

'His face is all over every newspaper, too,' said Mulcahy, slowly. 'We think that isn't fair, either.' He looked back at her.

'What else do you plan to ask me?' she asked coldly.

'Questions,' he said. 'I plan to ask you questions.'

'How clever.' She sighed. 'Well, you're not interested in fairness, but you may be interested in something else. All this trying to suggest I had something to do with Sam Whitaker's death because – what is it? Because Testa was my informant, as if *that* has anything to do with anything? Well, look, I want you to know something. My relationship with your client went beyond the professional. It went beyond the professional during the Idlewild closing.'

'And?' said Mulcahy.

'Just that. Just that if you are trying to link me to something that happened here, then you are linking him too. If there is any more questioning of me, I will tell the jury about our relationship. Wherever you mean to drive me, Ed, I'm going to take your client with me.'

'I see,' he said. Another gust of wind took hold of the posterboards, but he held them firm this time.

'You want to think about that before you put me back on the stand?' She leaned forward, almost as though she were a school teacher lecturing a wayward student. Her direct stare embarrassed him there in the plaza before all of those passers-by. He could feel their eyes as they passed, sense their curiosity, almost hear them thinking, Isn't that Libby Russell – the one on the news? – and that other lawyer? Some of them turned openly. She appeared to be used to it.

Mulcahy stood silently for a moment, turning this over. He had planned to play poker again with her today. He just hadn't known the game would start before court.

'Yes,' he said after a moment, 'I will think about it. If you will agree to think about something else.'

'What is that?'

He shook his head slowly to himself for a moment, looking past her left shoulder to the steps of the annexe. Then he spoke softly. 'John has been charged with murder. You have not. John may be convicted. If you tie yourself to him, you'd better hope I win this case. Not too many people think I'm better than O'Hanlon, you know. Just ask Stein. Among others. O'Hanlon isn't limited to one conviction per murder. And as far as I know, O'Hanlon doesn't know about your tryst with Shepard. I don't plan to tell him, unless I have to.'

Then he turned and looked at her again. 'But if you want to throw it on the table, I can't stop you.'

'I'm serious, I'm not going down alone.'

The breeze lifted her hair. He turned to the side, not wanting to look at her eyes for too long. 'Like I said,' he went on, 'I'll think it over. You should, too.' Balancing the posterboards on his toes, he extended a hand. But she ignored it, turned and walked briskly for the courthouse, and the posterboards fell to the brick, suffering more dents on the corners.

'Damn,' he said. As he righted his trolley and his posterboards again, he couldn't help but admire her long slim legs as she trotted up the steps and disappeared into the revolving door. I guess that constitutes poker, he thought. Wonder who was bluffing?

A pale John Shepard sat in the grim little tank behind the courtroom. His eyes were red. His face had lost that arrogant cast. Mulcahy wondered whether, perhaps, Shepard had slept even less than he that weekend.

Mulcahy wished him a good morning, but Shepard did not return the greeting. 'Sorry I didn't come in this weekend. We got something, John, maybe something big, and I had to go . . .'

Shepard cut him off. 'Look, I want her off the stand,' he said. He looked down at his hands.

'Makes two of you.'

'What?'

'Yeah, she kind of expressed that view to me just now.'

'And?'

'No,' Mulcahy said. 'I'm not finished with her.'

'I want her off the stand. That's an instruction.'

'No,' Mulcahy said again, evenly.

511

'What the hell am I supposed to say to that?'

Mulcahy's eyes narrowed. ' "You're fired",' he said. 'You're supposed to say, "You're fired".'

'Oh, fuck you, Ed.' Shepard shook his head and looked away. He closed his eyes and exhaled slowly. 'Where you gonna go with her?'

'Why?'

'Why? Why? Because it's my ass. I'm the damn client!'

'We're going to investigate her taste in men.'

'No we're not.'

'Oh yes we are.'

'Mulcahy, you're flailing, man! The defence was suicide, like I told you. And you guys did a half ass job with that and now you're flailing around, pissin' off the jury by going after this chick!'

Mulcahy didn't answer. He turned to go. 'Save it for the appeal,' he said. 'You'll have a great argument for ineffective assistance of counsel.'

'Ed, just tell me how in sweet Jesus's name it helps me to have the Senior Choir out there hear that I did the chick? How does that help me?'

'Don't assume her taste in men was confined to you. John, why have you, from the beginning, been steering me away from her?'

'Because it's a damn frolic and detour . . .'

'That's not it, John. What is it really?'

He looked down at the floor, and then said softly, 'Look, I was with her. During the closing, okay? Like I said. Now, we turn this whole case into Libby Russell's fraud on the mortgage, and you prove to 'em that it all went down the night I was with her, what do you suppose people are going to think?'

512

Mulcahy nodded his head. 'All that's productive', I think you said. It doesn't matter. I understand all about that. I understand that now. But it would have been better to know these things when we started.'

'All right, all right. Forgive me, Father, for I have fucking sinned!' Shepard sighed. 'Look, Ed, do you realise what you're saying? You're saying she's a killer!'

Mulcahy nodded. 'John, listen to me. This whole trial is her saying *you* are a killer. That's what she said on 16 May. Trust me. We had a busy weekend. We know what we're doing. This is going to work.'

Keys rattled in the lock. Freddie was behind them. 'He's comin' out,' said the little court officer.

'We're coming, stall him a little,' Shepard shot back.

'Sorry,' said Freddie.

'C'mon!'

But Freddie shook his head, and they began to move Shepard into the session.

'Yeah?' Shepard said.

'Later,' said Mulcahy. There was no time to relate Russell's threat to him. Probably it was malpractice to go forward without doing so. But at this point, what was a little more?

They brought the jury in, and Grosso entered briskly a moment later. 'Anything further with Ms Russell?' he asked.

'Yes, Your Honour.'

'Very well. Proceed,' he said, with the merest hint of impatience.

'Your Honour, excuse me.' It was Shepard. He was on his feet. 'Excuse me, but could I have a moment with my counsel before we proceed?'

The judge looked up, surprised. Sixteen pairs of

eyes flashed to defence table, and back to the bench. Grosso said, 'Certainly, Mr Shepard.'

Their heads were together, and Mulcahy didn't mind as much as he should that the jury could see his impatience. 'What is it?' he whispered.

'Listen, motherfucker, listen to me! You say it's going to work, then do it. I don't know what you're doing. I don't much like it. But you're my guy. I hired you, and I'm sticking with you. If I go down, I go down. On my own. You've done your job.'

'Why are you telling me this?'

''Cause I don't want you worried about your own backside. If you're going to go after her, go the hell after her!'

Mulcahy smiled again. 'Okay, John, I'll try. And John?'

'Yeah?'

'Thanks.'

He turned back to the stand. There she sat again, still regal, still lovely. Had she been bluffing? He'd know soon, by lunch at the latest. He looked once more at Shepard as he resumed the questioning. Shepard had his old colour back. They caught each other's eye, and Shepard smiled. It was time to bring it home.

'Ms Russell, did you have a personal relationship with the deceased, Mr Whitaker?' Mulcahy had decided not to settle in slowly.

'A relationship?' she asked.

'An affair, if you like.'

'That's outrageous,' she said.

'Perhaps it is outrageous. But the question is, is it true?'

'Your Honour,' said O'Hanlon, 'I would like to know whether counsel has any good-faith basis to put the question . . .'

In a moment they were at sidebar again, and Mulcahy was looking past the bifocals, up into the scowling face of Judge Grosso. Judges grow testy towards the end of trial. They want to see the thing wrapped up. They don't want anything new. 'Mr Mulcahy,' he asked, 'have you a witness who will say that this witness had an affair with the deceased, and that it had some bearing on this case? If you don't, I will not permit you to destroy her reputation. And his.'

Mulcahy measured his words and answered slowly. 'I have a witness.'

'You had better, Mr Mulcahy.'

'Yes, Your Honour.'

It was at that moment that the session door swung open and Kate appeared, followed by Emma Whitaker. Stevie rose to beckon to them from the seats he had staked out, and the pair made a mild stir as they squeezed by spectators to take their places. As the lawyers were returning from sidebar, Mulcahy took in the tableau. Stevie had seated Emma Whitaker in the front row, directly in Libby Russell's line of vision.

In the courtroom that day, she made a striking appearance. It wasn't just her fair hair and pale eyes. It was the way the whole cast of her features recalled her father.

'May I have a moment?' Mulcahy asked.

The judge nodded. Mulcahy stepped to the barrier and inclined towards Emma and Kate. 'I served

Hawley,' Kate said. 'I'd better go back to 100 Hancock to get him.' Mulcahy nodded as she rose to go. He killed a few moments more with Emma Whitaker, asking her in whispers whether her trip from the island had been uneventful, thanking her for coming. When he thought Russell had had long enough to watch, he returned to the lectern.

'Ms Russell, last week you said you couldn't recall going to Mr Whitaker's home. Isn't it a fact that you had dinner with Samuel Whitaker at his home in Sheringham one Friday night in February?'

Her eyes wandered to Emma Whitaker. 'It's possible,' she said.

'It was just the two of you, alone in the house, having dinner?'

'I believe so,' she said.

'And Mr Whitaker's daughter Emma arrived unexpectedly, do you recall that?'

'I do recall that she arrived on an occasion when Mr Whitaker and I were having dinner. I don't know whether or not he was expecting her at the time.'

'You recognise Ms Whitaker here in the courtroom today, the lady in the blue sweater seated in the gallery?'

'Yes,' she said.

'You were having an affair with Mr Whitaker?'

'What do you mean by that?'

'Did you sleep with him?'

Now she measured him coolly, glancing back to the daughter in the gallery. Nothing in her eyes or manner betrayed the speed with which her mind was calculating, exhausting the possibilities.

'Ms Russell?' Mulcahy interrupted.

'No, Mr Mulcahy, I did not sleep with him.'

They had faced off in the arena, and there was silence there. And Ed Mulcahy could see something that the jurors could not, something that comes of 'thinking like a lawyer', as the phrase is so often put. She had laid down a clear set of rules of engagement. She would give him only what she had to give, what her best estimate told her he could independently verify. There was a fatal weakness in this tactic, and he saw it.

He left the lectern for a moment, searched through his box, and removed a yellow pad.

'All right, Ms Russell,' he said, paging through the pad, 'you say you did not sleep with him. How would you characterise your relationship with him?'

'We were friends.'

'When did the friendship begin?'

'I don't know.'

'When was the first time you were alone with Mr Whitaker?'

'I don't recall.'

'Was it in 1992?'

'No,' she said, 'before.'

'In 1991?'

'Probably,' she said.

'On how many occasions were you alone with him?'

'I – I don't know.'

'More than ten?'

'Yes.'

'More than fifty?'

'More than fifty, Mr Mulcahy? I don't know.'

'You have been alone in his home with him?'

517

'Yes.'

'When his wife was not present.'

'Yes, when she was not present.'

'Did you ever meet him in his house when his wife was present?'

She paused, briefly. 'No,' she said. There was a rustling in the gallery. The Brooch lady looked across at Tie Pin man. Mulcahy went on.

'Did you ever meet him alone in your apartment?'

'My apartment?'

'Yes, that is the question.'

'I don't recall,' she said.

The magic words. The words he had been waiting for. The words lawyers use when others might lie in a simpler way. Now he paged through his yellow pad for a moment.

'Ms Russell,' he said, 'you live in an apartment in the Back Bay, don't you?'

'Yes.'

'And you did so throughout 1992?'

'Yes.'

'That's at 212 Clarendon Street?'

'Yes.'

'There is a doorman in your building, isn't there?'

'Yes, there is.'

He stepped away from the lectern again, so that she could see him as he turned the top sheet down from the yellow pad and tucked it behind the fingers of his left hand, see him as he studied the handwriting on the second page, watch as his finger traced down to the middle of the sheet.

'Didn't you meet Samuel Whitaker on the night of

Friday, 12 February 1992 at your apartment, at about 8 p.m.?'

He looked up at the witness stand. She looked back at him. She stared at the notepad in his hand. Then up at his eyes. But his eyes were blank. He returned her stare. Was he smiling? It was unclear.

Her eyes were again drawn to the pad in his hand. 'I don't recall,' she said.

'Is it, perhaps, Ms Russell, that you don't recall the specific date?'

'I don't,' she said.

'But you did meet Mr Whitaker on some night in February 1992 at your apartment, you remember that, don't you?'

She looked again, hard, at her antagonist, but his face was a blank. Her mind racing through the possibilities, she waited as long as she could, appraising him. But he gave no sign. 'I believe so,' she said.

There was a shuffle, a murmur in the gallery now. The doors swung as someone left. She had yielded a little. The next push would be easier. 'You met him there more than once, didn't you?'

'Yes.'

'The two of you, alone?'

'Yes.'

'Now, Ms Russell,' he said, and he walked slowly towards her, 'do you want to reconsider your prior testimony about whether you slept with him? You are under oath.'

'You don't need to remind me of my oath, Mr Mulcahy. I did not sleep with him. We were friends, close friends, that's all. We did not become lovers. And I would like to say . . .'

'Ms Russell,' he tried to interrupt, 'there is no . . .'

'. . . I didn't want to see the poor man's reputation tarnished in this trial . . .'

'. . . question before you,' said Mulcahy.

'Order!' shouted the judge.

'. . . and so I was hesitant to speak of these meetings here, for fear that people such as yourself and the media would misconstrue our friendship and seek to sensationalise his tragic death.' She finished blurting out her explanation.

And so she had recovered a footing. It was uneasy; the jury was uncertain, but there was at least an account, one which would permit them to dismiss the defence as character assassination. She looked at Mulcahy defiantly.

'Ms Russell, your friendship with Mr Whitaker was ongoing during the last week in March, when Idlewild closed, wasn't it?'

'Yes.'

He stood examining the yellow pad one more time. 'Did you meet privately with him on March . . . let me see here, excuse me, Judge . . . on 25 March, Ms Russell?'

Something was wrong. But she daren't trust her instinct now, looking at the infuriating calm of the advocate with his nose in his yellow pad. 'If that was the date,' she said.

'One last thing, Ms Russell. I believe Mr Whitaker's secretary testified that on the Friday before he died, Mr Whitaker directed her to schedule a lunch with you at the Bay Club. She said that she did so. Did you have lunch with him that day?'

'I don't recall.'

'Of course. You don't recall.' Mulcahy looked over at Paul O'Hanlon. 'Your witness,' he said.

But O'Hanlon had no questions. And as Libby Russell stepped from the witness stand, she noticed that Emma Whitaker had already left the session. Her bargain was complete.

It was mid-morning, and they had reached their final witness but one. There in the session stood the flimsy posterboard on the easel, with its hand-drawn schematic diagram of 100 Hancock Street, the schematic that Kate had traced out the night before with a pencil and a ruler, filling in the lines later with a black magic marker, with spaces for floors 18 through 26. In the parlance of trial lawyers, this was a 'chalk', a diagram which would not go to the jury room as evidence, but which could be used to help explain the case to them.

Fred Hawley had worked for building management for five years now. He was the shift supervisor for the day shift at 100 Hancock. He knew the security system well, and had helped the contractor debug it when it was installed three years before.

He had been a little surprised to find Kate Maher handing him a subpoena at 7.30 that morning. He couldn't figure out how she had a printout of the pass transit information, but checked it against his own program and it was accurate. Walking over to Pemberton Square later in the morning, Fred was thinking that it sure would make for an interesting day.

Just as they made the turn across Tremont and into Centre Plaza, he said, 'Think I got a call about this once before.'

'What?' she said.

'Yeah, I remember now . . .' He told her about it as they hurried into the courthouse.

On the stand, Hawley explained to the jury that each employee's card contained an electromagnetic fingerprint, which could be read and identified by the sensors which were installed at the elevator doors and the interior stairs on each floor of the building, as well as the front desk. When the sensor read a 'fingerprint' which had been input for clearance, it activated the unlock mechanism to permit entry. When a new employee was issued a pass, the pass would be input for acceptance, and the number recorded.

The same, he explained, was true for guest passes.

What most people didn't know was that the main-frame computer which co-ordinated the entire system recorded each engagement – each entry or departure as the pass engaged the sensor. When the computer downloaded its memory to disc each month, it downloaded not only the register of active and closed passes, but also this 'transit' information.

The printout was hard copy showing each engagement of a sensor by a registered pass during the last three days.

Now, with the sheaf of computer printout to refer to, Hawley was beginning to colour in the sketch on the easel, by placing the port number assigned to each of the sensors located on 26, 20 and 18. The sketch already bore the marks where Freer Motley's personnel director had sketched in the locations for Shepard's office, the Conference Centre on 26, and Samuel Whitaker's office. Soon it bore twelve additional five-digit numerals: on each floor, the two which flanked the fire stairs, and the two which flanked the elevator doors.

Mulcahy was almost ready for show and tell. But first, he asked for three more pass numbers. On 31 March, what was Samuel Whitaker's pass number? What was John Shepard's pass number?

Hawley read off the numbers.

Then Mulcahy asked this question. 'To whom was pass 702247 issued?'

The balding security officer looked at his sheet. 'That was a guest pass,' he said. 'It was one of the five passes issued on 24 March 1992, to attorneys for Fletcher, Daye & Symmes.'

'And to whom in particular was it issued?'

'It doesn't say,' he said. 'All five were issued to the law firm as part of some kind of big meeting or something, as I understand it.'

'Your Honour,' said Mulcahy, 'may I ask Mr George to help with the chalk?'

Judge Grosso smiled. 'We are always delighted to see Mr George,' he said, and Stevie gave him half a bow as he came forward.

'Now,' said Mulcahy, continuing, 'to assist the jury in understanding this, Mr Hawley, we've made up three Post-it Passes, one labelled Whitaker, for Mr Whitaker's pass, one labelled Shepard, for Mr Shepard's pass, and one labelled Fletcher, for the pass which was issued to Fletcher Daye. Referring, if you would, to Exhibit 56, I'd like you to take us through the movements of these three passes, starting from about the dinner hour on 30 March 1992.'

And so it began. Hawley called for a pass to be

moved, and Stevie unpeeled the Post-it and moved it up or down the board, pressing it back on the new floor. Both judge and jury stared in fascination. The Ancient Mariner, Mrs Watts, Tie Pin man, they were all craning forward to see. The blow-ups are never quite big enough when you get them to the court-room. And the easels don't fit right anywhere. But the jury was interested.

At 7 p.m., Whitaker's pass engaged the security port on the ground floor. Evidently he was leaving the office. Shepard's pass had previously logged in to 20. The Fletcher pass was on the 26th floor. At 10.30 p.m., the Shepard pass engaged the 20th-floor eleva-tor door furthest from his office, and then, four minutes later, engaged the one closest. A trip to the men's room, probably. At 10.45 p.m, the Fletcher pass engaged building security on the ground floor. Now Shepard was alone in the office. At 1.52 a.m., the Shepard pass engaged the ground-floor security.

There was a nod of heads in the jury box. They remembered the evidence about the computer changes made to the mortgage at 3.32 a.m. Mulcahy sensed an obvious question, and put it out of order, although his agenda now was different. 'Mr Hawley,' he said, 'when is the next engagement of the Fletcher pass?'

Hawley continued, 'The Fletcher pass engaged the south elevator door on 20 at 3.27 a.m.'

'All right, Mr Hawley,' Mulcahy continued. 'It's 3.27 a.m. The Whitaker pass has checked out. The Shepard pass has checked out. The Fletcher pass has entered the elevator door nearest Shepard's office. What happens next?'

'Well,' said Hawley, looking back at his printout, 'at 3.31, the Fletcher pass engages the north fire stair door on 18.'

Mulcahy cut him off. Was that the door nearest Whitaker's office? It was.

Stevie moved the pass on the chart. Down to Whitaker's floor.

'What happened next?' asked Mulcahy.

'At 3.43 a.m., the Fletcher pass engaged the fire door on 26.'

'Entering or leaving?' Mulcahy asked.

'Entering. Evidently, the person left 18, and when you leave, nothing registers – it's only when you are entering a secure area – and then walked upstairs to 26, where the person engaged the fire door.'

'What happened next to that pass?'

'It cleared security in the lobby at 4.01.'

'Thank you, Mr Hawley. Oh, sorry, I have one question more. Did anyone ever call you before to ask you about this?'

'Yes,' he said. 'Last spring, a man called to ask whether there was a computerised record of which passes activated the system. I told him there was, and that probably his own MIS department could access that, if they were sophisticated enough.'

'Did the caller identify himself?' Mulcahy asked.

'Objection!' said O'Hanlon.

'Grounds?'

'Hearsay, Your Honour.'

It had been going so well – he'd been trotting across a field in springtime. Now Mulcahy staggered as though he'd hit an invisible trip wire. Hearsay! To have Kate stumble on this fact through a chance conversation on the way to the courthouse, and then not get it in. He had to get this in! It was silent in the session for a moment. He had to get his bearings. O'Hanlon cut in to cite the hearsay rule, but Grosso waved him off. The judge knew it well enough. Someone not in the courtroom – the declarant – gives his name on a telephone – an out of court statement – and the defence offers the statement to prove that the caller was who he claimed to be – offered to prove the truth of the matter asserted. It sounded like hearsay.

Judge Grosso frowned, and looked down over the tops of his bifocals. 'Mr Mulcahy?'

Just then he felt paper slide into his hand, and looked down to read, '804-b-4' on the back of a subpoena form. Glancing behind him, he saw that Kate had stepped back towards the enclosure.

'Mr Mulcahy?'

He knew 804 was the rule on unavailable witnesses. But he didn't know section (b)(4). He glanced sideways at the table. His copy of the rules was eight steps away. 'Ah, Your Honour, it's just a statement as to who the caller is. I mean,' he groped, 'I would suggest that it comes in under the catch-all exception . . .'

'Excuse me, Your Honour, Catherine Maher, assisting Mr Mulcahy,' Kate interrupted from the back of the enclosure. The judge looked up. 'I believe it is a statement concerning the declarant's own birth, and therefore within the 804(b)(4) exception.'

The judge reached for his rules, and peered down at them. His lips were pursed as he read the rule.

'That only applies to unavailable witnesses,' he said, after a moment.

'The declarant is unavailable under Rule 804(a) (4),' she went on. It was a polite way of saying, without the jury understanding, that the declarant was dead.

'I see,' Judge Grosso said. 'I see. That's an interesting argument, Ms . . .'

'Maher, Your Honour.'

'That's an interesting argument, Ms Maher. But the rule applies by its terms to birth, not identity.'

'That is precisely the Commonwealth's point, Your Honour,' O'Hanlon weighed in. He had thumbed to his copy of the rule. 'We submit . . .'

'I have your argument, I think, Mr O'Hanlon.'

Kate went on. 'We submit, Your Honour, that birth *is* identity. It comes to the same thing.'

Judge Grosso nodded. 'I see the argument.' He was frowning as he looked back at Mulcahy. 'I must say, Mr Mulcahy, I don't see much merit in the catch-all exception here, as there are no circumstantial guarantees of trustworthiness. Ms Maher's argument is more interesting, however.' He was frowning again. 'I seem to recall that rule is used in will contests, that sort of thing. I wonder whether it might be stretching the rule somewhat?'

The judge sat for another few moments, frowning down at the rule book, as the lawyers, the witness, the jury all watched him silently. Mulcahy could see his hands fidgeting. Probably O'Hanlon was entitled to a ruling. Why Dave Grosso did what he did next was never clear to anyone, even to himself. But sometimes, to do justice, you have to stretch things a little.

'The objection is overruled,' he said. 'The witness will answer the question.'

Fred Hawley looked over at the jury. 'He said his name was Samuel Whitaker.'

'Your witness, Mr O'Hanlon.'

35

It would come down to this. It always came down to someone like this. The secretary who opened the mail. The clerk at the cleaners. Or the lady who lived on the first floor. Everything could turn on her, and no real rhyme or reason would govern how she would do. Cases turn on bystanders. Whether they can see, and hear, and remember, and speak, and stand up to Paul O'Hanlon: all of that is chance.

Mrs Lee walked slowly to the witness stand. The diminutive Korean-American lady clutched her purse, and nodded politely at the judge after she sat.

She kept her voice up, just as Mulcahy told her to do. The jury were interested in this. Someone who lived on the ground floor of Shepard's building. They leaned forward, politely.

'Mrs Lee,' Mulcahy was saying, 'directing your attention to 16 May of this year, were you home that day?'

'Yes, sir. I was home.'

'At about lunchtime?'

'Yes, sir.'

'What did you observe at that time?'

'Well, I look out of my kitchen window and I see a very pretty woman, in athletic clothes, walking down the street. Then I see Mr Shepard go outside in his athletic clothes. And they start running down the street.'

'I see, Mrs Lee. The woman, did you recognise her?'

'I had not seen her before, no, sir.'

'Have you seen her since?'

'Yes, sir, this morning.'

'Where did you see her, Mrs Lee?'

'She was right here,' she said, indicating the stand, 'she answers questions.'

'Ms Russell?'

'Yes, sir, I think that is the name, Miss Russell.'

'All right, Mrs Lee, returning to 16 May, after you saw Mr Shepard and Ms Russell go off running, what did you see next?'

'Right after, I hear the front door open. To the building. And I go to my peephole. I see a man go upstairs.'

'Had you ever seen him before?'

'No, sir.'

'Anywhere in the building?'

'No, sir.'

'Did he have anything with him?'

'Yes, sir, he had a bag with him.'

'A bag?'

'A – I don't know, a kit bag, you say? A cloth bag, you understand?'

'Yes. Then what did you observe?'

530

'I hear his footsteps go up two flights of stairs. Bang bang bang bang bang. Some steps. Bang bang bang bang bang. You see? Stairs are very loud in the building.'

'I see. Then what, Mrs Lee?'

'Then, few minutes later, I hear a door open. Open and close. Not right away. Few minutes.'

'Mrs Lee, have you been to the third floor before?'

'Yes, sir, certainly, I go to see Mr Shepard.'

'You go to see Mr Shepard?'

'Yes, of course. Mr Shepard a very nice young man. He take my grandson to see the Celtics.'

Bless you, thought Mulcahy. 'I see,' he said, out loud, 'and how many apartments are on the third floor?'

'Two,' she said. 'All floors have two.'

'Two, and one of the apartments was Mr Shepard's?'

'Yes, sir.'

'All right, then, Mrs Lee, what happened next?'

'Well, after few minutes, I hear the door, and the steps, and the man returns. With the bag.'

'Where did you observe him from?'

'I look through the peephole. Then I go to the window and see this man walk past. Down Joy Street.'

'Did you see his face?'

'Yes, sir, three times. Once, the peephole. Twice, the peephole. Once, outside.'

Mulcahy flipped over the photo array where it lay on his table. Just as he had done years before as a prosecutor, he carried it to the clerk's desk. 'I'd like this marked as Defendant's N for identification,' he said. The array of twenty photographs was marked.

531

He carried it to the stand. The court was quiet, now, with only the sound of his footsteps, squeaking on the tile. Mulcahy's stomach was churning. Would she get it wrong? Anything is possible in a courtroom.

'Mrs Lee,' he said, 'I show you what has been marked as Exhibit N for identification. Do you see a picture of the man you saw go by that day?'

'Oh, yes, sir,' she said, pointing to the picture of Vincent Testa. She hadn't hesitated.

Mulcahy let out a breath as Kelly marked it in evidence. The array was handed to the jury foreman, and they waited as the jurors passed it one to another. They all looked curious.

O'Hanlon came at her in a fury. He seemed to have lost all sense of proportion. He was tired. They had worked hard, terribly hard, on this case, and he wanted a conviction. To be upset now, by this! By this plant of a witness, this next-door neighbour polished up to tie in Vinny Testa!

He tried to bludgeon her, tried to rattle her, tried yelling, tried whispering, tried cajoling. He stormed this way and that in the courtroom. She had seen this man for seconds only, and she could remember him? She could. She had been told by the defence whom to pick out! She had not – Mr George brings the picture and she picks him out, just like in court. She had never reported this to the police! The police had never come to inquire. He was so angry, he blundered: she had never called his office!

'But Mr O'Hanlon, sir,' she said, 'I do not know your office. And you never call me.'

And with each answer, she smiled politely and said, 'sir'.

Mulcahy put his pencil down. At last, he thought, a witness for the defence whom the jury likes as much as Mrs DeSantis. We had to wait right through to the end of trial. There was no point in taking notes. She would need little help on redirect. But before O'Hanlon gave up, exasperated, he clawed his way back for one point.

'You say you had never seen the man in the apartment, Mrs Lee?'

'No, sir, I had not.'

'Now, you don't know everyone in the building, do you, ma'am?'

'No, sir, not everyone.'

'So you don't know if this man was visiting someone, do you, Mrs Lee?'

She paused. 'No, sir, I do not know that.'

'Nothing further,' said O'Hanlon, and sat.

'Redirect, Mr Mulcahy?' Judge Grosso asked.

'Briefly, Your Honour,' he said, rising. 'Actually, I have only one question. Mrs Lee, after you heard the man go to the third floor, and before you heard a door open, did you hear a *knock*?'

She inclined her head and considered the question very carefully. 'Oh, no, sir,' she said. 'I do not hear a knock.'

And when Paul O'Hanlon waved off re-cross, Mrs Lee left the stand.

At last, Ed Mulcahy faced the judge and said, 'Your Honour, we rest.'

As they ate pizza on that afternoon, the last afternoon at Stevie's, they giggled like schoolchildren for an hour of pure release before the last task. The evidence was in. In the morning, Mulcahy would argue to the jury.

For him, it was even better than that. The order from Judge Hughes had arrived in the morning's mail. He had his bank account again. The court had dissolved the injunction. But since Kate had discovered the provision in the statute prohibiting trustee process in slander cases, he also had a sanction against Parisi. Undoubtedly that was the basis for the judge's cryptic remark. It was just like him – he couldn't just dissolve the attachment because of what the statute said, he had to get a dig into the lawyers for not knowing it. They were to submit an affidavit of attorneys' fees: Kate's fees.

'So what should I charge for my time?' she asked.

'Whatever it is,' Mulcahy said, 'better be big, because it's the first and last attorney's fee to get paid in this case.'

Stevie had his mouth full. He nodded in concurrence. 'Gouge him,' he said.

'God,' said Mulcahy, rubbing his temples, 'isn't it great when the damn evidence is finally in? Think we'll get arguments and charge done tomorrow?'

Stevie nodded. 'O'Hanlon will put on a show. But Dave'll start early, and you two guys will be done by lunch. He'll charge in the afternoon, give'em the case by 3.30, I'd say. How long's your argument?'

Mulcahy shook his head. 'I'll know by about 9 tomorrow morning,' he said.

'So Eddie,' said Stevie, a moment later, his great blubber lips wrapped around a slice, 'I'm suppos' be the investigator here. Wheuh'd ya get them dates?'

'Dates?'

534

'Them dates on your yellow pad, the dates Libby bonked Whidukuh.'

'I didn't have anything on my yellow pad.'

'You didn't have anything?' Kate interrupted. She looked at Stevie incredulously.

'Good, heh?' he said, taking another bite, and raising his eyebrows. 'Fuckin' pokah playuh! Nuthin' on his yellow pad.' Stevie was smiling. 'He's pretty good for a shoht fat guy, heh?' And then he turned to Ed. 'Hey, Perry Mason,' he said, 'don't make a habit of that shit, heh? Jaysus.'

'I promise,' Mulcahy said.

'Jaysus,' said Stevie again. 'What if she'd a just said no?'

'She wouldn't.'

'Oh, she wouldn't! The Great Swami says she wouldn't. So enlighten us. Why wouldn't she?'

'Because she's a lawyer. She heard questions about specific dates, saw me reading from what looked like notes, knew I had Emma Whitaker for one of them. And so she would calculate, assume I was trying to set her up, and had a witness. The doorman. Somebody. Anybody else, probably would have said no. But a lawyer, I figured I had a shot.'

'Pretty good for a shoht fat guy,' said Stevie again, shaking his head. 'Have some pizza.'

It was late when Gitz came in and found Mulcahy in the kitchen. 'Tomorrow the day?' he asked.

'Tomorrow's the day.'

'You'll do fine,' said Gitz. 'You're going to be okay. I talked to Timmy. He said you were huge

535

today. Huge.' Gitz pronounced the word without the 'h', like a New Yorker, so that it came out, 'yooj'.

Mulcahy grimaced. 'I could be tiny in a heartbeat,' he said. And he could be in the snow slide for a long time. 'How's Denise?'

'Huh, Denise?' He shook his head. 'Miserable without me. Can't bring herself to call. She's overcome with animal lust. Just possessed with it. But intimidated, frightened. Eating herself alive with passion.'

Mulcahy chuckled.

'Truth? She blew me off,' said Gitz. 'You know, Ed, that was my last chance. I pretty much figure, that was the last girl on earth who might take a flyer on me, you know? I'm all done. I'm like Elko. Except for the six mil part. Washed up.'

'Terrible shame,' said Mulcahy.

'I have been thinking, however, that unless you show a little more interest in that Kate, I might take a shot, you know? Whattaya think? She a Celts fan?'

Mulcahy shook his head.

'Ixnay on the Celts with Kate?' asked Gitz.

'Ixnay on the Celts. Ixnay on Kate. Or I might have to kill you, and defend myself *pro se*, and not get paid again.'

'Okay, just checking. Give 'em hell,' said Gitz, and then he left, and his bedroom door slammed.

Mulcahy was alone again. In the morning he would argue to the jury: to Mrs Watts, to the severe matron with the plaid skirt and the pendant brooch, to the old fellow in the corner seat with the eyeglass case who leaned back and closed his eyes through so much of the evidence, to the man in the blue suit with the bald spot. To Ms DeVito. To the Ancient Mariner. To Tie Pin man. To all the others. Sixteen people with whom he had never entered into conversation, whom he knew only by jury questionnaire, only by handwriting and speculation, would have Shepard's fate, and his own, to resolve. He would speak to them once, and sit in silence as O'Hanlon offered the last word. And he would listen as the judge read them instructions, and then watch as they filed noiselessly from the room. And then the waiting would begin.

As they judged him, or his client? The line was indistinct to Mulcahy. He had nothing left to wager but the outcome of this case.

He couldn't sleep, listened as the sound of an approaching automobile below built and then faded, waiting in the interval of silence for the next, counting seconds.

It would all come down to this. This case. What would he do the next day, and the next, if Shepard were convicted? Go down to the Boston Municipal Court and troll for court-appointed assignments? His own prospects were too hopeless, so he tried to imagine Shepard, at this moment, in a cell, lying and listening to those shouts and the clattering and the yammering and doubtless the snores and the yelps and the hollers. At length he rose and shuffled into the kitchen and poured himself a tumbler of water, and sat in the darkness next to the stack of banker's boxes. A voice in him said that he should look at the outlines again, look at the witness files, reread something, hold a piece of paper in his hands. But the case was now beyond the paper. Every case reaches that point. The stacks of paper, the heaps of evidence, the cases and the arguments are all done now, and it is left to the advocate. It's left to the art of persuasion, and the faculty of truth.

He looked at the clock – 2.30 a.m. – and padded back down the hall to his bedroom. But sleep would not come that night. For some reason, all he could picture was Mrs Shepard. He wondered where she was. Poor woman, defrauded by Parisi, forced to endure day after day of the trial, on her own.

He flicked the light back on, and, after rooting through the bookshelf, returned to the bed with a book he hadn't opened in a long while. An old book. A good, old book, with a lot of good, old testimony.

36

'Members of the jury,' he began, 'the time has almost come.' Mulcahy looked about him. The courtroom was full. Gitz was there, and gave him a discreet thumbs up. A row of reporters sat in front, their pads at the ready. Kate smiled broadly at him from the front row of the gallery. How on earth was she still awake? On one side of her sat Mrs Shepard. And next to her on the other – the Captain! The Captain had come. He almost *never* came off-island. Mulcahy smiled back. He looked over at Shepard, but Shepard's gaze was locked forward, just as Mulcahy had told him it should be. The acoustics in 8b were terrible, but now his voice penetrated every corner. He turned and surveyed the jury, attentive in the box. It was 10 a.m., and the defence argues first.

'The evidence is submitted,' he went on. 'It is very nearly time for you to find the answers in this case. Or to say that there are none.

'For the answers have eluded the defence. And I submit that they have eluded the prosecution. Perhaps you will find the answers elusive as well. Perhaps, when you are finished, you will be able to say only that the matter remains mysterious. Can any of you say that he is left with no reasonable doubt as to the defendant's guilt? That he knows, to a moral certainty *knows* that John Shepard did this thing?'

He paused for a moment. Then he began more softly. 'I would like you all to remember one thing when you decide Mr Shepard's fate in this case.' And he stepped over to counsel table, where he picked up a canvas tote bag which he carried to the clerk's desk. He began to gather the six evidence pouches he had carefully laid out before the start of his argument, and placed them in the bag as though he were bagging groceries, holding each one up in his right hand, before dropping it in. 'This,' he said over his shoulder, matter-of-factly, 'is the prosecution's case. Six items. One suit jacket. One package containing a bar of soap. One credit card receipt. One package each containing hairs,' he dropped a package in the bag, 'fibres,' dropped another, and paused, to look back at the box, 'and pebbles.' He dropped the last pouch in the satchel.

'That's it. Oh, I know there was some testimony about arguments in offices, and some silly little man who wanted to tell us about a remark in an elevator, but none of that added up to anything. No, this is the prosecution case, right here. And I'd like you to remember,' he said, easily lifting the tote bag and carrying it over to the front of jury box, 'that the whole of the prosecution case . . . is portable.'

They leaned over the box, looking at the bag. 'The whole case fits in a tote bag, and can be carried from place to place.' He smiled and set the bag back on the counsel table. 'From Boston . . . to Sheringham, for example.

'We will talk about each item in the bag in a moment.

'Mr O'Hanlon,' he resumed, after taking a drink of water, 'is a skilful prosecutor. We watched at the outset of the trial as he gathered a mass of evidence, and arranged it, and presented it, as if he had all the pieces, and they all interlocked, like a jigsaw puzzle, smoothly and beautifully, so that no doubt was left as to the picture they fit together to form.

'And if, upon a close examination of those pieces, you are left with the firm conviction that they do fit together in only one way, that they combine to form but one picture, then you might vote to convict, and leave this place with a clear conscience.

'But if the pieces fit together but loosely, or if some are missing, and the pieces might just as well be rearranged to form a different picture, then none of you will be able to say, to a moral certainty, that Mr O'Hanlon's picture is the right picture. And, in that case, it will be your duty to acquit.

'If you are left only with answers, then perhaps – *perhaps* – you may convict. But if you are left with questions, you must acquit. This is your duty.

'Remember,' he said, and he spoke very softly now, so softly that they strained to hear him from the box, and barely could in the gallery. 'Remember how important you are. Only you can decide what becomes of a human being.' The room was perfectly quiet. 'The prosecutor tries to persuade you that his picture is the right picture. That is his job. But the prosecutor will never have to decide whether a man is guilty of murder. He will not have that on his conscience. That is for you.

'The answers are so mysterious here. At the outset of the trial, we suggested to you that Samuel Whitaker might have died by his own hand. There was much evidence to suggest that he had. His long marriage had reached an end. He had been forced from a position of power in his law firm, squeezed out by younger men. A suicide note was found on his typewriter. The Navy sidearm which fired the fatal shot was in his hand when the maid, Miss Biali, found him the next morning.

'And then, during the trial, other evidence came to light. Evidence of a different kind. Evidence of murder. But not a murder involving John Shepard.'

He walked back to the table to reclaim the tote bag. 'Let's start with the soap,' he said.

'A bar of Lifebuoy soap, bearing a partial thumbprint of John Shepard, is found in the washroom, scarcely a few feet away from the deceased.

'This seems damning, this bar of soap. It seems to fit into Mr O'Hanlon's puzzle. Until you start to look at it carefully. This is not the only bar of soap in the house. Scattered around the bathrooms and the kitchens are fifteen or twenty more. Many bars of soap. But this bar of soap *is* the only bar of Lifebuoy soap.

'Just for a moment, consider that trivial detail of household management. Whoever bought soap for the house bought packages of Ivory soap, packages of specialty soaps for the master bath, packages of Lava soap. But only one bar of Lifebuoy. When people shop for things like that, people shopping for a large house like the Whitaker house, do they buy a single bar of soap of one brand?

'It is a small matter, but sometimes it's the small matters which become the most troubling. That makes you ask yourself, how exactly did that bar of soap get there?

'And, members of the jury, there are other questions about the bar of soap. Mr O'Hanlon suggests to you that Mr Shepard did this terrible thing, and then, I suppose, washed his hands. Why? To wash away blood, perhaps? Well, all right, but think about that. A man has just fired a loud, percussive handgun. Does he remain at the murder scene to wash his hands?

'And where is the blood? Are any drops of it found in the sink? On the faucets? On the door, the doorknob, the floor, anywhere? On the *soap*?

'None.' Mulcahy nodded his head. 'Very strange, that bar of soap.

'But we do know one thing. We know where you certainly could find a bar of Lifebuoy soap bearing John Shepard's thumbprint. In his Joy Street apartment.

'Well, let's look at the credit card receipt.' He placed the package of soap back in the carryall, and withdrew the next exhibit. 'Five dollars and thirty eight cents, remember?

'Let's think about the Commonwealth's theory for a moment. Here it is. John Shepard has just murdered someone. He has in his Subaru wagon about nine gallons of gas, enough to get him to the Massachusetts Turnpike and then about another two hundred sixty miles. So what does he do?' He paused.

'He stops at a gas station not five miles from the murder scene to *top up*.'

He let them ponder that for a moment, before going on. 'Now Shepard is a graduate of the Harvard Law School. He's not stupid. And yet he stops at a filling station which would put him near the murder scene, and uses a credit card to cover less than six dollars, so as to create a written record that he was there? That is Mr O'Hanlon's theory.

'Only, before we leave the filling station receipt, let's look closely at it. Does it tell us that Shepard was there? No. The signature is illegible. And the blank for licence plate, the one at the top, is not filled in.'

Mulcahy handed the slip to the foreman and then waited, pouring himself another glass of water as each of the jurors looked at it briefly, handing it on to the next.

'So what do we really know?' he resumed. 'That John Shepard was at Lamartino's Sunoco? No. That his car was there? No. No, members of the jury, all that the Commonwealth can suggest with this evidence, is that the *credit card* was there. The credit card, like the soap, fits very comfortably in the tote bag, and like the soap, might have been found at Mr Shepard's apartment.

'What of the fibres? What of the hairs? Fibres from his jacket. Hairs from his head. But again, they fit in a bag, and the bag fits in the tote bag. The real question is, how did they get to the farmhouse?'

There were frowns in the jury box now. He anticipated them. 'But you may be thinking, all right, we grant you all of these things could have been planted. Fine. Why? Who would do this? Why?

'That is an important question. I will come back to it. I must first spend just a moment on the jacket. The jacket which Mr Shepard admitted looks like his own. Found in a dumpster on the Massachusetts Turnpike, stained with type A negative blood, a blood type shared by Sam Whitaker.

'Remember the evidence of the blood. It gets on to the jacket. But nowhere else. The breast is stained. Surely the blood which stained the breast of the jacket would have stained a shirt. But no one finds a shirt. Why isn't a bloody shirt discarded with the jacket?

'What happens next? Mr Shepard leaves the scene, with a bloody jacket. Does blood drip from the jacket on to the rear hall, the entranceway, the front door, the porch, the driveway? No. No drops of blood are found by police. What of the car? Mr Shepard gets into his car, according to the Commonwealth, with fresh bloodstains on his jacket. Colorado State Police later subject that car to a minute examination. They find no bloodstains. No drops at all.

'And so what do we have? The jacket very likely was at the murder scene. It may contain Mr Whitaker's blood. But there's no real proof of how it got there, and how it got away from there, and nothing to suggest that it was ever in Mr Shepard's car.

'And, you must ask yourself this question, for you met John Shepard. He is beginning a cross-continental drive in the springtime. Is he the sort of person who puts on a suit for that?'

Ms DeVito nodded. So did Tie Pin man, who *was*

the sort of man who might have worn one. But he knew that Shepard wasn't.

'There are the pebbles, of course. That was quite ingenious. But pebbles could have been collected from Mr Whitaker's drive, and carried to Boston. They could have been wedged into the tyre treads, dropped into the wheel well. By anyone who had been to the house.

'There was evidence that someone had been to the house. But it was not John Shepard.'

He paused again, and saw that the Ancient Mariner was frowning – the Ancient Mariner, who had seemed so often to be with him. He went on. 'What we have is six portable items, each of which could have been put at the scene of the murder by someone other than Mr Shepard. What the Commonwealth does not have is anyone who places Mr Shepard himself at the scene.'

He paused, again filling his glass. 'Let's now return to that question which I think is troubling you. Why? Who would do such a thing? I shall put a theory about that before you. I cannot prove the theory, but it is based on evidence you have seen and heard. And when I finish, I would like you to consider whether the theory I have placed before you is any less credible, any less likely, than the prosecution's theory. If you find this theory equally plausible, then I submit that none of you can say that the Commonwealth's case has been proved against Mr Shepard.

'Samuel Whitaker, a man who had achieved everything in his profession, from all we have learned in this trial, was not a man at peace when he died. Two relationships which, more than any other, defined him, had badly deteriorated: his marriage, and his partnership. The one had grown cold and lifeless. In the other, his power had slipped from him.

'Mr Whitaker had an affair with Elizabeth Russell, as we learned only yesterday. She denies sexual relations, of course, and we will never know. But she admits that there was a close friendship; that the two were often together, alone, and that they were sometimes alone in her apartment. A young, attractive, ambitious woman. An older man desperate for – for what – to prove something to himself? We'll never know.

'Ms Russell heads up the team of lawyers that almost literally lived at the Freer Motley offices during the last week of March 1992. She is issued one of the five guest passes issued to the Fletcher Daye attorneys. One of those five passes is the one which engages the fire stairs at 3.31 a.m. on 31 March. It engages that fire door, then re-engages, moments later, a window in time, sandwiched around the very moment that the Idlewild mortgage was called up on a computer screen for the last time. Recall that evidence, please, as you deliberate. I submit you will find that the mortgage error was not accidental. It was deliberate. And it was planted there by one of the Fletcher Daye lawyers.

'Was that Libby Russell?

'Was it Libby Russell who doctored the mortgage document? Remember her testimony. She found the error. But there was no record of her finding it on her time sheet. Did she find it because she knew where it was? Because she had put it there?

547

'This would certainly be a great advantage to her client – an advantage that client quickly seized. And where direct benefits accrue to clients, indirect ones accrue to their attorneys.

'Now I suggest that there was one man who figured out what the prosecution and the defence were unable to understand. He is not with us today. Sam Whitaker. He had been forced out of the senior partner's role, and younger lawyers have supplanted his key role at the bank. He wanders. He has an affair, as we said. With Libby Russell.

'He learns something about her. He knows her quite well. When the error is discovered, he follows the internal investigation. He guesses that the computer record is available, calls the security office. The record shows that a Fletcher Daye attorney was in the office at the critical moment. Sam Whitaker, in one evening, pieces together what eluded the rest of us throughout most of this trial. Not for nothing was he the managing partner of that firm for twenty years.

'Perhaps he confronts Libby Russell. He tells her that she must admit the matter. Remember the testimony of Mrs DeSantis. Recall that it was with Libby Russell that he arranged to have lunch on the Friday before his death.

'And if, as the evidence suggests, he confronted her that Friday with his suspicions, she was suddenly faced with a stark choice. On the one hand, bank fraud, disbarment, exposure, jail. On the other, well, this matter was about to be exploited to the considerable financial benefit of her client. And perhaps to herself. All until Sam Whitaker put the pieces together.

'On 16 May she gets John Shepard out of his apartment for an hour by insisting that he accompany her on a run around the Charles River. On that same day, Mrs Lee sees Vincent Testa climb the stairs past her first-floor door in the Joy Street apartment house. Testa returns a few minutes later. He carries a satchel.

'Who is Vincent Testa? He doesn't live there. Mrs Lee has never seen him before. He has connections with organised crime. He once was Libby Russell's informant, back when she prosecuted cases for the United States.

'Did Libby Russell use Testa to gather evidence from John Shepard's apartment, once she had him safely out of it? To gather hairs from a pillowcase, a suit jacket that wouldn't be missed from the closet, a bar of soap, a credit card from his wallet?

'Was it Vincent Testa who murdered Libby Russell's lover?

'Members of the jury, remember the conflicting evidence of the telephone calls. The records showed that a call was placed to Mr Shepard's apartment from the Whitaker exchange at 7.32 p.m. on the night of the murder. Mr Shepard testified that he received a call, from a salesperson.'

He paused, looking up at Tie Pin man, who was already nodding. So was Mrs Watts.

'And the salesperson was a sales*woman*. With an accent. Remember?

'Was that Libby Russell, using Whitaker's phone? Was she there that night? Had she found the service pistol, and passed it to her accomplice? Is that how the murderer entered the house and caught Samuel Whitaker unaware?'

Now Mulcahy paused again, for almost thirty seconds – an eternity in a courtroom – before resuming. 'Members of the jury, I want you to remember one thing. I do not stand here and ask you to convict Libby Russell of anything. I do not pretend that I can prove her complicity beyond a reasonable doubt. But I do say this. It is the law in this Commonwealth that John Shepard was entitled, at the beginning of this trial, to be presumed by you to be as innocent as anyone else in the courtroom. As innocent as me, as Mr O'Hanlon, or as Libby Russell.

'Libby Russell is entitled to no greater presumption of innocence than John Shepard.

'And if you weigh the hypothesis I just gave to you, and find it just as consistent with the evidence as the hypothesis vouched for by the prosecution, then you have found that there is reasonable doubt as to the case against John Shepard.'

He had finished now. As he wound up the argument, he felt a great weight pass from his shoulders. The room was hushed. Before he sat he spoke a few words more, the colour now filling his face and his jaw tightening. 'Members of the jury, John Shepard has spent every day since 12 June in the Charles Street jail. Every single day. Your verdict should be for his freedom. Let this man go home.'

A moment later Mulcahy had resumed his seat. He felt Shepard's hand on his arm. He placed his own hand over it and held it tightly.

Mulcahy was in the courtroom, at counsel table, for the rest of the day, and appeared to be listening as O'Hanlon closed, and as Judge Grosso instructed. He even went to sidebar to participate in the perfunctory charge objections. But his mind had wandered far away, even before the jury filed from the courtroom to begin deliberations.

That night he slept soundly for the first time in weeks.

Coda

Relief flooded over Mulcahy, and only far off in the distance was the judge thanking the jury for their service and bidding all rise and excusing them, and discharging the defendant. He scarcely heard any of it until a gavel fell and Shepard had him in a burly embrace.

And then it was all a whirl, all chaos, all fluorescence and noise. A tide swept into the enclosure and Shepard was engulfed. He found his mother, and she was weeping openly, and the others crowded around, and there were voices saying, 'Mr Shepard! Excuse me . . .' More faces were at Mulcahy's elbow and hands touched his shoulder: a television reporter, a microphone, another microphone, a shouted question. Someone was asking how it felt and someone else was asking what his plans were and what John Shepard's plans were and another voice in the din was saying, 'Mr Mulcahy, Mr Mulcahy!' And other voices and bodies pressed at Shepard, and said, 'Mr Shepard, Mr Shepard. Tell us . . .' There were strange faces and familiar faces and faces pushing into view, one after the other.

Stevie elbowed through the throng. 'Eddie, Eddie,' he was saying, 'ya did it, Eddie, ya did it!' He wrung his hand, and was pounding his back.

Now Stevie had been pushed aside, and Mulcahy had made his way into the lobby, where the television lights shone and the oddly familiar faces of the television reporters stood in a receiving line before him. Gitz was there briefly. 'Ed! Ed! I got Timmy here!' But he was drowned out and again a question from someone about how it felt, and he was talking at the picket-line of arms pointing pocket tape recorders toward him. Was it true that he had been fired by his law firm for taking the case? He had no comment.

'How does it feel?' he heard himself asked again.

'How does it feel? It feels, it feels ... where is Kate?'

'Mr Mulcahy? Excuse me? Could I ask ...' More din, and the crowd pressed across to Shepard.

But he had seen her across the lobby, by the elevator. He pushed through the throng and found her and they embraced very hard and rocked back and forth. She held him ever so tightly. A television gaffer was rushing over, camera jiggling, to film the embrace, and someone was saying, 'Who is she, you got a spelling?' But Mulcahy didn't notice. Nor did Kate. His mouth was close to her ear and her head was buried in his chest, and perhaps something was said, there in the lobby of the 8th floor of the New Courthouse Annexe, but there was too much din for anyone else to hear it.

It was some time later, when the well-wishers and the hangers-on and the reporters had all cleared out and gone, and the sound trucks parked out front of the annexe had retracted their dishes and driven off, that the three burst from the outside door and stood dizzily in the September sunswept brick of Centre Plaza, with nowhere to go, just that feeling of children liberated from school at the start of the summer holiday, three children giddy with delight. Shepard had put his mother in a cab and promised her he would meet her at her hotel in Cambridge in two hours.

'God,' he said, 'Jesus God, to be outside. To be outside again, Jesus God.'

And then he said, 'We've got to get away from the concrete.' They walked over to Beacon Street and turned into Tremont, heading upstream through the late-lunch crowd streaming from the Common. They walked past the Granary Burial Ground, and the Park Street Church and the T station and then they were in Boston Common, where they found a green patch of grass and sat beneath a sugar maple brilliant with red hints of autumn. 'Jesus God,' said Shepard softly again, and he shook his head, passing his hands in a loving caress over the grass.

'I love you both,' he said. 'You two took on all those motherfuckers. I'm so damn . . .' He broke off and turned away.

They were quiet for a bit and then Kate said that she would go off and find lunch. When she had returned and they were eating the hot dogs, Shepard said to his lawyer, 'So what are you going to do?'

557

Mulcahy said, 'I don't know. What are you going to do?'

'I know what I sure as hell ain't gonna do,' said Shepard.

'All I can do,' said Mulcahy, 'that's all I'm any good for.'

No one spoke for a time. And Kate stared at Ed and said quietly, 'Seeing as I don't have a job, I was kind of wondering would you be needing an associate?'

He looked back at her and said, 'No. No, Kate. I won't be able to pay an associate for the forseeable future.' He paused and took a bite from his hot dog, chewed it slowly, and looked off. Then he said in an offhand sort of way, 'I think I might be needing a partner, though.' And he grinned with the sun splashing through the maples on his extended hand. To which she said, in default of anything else coming readily to mind. 'Nuts,' and bearhugged him, spilling him sideways in the grass, as they all laughed. 'Deal!' she said, looking up suddenly, as if struck with second thoughts.

'Only, I refuse to do subpoenas.'

They all smiled.

They sat again quietly for a time before he said, 'All we need now is a case or two.'

'Well, hell,' said Shepard, 'you got a case.'

Mulcahy didn't understand and looked at him quizzically.

'Ed, you're a helluva trial guy, but Jesus! No sense of the deal. Who's the softest touch in the city? Who did Elizabeth Russell shake down without a peep? And who's still sitting on a pile of dough?'

'Yeah?' he said. It was a question.

Shepard continued. 'Now, I seem to recollect you having your sorry ass wrongfully booted out of the partnership, don't I? Wherefore the plaintiff was wrongfully deprived of a whole boxcarload of money. Make that three boxcarloads. And more importantly, the plaintiff will discuss with the good people of the jury the fuckin' dirty laundry of this law firm for a month or two, pausing for emphasis in all the right places so the gentlemen and ladies of the press will be sure to get the spellings right. And somebody might do a feature on the collapse of the whole white shoe house of cards: Whitaker, Idlewild, Russell. Hell, Ed, that's a case that makes sense to me.'

Mulcahy chuckled. 'Will you represent me?'

'Hell, no,' he said. And they sat in silence for a while, sipping Cokes. Shepard lay back and felt the sun warm on his face, and he shut his eyes hard but he could tell anyway that the two of them were staring at him.

And then Mulcahy said, 'So, John, are you thinking what I am?'

'Hell, no,' he said. 'I am definitely not thinking the bullshit you are thinking, so don't even think it.' He squinted at the two of them, 'And don't you think it either, Pippi Longstocking.'

They sat together a while longer, but Kate saw that there was something to finish, something that Mulcahy wanted to do with Shepard alone, so she rose and invented some excuse to leave.

'See you later, maybe?' Mulcahy asked. 'Would that be all right?'

'Yes,' she said, 'that would be very nice.' She rose, and Shepard rose too, and they embraced for a long time.

'I don't know what to say, Kate,' Shepard told her. 'You got it done. You got it done and it cost you your job and all. I owe you for the rest of my life. Thank you.'

'It's all right. It's all right. You take care,' she answered quickly, shaking her head as she felt the tears coming. They hugged once more. He lifted her from the ground. And then she waved and headed off for the subway station.

'Let's walk,' said Mulcahy when she had gone. They began to stroll across the Common towards the ball fields, walking in silence for a few moments. Shepard marvelled at the birds, stopping to look up in the branches at each new sound. For three months, he had seen only pigeons, and then only rarely.

'How close did I come, John?' Mulcahy asked at length.

'What do you mean?'

'I only had thirteen days before trial, remember, and I've been playing catch up the whole time. But I don't think I ever quite got there, even by the time we rested and the jury went out.'

Shepard looked at him uncertainly. Mulcahy walked a bit more before going on. 'Good thing for us O'Hanlon doesn't know much about computers.'

'What do you mean?'

'How about passwords, John?'

'Don't follow.'

'Well, we got Libby's pass in the building, and we

got her to Whitaker's terminal. Only, how'd she know the password?'

'Wondered about that myself. I suppose she got it out of Whitaker.'

'Maybe. Only, thing of it is that Whitaker never logged on to his computer system. They installed the thing in 1991, and he never even switched it on. Never ran the program to personalise his password.'

'Well, she might have known that. Them being such good friends and all.'

'Think that's it?' asked Mulcahy.

Shepard smiled. 'And the glory of the Lord shall be revealed,' he said, softly.

'For the original password,' Mulcahy said, 'she'd need help from someone who knew, somebody on the inside, familiar with the firm's computer system.'

'Someone like me, that what you're saying?'

'Well . . .'

Shepard was silent, so Mulcahy went on, digressing. 'It's good for us that O'Hanlon didn't have long to look at Hawley's printouts, and didn't know much about computers to begin with. But if he had, he might have had a question. The records would show you checked out just before 2 a.m. The witnesses said they found you in the conference room early the next morning. And I believe some witness or other reminded the jury that the firm doesn't open until 8 a.m.'

'Okay, Ed, so what's the question?'

'The question is, how come there's nothing on Hawley's record showing that you checked back in?'

Their footfalls crunched on the gravel between the ball fields. A little league team was taking swings.

Shepard chuckled, shaking his head. 'Now, there's a *helluva* question.'

'Amazing things, computers, keep a record of everything. But not of you coming back in that morning.'

They walked in silence for a bit, came to the crosswalk, and crossed to the Public Garden, threading through a crowd of tourists.

'So what's your theory, Counsellor?'

'Not sure,' said Mulcahy, 'but if I were a prosecutor, I might wonder whether you re-entered the building with someone else's pass. Maybe Libby Russell's.'

They had reached the bridge over the pond. Mulcahy fell silent, looking out. After a time, he went on. 'You know,' he said, 'here's what I don't get. Forget all the computer stuff. What I don't get is the *why* of the first part.'

'The why of the first part?'

'I understand that if she were involved in this, and Whitaker caught it, I guess I understand how she would have been faced with a dilemma between ruin and, well, making it go away. I understand the second part. But it's the first part I don't get. Why, if you're Libby Russell, and a partner at Fletcher Daye, and Snow White and all, and just – just *set*, why do you get involved in something like this? Why do you commit fraud? You've just bagged a trophy LBO. Who needs it?'

They walked some more. 'This privileged?' the big man asked.

'Probably. Can't be too careful, though, John, trial's over. And I used to work for the bank. I'd be

562

conflicted out if you were, hypothetically speaking, to ask me for advice on that. So it's not clear. Nothing's clear to me.'

'Well, I got to know her a little bit, like I told you. You know, her dad was a drunk, just like mine. Used to beat up the mother, she told me. He pilfered some Cleveland dowager's account, and the SEC caught him, shut him down. They lost pretty much everything. She went from dressage lessons at the country day to bagging groceries after the last bell at East Halfwit High. At thirteen. She knew what it was like to lose it. She remembered that feeling, and spent her whole life planning never to feel it again.

'And you know what? The night before the closing, she was a woman who didn't yet think she'd made it. Not even then. She was still looking over her shoulder, looking for trouble to catch up with her, looking for her clients to vanish, looking for the constable to come and grab the Lexus and change the locks on her. By God, she was determined it was never going to happen to her.

'I tell you, Ed, if you've ever had a drunken parent take a strap to you, and if you've ever seen the money pissed away in binges, you learn a couple of lessons. You learn to look out for number one and number one alone. And you learn that nothing in life is for sure.

'When it comes to it, Ed, you didn't have the right fairy tale. She wasn't ever Snow White at all. She was Cinderella. Cinderella waiting for the clock to strike twelve, waiting for that Lexus to turn into a pushcart, waiting to be chucked back into the ashes, and determined to stay at the ball.

'I should have seen it all long before the trial started,' he said. 'Sorry. Might have made things easier if I hadn't been so afraid of you getting near her. See, Ed, I wondered about her. I knew she was a funny human being. For all that Sweet Polly Pure-bread stuff, for all the white teeth and the hands on your forearm and the wide eyes, she was a calculating person. I knew – well, I knew after the Grenade, I knew that wasn't just an accident, put it that way. And I wondered too about this bullshit run. I ain't the complete airhead you may take me for. But I thought, you start to point at Libby, and we'll be in our own gunsights, you know?'

He was quiet for a moment. 'She must have cut some deal with Weiner. She planted it, and then cut a deal with him.'

'What, a kickback?'

'Maybe. She'd have dressed it up a little. You know, go on retainer, lock up his legal work for a while. Something. If I were Paul O'Hanlon, I'd get Sid Weiner's ass into my office, or before the grand jury, one or the other.'

Ed nodded. 'I still don't have you getting to work that morning,' he said.

'Well, no sense diggin' up what's done,' John said, 'particularly since the Founding Fathers gave us the double jeopardy clause. But before you go judging me too harshly, let's go back to the computers for a minute, Ed. Granted the sensor tells you what pass went past it. Doesn't tell you which human being had the pass. But it also doesn't tell you *how many* human beings.

'Libby let her guard down a little. "You have to

plan ahead, John," she said to me. And such a lot of questions about computers? More than I could credit, even if she *had* been appointed to Fletcher's technology committee appraising computer systems, like she told me. Which I suspected was bullshit. Maybe I got a sense then of where she was going. Maybe a fellow who was thinking that Freer was short on character in those days might have wanted to increase Freer's opportunity to experience misfortune, and maybe even Sam Whitaker's opportunity to experience it, since, as you know, misfortune builds character, and the sonofabitch needed a dose.

'And maybe I was a little negligent. Maybe I was a little goddamn tantalised. Maybe I had a drink or two and was too talkative about the goddamn computers – hell if I can remember.'

Mulcahy cut him off. 'John, let me ask you something. Ever heard of a case called *Swartout*?'

He looked genuinely blank.

'Come on. You know the case.'

'Sorry, pal,' he said, winking. 'Don't much care for library work. Never heard of the bastard. Why?'

Mulcahy sighed. 'Nothing. Just a little Parol Evidence chestnut from our contracts days.'

'Well, hell, why don't you ask Libby?'

'What do you mean?'

'She was in my contracts class in law school. She sat right in front, with her nose in the casebook. I spent most of the class staring at her bra strap.

'Now, I suppose I could have gone back to the office with her early that morning. Damned if I can remember. And, I'll admit, I'm the kind of sinner who might have said, "Fuck it, they don't want to make me a partner in this place, let 'em do their own proofreading." I do remember going to my floor, and parking in my office until almost dawn.'

Mulcahy nodded.

'I see it now,' he said. 'You're a careful guy. You also believe in the oath, for some reason. So. Maybe you never agreed with her to do anything. Maybe you come into the office with her and part company on the inside. For a while I wondered why the records show her going to your floor first. Anyway, maybe that way, you don't know if she did. She doesn't tell you. And, later that morning, you don't proof the documents. If they ever asked you about it, the truthful answer would be that you might have done it yourself, you can't remember. You don't know how it got there.

'But that morning you did remember to put Sam Whitaker on the circulation list. Had to create it from scratch, but you did it. And that afternoon, I believe your parting shot at the two of them was something about this thing being their mess, wasn't it? I guess I was a witness, after all.'

Shepard laughed. They walked on a bit further. He said, 'Ed, you're a helluva lawyer, you know that? Got a helluvan imagination, man. Got an imagination like mine, that's why I like it.'

Then his tone changed abruptly. 'Sometimes things just get out of hand.'

Mulcahy went on as though he hadn't heard. 'Whitaker figures out the guest book, and calls her. He suspected that Friday night that Libby had planted the error. So he confronted her with it and must have mentioned George Creel's name when he explained to her how he knew. That's what that Bay Club lunch was. And Libby works fast. That weekend her goon tried to hit Creel. The following Monday she gets Sir Sam alone in the farmhouse. And sets you up.'

'Hmmm,' was all Shepard said.

'I'll tell you what, John,' Mulcahy went on, 'I'm still kind of murky on the mortgage. At a minimum, it does seem to me that you have a habit of getting people into situations they can't handle. You did it with me. Maybe with Libby Russell, too.'

'No, I get people into challenges. You handled it. Both times. She, well, I didn't get her anywhere she wasn't already headed.' Their footfalls crunched on the gravel. 'Best not to get too philosophical. The deal has closed.'

So they sat by the edge of the footbridge in the sun, watching the swan boat ply lazily back and forth under the spreading willows, and the children toss peanuts into the water for the ducks. Shepard lay back and felt the warmth course through him, and felt the grass at his back, and shut his eyes. The warm grass felt good, and the quiet soothed him, even with the sounds of traffic up the hill and a city all around.

'There's one more thing I wanted to mention, John,' Mulcahy said.

'Jesus Lord, Ed, let's let it go.'

'Just one more thing. The jacket.'

Shepard sighed. 'What's to know about the jacket?' he asked softly. 'We've been through that.'

'Not through all of it. Not the part about what the jacket told you. And when. You knew it was yours when you saw it back in August.'

'I know, I know. I lied to you. I'm sorry that I did. I . . .'

'No, John, that's not it. That's not what I mean. John, back in August, you knew that they found your jacket in a dumpster on the Mass. Pike, and that you hadn't put it there. So you knew it had been planted by someone. And in your mind you played the whole thing through, played it all through, knew that this whole case was a frame. You knew Russell was involved. Or guessed it, anyway. But you didn't tell me.'

Shepard frowned, looking away at the pond.

'Why was that, John?'

'Aw, you're giving me too damn much credit, man. Look, you won the case, boy, don't retry it to death!'

But Mulcahy wasn't listening. 'No, John. I know why you didn't. There's only one explanation that makes sense. You knew that it was dangerous. You had been too close to Libby at the wrong times. You didn't – how did you put it? – you didn't want to be in your own gunsights. A lawyer who got into the truth would have to be a good one. You couldn't afford for him to make a mistake, to prove Libby's involvement without linking you to her.'

Shepard had shut his eyes, for he knew what was coming. Mulcahy went on softly. 'You didn't think your lawyer was up to it.'

They sat in silence, with Shepard neither acknowledging nor denying the accusation. Mulcahy went on. 'I was a plodder. I could be trusted with the nice simple suicide which Libby had laid out as her first line of defence. Framing you was her second line – the suspenders on top of her belt. It was clever, and you decided I just wasn't good enough to get into that without blundering into proof that you were with her at the wrong times. The odds for getting reasonable doubt there were better than the odds that I could beat the prosecutor if I got into the truth.'

They sat in silence. Shepard looked at him after a few moments more and said simply, 'Ed, I won't bullshit you.' Then he looked away.

It was time to go. The two men stood, Shepard stooping a little, and they embraced. 'Ed,' he said, 'I'm the debtor now.'

'The mortgage?' Mulcahy asked.

John Shepard smiled. 'Discharged,' he said. 'Redeemed. Paid in full.'

They stood uneasily for just a moment more. Mulcahy said to him, 'You once said I couldn't slip a verse by you.'

'Try me. I've had a little time to study up.'

' "Speak ye comfortably to Jerusalem, and cry unto her, that her warfare is accomplished." '

The brown eyes narrowed, but Shepard smiled. '*Book of Isaiah*,' he said. He turned, uncertain between leaving and staying. 'Ed,' he said, 'I'm usually not tongue tied, but . . . anyway, know that I can never, never repay, and never, never forget. And . . .' But he had no other words.

He stepped up the path, two steps, and then turned, smiling that ironic smile that sunk his narrow eyes into his cheeks. 'I guess the warfare *is* accomplished now. But you picked that passage for the next verse, didn't you?' And then he turned again and began to stride quickly away across the park.

For it had come back to the mortgage, in the end.

In a last act of bravado on 31 March, John Shepard, the Idlewild deal's driver, had sat back and loosed the reins. Just loosed them and folded his arms and laughed at the rush of events around him, laughed at the witless passengers in his coach, who would know too late that the team had careened astray. The line between loosing the reins and actually guiding the stage to disaster was a fine one, maybe a clever one, but too fine for Ed Mulcahy.

Mulcahy judged him. Objectively, dispassionately, even lovingly – but nevertheless he judged him. These things were to Shepard's account.

And yet it was almost October, now. Shepard had paid. He had paid with a long, hot stay in an iron box. He had paid with a career, and it was enough of a price. Mulcahy *had* chosen the prophet for the next verse. 'Cry unto her,' *Isaiah* says, 'that her warfare is accomplished, and her iniquity is pardoned.'

Judgment and pardon: Mulcahy felt a calm, a swelling peace settle over him, as he looked back towards the footbridge. He was free to go now, free of the mortgage, free of the memory, released from his indemnity to another man's approval. He judged him, and pardoned his iniquity. And what he knew then, and had not known even an hour before, was that in Shepard's pardon was his own release. He looked out at the bustle of the afternoon, and watched as the tall figure receded, mingling into the crowd, until it was lost to view. And then a smile spread across his face, as he turned his back on the Public Garden.

For John Shepard was gone.